MW00977530

Ms. Joyce Parks
286 Forest Valley Rd.
Lawrenceville, GA 30046-6072

Books by Fran Stewart

<u>The Biscuit McKee Mystery Series</u>:

Orange as Marmalade
Yellow as Legal Pads
Green as a Garden Hose
Blue as Blue Jeans
Indigo as an Iris

Poetry:

Resolution

For Children:

As Orange As Marmalade/
Tan naranja como Mermelada
(a bilingual book)

Non-Fiction:

From The Tip of My Pen: a manual for writers

A
Slaying Song
Tonight

Fran Stewart

Fran Stewart

A Slaying Song Tonight

1st edition: © 2009 Fran Stewart

ISBN: 978-0-9818251-4-4

This is a work of fiction. Any resemblance to any person living or dead is purely coincidental.

This book was printed in the United States of America.

Doggie in the Window Publications
PO Box 1565
Duluth GA 30096
www.DoggieintheWindow.biz

Dedication:

To former Gwinnett County Assistant District Attorney Alston C. McNairy, without whose inspiration this book would have ended three lines before chapter eighteen,

and in loving memory of Waldo, who passed over the rainbow bridge on 10/22/2009.

My Gratitude List

James Lord Pierpont 1822-1893 "A Sleighing Song Tonight" – better known as "Jingle Bells" first published in September of 1857

Clement Clark Moore 1779-1863 "A Visit from St. Nicholas" (1822)

The unknown author of **The Twelve Days of Christmas**, which was first printed in a children's book in 1780, although the song itself is believed to be much older.

Polly Hunt Neal, an extraordinary artist and fellow member of the National League of American Pen Women, who opened her house in the north Georgia mountains to me as a writer's retreat, and in whose gazebo I penned the first chapter of A SLAYING SONG TONIGHT.

Madeleine Ames, unpublished author and housemate of Glaze McKee, who – in GREEN AS A GARDEN HOSE – came up with the name of this book. Read the author interview at the end to see why *my* name is on this book instead of *hers*.

The following people from the Superior Court of Gwinnett County Georgia, who answered my questions with patience and humor, and all in all made my research at the Gwinnett County Justice and Administration Center an enjoyable experience:

    Superior Court Judge Debra K. Turner, whose good sense and superb jurisprudence, coupled with a wicked sense of humor, gives me true faith in the judicial system;

    Assistant District Attorney Alston McNairy, whose passionate pleading that justice be served moved me (and the jury), and sent me into a frenzy of rewriting so that the story I wrote became a story I could truly be proud of;

    Court Reporter Beth Cappell, who took time from her incredibly busy schedule to show me behind the scenes, and who was still as unflappable at the end of the trial as she had been the first day. (I borrowed your last name for my landlady in this story, Beth);

    Bailiffs Mandy and Leon Windham, who answered so many questions in between their shepherding of the jury; and

    Clerk of the Court Debbie Boyt, who shuffled through ancient archives, helping me find the right cases to quote as chapter headings and who said "bless you" every time I sneezed from breathing in old, old paper.

And while we're talking about Gwinnett County, **Allison Price** and **Stephanie Irvin** from the Gwinnett County Public Library System were indispensable in helping me with access to archived newspapers from the 1930s.

The original **Cheyenne**, who is the official greeter at Wild Birds Unlimited in Lawrenceville, GA. I look forward to scratching her tummy every time I shop at WBU. I apologize for aging you so much in this story, Cheyenne. And thank you for all the dog kisses you so enthusiastically bestow.

My two pre-readers, **Diana Alishouse** and **Millie Woollen**, who've gone through more drafts of this book than I thought they'd be willing to endure.

Jill Sensiba, my plant expert, who provided the idea for the wax myrtle hedge that hides the outhouse.

The *Toronto Star* **website**, which gave me clear information about the history of convertibles.

Woodward Mill Elementary School teacher **Laura Baynard**, whose name I purloined for my little town.

My editor, Nanette Littlestone, who encourages me, keeps my strange writing impulses firmly in line, and pushes me to exceed my dreams. She also tells me she'd rather have me throw things than cry when she makes her suggestions.

The dear folks at Doggie in the Window Publications, an independent press with a heart.

Quotations used at the beginning of each chapter are taken directly from documents in the Gwinnett County Superior Court archives.

STATESVILLE COUNTY CLARION
YOUR MORNING SOURCE FOR ALL THE NEWS WORTH READING
Friday, July 15, 1932

SUSANNAH LOU: TRIAL NUMBER TWO

by Nancy Remington

The State Capital: The unprecedented second trial of already-convicted murderer Susannah Lou Packard opens today in the courtroom of Judge Harvey McElroy. Miss Packard is accused of slitting the throat of State Representative Dominick Kingsley, in his Baynard's Mill office on December 23rd of last year. There were no witnesses to this gruesome crime, but Baynard's Mill Sheriff Jasper Fordyke arrested Miss Packard on December 25th, only two days after the murder. Sheriff Jasper's office informed the press that he would not comment on the case.

Last month a jury of ten men and two ladies found Miss Packard guilty of the sensational 1926 murder of State Senator Button Kingsley. Button Kingsley, named for a signer of the Declaration of Independence, was the father of Dominick Kingsley. Miss Packardslipped past door guards at a birthday party for Senator Button Kingsley, doctored his drink (said to be a martini) with cyanide, and left without being noticed by any of the other attendees. Scandal resulted, since the guests, many of whom were prominent political figures, were alleged to have been imbibing illegal alcoholic beverages in a secluded room prior to dinner. Miss Packard is currently serving a life sentence for that murder in the state prison just outside the state capital.

This second trial for Dominick Kingsley has attracted national attention. All the major newspapers and both radio networks are in attendance. Rumors are rampant about possible political motives for the murder of this powerful father-son duo. The Clarion's ace reporter Nancy Remington will give her first-hand account of the trial every day for as long as it lasts.

Chapter 1 - The First Day

State versus _____Susannah Lou Packard_____ :
. . . for that the said _Susannah Lou Packard_ , on
the _23rd_ day of_December_ in the year of our
Lord Nineteen Hundred and_Thirty-one_with
force of arms and a_knife_be-
ing a weapon likely to produce death, did unlawfully
and with malice aforethought _assault and stab_ one
Dominick Kingsley with said weapon which _she_ ,
the said _Susannah Lou Packard_ , then
and here held, cutting into his throat, resulting in
severe loss of blood and inabilitiy to breatheand
giving to the said _Dominick Kingsley_ a seri-
ous and mortal wound with intent then and there to kill and murder the said _Dominick Kingsley_ , contrary to
the laws of said State, the good order, peace, and dignity thereof.

They had the same middle name. Much later Nancy Lou
Remington wondered if that should have been a warning to her, a sign
that she was in danger of being seduced by Susannah Lou Packard's
skewed logic. The trouble was that Miss Packard didn't look like a murderer. She looked so inoffensive as she sat without moving behind the
defense table through her second trial, her gloved hands folded on her
lap. She was quiet and small, or perhaps it was just that her attorney was
such a large man. His bulky width made her look delicate by compari-

son. Surely someone that small couldn't be the monster Nancy's fellow press members made her out to be. Still, she was a convicted murderer.

Nancy had missed the first trial, the one for the murder of Button Kingsley; it took place while she was out of state on an assignment, one that she'd almost botched enough to cost her her job on the *Clarion*, and then where would she have ended up? Even if George hadn't fired her, he would have stuck her with the garden news or obituaries. A tornado saved her skin, so to speak. It was a minor tornado, as such things go, but she'd been the only reporter at the scene, having lost her way near the edge of one state and ending up in another one altogether. Her father always said she could get so turned around in a one-room apartment it was a wonder she ever found her door. But the tornado had touched down in the second state, right when Nancy happened to be there. She'd interviewed some of the survivors, found a telephone that worked, and scooped the other papers and both radio networks as well. As luck would have it, George was so delighted with the story, he'd hadn't thought to ask her what she was doing there in the first place. What would she have said: I'm really sorry, but I got lost, Mr. Smith? I just knew there'd be a tornado there that day, Mr. Smith? Aren't you glad you hired me, Mr. Smith? She was quite relieved when he neglected to ask.

Susannah Lou Packard's second trial packed the courtroom. With so many people out of work, this was as good a place as any to sit on a hot day, and it was cheaper than a Charlie Chaplin film, although not nearly as amusing. The cross breeze from the tall open windows was welcome. And then there was the novelty angle. It wasn't often that someone with a life sentence already pronounced was tried for a second murder. Nancy could have sat down front with the other reporters, but she'd chosen to head upstairs to the gallery seats. That way she could keep an eye on everybody at once, from the brisk judge to the obviously sore-footed bailiff; from the staid prosecuting attorney to the grim court reporter; from the rumpled defense attorney to his unflappable client.

Nancy had read the transcripts of the first trial. When she returned from out of state on the day Miss Packard was sentenced for the murder of Button Kingsley, Nancy had been appalled at the competition in the Clarion's press room for possible headlines. PACKARD SENT PACKING finally won out over LOU GETS LIFE and SUSANNAH TO SERVE. Luckily nobody had taken SUSANNAH BUTTONED DOWN seriously, although it generated numerous raucous comments. Nancy saw it as a measure of how well she was accepted as the only female reporter in the newsroom that the men there no longer watched their language in deference to her sex. But sometimes she wished they'd be a bit more gentlemanly.

After the second hour of this trial for the murder of Dominick Kingsley, Nancy wasn't even sorry she hadn't been assigned to the democratic convention two weeks ago. So what if she wouldn't be covering the presidential election? Hoover didn't stand a chance—the bonus army had seen to that, picketing the White House for their back pay and making Hoover look like a heartless ogre. Roosevelt was a shoo-in, with that brand new Happy Days song—everybody was whistling it—and his boundless enthusiasm. No, Nancy Lou Remington wasn't interested in covering a guaranteed deal. Susannah Lou Packard, though, was an enigma. If she hadn't slain Dominick Kingsley this past Christmas, Sheriff Fordyke might never have found the evidence linking her to Button Kingsley's 1926 murder. She killed the son in 1931 and got caught for killing the father half a decade before. Funny how those things work out sometimes. If she'd left Dominick alone, she might have gotten away with killing Button.

As the jurors filed in, ushered by the limping bailiff, Nancy took a few moments to sketch each one briefly. Her skill with a soft pencil was one of the reasons she'd been hired as a reporter. Her sketches often made the front page. A house fire, last month's tornado, the grand opening of the new and rather controversial train station in Statesville. She'd shown the detailed gingerbread trim that made the depot look more like a fairy tale cottage than a modern hub of transportation. The inside crown molding and inlaid patterns on the counters could have graced the governor's mansion. These exquisite touches had all been created by master craftsmen who had lost their jobs, been hired by the county, then poured their love of fine woodwork into a station where few people would ever stop to admire their handiwork. That was something the new president, whoever it turned out to be, ought to try—employing people who would be otherwise unemployed. Surely that was a worthwhile endeavor for the government.

But all that was beside the point. Nancy kept sketching jurors as they settled into place. She doubted these pencil sketches would ever show up on the front page, but one never knew. The first juror on the front row, the foreman she supposed, was a wizened little man with a bald head and a face furrowed and darkened by years in the sun. Nancy sketched his forehead, where a line divided his tanned cheeks from the place where his hat must have sat year after year. She was glad she could draw so quickly. Maybe there would be time for an overall sketch of the jury box, with the people simply suggested. She concentrated for a moment on the top edge of the wooden structure that formed the front of the box. Over the decades, as each jury member filed into the front row, he (and now *she*, ever since the 19th amendment was ratified twelve years ago) had placed a steadying hand on that top edge. The varnish was worn off in hand-wide petal shapes in front of each juror's chair. Nancy wasn't sure anyone without an artist's eye would even notice that small touch, but it lent authenticity to her drawing.

During the reading of the charge, Nancy took a few desultory notes and continued sketching some of the audience members. An old man with vacant eyes who looked like a derelict sitting in the back row. A rather gaunt woman with a bright emerald green scarf draped artfully over the shoulders of her black dress standing just inside the imposing double doors. A young man sporting a jaunty boutonniere that was entirely out of place at a murder trial. A tired-looking woman sitting behind the prosecutor. Her red-gold hair was piled so high she looked top-heavy. The green scarf moved steadily down the aisle to squeeze in beside the red-gold hair. They seemed to be acquainted, although they did nothing more than nod at each other. The boutonniere slipped into the last available space with the other reporters and whipped out a notebook.

When she tired of her sketching, Nancy pulled out her fountain pen and turned to observe the prisoner. Something about Miss Packard made Nancy wonder what was going on inside her head. Miss Packard kept on her old-fashioned kid gloves in a tired ivory shade, as if they'd been worn too many times for their own good. Her trim blue hat looked like the one Mrs. Eleanor Roosevelt wore in the news photo on page one that morning. The defendant seemed removed from the proceedings, as if all that testimony referred to someone else, someone Susannah Lou Packard had never met. Nancy pulled a blank note card from the collection she had tucked in her handbag. Half of them already contained questions for Miss Packard. Nancy jotted down *why the gloves?* and returned the card to the stack.

After the noon recess Nancy found herself paying attention to Miss Packard's hands. The gloves again, left on despite the heat of the courtroom. Did she keep her gloves on when she ate, or when she slept? Did she ever take them off? When had she bought them? Nancy pulled out the appropriate note card to add those questions, but was quickly drawn back to the drama below her. Even when the Sheriff showed the ghastly photographs, Susannah listened courteously. She never raised her hand to her mouth, never shifted in her chair, never even glanced around the courtroom.

She wasn't exactly dowdy. A single wisp of light brown hair had worked its way loose from the rather severe bun she'd wound up at the back of her neck. That one tendril peeking from beneath the hat brim made Susannah seem somewhat vulnerable. Nancy wondered idly about the length of her hair. She looked so innocuous. Nancy had to keep reminding herself that Susannah Lou Packard had killed two men in cold blood. She knew Miss Packard was presumed innocent until proven guilty, but the woman had already been convicted of the first murder—death by cyanide poisoning—and her attorney seemed to be finding the evidence for this second one hard to refute. He didn't stand a chance, no more so than President Hoover. There wasn't a whisper of a doubt in anyone's mind. The lust for blood—Susannah's blood—fairly oozed through the audience, especially after the photographs came out, blown up to bigger-than-life-sized proportions. The black streams of blood down Kingsley's neck and the front of his shirt. The ice-blue eyes, gray in the photograph of course, half shut. The mouth gaping open in a silent scream. A woman seated just to Nancy's left gasped and fell sideways from her seat, bumping into Nancy on the way down. The court proceedings paused while she was revived and ushered outside into the fresh air. The woman sitting on Nancy's right leaned closer and whispered, "I wonder if Miss Packard wanted to get caught the second time."

Nancy murmured something indistinct, and the woman added, "What I mean is, how can anyone live with that kind of knowledge, with that kind of history, without wanting to be punished for it?" She had a point. Susannah had run, but not very far. She had hidden the evidence, but not very well. She never even denied it when the Sheriff arrested her. Her attorney tried to confuse the issue, saying that she had given in too easily, that she must have been trying to shield some other person or persons unknown. He was full of hints, full of suppositions on his cross-examinations, trying to cast that doubt that would allow the jury to find her *not guilty*. The general agreement among the onlookers seemed to be that her attorney was an idiot.

How could he explain away the small wooden box Sheriff Fordyke had found beneath her bed? About the size of two hefty books, it was stuffed with a bunch of junk—a pebble, a miniature model car, a blue feather, a short length of twine—the kind they put around bales of hay. There was a button, three inches of handmade lace, even a clothespin and a piece of straw; but it also held a vial of cyanide crystals, the poison that had killed Button Kingsley. Prosecuting Attorney Stevens and Sheriff Fordyke were very careful not to mention the first murder, but everyone who'd followed the story of the first trial—probably every person in the courtroom—knew how that cyanide had been used. The damning evidence for this second trial was a knife, a wristwatch engraved with Dominick Kingsley's name, and a blue dress the sheriff had found at the back of Miss Packard's closet. It was stained with more blood than could be explained by the feeble excuse of a chicken killed for Christmas dinner. Sheriff Fordyke demonstrated how the pockets on that dress were deep enough to easily secrete the knife. Nancy thought about her own ridiculously shallow pockets. She could barely fit her hand in there, much less anything like a knife. Not that she'd want to carry a knife. Still, it would be nice to be able to carry her fountain pen in there instead of having to keep it in her shirt pocket. Every time she put it in her handbag, it got lost at the bottom. She shook her head to bring herself back to the present. What had she missed? The prosecuting attorney asked the jury to imagine themselves in Dominick Kingsley's shoes as he greeted Miss Packard with a handshake, only to be skewered a moment later.

Susannah watched the photographs with a detached air, as if they were interesting specimens, collages of blood and flesh composed in a first-year art class at the local college, the one that had denied her application for admission, based on her advanced age. Nancy made a note about the way Susannah shook her head when the prosecutor mentioned the college application. She turned away from him when he said that, the one and only time she shifted in her seat that whole long day, except for the times she reached up to adjust her hat. Nancy wondered about that. Why wouldn't it stay in place? Hat pin, Nancy thought. Of course they would have taken away her hat pin, that potentially lethal implement most women routinely donned before stepping outside.

Susannah Lou Packard did not look insane, although her attorney hinted that his unprepossessing client might somehow have been pushed over the edge by the disappointment of not being admitted to the college. Despite repeated objections from the prosecutor and warnings from Judge McElroy, he kept sneaking in inadmissible comments, first saying she didn't do it, then saying she had a good reason to. He was arguing both ends against the middle in Nancy's opinion. Several members of the jury looked downright disgusted with him.

Still, Dean of Admissions Dominick Kingsley (part-time politician) was dead. His throat had been slit, and the links Susannah had with him were that letter of rejection folded around his wristwatch in her wooden box, to say nothing of the slender knife honed to razor sharpness that they'd retrieved from her left front pocket.

Nancy listened. She looked at the photographs. She was very glad she wasn't on the jury. The thought of interviewing Susannah Lou Packard was enough. What a plum assignment.

The judge adjourned the session early Friday afternoon and sent the jury home with strict instructions not to talk to anyone about the trial. Fat chance, Nancy thought. She approached Susannah's attorney on the courthouse steps. "Excuse me, Mr. Pinkney. I'm Nancy Remington with the *Clarion*, and I understand George Smith spoke with you by telephone about letting me interview Miss Packard about her first trial." She didn't mention how long it had taken her to convince George to let her take on this assignment. He'd intended to give it to one of the men in the press pool, but she stood up for herself and managed to make him see that a woman would have a better chance of getting an in-depth story from another woman. To her everlasting surprise, George had agreed to pay for her stay at a rooming house he knew of in the capital, so she wouldn't have to spend an hour driving the twenty-eight miles each way from Statesville and home again. What luck. The rooming house was less than a mile from the courthouse.

Pinkney started to bluster his way through a plea about his

client's innocence, but then seemed to recollect that his argument was unnecessary. "Yes, well, I know I told George . . . old school friend and all that . . . understanding that you're not to print a word . . . after the trial, you know."

What school gave this incoherent man a law degree? "Yes, I completely understand the need for confidentiality. Once Miss Packard is found innocent, as I'm sure she will be," Nancy managed to keep a straight face, "we'll tell the whole story."

"Yes. . . . Surely. . . . Should help the . . . the appeal process for the first trial."

Nonsense. Appellate courts don't pay attention to the newspapers. "Oh? Have you filed an appeal? I hadn't heard about that."

"Yes, yes; well, it's . . . shall we say . . . in process. Can't rush things too much, you know."

Which means you're lying through your teeth. Nancy smiled. *You either know it's hopeless or you lost the paperwork.* "Thank you, sir." She wondered idly if George had bribed Attorney Pinckney to get this interview. Did she even want to know?

A guard at the outer fence waved Nancy to a stop, asked her name and her reason for visiting the prison. He jotted down her answers and directed her to park in front of the three-story brick building off to her right. The gravel parking lot was less than half full. Nancy would have preferred to park in the shade, but there was only one rather short tree. The shadows beneath its gratifyingly wide branches spread over a Model-A Ford on the tree's left and, on its right, another car that defied identification. Nancy parked beside no-name, hoping the shade would work its way around to her car as the day went on. Given her sense of direction—or rather her lack thereof—perhaps she should have voted for the Ford side. She'd find out soon enough. When she was through with her interview for today, her car would either be relatively comfortable or it would be an oven.

If there were no high fences branching out from the sides of the building, it might almost have looked like a benign school of some sort. The barbed wire on top of the fence negated that impression. A flight of fifteen steps—Nancy counted them—led up to a tall and exceedingly heavy door. She entered a bare chamber, brightened only by two flags, and dominated by a scarred oak counter that was presided over by a sour-faced uniformed guard. He watched her closely as she crossed the open space, and Nancy felt self-conscious about the way her high heels tap-tapped so loudly on the wide wooden floorboards. He indicated a roster where she entered her name, address, phone number, and purpose of visit. She toyed with the idea of writing *Sheer Curiosity* as her purpose, but settled for *Interviewing Miss Packard.* The guard, still without speaking, turned the book so he could read it, made a non-committal grunt, and motioned for her to place her handbag on the counter. After searching it thoroughly, he passed her through a barred gate and on through a metal-reinforced door. Her fountain pen made a suspicious bulge beneath her suit jacket. It would have made a fine weapon if Nancy had been so inclined. The prison matron who awaited her in what turned out to be called the Processing Room found it immediately. "I'm a reporter," Nancy said, brandishing her press pass.

The matron—Nancy couldn't read her name tag—shook her head. "Guess I'll have to allow it, then. I do need to keep your hat pin out here, though." Nancy pulled out the seven-inch piece of sturdy wire. It was her favorite hat pin, decked on one end with three half-inch wooden beads in graduated shades of gray. The matron gave Nancy a signed receipt—the signature was illegible—and led her to yet another barred door. Nancy paused. "May I ask your name?"

"Why?"

"I'm a reporter. I like to have all the facts."

"You're not going to write about me, are you? They don't like us to get noticed too much, and I wouldn't be comfortable seeing my name in print."

"No, it's not that. It's just that I'd be more comfortable if I knew what to call you."

The placid-faced woman seemed to withdraw into herself a bit. "My name is Charlotte Curtis," she said, "but you can call me Matron. That's what everybody calls me."

"Thank you, Matron." Nancy smiled and stepped into a gray-walled room. It was empty, just two uncompromising straight wooden chairs bolted to the floor, one on either side of a sturdy and equally immovable table. The matron offered Nancy a cup of coffee. "No, thank you." She would expect coffee in a place this bleak to taste like tar. Or salt tears.

The table was grimy, as if thousands of sweaty hands had held onto the edge of it in desperation. She took a utilitarian white handkerchief from her purse and spread it open on the table in front of one of the chairs before setting down a narrow-lined steno pad. Then she pulled out two more handkerchiefs and one pencil and put them beside the pad. Nancy left the cap on her fountain pen but laid it ready on top of the note pad. She sat down. Stood up. Rearranged the pad, the pen. Added her stack of note cards with the proposed questions. *I wish I had one of those new-fangled Blattnerphones.* Nancy could see that taped recordings would eventually revolutionize the newspaper industry. Any fool could see that. She tugged at her suit jacket and rearranged her hat. Sat back down. And stood up once more when the door opened.

Susannah Lou Packard paused there, framed by the gouged wood around the door opening, looking Nancy up and down. Miss Packard wore the same short-sleeved blue shirtwaist dress she'd worn in the courtroom and what looked like the same low-heeled black shoes. Her hat was missing, though. Nancy was surprised at the thinness of her hair. The curl that had escaped her hat had looked thick in court, but now it simply hung lank and somewhat sad. Miss Packard nodded once, and Nancy smiled; she felt as if she had passed some sort of test. "Thank you for agreeing to this interview, Miss Packard."

Susannah inclined her head and waited for the matron to leave.

"I'm going to lock this door after me," the woman said in a nasal twang. "Knock or call out if you need me. Someone will be stationed in the hall outside." As she closed the door, she said, "Lavatory is across the hall. It has only one door."

Susannah sniffed and raised one eyebrow. "Suspicious soul, isn't she?"

Nancy motioned to the chair across from her. "As you probably know, I'm Nancy Lou Remington from the *Clarion.* I'm—"

"Your middle name is Lou?"

"Yes, it is. As I was saying, I'm glad you're willing to talk with me, Miss Packard."

"Call me Slip."

"Slip?"

"My initials. SLP. My pa said it was because I was just a little slip of a thing when I was a girl. My mother said it was because everybody was too lazy to say Susannah Lou Packard. She didn't hold with nicknames."

"And you may call me Nancy. I'll be taking notes as we speak, so I can get all the details right."

Slip stared for a moment at the collection of items Nancy had placed on the table. "Why the handkerchiefs?"

"If I need one, I want it handy." Nancy shrugged. "I always have three or four with me. That's just the way I work. I hate to rummage around in my bag when I'm talking with someone."

Susannah looked around the stark room. "Talking."

"Well, yes, Miss . . . Slip. I was hoping we could have a regular conversation. That's much better than my just asking questions and writing down your answers, don't you think?"

"I suppose." She walked quietly to the far side of the table, her shoes barely making a sound on the dull gray linoleum. She tried to pull the chair out, grimaced at its immobility, and slid onto the seat. "This," she glanced around the room again, "doesn't seem real yet. At least they've let me keep my own clothes. They didn't have any prison garb that would fit me." She clasped her gloved hands on the table in front of her. "What would you like to know?"

"First," Nancy adjusted her hat, which had slipped to one side, and settled into her own chair, "I want you to know that I'm under strict orders not to reveal any of our conversations until after the trial is finished." Even George, her editor, knew that she couldn't risk telephoning in any of her findings. If Miss Packard said anything about the current trial, and if someone overheard her and word got out, there could be a mistrial. Nancy personally thought Susannah's attorney was a fool to allow this interview, and this might even be illegal, although Nancy's knowledge of the law was vague at best. Nonexistent if she were being candid about it. Pinkney had apparently known George for years and must have trusted him implicitly. Either that or the bribe was big enough for him to risk it. Of course, Susannah already had one life sentence that hadn't been appealed, so maybe this wasn't such a risk anyway. *What harm could it do to tell the behind-the-scenes story while she was already serving time?* "Unlike some of my fellow reporters, I value my word as a journalist." Susannah nodded, and Nancy went on. "I'd like to ask you about the previous murder." Once again, that quick nod. "Were you really guilty of killing Button Kingsley?" A jury of ten men and two women had already convicted her, but Nancy needed an admission to quote directly. It was a matter of pride with her that she never made up quotations, unlike several of her competitors at the *Midwest Times.*

"Yes. I killed him." Susannah's voice was quiet, confident. "That's why they found me guilty."

"Did you kill him the way they said you did?"

"Yes. They got the details right. My attorney insisted on entering a plea of not guilty. I think now that it was just so he would be paid more, but he implied that there's some sort of law that says a murderer has to be tried."

"Don't you mean someone *accused* of murder?"

Susannah drummed her gloved fingers on the table in a muffled rat-a-tat. "Look, I don't have time to play word games, Nancy. I'm prepared to give you the entire story if you're willing to sit and listen, and refrain from unnecessary questions."

For a moment Nancy felt like she was in front of her grammar school teacher again, caught trying to peek at Sarah Atchison's geography test answers. "Yes, ma'am," Nancy intoned, and pushed her hat more firmly in place. She tried in the interest of professionalism to quell the surge of resentment at the reprimand.

Susannah's head twitched slightly. "There's no need to go all school-girl on me." She laughed. "Yes," she said, "I sometimes seem to be able to read minds, but it's really just that I'm observant. That's what comes of being so easily overlooked all my life." She steepled her hands and gestured with them at the blank steno pad. "That thing won't do you a bit of good if you don't use it."

She waited until Nancy's pen was poised expectantly, and then repeated herself, as if to be sure Nancy got it right. "I'm easily overlooked. Nobody notices me." She put a gloved hand up to her graying hair. "It was that way when I was a child. It's that way now that I'm in my fifties. Nobody remembered that I was at the party. That's probably the only reason I got away with poisoning Button's martini." She shuddered. "Vile drink."

According to the transcripts, her attorney had wasted a good deal of time trying to convince the jury of the sheer impossibility of her poisoning the man right in the middle of a party for his 50th birthday without her being noticed. "There were so many people at that party," Nancy said. "What if someone *had* remembered you?"

Slip cocked her head to one side, like an eagle examining a mouse before disemboweling it. "They were all so concerned about being seen themselves, I knew they wouldn't pay a bit of attention to me. Surely *you* can imagine what that sort of invisibility is like. You'd never stand out in a crowd with that bland hair of yours."

Nancy's hackles rose at the casual insult. *My dad didn't think so. He always told me my hair is like a wren's feathers, all golden brown and soft.* Her innate respect for the facts, though, won out over her resentment. Her dad was undoubtedly biased, so she felt she had to admit, "I guess you're right. I have a way of blending in with a crowd. Sometimes I manage to overhear interesting conversations that way. That's convenient for a reporter."

Slip smiled and pulled off one glove, then the other. She folded them and tucked them inside the left pocket of her skirt.

I can cross off that question. "Big pockets," Nancy said to keep the conversation flowing.

"I like big pockets. They come in handy."

The prosecution said she'd hidden the knife that killed Dominick Kingsley in one of her pockets. She might have carried the poison for his father's martini six years ago in the same pocket. Did all her dresses have such deep accommodation?

"Yes," Susannah said to Nancy's unspoken thought. "I make my clothes myself, and I always put in pockets that are extra deep."

George would love a touch like that. Here she was, ready to get all the juicy details from Susannah Lou Packard, the headliner on trial. The woman who had single-handedly eliminated the father-son political team of Button and Dominick Kingsley, the duo that could keep a whole state tied up in red tape until they got their way on key legislation. Some of Kingsley's political opponents thought Miss Packard should be given a medal instead of a protracted trial, although not many of them said it out loud.

Susannah sat quietly as Nancy pushed her hat back in place and tried to frame another question. Such patience seemed to be as natural to Susannah as a hen on a clutch of eggs. It was downright relaxing, and Nancy had to remind herself that she had a story to write, even though she wouldn't be able to publish most of it until after the trial was over. She wrote *Button Kingsley* at the top of the page. "Could we start with the first murder? I'd like to know your reasons."

"No," Susannah said. "I'm not quite ready to talk about that yet." Nancy frowned, and Susannah shook her head. "Take off that fool hat of yours, and then we'll start with the last one first. Tell me, though, where are you from?"

"I was born in Statesville, grew up there, never really left."

"Have you ever been to Baynard's Mill?"

"No."

"Well, good. You haven't missed much. I don't recommend it."

The hat joined the hankies on the table. Nancy heaved a sigh, crossed out *Button,* and wrote *Dominick* above it. She underlined the name.

"He was born in Baynard's Mill," Susannah said. "Did you know that?"

"Was that important?"

"Oh, yes. You see, I'd known him most of his life. He was so much like his father it was like watching a badly-scripted play, with him moving in to take over his father's place in the community after his father died."

After you killed the father, Nancy thought, but didn't it say aloud.

"His father had pulled strings to get Dominick elected to the State House of Representatives. With Button in the State Senate and Dominick in the House, they could push through just about any bill they wanted to. Once the father was dead, some of his political clout still seemed to hang around his son. Nobody could stop Dominick when he wanted a bill passed. He may have been a successful politician, but between sessions he was only a second-rate Dean of Admissions at a second-rate college."

"If the school was second-rate, why did you want to go there?"

"It was convenient, and I wanted some letters after my name. I always thought that would look nice on my gravestone when I got around to dying, don't you know?"

Nancy wasn't sure how to answer that. She'd give anything for a degree in journalism, and she couldn't imagine taking it lightly. Some day, when journalism schools were more accessible to women, and when the Depression was over and she could afford it, she'd get those letters, but she'd do it for better reasons than a tombstone engraving. Nancy Lou Remington, college graduate. She scribbled something illegible so she wouldn't have to look at Susannah.

"How did you manage to get close enough to him to slit his throat?"

"I didn't slit it. I simply reached out to shake his hand and held on tight. Then I stepped closer—I'm left-handed, you see—and stabbed him, right above that obnoxious necktie of his."

"How could you be sure nobody would see you leave his office?"

"That was easy. I'd gone there once before, asking him to support some meaningless farm bill. I saw then that his office had a washroom and a back door. After I stabbed him, I cleaned myself up, put on the dress I had stashed in my handbag—it's quite large—and left by the rear entrance."

"But what if someone had come in from the front office while you were still there?"

"I waited until his secretary left for lunch. Then I locked the door as I walked in. The outer office was empty. The secretary never saw me, and nobody knew I was there."

"Wouldn't it have been easier to stab him in the back?"

"Oh, no," Susannah said. "It's obvious you've never stabbed anyone from behind. That requires very precise placement of the knife. It's amateurish to say the least, since the first stab often gets stuck on a rib and misses the heart entirely. Or so I've read." Susannah frowned. "Also, I wanted to see Dominick's face as he died. I missed that with Button, his father."

"You took his wristwatch. May I ask why?"

"I'm not a fan of melodrama, but it seemed to me that his time had run out."

Nancy refrained from rolling her eyes. "You said you'd known him all your life?"

"All *his* life." She clenched her teeth. "He was younger than I was by seven years."

"What did you have against him?"

"Why do you ask that?"

"Well . . ." Nancy stammered a bit. "I . . . I assumed that if you . . . if you killed him, you must have had a reason, and a better one than what the prosecuting attorney said."

"I think I'd like to defer that information until you've heard more of my story." Susannah pulled those old gloves of hers out of her pocket and passed the lump of them from one hand to the other. "I can tell you this. I did have a reason. You see, it had been awhile since the last killing, and my gloves weren't getting any use at all. It seemed a shame to let them waste like that."

"Your gloves?" Nancy obviously was missing something here. She wondered if this was a code of some sort.

"My gloves." Susannah opened her fist and the gloves uncurled like a fern frond in the early spring. "For some reason regular dousing with blood appears to have an amazing preservative effect, but the gloves need rigorous cleaning, you know. To keep them supple."

"Rigorous cleaning?" Nancy felt like a parrot, echoing Susannah's words this way, but what on earth was she to say? How could she ask an intelligent question when they were talking about cleaning gloves once, no twice, in five years? "Why would you have had to clean them after you poisoned Button in 1926?"

Slip shook her head—a gesture that Nancy was getting used to—as if she disapproved of Nancy's question. "You don't understand, do you?"

"I'm trying, but I need more information."

"You're so sure of yourself, waltzing in here like Miss Professional herself, but you don't have any idea what you're in for. You think you can wind me up like a toy and have me spin your story for you. What gives you the right to intrude on my time like this?"

"But you're not—"

"The fact that I'm not going anywhere, as I'm sure you were about to observe, is completely beside the point."

"I didn't mean to—"

"Of course you meant to! You meant to drain me. You meant to use me. You meant to spatter my story across the headlines of your newspaper. You don't care whether or not I'd want it that way. You probably never thought about what my family would think, having their names linked to mine in such a public way."

"I'm sorry, Miss Packard. I certainly didn't intend it this way." *Of course, if you didn't think your family would want their names linked to a murderer, you should have thought about that before you killed anyone.*

"I know your type. You think you can apologize, all meek and timid sounding, and I'll just cave in."

"Your lawyer assured my editor that he had cleared this interview with you."

"I find it hard to comprehend how someone—even someone as malleable as you appear to be—would believe my lawyer."

"I believed my editor. That was good enough for me." *I do trust George, even though he adds outrageous adjectives to my news stories.*

"Did it ever occur to you that he might have been lying to you?"

"No. George doesn't lie."

"Well, in that case, then, I suppose I can forgive you."

Forgive me? For what?

Slip shifted smoothly to a less belligerent tone. Nancy might have thought she'd imagined the animosity, except for the nasty taste the exchange had left in her mouth.

"I honed the knife at least once a month, just to be sure it kept its edge. My father taught me that. I don't suppose I'll get it back, do you?"

"No. I imagine not. Not unless this jury finds you not guilty. Then you'd have to win the appeal on the first trial."

Susannah looked up at the ceiling. Nancy's mother used to do that. One day Nancy asked her why she did it, and Mom said she was praying for patience. Susannah's gaze moved to the locked door. "I wonder what will become of it?"

"Your knife? I don't know, but I suppose I could ask Sheriff Fordyke for you. I'll need to interview him."

"Jasper? Don't waste your time."

Nancy couldn't identify a reason for the sharp undercurrent. "Do you know the sheriff? I understand he's been around a long time."

"Heavens yes, child. He and his brother and I grew up together.

Jasper and I are the same age, fifty-seven now."

"I've never met the sheriff."

"You don't need to. There's not much to know about him. Men are all pretty much the same." She curled her lip in obvious scorn.

Nancy didn't agree with that, but she couldn't see what would be gained by arguing the point. She thought about her father, how he used to take her with him to his hardware store. Maybe she should have followed in his footsteps and worked in the store alongside him. He had taught her always to give the customer a few extra nails or an extra measure of lamp oil. He'd taught her to respect the other person's point of view, even if she didn't agree. Nancy had been so full of her own importance, getting hired by the *Clarion*. She wanted to make her mark in the world. But she wanted to do it abiding by her father's principles. He'd taught her not to lie, but then again, he'd taught her to be polite to her elders. So, it was fairly obvious that Susannah Packard didn't like Sheriff Fordyke, but then again, he'd arrested her. Maybe she'd transferred her scorn for him to all men in general. "You may be right," Nancy said diplomatically. "Is his brother much like him?"

"Jethro?" She studied Nancy for a full minute. Nancy wanted to ask a question, but felt almost hypnotized by Susannah's steadfast gaze. Just before Nancy started squirming, Slip broke the silence. "I'd say Jethro Fordyke was the only real friend I ever had."

Nancy combed her memory for an elusive bit of information. *Jethro Fordyke*. It was an unusual name. "Wasn't there something about a Jethro Fordyke in the news a couple of years ago? He was hurt in a freak accident, if I remember rightly."

Susannah rolled her shoulders back, and Nancy was surprised to see how her breasts strained against the dark blue of her shirtwaist dress. Nancy had thought of Susannah as shapeless and sexless. Now she wasn't so sure. "The accident didn't happen the way it was reported. Jasper always suspected there was foul play—that's how he put it—foul play. But he could never prove anything. He needed evidence, but *he* never had enough evidence to be sure . . ." She let the sentence hang there.

"Are you telling me you know who killed Jethro?"

"You catch on fast," Susannah said. "We'll talk about that later."

Chapter 2 - The First Time

A Crime of Malicious Mischief
. . . unidentified person or persons, on December 1ˢᵗ in the year of our Lord Nineteen
Hundred and Ten with force of arms did unlawfully, illegally, and maliciously,
remove, injure, and destroy the syrup mill of J. W. Mitchell, Esq.

Signed by J. W. Mitchell, Prosecutor
--from the 1910 archives of the
Gwinnett County Superior Court

Nancy could tell that subject was closed, so she turned to a new page and once again wrote *Button Kingsley* at the top of it. "Now will you tell me about Button's murder? I read the transcript of your first trial, but I'd like to hear it from you." Susannah sat in silence, and Nancy repeated herself. "The first murder?"

"The first murder? Are you sure you want to go back that far?" Slip smiled as Nancy mumbled her agreement.

Nineteen-twenty-six wasn't that long ago, even for me, and I'm only half her age. Still, I can certainly use the background, although cyanide in a birthday martini couldn't take too long to relate.

Susannah turned slightly in her chair, as if she were settling in for a long story. "Why do you want to interview me?"

"Why?" Nancy hesitated. She had nothing to lose, though. "I want to tell your life story, if you're willing to share it with me."

"Why *me*, though?"

Because you're a murderer. Because it will sell papers. Because I'm curious. Because I want a name for myself. Headlines. "Because I'm a reporter, and people have a right to know the truth."

"Do they? Even though it means prying into my private life?" Susannah wiped the back of her hand across her mouth. "What do you think gives you the right to feast on . . ." she swept her arm in a wide circle, ". . . on my misery?"

"I'm not . . . that's not what I . . . I'm so sorry, Miss Packard. This isn't at all what I intended." Nancy shuffled her steno pad from one hand to the other and back again. "I just wanted you to be able to tell your story. I thought it might help people to understand."

"Understand?" The scorn in her voice was almost palpable. Nancy pressed her back against the chair as if she could distance herself from the waves of dislike. "Why would anybody want to understand me?"

"Of course they would! People are talking about nothing but your trial. Even President Hoover has taken a back seat to this."

"But how do you know my whole story would be just as interesting as the trial?"

"I think anything about you would catch people's attention. If I could give some background—how you grew up, what molded your personality, how you see life, things like that."

Susannah subsided and pushed the wayward curl back toward the bun at her nape. "I certainly have plenty of stories."

"That would be wonderful."

Susannah narrowed her eyes and regarded Nancy without blinking. "If I agree to this," she lowered her eyes and lifted one of the gloves on top of the other, "will you promise to write the story exactly as I tell it to you?"

Nancy thought about the edits that were a necessary part of any reporter's job. Miss Packard didn't need to know about that qualification. "Yes. I'll write it just the way you tell it."

"Is that a promise?"

Nancy was taken aback by the intensity of Miss Packard's gaze. "Yes. Yes. It's a promise."

"In that case, you need a little background information." She pointed to the note pad. "Can you write fast?"

Nancy smiled. "As fast as you can talk."

"Get ready then." Susannah held up both hands, fingers spread wide apart. "There's one more promise you have to make."

"What is it?"

"Don't share this story with anyone until it's time to print the whole thing."

"All right."

"Promise?"

What am I getting myself in for? "Yes."

"Baynard's Mill isn't much of a town. Nothing much ever happens there, and the people are a lot like the folks in almost any other town around these parts." Slip met Nancy's eyes and held them for an uncomfortable half a minute. "You never had to work hard growing up, the way I did. You're a city girl, aren't you?" The scornful tone was back.

"Not exactly *city*. I already told you, I grew up in Statesville, and I still live there."

"Never went away from home?"

Nancy thought about her dream of Harvard. "No. I've travelled some for my job as a reporter, but with the times the way they are, the paper doesn't pay for many trips."

"Just as well. You stick close to home. It's safer that way."

But not as much fun. "The last trip I went on, I got lost." *Why did I tell her that?* "But I got a good story out of it," she added to cover her embarrassment.

Susannah nodded, as if answering a silent question. "Lost, eh? All the more reason for you to stay away from Baynard's Mill—it's on the back end of forever. Not an easy place to find."

"Well, then, I guess I won't be heading that way."

"Promise you'll stay away from there."

"What?"

"I want you as far away from my family as possible. Promise me you won't go to Baynard's Mill."

Could she get all the background information she needed for the story without going to Susannah's home town? Probably. "I promise."

Susannah nodded. "Good. Now then, about that first murder." I'd planned it all, maybe not down to the very last detail, but most of it

I'd already decided on a good month before it happened. I knew what I was going to wear, my dark blue dress with the deep pockets. I knew there would be blood, of course. I didn't want it to show. I even planned to put a soft rag in my right-hand pocket so I could clean myself up afterwards."

"Wait a minute," Nancy interrupted. "Blood? From a poisoned martini? There wasn't any blood. Or did you just not know what to expect?"

"You're getting ahead of yourself," Susannah said, with a hint of irritation in her voice. "I knew there *would* be blood to clean up that first time. I knew what shoes I'd have on, my sturdy everyday work shoes. I'd need them for the walking beforehand. For a touch of elegance, I decided to wear my Sunday kid gloves, the nicest pair I owned." She rearranged the gloves in front of her, stroking them softly. "Hattie's mother gave these to me when I was just a child."

"Hattie?" Nancy searched her memory for that name and couldn't find anyone to match it. "Who's Hattie?"

"Quit interrupting me," Slip almost barked. You'll find out sooner if you'll hold your peace." She glared at Nancy, then shifted once more into a reasonable tone. "If you want to hear my story, you're going to have to let me tell it my way. Just settle into it, and remember to take good notes. I don't want to have to tell this again."

"But what about questions?"

"You can ask them afterwards. I will not be interrupted." She narrowed her eyes and leveled a disconcertingly direct gaze at Nancy. "I hate being interrupted, and if you badger me with questions, I won't tell you anything. Is that understood?"

Nancy refrained from saying *yes, ma'am* and bent over her note pad instead. Susannah Packard might hate being interrupted, but Nancy hated being lectured as if she were a child. She hadn't achieved her status at the paper by standing back and waiting for stories to come in. She'd gone after them, the way she'd gone after this interview. She raised her head in what her father had always called her stubborn stance. Glaring at Slip did no good, though, because the woman, the murderer, wasn't looking at the reporter. She hated the feeling of being a secretary taking Slip's dictation. On the other hand, Nancy thought she could live with these ground rules, as long as she could ask questions later. She'd just have to think of it as an efficient way of getting a powerful story. If she could provide some insight into the reasons for Button's murder, something the prosecution had never been able to establish, she'd have a chance at having her name under national headlines. Maybe even more.

Susannah seemed to be gathering her thoughts. She certainly wasn't paying any attention to Nancy. Nancy sank against the back of her chair and raised her pen.

When Susannah spoke, her voice followed a sing-song cadence.

I'd had those gloves since I was a child, but finally I'd grown into them. Now they fit. Perfectly. They didn't go with the work shoes, but those wouldn't show much beneath the hem of my everyday dress. It would be a shame to mess up the gloves, but they provided that certain flair I was looking for, almost like a celebration.

I wanted my first time to be the best. I'd never talked with anyone about this. It wasn't the sort of thing anyone could talk about. That just wasn't done in polite circles. Not that I lived in polite circles. No. But we were raised right. We were just a farm family. Ma, Pa, Mary Louise, the younger boys, our little sister, and me. I shouldn't say *just* a farm family. We fed ourselves and the county too. That's what Pa always said. He was proud of his land, and he made sure we were proud of it. There wasn't a one of the boys that couldn't care for the livestock and tend the crops from tilling to planting to harvesting. Each one could repair the tools and maintain the buildings. They knew how to haul the grain to market, and how to read the skies for hints of rain.

The girls all cleaned and canned and cooked. We made our butter and sewed our clothes and tended the vegetable garden. We cared for the chickens and turkeys and gathered the eggs. It was a busy life. I was the second oldest girl left at home. Our other two sisters and our oldest brother were all married and living nearby, not any of them more than half an hour away on foot. Pa didn't like for me to ride the horses, since he needed them to work the farm. He also didn't like me to be away too much because of Ma needing so much help. She was plumb worn out all the time. Seems to me if I'd ridden Old Ned, I could have made the trips back and forth much faster, but Pa didn't see it that way. Still, Mary Louise and I visited each of our older sisters at least once a month, and we saw our older brother about as often, not for visits, just in passing when we walked past his fields. Of course, we saw everybody at church on Sundays and for the big family dinner after the services.

Sundays. I'd have to do some thinking about that. I knew that what I was planning would be frowned on if anyone had known about it. I sat in church the two Sundays before I was going to do it, and I thought about what my life might be like afterwards. Pastor Jacobs used Chapter 17 of First Chronicles, verse 33 as his text. *He shall judge the world with justice and reprove the peoples in faithfulness.* I have never liked it when Pastor Jacobs quotes only part of a verse and takes it out of context. He preached on and on about judgment, but never mentioned the very next verse that says, *Oh give thanks to the Lord, for he is good; for his mercy endures forever.*

I was rather hoping, you see, that God would act in accordance with verse 34 when He saw what I'd done. I have to admit, though, that when the crowning moment came, I wasn't thinking much about God.

The next Sunday was even worse. Pastor Jacobs preached on Psalm 119 that starts *blessed are the undefiled.* I knew what defiled meant. At least he hadn't preached on the Ten Commandments. I'd get into big trouble over one of those shalt nots.

Nancy didn't like the way this was sounding. She'd been expecting to hear about a murder, and now it sounded like . . . well . . . like Slip was talking about something else entirely. Nancy kept writing Slip's words, but she wasn't comfortable at all.

"I leaned forward and peeked past Ma at my sister Estelle. She had always been my favorite sister. She was closest in age to me, except for Mary Louise, and it felt like the end of my life when she married Franklin. It seems strange to speak his name. I usually called him *that man.* I couldn't imagine her making babies with him. Even though I had never experienced it, I did live on a farm. I'd seen what the horses did, and the bull, and even the goats. And of course, I'd seen Hattie."

"Hattie?"

"Stop breaking into my story like that! I warned you to hold your tongue. You'll find out soon enough. Do I need to quit talking right now?"

"No, please don't stop. I just need to be sure I have the facts right."

"Trust me. I'll give you a good story that your readers will love. And I'll tell you everything you need to know. Just let me do it my way."

Nancy nodded, somewhat mutinously, but it was still a nod, and flipped to a new page.

"Now, when Estelle's babies started getting born, one after another like stair steps, and Estelle kept getting more and more tired and more and more sad-looking, I decided right then I didn't want anything to do with any man, ever. That was three years before, when I was fourteen."

"Fourteen? I thought we were talking about Button Kingsley."

Susannah clamped her mouth shut. Nancy saw her story going down the kitchen sink with the wash water. Why couldn't she keep her mouth shut? "I'm sorry," she said. "I just thought I'd made a mistake in the timing."

"There's no mistake." Susannah brushed at the table in front of her, although Nancy couldn't see any dust there. When she spoke again, her voice was somewhat less haughty. "As I was saying, I'd changed my tune. I knew I'd have something to do with a man. *That man.* Even though I knew it might hurt Estelle if she ever knew what I had done. She never had to know, though. That's why I planned so carefully.

"That same Sunday, right after church, Estelle asked me to visit with her the next day and stay the night so we could string cranberries and popcorn to decorate the house for Christmas. When I walked in, Estelle smiled, the children swarmed around me, and that man— Franklin—nodded his hello. He had a way of looking at me that I don't think Estelle ever noticed. I took off my overcoat and my wrap, but made sure my collar was buttoned all the way to the top. When I went to sleep that night, I moved a chair against the door and lay down in the middle of the children's bed with three little girls and two little boys around me. Most people thought I was invisible, which is why I suppose I was so surprised when Franklin looked at me like that."

Susannah fiddled with the collar of her dress. "You're a lot like that too, you know," she said.

"You mean invisible?" Nancy had, as a matter of fact, felt invisible the whole time Susannah—Slip—was speaking, as if her only function was to transfer Slip's words onto paper.

Slip nodded.

"Yes," Nancy said, "I do know that. But what does all this have to do with Button Kingsley?"

"I thought you wanted to hear about the first one."

"The first one?"

"That's what I said." She smiled that tight smile of hers and went on. Once again, her eyes focused on something or someone other than Nancy. Her voice took on that sing-song quality again. Susannah Lou Packard was somewhere else than in that dreary interview room.

That Thursday, that special day, the day before Christmas, I hurried through my chores and asked Ma if I could walk to Estelle's house again. I knew that man had butchered a hog, so Estelle would be busy rendering the lard. Our oldest sister, Lucy, had agreed to be there to help keep the younger children from falling into the fire, and Mary Louise, the third oldest girl, six years younger than Lucy and a year older than I was, said she'd walk over early and help Estelle with the cutting up and melting down. Between Lucy and Estelle, those two already had nine children, so Estelle's farm house would be busy indeed. "Wear your long shawl, Susannah Lou," was all Ma said. "And take some of this fresh bread to Estelle." She wrapped a loaf in a clean towel and handed it to me. "Why are you wearing your good gloves to go to a hog-rendering?"

"It's cold enough for gloves on the walk there, Ma," I said. "I'll take them off before I get to working. It'll be warm beside the fire."

On the way there, Pastor Jacobs stopped me when I walked by his house and said he hoped he and the missus could count on me to teach Sunday school starting the next month. I told him I'd be happy to do that and thanked him for asking me. He said his wife was impressed with how studious I was. I figured she might change her opinion of me if she'd known what I was planning, but of course she'd never know. I hurried away, glad that Estelle's place was over a couple of hills and out of sight of the pastor.

Just before I reached the top where the farm would be spread out below me, I moved into the trees, so none of the women would look up and see me. Estelle had a pair of geese that were better watchdogs than any mutt I ever knew. If they had spotted me, I never would have gotten away with it. I paralleled the right fork of the path, the one that led around behind the barn, and once I could see that the geese were nowhere in sight, I edged out of the woods just a bit. I walked with a casual air, swinging my bonnet from my gloved hand. It wasn't too cold, despite what I'd said to Ma. The snow from five days before had mostly melted away, and I dodged mud puddles in the track. I took a quick look and could see that man watching me from the back door of the barn. His shape was outlined by light from the afternoon sun that fell through the door at the other end of the building. Even though I couldn't see his face clearly, I knew him from his broad shoulders and the way he slouched a bit, leaning against the horse stall closest to the end.

I paused for just a moment, glanced toward him, and then turned away from him. I lifted my skirts well off the ground so I wouldn't leave a trail other than my shoe prints. The barn stood between me and the house, and the pine woods weren't too far from the barn at this point. There was a small clearing back in the woods, beginning to be overgrown, that I'd seen once when I was four or five and then again last year when Estelle and I took the children to look for the goats. They were always eating the fence and getting out of their pasture, and they seemed to love the woods. Today, those woods were exactly what I wanted. I slipped my hand in my pocket and made sure I had what I needed, then stepped under the shelter of the trees. I didn't look back, but I knew he was following me. I heard his heavy step, and as he got closer to me, I could hear him breathe. Have you ever had that feeling of consciousness of every living thing? If I'd stopped walking, I'm sure I could have heard his heart beating.

I wound my way through the trees, stepped into the edge of the clearing, and stopped just short of that old fallen hickory tree; you can still see it if you visit the place, where the birds sit to chip away at weed seeds they've gathered from the overgrown yarrow and thistles. The weathered bark is covered in bird droppings, as if they've designated that their outhouse. This was the perfect place for our meeting. Dead grasses with just a light dusting of snow. Far enough from the house that nobody would hear anything. Easy enough for me to slip back unseen afterwards.

Slip. A good word. Slip had been my nickname for as long as I could remember. I already told you why. That year I was still only a slip of a thing, but I knew that today I'd feel grown up somehow in a way I hadn't been before.

I reached into my left-hand pocket and made sure one last time. I spread my shawl across the fallen tree trunk and set my bonnet and the wrapped-up bread on top of it. A single bright feather, from the tail of a blue jay, lay there like an offering. Like a gift. Like an omen.

When I turned around, he loomed in front of me, closer almost than he'd ever been before except that time when I was helping Estelle with birthing her third and I'd walked out to get another pail of boiling water. He'd moved close to me then, but I brushed past him and he let me go, knowing perhaps that I was doing women's work and he'd best not interfere. This time, I still had women's work to do, but he didn't know that. I leaned my head to one side and looked around him as if to check to see that no one had followed. He was so sure of himself he didn't turn.

"We're here alone, Slip," he said. "Just the way you wanted it."

I hardly trusted myself to speak. "Yes," I said. "This is the way I want it."

My hand was still in my pocket. He threw off his coat and struggled out of his suspenders, unbuttoned his pants, and grabbed my shoulders, blinded to everything around him by the full tide surging within him. At least, that's what I imagined he was feeling. He wasn't very gentle when he pushed me down away from the tree, although I couldn't tell for sure. Maybe he didn't want me to brain myself on the heavy branch. I should have placed myself farther away from it, but this was part of the script I couldn't have planned out exactly. I wasn't sure how he was going to go about it. He reached up under my dress and put his right hand where Ma said nobody should ever put a hand. And then he was fumbling around with his pants, leaning on one elbow above my shoulder, and grunting like the hog must have done just before he'd butchered it. I made sure my arm was free, pulled the knife from my left-hand pocket, and slammed it as hard as I could into his back. The kid gloves had been a good idea. My hand never slipped even once on the wooden handle. There's something really special about the first time. Those oh-so-magical goose bumps that run up and down your body inside and out. Your brain gets a little hazy afterwards, and your eyelids get a little droopy once it's over, like finding yourself with a few stolen hours on a lazy sunny afternoon sitting by the creek, with flies buzzing around you. That one supreme moment, though, *that* moment is completely divine, as if you've stepped into the company of angels. As if you've started a conversation with God himself. At least that's how it was for me my first time. Even the moments leading up to that one moment felt so delicious. I knew what was going to happen. At least I thought I did, but I have to admit it was even better than I thought it would be. Much better.

His mouth opened in a ridiculous O, and he looked surprised more than anything else, until his eyes went wide in pain. Served him right. He rolled away from me, which turned out to be good, because that way his blood didn't get on my skirt. I must have hit him in exactly the right spot. Now, looking back, I know it's not that easy, but at the time I had no idea. It was luck, I suppose. What do they call it? Beginner's luck? He was heavier than I expected. For a second I thought I might be trapped there, but luckily he rolled off, right onto the knife, and his own grunting weight pushed it farther into him. By the time I stood and shoved him over onto his stomach so I could get my knife back, he was pretty close to being dead. Still, his moans sounded desperate, like he wanted help. He was in the wrong place for that.

"That was for Hattie," I said as I wrenched the knife out, but I'm not sure he heard me. I should have told him sooner. I wanted him to know why.

His blood was warmer than I'd expected it to be. Even through my kid gloves I could feel the heat. I thought about twisting the knife in one more time, but that might kill him too soon. I'd thought his blood would flow like the creek that ran through the woods behind my sister's house, only this one, of course, would be red, and would eventually stop. His blood didn't flow, though. It oozed. The hole wasn't very big.

The trouble with that man, lying there with his right ear in a snow-crusted patch of brown winter grass, his arms splayed out to the side in a spreading pool of his own blood—the trouble with him had always been his lack of imagination. He thought his wife was stupid.

He thought she and his children would respect him for the beatings he gave them. He thought nobody had seen him with Hattie. He thought he could keep getting away with it. Everything about him was arrogant. Or had been. Now he looked pathetic. His eyes, I thought, would have the same glazed look that Estelle's held when she tried to hide the bruises from me. No. That was wrong. They'd have the same look that Hattie's eyes had the day she died. It was just as well I couldn't see his eyes. The left side of his face was bad enough, with blood leaking from his mouth, its flow interrupted by his stiff black beard, like the stones just below the creek crossing that stirred the water into whirlpools and channeled it to a new course.

Susannah fell silent for a moment. "Do you think you could ask the matron for a glass of water for me?"

Nancy fumbled with the cap of her pen and set it down. Then she thought about Slip's sudden shifts from quiet storytelling to explosive anger. She pictured the knife that had stabbed Franklin, and picked the pen back up. She carried it with her to the door.

"Can't have glass," the matron said as she handed over two tin mugs. That suited Nancy just fine.

Once they were settled, Susannah picked up her gloves and rolled them back and forth in her hands. "Have you ever experienced anything like that?" she said. "Seen someone get away with something they should have been punished for? You have, haven't you? I can see it in the way you're looking at me."

"No, I've never felt that way. I'd never kill . . . I'd never want . . . I wouldn't . . . I couldn't."

"Who was it?" Susannah asked in almost a whisper.

"No," Nancy said. "Nobody."

Slip raised one expressive eyebrow and waited.

"When . . . when I was in fourth grade, a man who was drunk . . . went through Statesville taking potshots at the sides of buildings. Josie, my best friend, was . . . she was in the wrong place at the wrong time."

Susannah nodded. "So you do understand." She didn't wait for an answer.

The whole time I was killing him I felt that sunny-afternoon feeling, almost grateful to him for giving me this bright event. Every moment of it, the heft of the knife in my hand, the arc of the blade. Even though I hadn't been able to see it moving toward his back—his shoulder blocked my way—I'd known, as surely as I knew my own way from my bed to the outhouse on a spring night, just where that blade was headed. I felt the world passing as slowly as a tortoise. I had time, plenty of time, to focus on the call of a blackbird from the other side of the clearing, to see a shower of snow fall from a pine branch off to my right, to feel the cold of the snow and grass beneath my back. I heard the swoosh as the knife ripped his shirt. That was a shame. Estelle had worked long to make that shirt. Maybe I could make it up to her somehow. I thought about that as I listened to the start of his scream, the way it built until he choked. I tasted the salt of his sweat that fell from his forehead onto my mouth. His hand clutched at my shoulder and pulled at it as he collapsed to one side. The white cotton of my shift rubbed hard against me in a way that almost burned and was almost cold. Both at the same time.

He'd underestimated me, the way everyone did, even back then. I knew I was unprepossessing. Practically invisible. Everyone tended to look right through me. They always had, from the time I was a skinny, knock-kneed school girl with mousy brown hair. Then I grew into a skinny young woman, gliding mostly unseen through the crowds on the sidewalk outside the general store when we drove to town for supplies or alongside the neighbors on their way to church on Sundays. Whatever would Pastor Jacobs think if he could see me now?

Once I rolled him over, so I could retrieve my knife, his blood didn't really look wet. It looked soft. I lifted my skirts and bunched them between my legs to avoid any stains. I trailed my index finger across his back and drew a swirl of vermillion on his heavy cotton shirt. I did feel bad for that, as I said earlier, but only for a heartbeat. The bright red reminded me of my sister's roses. The coppery smell of his blood was not as sweet a fragrance, but at that moment I would have chosen that odor over roses or fresh bread or new-mown hay or the clean scent of a tiny baby. Blood that I had drawn. Life that I had taken.

My gloves were a mess. How hard would it be to clean blood from soft leather? Estelle would know how to do it, but I couldn't very well ask her. Not with her husband lying dead there in the clearing and his blood on my gloves. Estelle knew everything. She grew the largest, juiciest tomatoes. Her lard was the creamiest in the county. The clothing she stitched was perfect in every way. Estelle had a flair for turning the ordinary into the beautiful. The only things she hadn't known were how to keep from having five children in four and a half years and, before that, how to choose a man. I had tried to talk her out of marrying him, but she wouldn't listen, and I couldn't find the words to make her understand. I couldn't tell her about Hattie.

I can see you want to ask me about Hattie. Don't. It's not time to tell you that yet.

I wiped the knife blade on the grass nearby. Other than my gloves, I didn't seem to have any blood on me. I wrapped the knife and the gloves in the rag I'd brought and returned the bundle to my pocket, grateful to my mother for sewing in a pocket that was so deep. Ma believed in substantial pockets. She was always gathering herbs along the roadside or picking up an interesting rock to place for a week or two on the window sill beside the cook stove. I rubbed snow on my hands to get rid of the red.

A swirl of snow skittered around me. I thought at first it was something blown from a nearby branch. The sky had gone that slate color of an impending storm. Good. More snow would cover our tracks. I lifted my skirts again and scuffed my way back through the trees. I backtracked a bit just inside the cover of the trees, stepped out onto the road near the top of the hill, and walked through the gathering snow to where my sisters bent near a fire in Estelle's open side yard. The younger children saw me coming and flew at me in a frenzy of greeting. They saw me. To them I wasn't invisible. The gander added his two cents' worth, and the goose joined in, which set all the other barnyard fowl to clucking. It was quite a welcome.

"Slip, you took a long time getting here." Lucy's red face looked stern, as it always did, but she had a soft heart. She let the children run all over her, whether it was her own or one of her sister's brood. "You look all dreamy-eyed." She poked my arm and pursed her mouth. "Thinking of a beau?"

"She was most likely reading," Estelle put in. "I see that lump in your pocket, Slip. Is it a good story?"

That was something to remember. I should have put a book

in my pocket to help waylay suspicion. "No," I said, afraid that if I'd claimed to have a book, they might have asked me to read it to them after our evening meal. "Just my gloves. And here's some bread from Ma. I'll put it in the kitchen."

Later when Lucy sent Joshua, her middle son, to call his Uncle Franklin in to eat, I made sure I was busy slicing Ma's fresh bread, to keep my hands from shaking in anticipation.

The snow slowed down the search some, but Lucy's husband, William, found what was left of the body the next day, on Christmas morning, near that fallen tree. He came straight to our place to tell Pa. I was in the hayloft at the time and heard them talking about it. He said it was pretty clear that something big, like a bear or a mountain lion, had gotten hold of him. The two of them went to the house to tell Ma, and then Ma went with William to tell Estelle. I stayed in the barn, happy to know that a bear had a good meal or two.

My gloves were hardly stained. I had soaked them in cold water, and they were stiff for a while and maybe a bit browner than they had been before, but nothing anyone would notice. Of course, I didn't wear them again until the next time.

Slip paused and rubbed the back of her neck. "I'm not used to sitting this long in one place." She frowned. "I guess I'll have to get accustomed to it."

Nancy mirrored her action and bent her head to the left and to the right. She wondered if she would have to tell the sheriff about this. Was she obliged to report a crime that was—what?—forty years old? Ridiculous. The woman was on trial for murder. A different murder. And she already had a life sentence ahead of her for the murder of Button Kingsley. Nancy could run this story as an exclusive after this trial was over. It not only would get her a headline or two, it ought to bring nationwide recognition. She decided to sleep with her notebook under her pillow, just in case. That boutonniere-toting reporter from the *Midwest Times* was staying in the same rooming house for the duration of the trial. She wouldn't put it past him to try a little pilfering if he got wind of her interviewing Miss Packard.

"Did you get every word?"

Susannah's strident voice, so different from a moment before, jerked Nancy back to reality. "Yes. Yes I did. Every word."

"Remember your promises—not a word of this to anyone until you print the whole story."

Nancy mumbled some sort of an excuse about having to organize her notes, grabbed her hat, and stumbled over her chair in her haste to leave. The matron responded to her knock.

"Come back tomorrow," Slip called out as Nancy left. "I'll be right here. I'm not going anywhere soon."

The matron handed Nancy her hat pin and clanged the heavy door shut behind her. The same officer who had signed her in before still sat hunched over his desk. "You'll need to sign out, miss." His light auburn eyebrows, the color of a weasel, came close to touching each other. One deep furrow separated them, like the parting of the Red Sea. He pushed the book to her side of the desk and scowled at her.

She glanced at his name tag as she signed out. "Thank you, Officer Jolly." It was considerably later than she had expected, and light clouds obscured the sun. Nancy's car was only moderately hot, but she still had no idea whether or not she'd parked in the right place. She needed a course in directions. She'd often regretted not signing up for that troupe of girl guides when she was ten.

Back at the rooming house, which she found after only one wrong turn, Nancy hurried past Mrs. Cappell, who put out a hand to stop her. "You made it back on time. Dinner will be served in twenty-five minutes."

All Nancy wanted to do was hide in her room. "No, thank you. I have too much work to do." Her stomach took that moment to growl in open rebellion. "I'll take something up to my room if that's all right with you."

"I have some new boarders you might enjoy meeting," Mrs. Cappell crooned. "Two lovely sisters who've come to stay for a few days, and there's that polite young man from the newspaper—the other newspaper." Her voice took on a wistful note. "Yesterday when he arrived he gave me the boutonniere from his lapel. I love the smell of carnations."

"That's nice, but I really do need to get my notes together. I'll be happy with a sandwich."

Mrs. Cappell wasn't to be put off. "I know I'm supposed to prefer the *Clarion*. My brother George is always extolling its virtues, but I must say that the young man from the *Midwest Times* is such a gentleman. It just makes me want to read his paper."

Nancy mumbled her apologies again and fled upstairs. So George, her boss, was Mrs. Cappell's brother. No wonder he'd been willing for Nancy to stay here during the trial. Mrs. Cappell probably gave him the room for next to nothing.

She pulled out her tidy stack of largely useless note cards. Susannah Lou Packard had led Nancy through that first interview like a general leading his troops. Nancy lay across her bed and wondered if she had chosen the right profession. It would have been a lot easier if she had gone to work for her father. Finally, she sighed, got up, and called in a very boring summary of the day's courtroom events for the Saturday edition. At least, it was boring compared to what she'd heard at the prison.

STATESVILLE COUNTY CLARION

FORDYKE FORKS OUT FACTS

by Nancy Remington

The State Capital: The first day of testimony in the sensational trial of Susannah Lou Potts brought gruesome surprises yesterday after District Attorney Paul W. Stevens and Defense Attorney Rupert Z. Pinkney offered their opening statements. Mr. Stevens then called Baynard's Mill Sheriff Jasper Fordyke to testify at length regarding his investigation of the brutal slaying of Senator Dominick Kingsley on December 23, 1931. The evidence he presented included a blood-stained dress and a slender knife, as well as horrifying and extremely explicit photographs of the murder scene. One lady in the gallery swooned when the terrifying photographs were shown and had to be helped out into the fresh air. She did not return to the courtroom.

Sheriff Fordyke displayed a wooden box of mementos (for a list of the contents, see accompanying story on page 2 of this edition) that he said had been hidden underneath Miss Packard's bed. The jury was dismissed at 1:00 p.m. and asked not to discuss the case. The trial will resume on Monday, July 18th.

Chapter 3 - Tomatoes

On <u>September 11th</u> in the year of our Lord Nineteen Hundred and <u>Nine</u>, the aforesaid <u>James Garrett</u> did use opprobrious words and abusive language in the presence of one <u>E. S. Camp</u>, to wit: <u>"You are a suck-egg pup" and "You are a rascal."</u>

--from the 1909 archives of the Gwinnett
County Superior Court

🛷 **Slip had said she'd be happy to continue the interview over** the weekend, not having any place to go. As Nancy ate breakfast Saturday morning, she debated whether to pack a lunch. She should have asked about the prison policy. Surely there was a quiet corner office where she could eat in peace? Mrs. Cappell fluttered around, offering more eggs, more sausage, more toasted bread. The other boarders must have slept in, leaving no one else for Mrs. Cappell to hover over. Berating herself for not having planned ahead, but glad she was in a rooming house where she had kitchen privileges for preparing her own lunches, as long as she bought her own food—Mrs. Cappell's generosity only went so far—Nancy cut two slices of bread and a good-sized hunk of cheese, wrapped each in oiled paper, and swaddled them in a page from yesterday's *Midwest Times*, their major competitor, worth not much more than its current use as far as she was concerned since the *Times* had refused to hire her three years before. She bundled her now compact meal into her capacious handbag.

On the way to the prison, she stopped by a newsstand for a copy of the morning's *Clarion*. She cringed at the flippant headline above her short factual rundown. George had added some adjectives as well: gruesome, brutal, terrifying. He berated her frequently for her tendency to recite just the facts. "Readers want to see the scene, Miss Remington," he'd said. "You have to draw it for them. That's what sells papers." Still, she deplored the sensationalism. It could have been worse, though. The headlines could have read something along the line of SHERIFF SHARES SHENANIGANS or JASPER WON'T JEST ABOUT JUSTICE. *Ridiculous, Nancy. You sound like those jokers in the press room.*

She parked beside a Willys automobile near the prison entrance. All the potential shady spaces near the tree were already taken.

When she checked in at the oak counter, the still-sullen guard rummaged through the lunch package. Nancy hoped his hands were relatively clean. If not, maybe she could poison the cheese next time, some sort of acid that would rot his hands away. He'd writhe in excruciating pain before she . . .

"Step through the door there, miss, and someone will be right with you."

She was patted down by the same matron, given a receipt for her hat pin, and ushered to the familiar interview room. This time Nancy and Susannah both accepted the offer of coffee after Matron said, "The coffee's fresh, if you want some. One of the other guards brought in a new percolator because he couldn't stand the tar we had before. I perked it myself a few minutes ago."

Nancy took a sip, sighed, and turned to another page. *Button Kingsley* she wrote at the top. "Okay. I'm ready. Shall we begin?"

"Oh, yes." Slip wore the same blue shirtwaist dress as before; either that or she had several duplicates in her wardrobe. Nancy wondered where she had left her blue hat, the one like Mrs. Roosevelt's, the one with no hat pin. Were there hat racks in prison cells? Susannah pulled her gloves out of her pocket and laid them on the table, one on top of the other.

Nancy's high school stenography course allowed her to keep up with Slip's monologue yesterday without any trouble. She was looking forward to today's story of Button's murder. She'd begun to think of Button as *number two,* the middle victim instead of the first one, now that she knew about Franklin's death. That knifing would be the first installment in her story for the *Clarion*. She'd have to watch herself when she got to the courtroom on Monday, not to let anything slip about that extra murder.

Susannah smoothed the gloves, lifted one of them, and laid it next to the other one. They resembled handprints, with the thumbs pointing to her coffee cup. "You know how there's always one stuck-up girl in a schoolroom? And then she grows up to be the one truly arrogant woman in the community."

Nancy nodded. She'd read enough about Button Kingsley's snooty second wife to know exactly what Slip was talking about, although she had wondered if Mrs. Kingsley might just be painfully shy. Sometimes that made people seem aloof. She knew that Mrs. Kingsley was a good thirty years younger than Button, making her ten years younger than Button's son. Nancy could just imagine the difficulties that would have caused. Had Dominick been required to call her *mother*? Nancy missed a sentence or two and hoped none of it had been critical to the story. Slip didn't seem to have noticed the lapse. She went right on speaking.

"... one who shakes her head and purses her lips when somebody sings off-key at choir practice. She's the one who gets her shoe buttons in a tangle when somebody else wins a blue ribbon for the best canned green beans at the county fair."

Nancy smiled at the old-fashioned analogy. It wasn't appropriate since Slip was talking about Imogene Kingsley, a wealthy woman who had most likely never canned a single bean and wouldn't be caught dead wearing anything that wasn't the latest fashion. Thirty years from now, Imogene would probably still be trying to pass herself off as thirty-four. *Button-up shoes. How did women ever manage to put up with those monstrosities?* She looked at Susannah carefully and registered the woman's age. Her comment about the shoe buttons had dated her. Creases wrinkled the skin around her eyes and ran deep furrows from her nose to her mouth. Nancy's notes said that Susannah was fifty-seven. She would have been born in 1874. She'd have her fifty-eighth birthday coming up in early November, right about the time of the election. Nancy was half her age. Not married, just like Slip. She wondered if Slip had ever loved someone, if she'd ever had a chance at marriage. Would she be where she was today if ... At that thought, Nancy wasn't sure whether she was referring to Slip or to herself. She cleared her throat unnecessarily. "You were telling me about Button's wife?"

"No, I wasn't. I was talking about Dotty."

Dotty, Nancy wrote. She wondered when she'd find out who that was.

"I can tell you're wondering who Dotty was," Susannah said. "Well, I always knew how to deal with pushy people like Dotty Farraday. . . ."

Being invisible helped. I never sang loud enough to be noticed, and my canning skills were mediocre at best, so I never had much trouble with her, even though we grew up together and I didn't like her much. I guess my opinion didn't count.

The one I did have a problem with, though, was Dotty's hanger-on. You know that kind too, don't you? Maude Reynolds was plain next to Dotty's pretty face. She was skinny as a fence rail compared to Dotty, who managed early on to show interesting curves in all the right places. Maude was not exactly dumb, but our teacher always repeated herself two or three times just so Maude could catch on. Maude never could think of a cutting thing to say until Dotty said it first. Then Maude would snicker. She didn't have the gumption to laugh out loud, just that simpering hee-hee to let Dotty know Maude thought she was so clever.

One day when we were nine or ten Maude asked me if we could walk home together after school. She lived just a ways beyond our farm. Of course I said yes. I was, I must admit, flattered that somebody wanted to walk with me, even if it was only Maude. I guess I hoped she'd finally gotten tired of Dotty. We talked about everything, the way little girls do. I thought it was the start of a good friendship. She asked me about my secret dreams for when I grew up. Nobody I knew used to talk much about dreams. We all knew we'd grow up there in Baynard's Mill and probably get married, raise a family, live our whole lives no more than fifteen miles from where we were born, and then die there too.

But I'd seen a newspaper picture once, a drawing of a lady ballet dancer. She was a real lady too, not one of those circus performers in a scandalous outfit. No, this lady was elegant, the most elegant person I'd ever seen. I told Maude about the picture. Told her how sometimes when I was alone I tried dancing up on my tiptoes. I even twirled around right there on the road with my hands stretched up high, like I could touch the sky and turn the dark storm clouds into sunshine. It didn't work. The rain started falling as Maude said, "That is so exciting." Her eyes got really big. "I never knew a dancer before."

The next morning, Dotty and Maude stood up as I walked into the school room. They both put their hands way up over their heads and twirled around and around. Everybody laughed, which wouldn't have been so bad, but then everybody in the classroom turned and looked at me. Even my little brother Silas. He sat there like a traitor next to Maude's brother Johnny and laughed his fool head off. The two of them always played together whenever they had time away from their chores, but that was no excuse for Silas laughing at me. Johnny was a scrawny little kid with a pointy nose and pointy chin. Silas always did what Johnny wanted. And right then Johnny wanted to laugh at me along with his sister and Dotty and everybody else. Everybody except Jethro. Jethro never laughed at me.

The summer I turned eighteen, that was the year after Franklin had the run-in with the bear, my sister Mary Louise grew the biggest, most beautiful tomatoes I'd ever seen, even better than Estelle's, and that was really saying something. I'd heard from a traveling peddler that in a lot of states, people thought tomatoes were poisonous, but we'd been eating tomatoes in our stretch of the woods for as long as anybody could remember. Mary Louise had some beauties in our garden that year. She'd staked out the finest plants and already had her eye on the three best tomatoes, planning to pick them the morning of the county fair judging.

"When I win that blue ribbon," Mary Louise told me, "I'm going to put it in my treasure box to keep forever."

"No you're not," I said. "We're going to hang your blue ribbon on the parlor wall where everybody can see it. Then when you get married, you'll take it with you to your new house."

Mary Louise and I both had treasure boxes, small wooden crates that our brother Tom had made for us a long time ago when we were little. We kept them under the bed we shared. I had no idea what Mary Louise had in hers. Mine held a picture postcard Tom sent me that time he traveled all the way to St. Louis and the blue jay feather I'd picked up last year.

We spent the week before the fair working extra hard to get everything caught up so we could take the whole day off. The day before the fair Ma set us girls to work doing laundry, even though it wasn't Monday. We knew we'd have to spend the following Monday canning tomatoes—they were ripe enough almost to bursting. So that Friday we boiled the clothes, wrung them out as they cooled down, and strung them up to dry. Thank goodness there was no rain or we'd have had to hang everything inside, which could turn the whole house into a steam bath in a hurry. Pa sent Silas and Joseph off to clear out a patch of water hemlock he'd seen growing down by the marshy area in the back forty. Everybody called the plant cowbane, because it could kill a cow faster than anything. "Dig up the roots," Pa told them, "so it won't grow back." Even little Emmeline had a chore. Ma had some problems when Emmeline was born, and Doc Breslow told her she'd never be able to have any more. Emmy was six that year, and her job was to sprinkle flea powder on all the kittens down in the barn. Mary Louise and I laughed at how they wriggled to get away from her. Emmeline got more of that white powder on herself than on the kittens. We made her wash up real good afterwards. At least she wouldn't get fleas.

That evening when we gathered to read the Bible before bed, Pa asked us whether all our chores were caught up. Emmeline told him all about the kittens, rather more than I think he wanted to hear, but Pa had an extra softness when it came to Emmeline, maybe because she was the youngest and the last. Silas reported that Johnny Reynolds had helped him and Joseph clear out the cowbane. They'd cut it down and burned it.

"Did you wash your knife real good?" Pa asked.

"Of course," Silas said. "I know that stuff's poison. We dug out the roots too."

Pa turned to Mary Louise. "What about you and your sister?"

"Everything is done, Pa. We even packed the wagon with some blankets for us to sit on."

"I'm never going to stop long enough to sit down," Silas said, and we all laughed. "I want to see the hot air balloon go up. Maybe I could even ride in it."

Ma pointed her finger at Silas. "You keep your feet on solid earth, young man. The farthest off the ground you'll ever get is to the rooftop of the hotel on Independence Day to watch the parade. Three stories is high enough for anybody."

Everyone got up extra early the next morning. Pa and the boys tended the stock while Mary Louise and I helped Ma load food for our dinner into the wagon. Once all those chores were done, we were ready to join the train of families on their way to the fair. Old Ned, the horse we'd grown up with, had finally gotten too slow to pull the wagon, so he missed the fair that year, the first time he'd ever had to stay home in the pasture as all our friends and neighbors rattled past and called to us to join them. We knew he'd be dying soon, and Pa had already told us that if Ned got too feeble, he'd put him down, something none of us wanted to think about that fine day.

Mary Louise waited until the very last minute to pick her prize tomatoes. I went running when I heard her shriek. Every single tomato that was anywhere near ripe had a big knife slit across it. Not just the good tomatoes, either. Even the second best ones. Dozens of them. We couldn't leave that many tomatoes to rot on the vine while we went to the fair. We'd be gone all day. So Mary Louise and I missed the fair that year. We stayed behind and canned every slashed tomato we could find. I pumped a bucket of water and set it boiling so we could dunk the tomatoes to loosen the skins. It wasn't easy to slip the skins off because the knife slits got in the way. We lost a lot of the juice, but we still thought it would be all right. We canned seventeen jars of tomatoes that day, knowing at least that they wouldn't go to waste. Mary Louise tried to pretend that the water running down her face was sweat from the hot fire in the cook stove, but I could tell she was crying about losing her prize tomatoes and the blue ribbon that should have been hers.

Parsella Myers stopped by and asked if she could stay with us while her husband took their produce to the fair market. She said she didn't mind missing the fair since she wasn't entering any of the contests. She'd been feeling a bit tired with the baby she was expecting, her first one, so we didn't let her do any of the heavy lifting and pouring. She just lined up the canning jars straight out of the hot water and made sure the lids were on tight.

We could tell Parsella was worried about birthing her baby. Her mother and mother-in-law both were long dead. She and Ronald were the only family they had. "My mother and Mother Meyers both had so many stillborn babies," Parsella whispered. She cradled her arms around her still slender stomach. "I don't think I could bear to lose this child."

"You hush now," Mary Louise said. "Slip and I both have helped our sisters birth their babies. There's nothing to it. We'll help you too."

Nothing to it, I thought. Nothing except blood and screaming and a terrible mess to clean up and a squalling baby and then you do it all over again a year later. "Yes. We'll help," I said.

Parsella was only partly comforted by that offer. "What if it comes sudden like? I don't want to be alone while Ronald comes to get you."

Mary Louise looked at me, and I nodded. "About a week before your baby is due, Slip will come to stay with you. Then when you go into your labor, she'll send Ronald to get me. Men are no use around a birthing anyway, and this will help him feel useful. He can always get Dr. Breslow too, if he has to, but everything will go just fine. Don't you worry."

We laughed, and Parsella wondered if her baby would come on Christmas morning. On that happy note, we kept on canning.

We gave her four of the jars as a thank you when her husband stopped by to pick her up on his way home shortly after sunset. Lucy, our oldest sister, was madder than a wet hen when she walked in not five minutes later. She threw her shawl over the peg and slammed her bonnet on top of it. "That Dotty Farraday!" She practically spit out her words. "Not only did she win a blue ribbon for her tomatoes, which everybody knows you should have gotten, Mary Louise. Not only that, but her canned green beans won too."

"Ma didn't win with her beans?" I could hardly credit the news. Ma's beans outshone everybody's in the county.

"Maude's brother Johnny let loose a slingshot in the judging tent. He claimed it was an accident, but the only jar that got broken was Ma's, and later on I saw Maude buying him some taffy. I think Dotty put Maude up to it, and Maude got her rat-faced brother to break Ma's jar. For all I know, he's the one who ruined all our tomatoes too."

"I think you're wrong," Mary Louise said. "Dotty's not mean enough to do something as evil as that. I'd be willing to bet—of course I wouldn't bet—but I'm sure you know what I mean. I just know that Maude thought of it, and probably bribed Johnny to ruin our entries."

It sounded like just the sort of low-down thing Maude would do. It made me wonder if maybe Maude had been the leader all along, just letting Dotty think that Dotty was in charge.

Just before we went to sleep that night, Mary Louise told me she was going to put Maude and Johnny on her Rectification List. She kept a sheet of paper in her treasure box—I never looked at it, but she told me about it once—where she listed all the people she didn't like and all the situations that needed rectifying. That's the word she used, *rectifying*.

Three months later, in the winter, we found out the extent of Maude's meanness. That Sunday I got up early and packed a bundle of clothes to take to Parsella's for the week. I was looking forward to delivering her baby. It was hard work for sure, especially with a first child, keeping the mother up and walking so the baby would move more quickly down the birth passage to where it needed to be. Parsella was going to be mighty tired. It felt good to know I was needed. She'd asked me to stay with her the night before, but I told her I had to wait until Sunday. She tried to lure me with the promise of meatloaf—Parsella was a good cook for sure—but I had sewing chores I needed to complete before I left, and it took me all day Saturday to finish them.

Parsella made a sauce for the meatloaf using one of those jars of our tomatoes. We hadn't opened any of our jars yet, since we still had half a dozen jars left from the previous year's canning season. We always used the oldest jars first, and we had every jar dated. It was a good system.

Well, Parsella and her husband Ronald didn't show up for church that Sunday. We thought maybe the baby might have decided to come a few days early, and I felt bad for not being there with her. Doctor Breslow was in church. When we asked him about the baby, he said he hadn't heard a thing. He offered to stop by their house to be sure all was well.

All was not well. Doc found Parsella's husband stretched out on the kitchen floor, rolling around in his own vomit, retching his head off. "I tried to keep him from choking on his own tongue," Doc told us that evening, two weeks before Christmas, when we came over to clean up the house and lay out the bodies. "But he died within minutes. I went looking for Parsella, and found her curled up in a tight ball, almost like she'd been trying to protect the baby inside her." She'd thrown up everything. It was all over the bed and splattered around the floor. Doc said he'd never seen anything like it. Half-digested meat and red sauce and yellow bile all thrown around the room as if a demon had pulled her insides out. It took Mary Louise and me, and three other women who'd come to help, a couple of hours just to clean up the bedroom. Then we started on the kitchen. I took the counter. The pump handle and the sink had awful vomit mess splashed all over it, as if Parsella's husband had tried to pump himself some water. It fair turned my stomach, but I had to clean it before I could wash up the dishes. A glass canning jar stood to the left of the sink. Parsella had pried off the lid and left it lying upside down just beside the sink. I noticed my handwriting as I tossed the lid into the garbage. 26 August 1892. At least she had a good meal from our tomatoes before she died.

Normally when a group of us women were together around Christmas time, we'd get to singing some of the old carols and that new song we'd learned, *Jingle Bells*, which everybody liked so much. But this year we didn't do any singing, and not too much talking either.

Parsella's husband had an old hound dog that everybody liked. Trip had this lopsided look to his head, like one long ear was heavier than the other. Every time he looked at me, I thought he was asking a question. While the men were hauling the coffins into the living room, they left the door open, I guess to help clear out the smell. Old Trip walked right in the front door and into the kitchen. Guess he decided it was his dinner time, and maybe nobody thought to feed him the day before, because he reared up on his two hind legs and planted his feet on the table where the meat loaf platter still sat. Parsella would have tanned his hide—tell the truth she never would have let him into her kitchen to begin with. Trip grabbed what was left of the meatloaf and ran with it. It wasn't half an hour later we heard him upchucking and whining out in the yard. Listening to him at the end was a terrible thing. He'd crawled under the porch, and it took two men to finally drag his body out of there once he was dead.

At the funeral, which everybody for miles around attended, Pastor Jacobs talked about the waste of such a promising young family. After the burying, we went back into the church, where everybody had a story to tell about Parsella or her husband. Doc stood up in the middle of all this and said he was sure the meatloaf had caused their deaths. He warned us about the danger of meat that hadn't been smoked long enough and of canned goods that hadn't been prepared correctly. He went on for some time about some new-fangled medical ideas, and we all listened to him because Doc was a good man. I could tell the instant Mary Louise thought of it. She grabbed my hand and sat there beside me, hanging on for dear life, like she was afraid to speak anything out loud but had to say it through her grip.

Doc told the whole story all over again. He left out the details about all the vomit, but he did mention Parsella's unborn baby, and the dog. Maude Reynolds and her brother sat two rows in front of us. When Doc told about Trip dying, I saw Johnny turn to his sister. For such a tough guy he sure looked like he was going to cry. Seems he had a real attachment to that dog, and nobody had told him Trip was dead.

Mary Louise and I stopped by Parsella's kitchen after the funeral. Somebody had left a good fire in the cook stove so nothing would freeze before it could be packed up. Half a dozen women were there before us, placing all the food and utensils in piles on the tables and counters. We decided to divide it equally between all of us. Mary Louise and I volunteered to clean out the pantry. There were three of our jars of tomatoes among the other canned goods on the shelves. We made sure we took all three of them as part of our share. It could have been the meat, of course, but we didn't think so.

After our family supper that night, Pa told us Old Ned had barely made it to his feet that morning. "I can't watch him suffer any more," Pa said. "I'm going to take him out to the swamp and shoot him tomorrow morning. Silas, I'll expect you to help me."

Even without talking too much about it, Mary Louise and I knew what we had to do. Just before bedtime, we took Emmeline and the boys to the barn to say goodbye to Old Ned. He stuck his head over the rail of his box and nickered softly when we walked up to his stall. I'd brought him one of the carrots from our root cellar. We watched him munch on it, feeling his soft breath whoosh out of those big nostrils of his. It was like the last meal that a condemned man eats. We'd heard about that from Jasper Fordyke, who knew about such things. Old Ned nuzzled at Mary Louise's golden red hair, like he always did, and she laughed through her crying. Emmeline was excited to be staying up so late, but the boys understood what was happening. They patted Ned's neck. Joseph . . . little Joseph cried, but Silas turned away and swallowed his tears before they could embarrass him.

I'm the one who had to do it, even though it was all Maude's fault. As soon as everyone else was in bed and asleep I whispered to Mary Louise to close the window after me. Our bedroom was just off the big back porch. As long as I didn't bump into the swing, which did tend to squeak, I could sneak out without anybody knowing. The stars were too bright, watching me all the way down the path. I could hear Old Ned thumping around in his stall and hoped he wouldn't wake up Pa. I took a small scoop of oats and slipped inside his stall. I pushed his big inquisitive head aside so I could pour a whole jar of tomatoes onto the oats. Ned always did like sweet things, and I wasn't sure he'd eat the tomatoes, so I added a cup of sugar I'd taken from our pantry. I stirred it up, and Old Ned looked at me, like he almost understood what I was doing and why I was crying. He snorted once or twice when he tasted the tomatoes, but he ate the whole thing.

It took a while for the tomatoes to take effect. I spent the time currying him; he always did like that curry comb. When Mary Louise and Estelle and I were little, we used to brush him and then braid his mane and tie little bows on the end of it. We'd take them off our pigtails and put them on him. I reminded him of that, and told him how handsome he had been. Now his old bones were showing through, and I made sure to brush very carefully over the places on his hips where the firm muscles from years before had caved in to make hollows that were shadowed by the lantern I'd lit. I was almost angry with Pa for waiting so long. Surely Ned had been hurting for a long time just from being so old. As if he understood my thoughts, he turned his head and nibbled at my dress, almost as if he were asking how long this would take. He was so gentle. He always had been. We never needed to worry about him biting us accidentally. He used only those soft lips of his whenever he snuffled through our hair or nibbled at our skirts or shoulders. I'd had more horse kisses from that old boy than I could count, and I took a moment to stop the currying and kiss him back, right on the top of his shoulder where his neck started. He was a tall horse, and I've always been a bit on the short side. I laid my cheek against his side, and slowly I began to feel little ripples making his skin twitch. He started weaving his head back and forth and blowing out puffs of air, as if the hurt was building inside him. I would have done anything to ease his pain. All I could think of to do was to sing *Jingle Bells*. He settled down a bit, and I'm sure my voice brought him some comfort. It wasn't enough, though. No matter how hard I tried.

Everybody knows that horses can't throw up. But there's nothing to stop the other end from working overtime. It wasn't pretty, but fortunately he didn't last long. Maybe five or ten minutes that took a century. I finally had to let go of his head, because the convulsions were too strong. At the very last, he looked at me like he was wondering why this had to happen.

"It's not my fault," I told him, my nose running and my eyes overflowing. "Maude did it, somehow. She could have killed our whole family, just like she killed Parsella and Ronald and the baby and the dog too. She's the one who's killing you. She's the one. She's the one." His body jerked and his foot thrashed out as he fell onto his side. I jumped back in time to avoid being kicked. Some of his slobber sprayed across my dress. "I had to do this, Ned; I had to know for sure before Ma and Pa and Mary Louise and the boys and I ate those tomatoes. I *had* to know. I *had* to. Emmeline was the only one who would have survived. She hates tomatoes and won't eat anything red. Maude would have killed us all, just like she's killing you." I paused to take a breath and choked on my sobs. Then I remembered that Parsella had tried to get me to come over there for a meatloaf dinner on Saturday night. Maude would have killed me first, and my family would have had to hold a funeral for me.

Old Ned would have died the next morning anyway, but that would have been a clean shot in the head. Pa would never let an animal suffer like this. Heartless Maude. That's what she was. Heartless and evil and mean and despicable and hateful. Ned rolled his eyes that looked ready to pop out of his head. At the end his legs went rigid. He lifted his head one last time, and it crashed down beside me where I knelt next to him. One big final shiver raced up his body, his ears twitched, and he was gone. I brushed a few grains of sugar off the bristly hairs under his chin. I don't know how long it took before I was able to stand up and face the chores ahead of me. Every step I took, every shovelful I lifted, I cursed that Maude Reynolds. Old Ned didn't deserve to die like that. He'd sacrificed himself to save our family. Maude would have killed our family, just like she'd killed Ned.

I didn't sleep at all the rest of the night. It took a long time to clean up the mess around the stall. I shoveled up the worst of it and scraped the remainder of the soggy red oats out of his food trough. Even through my tears I made sure I'd gotten it all. I dumped it in the privy, cleaned out the wheelbarrow, and stuck the shovel back where it belonged. Then I sat down on the floor next to Old Ned and leaned my back up against him, absorbing some of the leftover warmth of his big old body. I stayed there until he went cold. Just before dawn I stroked his soft ears one last time. "Don't you worry, Old Ned," I told him. "She'll pay for what she did. I promise you that."

On my way up the path to the house I met Pa and Silas. Pa had his rifle slung under his arm, with the barrel pointing down to the ground. Pa was always a careful man.

"What are you doing up this time of the morning, Slip?"

"I wanted to say goodbye one more time. But you can put up your rifle. Old Ned's already gone."

Silas's whole face scrunched up. He'd never forgive me if he found out what I'd done. What Maude's hatefulness made me do. Pa let the silence settle around us for a bit. "I'll miss the old fella," he said. "Now you run on up to the house and send Joseph down here, then you go to your sister's house and round up the men folk. It's going to be a job to get Old Ned out of that stall, and I'll need all the men you can muster."

Before I ran down to Lucy's house, just a mile or so over the hill, I woke Mary Louise and told her about Old Ned.

"I'll take the other two jars down to the privy," she said. "But what are we going to do about all our own tomatoes? We still have the thirteen jars from that batch."

"It's not like we're going to lose a year's supply," I said. "The other batches we canned later in the season must be okay. We'll just have to rearrange the pantry and make those thirteen jars disappear."

"Ma's not dumb," Mary Louise said. "We have to tell her."

Mary Louise was right, of course. We ended up telling Ma, and Lucy too, since both of them knew exactly how many tomatoes we'd canned. They helped us pull out every single jar labeled 26 August 1892. Then we dumped the contents down the outhouse hole. I held back one jar and hid it behind my treasure box under the bed. Mary Louise and I never looked in each other's boxes.

When we washed and scrubbed and boiled the poisonous jars, I slipped a clean one from the shelf so we'd have just the right number. There was no need for Ma and my sisters to know what I planned to do.

Ma said she thought we ought to own up to what we'd done—at least to Pastor Jacobs—but Lucy reminded us that murder was a hanging offense.

"We didn't want to kill Parsella," Mary Louise said. "It's a wonder we aren't dead ourselves, what with all those jars from the same batch."

"I don't know what could have gone wrong," Ma said. "You girls have been canning for years. You know what to do."

"And tomatoes are easy," Lucy said. "They have so much acid in them, nothing much ruins tomatoes."

I refused to be blamed for a bad batch of canning. "Isn't that the batch," I started to say. Ma and Lucy and Mary Louise all turned around in surprise. Even my own family sometimes forgets that I'm around. "Isn't that the batch that had all the knife slices? There must have been something wrong with those tomatoes. Something that wasn't our fault."

Lucy shook her head. "That's good to know, but it won't matter," she said. "A hanging judge won't care that we didn't mean to kill Parsella."

Two weeks before Christmas I rode with Pa into Baynard's Mill. He stopped the wagon in front of the general store, and I walked down past the lending library. Johnny Reynolds, Maude's brother, shifted a sack in the back of his wagon. I could feel the heat from the blacksmith's forge wafting out the open doorway, and I stopped to absorb some of the warmth. Johnny startled when he noticed me, but there was no way he could avoid me since he was already in midair, jumping over the tailgate of his wagon. He stumbled when he landed. He tried to smirk, but it didn't look as brave as he wanted it to.

"I know you broke my ma's green bean jar with your slingshot," I said, "and I know you slit Mary Louise's prize tomatoes too."

"I did not." He practically spluttered, but then he seemed to think better of it. "I did break the jar, though," he admitted.

I wondered why he'd confessed so readily, but then he did that man thing I've never understood, where he puffed up his scrawny chest—he was as skinny as his sister Maude—and dropped his voice a couple of tones. He couldn't quite get it out of the tenor range, but he did a fairly good imitation of a squeaky bass. Just like a boy, to be proud of acting bad.

"It took a really good marksman to get just the right jar without hurting any of the others," he bragged. "Maude knew she could trust me for that."

I must not have looked like much of a threat, so he kept on. "Anybody," he said, "could sneak into a garden early and mess up a few tomatoes, even a girl."

"So Maude did it?" I said as if I didn't care one way or the other. Then I let the corners of my mouth tilt up a little, like it was one big joke.

He laughed. "Yeah, she really got you good with that prank, didn't she?"

I thought about Parsella, curled in her own vomit, trying to cradle her unborn child, and I thought about Old Ned taking so long to die so hard. "Yes," I said. "She really fooled me with that prank. My sister too." I paused so it would sound like an afterthought. "Did you loan her your knife, or did she use her own?"

"Her own? Not hardly," he said. "Girls don't have knives. She had to ask me to let her use mine." He added, "She's the one who thought of ruining the garden. I wish I'd thought of it first, but she needed me to use the slingshot. Girls can't do that."

I looked at him and wondered where I could get a slingshot of my own.

Maude's mother looked surprised when I knocked on her kitchen door. "Why Slip," she said, "I haven't seen you in a blue moon."

"We all keep pretty busy. Is Maude home?"

"Well, of course she is. Today's Monday. You can head out back to the shed. She's just finishing the laundry."

I nodded politely and murmured my thanks. "I brought your family some muffins I made," I said, and handed her the towel-wrapped bundle.

"Why, aren't you sweet," Maude's mother said. "They smell delicious. We'll eat these with our supper."

Maude was even more surprised than her mother had been, especially when I stooped to pull one of the shirts from the basket and clipped it to the clothesline. Cold as it was outside, the steaming shirts would freeze before they'd dry, and they'd hang on the line for two or three days before they could be brought in for ironing.

It was a stiff beginning, but Maude seemed ready to try out a new friend. She probably thought she could weasel more secrets out of me, like she did before when we were schoolgirls. I didn't say anything I couldn't have said out loud in church, though. She finally loosened up. When I told her about my conversation with Johnny, she snickered. "Slicing open those tomatoes was a good joke," she said.

"Yes," I agreed. As a general rule I hated to lie, but it seemed necessary at this point. "It was a good joke, but we all got a little bit sick after we ate some of them. That was really clever of you. What did you do to them?"

"Oh, I never heard you got sick." She leaned in close to me, like it was a big secret. "Do you remember how Johnny helped Silas clean out that patch of cowbane the day before? Johnny's sloppy; he never cleans his tools the way he should. So I just took his knife and used it on the tomatoes. I sure didn't want Mary Louise to beat Dotty in the judging. And I guess she didn't."

"No," I said, "Dotty won for sure. Maybe she would have won anyway."

"Not hardly," Maude said. "I had to make sure. Your family always wins everything at the fair."

"Not everything," I said, "especially not this time."

Maude laughed again. "I knew you wouldn't let all those tomatoes go to waste, and I sure did want to make you get sick. Just a little." She stopped and looked at the bed sheet I'd just hung up for her. "I guess I'm sorry for that," she said.

She didn't look too sorry to me.

The next Monday, not long before supper time, I took another batch of muffins to the Reynolds family.

"You always come on laundry day," Mrs. Reynolds said. "Maude's probably almost finished. Will you join us for supper?"

"No thank you, ma'am. I need to get home, but I'd like to see Maude if I could."

"You know where she is."

The timing was perfect. I helped hang the last sheet and a few undershirts. Maude complained about the cold spell. "I always have to get up at night to use the privy, and I hate going outside in the cold, but Mama won't let us keep a thunder mug under the bed."

"Maybe that's just as well," I said. "You'd have to go down to the privy to empty it anyway, and those things are no fun to clean out." Before she could change the subject, I asked her, "Do you really have to go every single night?"

"Just like clockwork. Midnight comes and I'm down there." She waved her hand toward the privy, which was set a good ways below the house behind a big wax myrtle hedge.

"I have to head on home," I told Maude, "but before I go, do you want a muffin to celebrate?"

"Celebrate what?"

"The way we're getting to be friends," I said and pretended not to see the sneaky look she gave me.

We sat on the bench behind the laundry shed. I pulled a muffin, wrapped in a red napkin, from my left-hand pocket and handed it to her. Then I reached into my right-hand pocket and took out another muffin, this one in a white cloth.

"Why didn't you wrap them together?" Maude asked.

"I didn't want them to rub against each other and crumble."

Maude nodded. "That was very smart of you."

"I have a book I'd like you to see."

"What is it?"

"I'll bring it next week," I said, knowing full well that for Maude there wouldn't be a next week.

The breakfast bacon splattered the next morning, and I jumped back, but not quickly enough. I wiped at the dot of hot grease and pressed a damp towel against my forearm. Stupid fat hog. I rolled down my sleeves and moved the cast iron skillet away from the direct heat.

Someone pounded on the kitchen door. I turned to Mary Louise and nodded toward the noise. "Get that, will you?"

"You're closer."

When I didn't say anything, she rose and set aside her mending. The boys were getting entirely too active; Ma and Mary Louise and I could barely keep up with all the rents and scrapes, the torn collars and lost buttons.

"Dotty Farraday," Mary Louise said, "whatever are you doing here this early in the morning?"

Dotty pushed her way past my sister. "She's dead," she said. "Drowned."

"Drowned? Who?" My voice had, I thought, just the right inflection. "The ponds are all frozen," I said. "How could anybody drown? Who was it?"

"Stop being so logical, Slip. Maude is dead."

Mary Louise placed her hand over her heart. "She drowned? How?"

Dotty spread her hands wide, palms up, as if asking for forgiveness. I'd never seen her look so unsure of herself.

"They said she got really sick awhile after bedtime and ran for the outhouse. Her sister went out to check on her later, but Maude told her to leave her alone, so she went back into the house."

I had to step aside. They thought I'd gone back to the stove to turn the bacon, but really I just needed something to do to keep from laughing. I was the one inside the outhouse with Maude, who was already dead by that point. I'd been afraid that the muffin wouldn't be enough to kill her, so I snuck out of bed and went to her house. I had my knife in my pocket, but I didn't need to use it. When I saw Maude careening down the path to the outhouse, I just followed her. While she was retching into the hole, I picked up her feet and dumped her in. I had to make sure her head was beneath the surface, but luckily it was about time for them to dig a new outhouse, so I didn't have to shove her too far down. I did have a bit of a worry when her sister came outside, but I just coughed and retched. I disguised my voice and told her to go away. She believed me.

I didn't think Mary Louise had heard me leave by the bedroom window that night, but when I snuck back in well after midnight she told me I'd better not be off meeting a boy. As if that were the only thing I'd be doing. What's wrong with a little sleep lost, though, in exchange for something so worthwhile?

I moved the bacon around in the pan and turned back to Dottie. "When did they find her?"

"Maude's sister woke up again a few hours later," Dotty said, "and went looking for Maude. She found her in the outhouse with her legs sticking out of the hole."

"Maude always was skinny as a rail," Mary Louise said.

"Is that all you can say?"

"Maude *was* skinny, and you know it—don't slap at me like that."

Dotty's sneer was back in full force, all grieving left aside. "My very best friend is dead, and you're calling her skinny?"

"Dotty, settle down and quit shouting. I'm sure you're very upset about this." Mary Louise paused to let Dotty settle down. "I'm sorry you lost your friend," she said.

Dotty wrung her hands, like a third-rate actor in one of those traveling stage shows. "How could she have fallen into the privy?"

"If she was horribly sick and throwing up down the hole, she might have lost her balance." Mary Louise looked at me as if she wanted help.

Even though it pained me to say anything good about Maude Reynolds, I spoke up. "That couldn't have happened," I said. "Maude had really good balance. Remember how well she used to dance?"

Dotty looked at me long and hard. I kept my face decidedly neutral. It wouldn't sit right if I'd started acting like I was really sad Maude was dead, but I didn't need to crow about it either. I wrapped my fingers around the kid gloves in my left-hand pocket, glad that they hadn't gotten wet.

"She might have fainted," I said, "since she was feeling so sick." Especially since I hit her over the head with a big rock while she was throwing up, just before I grabbed her legs and dumped her into the privy.

I paused a few seconds while Dotty looked me over, then I turned to Mary Louise. "You don't think she had anything catching, do you? What if it's scarlet fever? We'd better stay away from the funeral since we don't know for sure."

Doctor Breslow was out of town, so there wasn't anybody to say one way or the other what she was sick with. The body wasn't pretty—or so I heard—what with its having been headfirst upside down in the privy sludge for hours. Luckily nobody noticed the dent in her head under all that hair. Not many people showed up for the funeral. With a scarlet fever scare in the community, nobody wanted to risk it. Even Dotty stayed home while her best friend was laid to rest.

While the funeral was going on, I pulled my treasure box from under my bed. Next to the blue jay feather, I put one wooden clothespin. Mary Louise said that night that she wondered if her Rectification List had made Maude fall in the privy. I assured her it was just a coincidence. Mary Louise never was that powerful.

Nancy massaged the cramp in her hand. She groped around for a question to ask, but nothing that came to mind seemed pertinent. *Do you enjoy murdering people?* She thought back to the story of the first murder. The *divine moment*—that was what Slip had called it. Nancy decided not to ask that particular question. She wasn't sure she wanted to hear the answer. "That blue jay feather you just mentioned. Was that the one on the hickory stump in the meadow the day you . . . you were there with Franklin?"

"Well, of course it was. It's nice to know you're paying attention. Now, just give me a minute or two, and then we'll go on."

Chapter 4 - The Twins

October 25, 1935 . . . and 1 blue black horse mule weight about 1000 pounds named Bell; also 1 bay horse mule named Pete, weight about 800 pounds. All of said property levied on as the property of the defendant, H.A. Moore. Also 1 two horse wagon and bed unpainted and 2 sets harness.

--from the 1035 archives of the
Gwinnett County Superior Court

While she waited for Slip to take a turn around the cell—"I have to stretch my legs, you see"—Nancy opened a new steno pad. Thank goodness she'd brought an extra one. She wrote *Button Kingsley – Murder #3* at the top of the first page. She crossed out the *3* and changed it to a *4*. Old Ned. Slip had murdered Old Ned, too. Sure, she'd been sad about it, and maybe that old saying about the end justifying the means applied here, but somehow Nancy couldn't quite see it that way. Why hadn't Slip talked to the sheriff? It wouldn't have been Sheriff Fordyke that long ago, but there must have been another sheriff before him.

She felt prickles up the back of her neck. Susannah had stopped her pacing. Nancy turned and Slip smiled at her. "Let's keep going," she said. Slip didn't want to discuss Button, though, as Nancy found out soon enough. "I've been thinking about Jasper and Jethro Fordyke," Slip said. "You probably ought to know how they figure into all of this."

"I know that Jasper is the one who arrested you for the Kingsley murders, but what did Jethro have to do with all this?"

"You're getting ahead of yourself again."

Nancy silently agreed with her, mainly because she knew she'd have to report both of these other murders—Franklin and Maude—to Sheriff Jasper Fordyke before she gave the story to George to print. She wondered if she ought to tell him about Old Ned. She'd probably have to eventually. In the meantime, though, she might as well learn as much as she could about the sheriff beforehand. She didn't dare tell Susannah what she was planning. Slip would think she was reneging on her promise not to tell anyone anything until the stories were in print. But surely reporting these other murders to the sheriff didn't count.

"Jasper and Jethro Fordyke had more freckles between the two of them than a dandelion has seeds." Slip smiled, as if at a happy memory. "Jasper was the older one, by about five minutes. From behind it was hard to tell them apart. They both had that shock of sandy-looking hair, like dried-out corn husks. They both always had their jaws going. When they were little, it was them chewing on beeswax they'd stolen from the hives. Later on Jasper moved over to chewing tobacco, but Jethro never went that direction. Just as well. Jasper's teeth turned brown as mud, while Jethro could practically blind anybody, anybody except me, with that sun-white smile of his, another way to tell them apart."

"His teeth didn't look all that brown to me."

Susannah's head snapped up. "I thought you'd never met him."

"I haven't. I saw him in court, when he was testifying."

"Oh. Well, I suppose they've lightened up a bit in recent years. Maybe he's not chewing as much as he used to do." She lapsed into silence.

"You were talking about Jethro's smile," Nancy reminded her. "It sounds as if you liked him a lot." *Could murderers—four-time murderers—fall in love?*

Slip didn't answer. She looked right through Nancy, as if she hadn't heard the question, and went on with her train of thought. "They lived on the old Anders spread, the one that went up for sale when Mr. Thomas Anders died. It was on the other side of Baynard's Mill from our farm. I guess I should explain all this, since you'd have no way of knowing it, what with you not being from Baynard's Mill."

"I could go take a look at the town tomorrow."

"No!" Susannah slapped her hand on the table, and Nancy jumped at the gunshot sound. "I'll tell you everything you need to know." She clenched her jaw briefly. Nancy could see the muscles contract and release. "You'll need to be here tomorrow to take down the rest of my story." She picked up her gloves, folded them over once, and put them in her pocket. "Yes. I'll tell you everything. You need to know this." Slip's anger seemed to dissolve, and her voice softened into what Nancy was beginning to think of as *story mode.*

    The Anders land abutted the side of the Fordyke property, so Mr. Fordyke more than doubled the size of his farm in that one deal, making him almost the biggest landowner in these parts. Mrs. Fordyke insisted that they move into the Anders house because it was so much bigger than the one Mr. Fordyke had built when they married. She promised Mrs. Anders that they'd care for her like a loved grandmother. And they did too. Everybody knew that Mr. and Mrs. Anders had been practically destitute toward the end. That's what came of having only one child to survive them, and then he went off to join the War Between the States twenty years back and didn't return, leaving them with nobody to help out on the farm.

    Of course, many of the neighbors helped Mr. Anders with the haying, and we made sure they had enough food and firewood, but we all knew that Mrs. Anders would be in a bad way when her husband died. All she had was the farm, the house, and a collection of knickknacks she'd started amassing when John left for the war. That was why it was so good of the Fordykes to buy her farm and take her in to live with them. They rented out their old house to a tenant farmer with the idea that whichever twin married first would take it over. Of course, they had awhile to wait for that to happen.

    The only joy Mrs. Anders seemed to have, other than the Fordyke children, was riding into town whenever one of the Fordykes hitched up the wagon to head that way. She'd always visit the bank and then go across the way to buy another knickknack or two in the general store. "They're for John," she'd say. She never gave up hoping that her son would come back from the war, although nobody knew why she thought he'd want all those tacky little statues.

    Mrs. Anders helped Mrs. Fordyke with the cooking as long as she was able to. She tended to the younger children, and told Jethro and the others rousing stories about the old days before we became a state. The only thing she was truly strict about was her doodads, as she called them. She would never let the Fordyke children touch her collection of figurines. She had more of those little statues than a barn had rats. She seemed to prefer large ones—sad-eyed cows and brightly colored roosters and fat-bellied clowns. After she died, Mr. Stybard—the general store owner—told us that every time she came into his store, starting right after the War began, she would ask him to order more of those figurines for her.

Jethro and all his brothers and sisters were brokenhearted when Mrs. Anders died. She was like a grandmother to them, the only one Jethro ever knew.

Her son John, who we all thought had died long before in the War Between the States, returned to Baynard's Mill shortly after her death, demanding his inheritance. Mr. Brown Markham, the bank owner, told John Anders that his mother had withdrawn, over the course of the twelve years she lived with the Fordykes, almost all the money Mr. Fordyke had paid her for the farm. The Fordykes swore they'd never seen a bit of money from her. All that was left of Mrs. Anders, besides the good memories she'd left with Jethro and his siblings, was that collection of those dad-gummed knickknacks. Mrs. Fordyke hadn't had the heart to throw them out, even though they cluttered up her house something awful, and who was John to say his mother hadn't spent all her money on all those doodads? Mrs. Fordyke packed them up and made the twins haul the boxes into town to where John had taken a room above the livery stable. Not much of an inheritance, although if he'd thought about it, he should have come back home to work the farm after the war instead of hanging about back East. He said he'd been employed as a bookseller and a journalist, but I'm not sure I believed him.

I happened to be leaving the dry goods store when Jethro and Jasper drove into town with those boxes. I went next door to the general store to pick out some penny candy for Emmeline, but I could see Jethro and his brother unloading at least a dozen boxes, maybe more, and carting them into the livery stable.

"What's so interesting, Slip, that you have to be peering out the window like that?"

"Nothing much, Mr. Stybard." I was surprised he said anything to me. Usually he acted like I wasn't around until it was time to tally up my purchases. "I just like to watch the comings and goings outside."

"Anybody coming or going in particular?" He peered over my shoulder.

Old busybody. "No, sir. It's just a nice day to be looking out the window."

Mr. Stybard watched Jethro hoist another box onto his shoulder. "Uh-huh," he said as he turned to shuffle back to the counter. "Nobody in particular. Nobody in particular."

John Anders drove out of the livery stable as I left Stybard's and headed down the street that went toward the south. When he rode past me I ignored him, but Jethro stepped up onto the sidewalk off to my right and called out to him. "Where you going with all those boxes I just brought you, John?"

"I plan on getting in some target practice down by the graveyard. I reckon these thingamabobs aren't good for anything else."

Jethro nodded and ambled over to stand next to me. "He had us unload them from our wagon straight into his," he told me. "They were all pretty heavy. I asked Mrs. Anders once why they were heavier than they looked, and she told me she packed a couple of rocks in each one to weight it down so it wouldn't knock over easily. Then she stuffed paper in the bottom to hold the rocks in. Before Mother packed them up, I asked her if she wanted me to take out all the rocks, but she said that would be a waste of time."

"I guess he didn't think much of his inheritance."

"I don't see why not. Those fat-bellied clowns look a lot like him."

I thought about John Anders' scarecrow frame. "Jethro Fordyke, you are absolutely crazy."

"I never thought you'd notice."

It wasn't long before we heard John's rifle picking off those rock-laden figurines one by one. Jethro stood there, chewing away on a wad of beeswax, apparently content with the silence between us. I glanced through my library book. *Middlemarch*. "Have you read this?"

Jethro glanced at the cover. "Yes. I like the way she weaves the different subplots together."

Ha! I looked again at the author's name. Some man named

George Eliot. Jethro obviously didn't know what he was talking about. I was about to comment on it when the shots abruptly stopped.

It stayed real quiet for a spell. Jethro looked over at me and I returned his stare. He scratched at his chin. "Maybe he got fed up with it all and shot himself, do you think?"

"Leave it to a boy to think like that. He probably ran out of ammunition."

"After only a dozen shots? Not likely. Maybe I'd better go look."

"You stay away from there, Jethro Fordyke. You're liable to get yourself shot."

Jethro didn't have time to ignore my advice or to take it either. Mr. John Anders came racing back into town and drove straight up to the bank, toting a big box in with him. We headed over that direction. I tried to look nonchalant about it, as if I'd been planning to go that way in the first place, but Jethro kept pulling me along to make me rush. Before we got there, John must have hauled seven more boxes inside.

We had to wait quite a spell. "Hoo-boy!" John Anders clapped his hat on his head and closed the bank's big front door behind him. He looked around at the crowd that stood stock still like a bunch of puppies confronted by a honking gander. "I done made me a fortune! My ma's been stuffing money in those doodads of hers, looks like for years. The second one I shot, this big bunch of bills exploded into the air. All I had to do was break open all the rest of them. Mr. Markham here tells me it's good money, and I opened me a big fat bank account." He glanced around the crowd, settled on Jethro, and hooted again. "Bet your pa's going to have himself a fit when he finds out he made your ma get rid of all those things. It's a whole lot more money than I would have gotten for selling the farm."

I didn't like that smirk on Mr. John Anders' face, but I will say this much for Jethro. He grinned back instead of arguing. "I figure you deserve it, John," he called out. Under his breath, so only I could hear, he said, "Twelve bullets to hit only two figurines? What a lousy shot." He stood there for a moment, scratching at the scar on his chin. "I should have taken out all those *rocks*."

I turned to go, but Jethro put out a hand to stop me. "My father isn't as greedy as most people think he is, but even so, I don't want to be the one to tell him, especially after he let Mrs. Anders stay there for free, with us feeding her and Ma taking care of her." He looked around, took off his hat and slapped it against the side of his leg, raising a minor dust cloud in the process, then brushed at a bit of dandelion fluff caught in the heavy felt. "You wouldn't want me to walk you home, would you?" He reached for the package of dress fabric tucked under my right arm.

"Jethro Fordyke," I pulled back away from him. "You know I'm quite capable of carrying my own packages. It not even three miles."

"I know that, but if I don't walk you home, I'll have to head in the other direction and walk myself home. I need a good excuse." He scratched at his jaw and looked back across the square. I followed his gaze. The top of Jasper's head was unmistakable with that corn-husk shock of hair. "My good twin will be delighted to hurry home to give Father the bad news, but he has to see Sheriff Lundstrom first. By the time I walk you home, he'll be through with his interview, and he'll beat me home by a good hour or more, just long enough for me to avoid the tirade."

I thought about it, unsure if he was flirting with me. Jethro ignored my scrutiny. He wasn't blushing and didn't look particularly nervous. The deep scar on his chin had a tendency to twitch when he was anxious, but today it was still. I decided to take his request at face value. "Here." I held out the package and let go of it before our fingers could touch.

He frowned, but that might have been because he had to scramble to keep from dropping the gingham. I walked around him and headed up the sidewalk, leaving him to catch up with me. It wasn't that I didn't trust Jethro. We'd pretty much grown up together. Being in the same town, we'd gotten to know each other as well as anybody. In school he'd always sat one aisle over and two desks back from me on the boys' side of the classroom. Now I saw him only when our paths crossed in town. At church too. And whenever he had call to walk or ride past our farm. He and Jasper did seem to have a lot of business on our road.

We walked the first two miles or so in silence, until my curiosity overcame my determination to make him sorry for his offer. "Why is Jasper meeting with Sheriff Lundstrom?"

"He's applying to be a deputy."

"Jasper? A deputy sheriff? That's a laugh."

He stopped walking, but I kept right on going. "Why don't you like my brother?" he asked my receding back.

"He's like the air in that high-flying balloon they had at the county fair last year. He needs a lot of heat to get him moving."

"You weren't at the county fair last year."

"How would you know that?"

"No particular reason," he said. "I just notice things."

It made no sense to narrow my eyes at him because he wasn't looking at me. "Well, if you must know, Silas told me all about that dad-blamed thing. He thought it was wonderful. Bunch of nonsense if you ask me."

"Your brother's right. I'll take you up in one someday."

"You'd be better off taking Silas. He's the one who wants to go."

"I'd rather take you, so you'll see how much fun they are."

"How would you know?"

"I have an imagination," he said. "I can see you in a hot air balloon, carried along with the wind. It won't even mess up your hair, because there's no breeze when you're going the same speed as the wind." He gestured up toward the sky. "I'll take you above the clouds."

"You'll take me no such place, Jethro Fordyke."

"You don't need to holler, Slip. I can hear you just fine."

"If you'd start talking sense, I wouldn't have to point out your mistaken assumptions."

He stopped walking again and muttered something I couldn't hear. I probably wouldn't have wanted to know what he was saying anyway, so I ignored him, other than to say, "You look like a jackrabbit, Jethro Fordyke, starting and stopping like that, over and over again."

"It sure is hard to carry on a conversation with you," he countered.

"Well of course it is, and whose fault is that? If you'd walk along like a normal person we could have a decent conversation."

"Maybe we should talk about something neutral, like the weather."

"Of all the ridiculous ideas, Jethro Fordyke, that takes the cake. The weather never changes around here. In the summer it's hot and in the winter it's cold, and in between it's . . . well, it's in between. We could say all there is to say about the weather in two minutes, and then where would we be?"

"Right here in front of your house," he said, with a hint of a smirk.

"I'll thank you to give me my gingham now," I said, "and then you can leave."

Mary Louise chose that moment to walk out on the front porch. "Jasper!" she said. "Come on in here and get some lemonade."

Why my sister can't tell them apart the way I can, I have no idea. That scar on Jethro's tanned chin stands out like a white horse in a field full of brown Jersey cows. Mary Louise was always just a little bit slow, so maybe that explains it. "It's not Jasper, Mary Louise. It's Jethro."

"Well, come on up here anyway and set a spell."

Jethro took off his hat and flashed his bright teeth at her with more enthusiasm than the invitation warranted. "Thank you, Mary Louise. I don't mind if I do."

It was my turn to look him up and down. If I didn't know better, I'd think he was flirting with my sister. She was in a fair way to flirting herself, inviting him in for lemonade. Usually a long walk on a mild day lifted my spirits but today, for some reason, I felt grumpy. She didn't make a fool of herself, thank goodness. Didn't fawn over him once we got up onto the porch, which was just as well, or I might have said something that would start us snipping at each other. She wasn't my very favorite sister, never had been, but when Estelle left home to marry that man, I moved off the trundle I slept on with little Emmeline and started sharing a bed with Mary Louise. We'd talk at night before we fell asleep, and I guess that helped us get closer. There was that business with Old Ned and the tomatoes too. Having something like that in common made us understand each other better. We still argued some, but it wasn't too serious usually.

Still, she hadn't confided much in me lately. It cheered me only for a moment to think that I probably wouldn't have been that much interested in anything she had to confide.

Jethro waited until Mary Louise brought out a pitcher and three glasses on the green glass tray that came all the way here from eastern Pennsylvania with great-great-grandmother Thornton when she was a little girl. Then he settled into the rocker. I reached for my glass. Mary

Louise handed one over to Jethro, once he'd placed the bundle of fabric on the floor beside his chair.

"I declare I thought you were Jasper," she said. "What's he been up to lately?"

Jethro's scar twitched. "Not much different than a couple of days ago when we talked to you out by the fence."

"He's in town now applying to be a deputy sheriff," I said.

Mary Louise didn't look at all surprised. "I sure hope he gets it," she said. "He'd make a fine sheriff."

"Deputy," I said.

"For a while." She sipped at her lemonade. "Someday Sheriff Lundstrom will have to retire. I think Jasper would make a real good replacement for him."

"Aren't you getting ahead of yourself?" I asked. "Jasper might get shot in the line of duty."

Mary Louise turned a fine shade of gray. Jethro threw his hat at me. "That's not a nice thing to say, Slip."

"Well, it's true, isn't it?"

Before he could answer me, Mary Louise stormed into the house and let the screen door slam behind her. I had a feeling I might turn up on her Rectification List that night.

"What did you do that for?"

"She sounds like she's getting sweet on him."

"So what if she is? He likes her."

"He does not," I said. "Not that way."

"How would you know? Your face is always buried in a library book."

"Jethro Fordyke, that's not true and you know it."

Slip stopped talking. Nancy thought she'd just paused to take a breath, but the silence stretched out. Once again, there didn't seem to be a pertinent question to ask since Nancy had no idea where this story was headed.

Slip had a way of breathing loudly, as if she had to force the air in and out. Nancy listened to that for a bit and tried to figure out how many breaths she took in a minute, which was hard to do since there was no clock in the room, and she didn't want to break the spell by looking at her wristwatch. It had slipped around on her wrist, and the face sat in her lap. She found herself matching her own breath pattern to Slip's, like one of those lizards that takes on the color of every leaf it sits on. *Was a taste for killing an acquired taste? Did it seep into a body the way a breath of air did? Once you caught it, could you ever get rid of it? Would you ever want to?*

"So now you know," Slip said, breaking into Nancy's reverie. "Mary Louise got worse instead of better. She'd always liked Jasper best, but now she started preening like a lovebird every time he was nearby. It was disgusting to watch. He was completely smitten with her, up until the Colper family moved here from Indiana."

"The Colper family?"

Nancy started to say more, but the matron interrupted with the news that the prisoner was expected back in her cell to eat lunch. "You'll have to leave," she told Nancy. "We don't hold lunch for anybody." In a slightly less grudging tone she added, "I suppose you could come back later if you aren't finished with . . ." she swept her hand in a non-specific arc that might have indicated anything from a nefarious meeting to a Sunday School lesson, ". . . with this."

Nancy leaned forward to stand up, but Slip motioned her back down. "My guest would like to eat with me in my cell," she said.

Nancy's eyes widened. *I would?* She nodded. "Yes. I would. I have my own food with me," she said and patted her handbag.

Chapter 5 - Summer Cotillion

**William F. Jennings, Plaintiff, vs. Mabel Maddox Jennings, Defendant -
September 1938**
Plaintiff made Defendant a true and affectionate husband and gave her no just cause
for complaint. . . .

> *--from the 1938 archives of the*
> *Gwinnett County Superior Court*

🛷 **When the cell door clanged to behind her, Nancy had second** thoughts. The space before her was cramped indeed. A cot, a flimsy wash pan on a small table with a covered chamber pot underneath, a screen apparently intended for the prisoner to dress behind, Slip's blue hat perched over one corner of it with the hat pin noticeably absent.

"It's good you used the lavatory on the way here. That screen's not much to hide behind. We'll both have to sit on the bed, if you don't mind. They won't let the women eat in the same room with the men prisoners, so the matron brings our food and we have to eat it in here." Susannah picked up one folded dress and moved it to the table.

I wonder if she has extra underthings tucked inside the dress?

Susannah leaned back against the cell bars at the foot of the bed and balanced the metal tray across her lap. Her lunch looked singularly unappetizing.

Nancy nodded, took her seat at the head—she noticed that there was no pillow—and pulled out the newspaper-wrapped packet. She looked at Susannah's lunch and grimaced. "I'd be happy to share with you."

"Oh? Did you notice how well this great state feeds its guests?" She pushed the drastically overcooked mess around on the plate. "You wouldn't think anyone could ruin peas, would you?"

Nancy handed her a slice of bread. "I don't have a knife to cut the cheese," she said without thinking. "You wouldn't happen to . . ." At Susannah's cackle, she stopped and added, "No, I suppose not."

"Even if I had my knife with me, I don't suppose you'd want to cut any food with it, considering where it's been." She tilted her head to one side as she inspected Nancy's face. "Oh, don't look so forlorn. I could cry about my situation or I could laugh." She glanced over her shoulder at the empty corridor and lowered her voice. "I never used that knife for food myself. Not once after it had been buried," she lowered her voice even more to a bare whisper, "in that man's back."

"You know," Nancy said, "I'm hungry enough that I'm not going to let this conversation stop me from eating."

"Good for you, girl. That's the spirit." Nancy munched happily for a few minutes. Then she reached for her notebook. "Should we keep going with the interview?"

Once again, Susannah looked over her shoulder, as if gauging the interest level of the inmates in the cells on either side of her. The walls between the cells were solid, but Nancy could hear vague shufflings from up and down the hallway. The woman in the next cell sneezed. A muffled *bless you* sounded from a cell on the other side of the corridor.

"Let's just wait until we get back into that private room," Slip said.

Nancy referred to the last comment she'd written. "The Colper family from Indiana," she said. "What about them?"

"Well, Jasper was sure making a fool of himself over Minnie Colper, almost from the moment those Colpers rode into town. They were related to the Stybards, and when a friend of the Stybards died, the Stybards talked the Colpers into moving to Baynard's Mill and buying her old house right there off Havering Street. Mr. Colper was a lawyer, and he opened himself an office in the front room. I never saw much sense in lawyers." She rubbed her hand across her forehead. "Even now," she said, "I can't think they're doing me much good, and they may be leading me to a lot of harm."

Nancy kept her eyes on her notebook.

"That said, Mr. and Mrs. Colper were nice enough, I suppose, but that daughter of theirs was something else. I remember one particularly awful Sunday . . ." Her eyes took on that unfocused look that Nancy had seen before.

I deliberately tried not to look at Mary Louise that Sunday morning, but her Bible was shaking in her hands, and her elbow kept poking me. I doubted she heard a word of Pastor Jacobs' long-winded sermon, which was just as well, since he'd been yammering on about forgiveness for the last half hour or so. His ideas about forgiveness dwelt more on the wrath of God, so I couldn't see what good it would do for me to ask to be forgiven if that was all that was in store for me. Every time Pastor Jacobs paused to take a breath, which wasn't too often to tell the truth—that man had lungs like the blacksmith's bellows—Minnie, three rows in front of us, tilted her head to look up at Jasper with a prim self-satisfied smile, and Mary Louise's thumbnails dug deeper into her Bible, leaving its cowhide binding covered with three-quarter-inch half-moons of disgust. Mary Louise wasn't about to forgive Minnie for moving in on Jasper's affections.

Minnie was eighteen, which right away was enough to make twenty-three-year-old Jasper drool and twenty-four-year-old Mary Louise simmer. Minnie had that frothy kind of sweetness that made me want to shake her. Of course, Jasper was so entranced by her long eyelashes and her round bottom, which believe you me she managed to show off even through her long skirts and petticoats, that he was blind to any other female in town. Even I had to admit her ankles were trim above her dainty feet. None of us would have been able to see them if she'd worn sensible shoes that buttoned up properly, but she'd sashay those delicate lawn skirts of hers getting in and out of her Uncle Denver's wagon, and everybody in the churchyard knew she was wearing silk stockings and ribbon-tied satin shoes that wouldn't make it through one rainstorm.

Of course, it wasn't raining that Sunday, although if it had been, Jasper probably would have picked her up and carried her from the wagon to the church, and poor Mary Louise's Bible would have been in tatters. Rain wasn't likely, though, which was a good thing because of the Cotillion planned for the following Saturday. We'd heard there was plenty of rain over the rest of the Great Plains, floods even; the weekly newspaper said so. That day, though, there wasn't a puddle in sight anywhere around Baynard's Mill to mess up Minnie Colper's shoes, more's the pity.

That first Summer Cotillion was set to be the high point of the town's social season, if you could call it that. We had barn dances every so often, and harvest festivals, and of course the county fair. And usually a big Christmas gathering if nobody had died recently, but Meribelle Smith decided we needed a Summer Cotillion to be the fanciest of all the town gatherings. I'd had my work cut out for me to convince Mary Louise to attend. We'd be going with Ma and Pa, of course, and all our brothers had promised me they'd ask Mary Louise to dance so she wouldn't feel like a wallflower. It's one thing not to dance because you know nobody's going to ask you anyway, like me. But dancing with your brothers when you knew Jasper would have his arms around Minnie Colper must have been discouraging to say the least. Mary Louise probably wouldn't even appreciate all my efforts, to make sure she'd have a good time despite Jasper and his new lady love.

I never could figure out what Mary Louise saw in Deputy Sheriff Jasper Fordyke. He was good-looking enough, I supposed, as long as he didn't smile and show off his tobacco-stained teeth. And, he had a singing voice that could make a corpse want to sit up and praise the Lord. But as far as I knew he'd never read a book once he was out of school. His brother did all the reading for that whole family. Still, it seemed unfair that just when Mary Louise figured out how to tell Jasper and Jethro apart from a distance, he went and took up with such a shallow-minded doll. Mary Louise was worth ten of her.

As soon as the last reading finished and the last hymn faded away, Mary Louise grabbed her badly dented Bible and headed for the door. She had to pause to say a few words to Pastor Jacobs, of course, and I wasn't close enough to hear her, but either she'd been listening to the sermon more closely than I thought she had, or else she dredged up some generic observation that passed for true evaluation, because Pastor Jacobs boomed out his thanks along with the obligatory disclaimer that they were the Lord's words anyway. As far as I was concerned, the Lord would have been bored silly the same way I was, but the good reverend seemed mighty pleased with himself despite the Lord's supposed contribution. There was no way the Lord could have kept those twelve young disciples of his interested in what he had to say if he'd preached at them in Pastor Jacobs' style. But that was just my opinion.

I made it through the line and complimented the Pastor rather graciously considering what I'd really thought of his sermon. I wasn't too enthusiastic about this idea of forgiving people who didn't deserve it, but then again, I certainly hoped the good Lord would see that some people needed to be eliminated. I was doing the Lord's work in many ways.

I headed toward the road, hoping to catch up with Mary Louise, but Jethro put up a hand to stop me, and he reminded me of that big cactus on a picture postcard from Texas that Mrs. Reynolds sent home five years ago when she visited some of her relatives after Maude drowned in the privy.

I stopped, of course, Jethro being considerably taller and much broader in the shoulders than I was. He'd shot up and filled out quickly in the past four or five years, so now the top of my head was about even with his nose. He lowered his arm. "Are you going to the Cotillion Saturday?"

"I suppose," I said. "Isn't everyone?"

He glanced over my shoulder, and I started to turn to see what had caught his attention, but just then Minnie Colper's twittery, tweety little-girl voice pierced the late morning quiet. "Oh Jasper," she simpered, "I can't wait to go dancing."

I deliberately did not grimace, but Jethro did, and I caught him at it.

"I was wondering . . ." he paused, leaned toward me, and lowered his voice, "if you'd think it was a good idea if I asked Mary Louise for a dance or two."

"That's real thoughtful of you. I'm sure she'd be pleased." And this would save me from having to ask him to do it.

"Yes. Well. While we're at it, I guess I could ask you if you'd want to dance too."

Dance with Jethro? I was spared a reply, though, because Minnie tripped up beside him, with Jasper in tow like a hound dog on a short leash. "If I'm going to dance with one brother," she said, "I might as well dance with the other one too."

I watched Jasper's eyes narrow and wondered what sort of signal passed between the two brothers that I wasn't quick enough to catch. I sure couldn't figure out men. Jethro swept off his hat and gave a rather good imitation of a courtly bow. Not that I'd ever seen a courtly bow, but I'd read about them, and I knew Jethro had too, because we'd had a bit of a tussle at the lending library one day when we both wanted to check out a book about Shakespeare and Queen Elizabeth. I won and got the book first, but Jethro read it right after I did. "I am willing to let the evening breezes blow howsoever they choose," he said, which had nothing to do with an answer, but it seemed to impress Minnie and mollify Jasper who, I was sure, wasn't going to let any sort of breeze blow Minnie in his brother's direction. As long as Minnie was around, Mary Louise didn't stand a chance.

I did think the infatuation would peter out naturally. I couldn't believe that Jasper wouldn't wake up one day soon and see that Minnie had about as much sense as a pea pod.

That Saturday, the ladies of the town spent hours bullying their husbands into stringing ivy around the posts that held up the roof of the pavilion. Why a town as small as Baynard's Mill needed a pavilion, I'd never figured out. But even I could see it was going to look especially festive this year. I did as much as I was expected to do, and then faded away from the busy clumps of females. I decided to cut through the back way to get home in time to finish my chores and clean up a bit before the dance. Mary Louise and I both had new dresses. Hers was a soft pink and mine was my usual blue. I always wore blue for some reason, but this was a lighter shade than I was used to. Mary Louise had insisted that I get a new one, even though I thought it was nonsense. She even helped me sew it, but she showed no interest in her own dress at all. I was the one who attached the lace around her collar and hem. I ducked across the square, hoping to be out of sight before Meribelle Smith looked up from the white tablecloths she was spreading over the long table where gallons of lemonade in glass punch bowls would be served all evening. Minnie Colper, I noticed, was nowhere in sight. She'd been no help at all.

The Colper house stood on a corner about two blocks from the square. On the side away from Havering Street, a sturdy trellis covered in ivy shielded most of a second-floor balcony from view. At the rear of the balcony, though, Minnie leaned over the railing, toweling her hair. She'd obviously just washed it, and the blond tangles cascaded almost to the bottom of the white spindles that supported the top rail. I wasted a few moments hoping the railing would give way with poor Minnie leaning against it like that. We'd have to dry her hair before we could lay her in her coffin. The railing was better built than my wishful thinking called for, though. Minnie kept drying her hair, and I walked home to finish my chores.

The night of the Cotillion was like a dream for most of the girls and women in the town. Meribelle Smith and her decorations committee had raided every rose bush in Baynard's Mill and convinced every girl under the age of twelve to spend the evening strewing rose petals around the floor. Not that they needed much convincing at first. It looked like we were in the middle of a pink and red blizzard. Trouble was, the girls pretty soon got bored with the process and reasoned that as long as they were strewing petals they wouldn't be able to hold a glass of lemonade at the same time. Within minutes huge globs of rose petals littered the floor between the tables like blown-down nests of baby robins after a heavy wind storm. Meribelle Smith descended on Holden, her husband, and demanded that he do something.

"What would you like me to do, dear?" His buddies didn't even pretend not to be listening.

"Make them stop that petal throwing!"

"But you're the one who convinced them to do it in the first place, dear." I stood nearby, listening too. His first *dear* was pleasant. His second one had an edge to it. By the time he got to the third and fourth, even Meribelle could tell he wasn't going to stir away from his cronies. Finally she stormed off, caught herself, and slowed to a dignified stroll, nudging mounds of rose petals aside as she went, as if she'd planned it all along.

Jasper and Minnie got there late, after the roses had been rather mangled by dozens of feet. But when Minnie showed up, nobody looked at the floor. Minnie glowed. Her newly-washed hair was wound up into the most elegant of chignons, with tiny white asters tucked into the strawberry-blond twists like stars twinkling above a summer sunset. She floated into the room with Jasper beside her. He was grinning like the Cheshire cat in that new book by Lewis Carol. I could have happily kicked our deputy sheriff. First one couple and then another moved aside, and pretty soon there was an empty dance floor. Jasper took Minnie's hand and flowed into the waltz like he had been born to it. Jasper, the deputy sheriff, dancing? All I'd ever seen him do was square dancing. Of course, if his singing voice was any indication, he certainly had musical talent, and maybe waltzing wasn't that far from singing.

Silas and Mary Louise had stopped a few yards away from me, and I tried very hard not to look at my sister in her despair. Because that's what was written all across her face. My vision of my brother and sister was blocked for a moment when Jethro stepped in front of me. He walked over to Mary Louise, cut an awkward bow, and asked her to dance. She drew back, but then she glanced at me, and I nodded. If she were dancing, she wouldn't be able to watch Jasper and Minnie together, and maybe she'd stop grinding her teeth. She put her hand in Jethro's and let him lead her onto the dance floor just opposite from where Minnie twirled in her lacy dress that showed off her slim ankles. I hoped Minnie would trip and break one of them, but that didn't happen. The musicians were already near the end of the song, but the lead fiddle player must have cued everyone to keep going, because they circled back to the beginning and kept playing.

Jethro took about three turns and you could have knocked me over with a dry wash rag. If anything, he danced better than his brother. Mary Louise lifted her head, smiled at Jethro, and proceeded to outshine Minnie Colper simply because she started enjoying herself so much. I could swear she forgot completely about that little snit, at least as long as the waltz lasted.

After it was over, Jethro escorted her back to where I was and offered to bring her some lemonade. "Yes," she said. "Thank you." As he walked away, she looked at me and smiled. I had to lean closer to hear her whisper, "Minnie Colper will be on my Rectification List tonight, and may she waltz in hell." Ma would have washed her mouth out with soap, but Ma was nowhere close.

I danced three dances with Jethro, one with my brother Silas, and one with Pa. That was enough dancing for one year.

It wasn't two months later, before church one Sunday, that Jasper announced that he and Minnie were engaged. I singled out Jethro right after the service was over. "How could you let him do a fool thing like that?"

"Stop hissing at me, Slip. There's no way I could have stopped him. She's got him so starry-eyed it's a wonder he doesn't walk into the outhouse wall in broad daylight on his way to take a . . ."

I cut him off. "You don't need to be uncouth. All I did was ask you a simple question."

"In all the years I've known you, you've never once asked a *simple* question. They're always loaded with multiple implications."

"*Loaded* and *multiple* imply the same thing." If I couldn't refute him, I could at least confuse the issue.

He had the audacity to laugh at me. "I'm glad I'm not the starry-eyed type. No telling what you'd do if I went all gaga over some flirty girl."

"I always assumed you'd have more sense than that," I said. "But looking at your brother, who I thought at one time was sane, now I'm not so sure. Have they decided on a date yet?"

"Not that they told me, but I'm just the younger brother."

"By five miniscule minutes. You must have spent that extra time ingesting more sense than your sibling."

"Ooh, we *are* angry, aren't we?"

"What do you mean?"

"The madder you get, the more syllables you spout."

"How would you know that?"

He covered his cornhusk-colored hair with his new straw boater. "I'm observant," he said. I had never thought of Jethro as a fashion leader, but his was the first straw boater in town. The red and blue ribbon around its crown was particularly jaunty. At that moment, though, I was in no mood to compliment him on his sartorial splendoriferousness. That was the most syllables I could think of.

They set the wedding date for New Year's Day, eighteen-hundred-and-ninety-seven. Everywhere I went, people gossiped about how beautiful a bride Minnie was going to be, what with her blonde hair and those big green eyes. I got sick and tired of hearing it after about the first three days. Having three more months to endure was a sickening thought. And then there was Mary Louise. She tried to act like nothing was wrong, but she started losing weight. Jethro and I tried to cheer her up whenever we could, but there was an emptiness in her eyes. Lots of nights I'd hear her crying after she thought I was asleep. I couldn't see any sense in losing either sleep or weight over Jasper Fordyke, but Mary Louise had loved him ever since he beat up Samuel Markham for pulling her pigtails in grammar school.

Thanksgiving was just around the corner, and we'd had good harvests for a change. The turn of the century was coming up in a bit more than three years, and everyone was hopeful that the hard times were over. Of course, farmers all knew that the weather could turn against us any time it wanted to, but still, our hearts were lighter, and we felt we truly had something to be thankful for. Most of us could remember the five years of bad winters we had after that Krakatau volcano erupted back in 1883. We knew something like that could happen again at any time, but with the new century coming up, we were all more hopeful that the volcanoes would behave themselves, the winds would stay mild enough not to parch the fields, and the sun would shine enough but not too much.

Mary Louise managed to make it through the day of Thanksgiving, but got droopier and more tired as the end of the year approached. Everyone in town sang carols. You couldn't walk ten paces without hearing *Oh Little Town of Bethlehem* or *Silent Night*. But I'd already adopted a different winter song for myself. I liked its perky lilt. I knew most people called it *Jingle Bells*, but I'd begun to think of it as *A Slaying Song Tonight,* with an a-y instead of an e-i-g-h.

An unseasonably warm spell hit Baynard's Mill in mid-December. Krakatau weather was a thing of the past. Bright sunshine. Open windows. Mild nights. No snow, no woolen scarves, no heavy mittens. I brought out my kid gloves.

The night that Minnie Colper died was another one of those warm days. The poor dear must have leaned too far over the railing while she was out on the balcony, maybe looking at the stars and dreaming of her upcoming wedding. Nobody heard her cry out, and Doc Breslow said that the dent on her head most likely happened when she hit a rock beside the path just below the balcony. The ivy had stayed particularly dense for some reason, and the shrubs along the path hid her body from the sight of anyone passing by on Havering Street. Not that anyone was passing by that late. The timing had been perfect, and the trellis didn't even squeak.

The next morning I took a few minutes to add one ivy leaf to my treasure box. The green stains on my gloves took a bit longer to deal with.

Slip shook her head, as if she was just waking up. She patted her gloves and smiled in a languorous way, as if she had a lovely, deep secret. "Did you get all that?" she asked.

Nancy lifted her notebook. "Shorthand. But I do have one question, if you don't mind."

She inclined her head.

"How did you climb a trellis in a long-skirted dress?"

Slip frowned at first. Then her face relaxed and she laughed a deep, throaty chuckle that was downright infectious. "I stole a shirt and a pair of my brother's knickers off the clothesline and hid them behind the barn where I could change into them before I set off to town. It's a good thing Pa slept so soundly. If he'd ever caught me climbing out of the window in my flannel nightdress, he would have whupped me good, even though I was grown up by then." She thought for a moment. "Twenty-three. I was twenty-three that year."

"She must have heard you climbing up there. Didn't she scream or call for help?"

"She heard me all right, but she pretended she didn't. I'm sure she thought I was a young man, especially when she noticed my pants. I wondered later if she'd been expecting someone. That trellis must have been a well-used corridor. Luckily nobody else used it that night. She let me sidle right up next to her before she turned to look at my face. All I had to do was pull the hammer out of my waistband where I'd tucked it. She was so surprised to see me instead of a young man, that she never noticed the hammer. Just before I hit her—one time was all it took—I whispered, *This is for Mary Louise.* I wanted to be sure she knew why she was dying."

Nancy shivered, despite the stultifying heat of the room, as she scribbled the last few words. "Jasper's heart must have been broken," she said. When there was no answer for several seconds, she looked up.

"He got over it real fast," Slip said in a dry tone. "He sang at her funeral and never missed a note. I tend to think that once she wasn't around to hypnotize him, he smartened up. He married my sister not six months later. She didn't even seem to mind being a second choice, fool that she was. Any more questions?"

"No."

"Good, because we still have some time." Slip stood and walked into the shaft of afternoon sunlight. The window was too high to offer any view, but the sun was a welcome presence in the barren room. "Don't even bother writing *Button* at the top of this one," she said. "You're just going to have to wait until it's his turn. Write *1899, the Turn of the Century.*"

Chapter 6 - The Turn of the Century

William F. Jennings, Plaintiff, vs. Mabel Maddox Jennings, Defendant - September 1938 . . . After Plaintiff and Defendant had been married about one year, Defendant apparently became dissatisfied and left Plaintiff on the pretense of coming to Lawrenceville to see a doctor and to visit her mother; the Plaintiff did everything in his power to persuade Defendant to return and live with him; . . .

--from the 1938 archives of the
Gwinnett County Superior Court

Nancy tried to imagine what it had been like – a new century on its way. She supposed she'd never see the next century, unless she lived to be ninety-eight—not an unreasonable hope, since her family were all long-lived. Her great-grandmother was widowed at ninety-seven and lived another five years. Nancy knew enough about the growth of technology to see that newspaper interviews would someday be recorded, and cars would travel a lot faster. Even now, that Cadillac was very impressive, and Ford seemed poised to revolutionize the way America moved from one place to another. It made sense that in another seventy years, when the twentieth century moved into the twenty-first, people might be traveling routinely at fifty miles per hour. They might be living in buildings that stretched twenty floors above the earth. That new Chrysler Office Building in New York City was more than a thousand feet high. Who knew where we would be in another seventy years? "What was it like, at the end of the 1800s?"

Slip took a moment to organize her thoughts. "It wasn't much different than the decade before," she said. "Or the one after. Oh, clothing was getting lighter and less restrictive. We heard rumors about gas-driven automobiles, but we'd never seen any in our town. We kept to the same old ways of thinking. Lots of people had been ruined in the crash of 1893, but it didn't hit the farming communities as bad as it did the cities. We still produced the food for ourselves and most of us were able to make our own clothes and handle all our own repairs, or we had people in the community to barter with for any services we needed." She shook her head. "Things are moving too fast nowadays. Too fast."

"This Depression doesn't help."

"No," Slip agreed, "it doesn't. But a lot of our problems today were caused by greed, by people who weren't careful with their money, and by other folks who thought they were entitled to more than they'd earned. We need this hard time to wake us all up and teach us to take better care of our money so we can provide for our families."

This sermon brought to you by your local friendly murderer, thought Nancy in a parody of a radio commercial. "The way you cared about your family?" she said aloud.

"Exactly. Nobody hurt my family and got away with it."

"Can I quote you on that?"

"I wish you would."

"So . . ." Nancy wondered how to phrase her question, "what did you do to bring in 1900 on a high note?" Half of her felt morbidly interested in the answer, and the other half, the half that was her father's daughter, wanted to run screeching from the room. She kept her eyes on her notepad.

"It didn't seem fair to let a new century come in without doing something special to celebrate it, but I'll have to go back a few months so you'll understand who needed killing."

I was twenty-five that year, and I'd killed only a few people, which was something of a shame considering how many folk there were who deserved it. Baynard's Mill was growing, and some of the old ways of doing things were slipping away. The new mayor was to blame.

He acted like he'd earned all that money himself, but we all knew his mother had squirreled it away year after year in those fool china statues of hers. John Anders, Mayor John Anders that is, bought the general store from old Mr. Denver Stybard, whose health had gone downhill steadily after his niece Minnie passed away in such a tragic fall. I never did understand why Mr. and Mrs. Stybard both were so attached to that girl, but there's no accounting for bad taste, is there?

At any rate, when Mr. John Anders bought the general store, he got the lending library next door too, and decided to expand his store by knocking out a good portion of the wall that separated the two. Mrs. Stybard was in shock. Jethro and I helped her move most of the books back to her house, but that was quite a ways outside of town to begin with, which made it plain inconvenient for most library patrons, and then too, her house didn't have enough room for all those books. We squeezed everything in as best we could, but we all knew the lending library was as good as dead.

"It's just as well, I suppose." Mrs. Stybard motioned the two of us to join her for some lemonade on the front porch. She settled into one of the rockers and fanned her red face. The heat had been something awful that summer. "Mr. Stybard needs me here since he's gotten so poorly." I thought he should buck up, but his wife had a different idea. She rotated her glass, looking like she was mesmerized by the lemon slices floating in it. I was glad it was lemonade weather; Mrs. Stybard's coffee was strong enough to eat the shine off my teeth. "I don't know how I'll manage to keep him occupied, though," she said. "That store was his life. When he talked about selling it he got so sad, but at least he knew he could help me in the lending library. Now that's gone too, and there's nothing for him to do."

Jethro shifted around in his chair like he had sand in his britches. "I'm so sorry, Mrs. Stybard," he said. "I was kind of surprised when you sold the library building."

"So was I," she said, grinding out each word.

I couldn't figure out what she meant, but she didn't keep us guessing too long. "You know how all those buildings in that block are connected? They look like different buildings, because all the store fronts are different. Our general store was painted dark brown and the library was white. The dry goods store has that pretty yellow paint with the white trim, and the post office is bricked, even though it's nothing but a hole in the wall, not even twelve feet wide."

Jethro and I nodded, and Mrs. Stybard stood up, motioning Jethro to keep his seat. She leaned against the porch railing and looked out across the yard where her chickens squabbled over something, probably a juicy bug.

"Of course, the blacksmith's shop was completely separate, with that wide alley between it and the post office." We nodded again, but she didn't pay any attention to us.

"Mr. Stybard owned what we thought of as our two buildings, the general store and the library. What we didn't know was that when the deed of sale was drawn up, it described the property as so many feet of frontage. My poor Mr. Stybard didn't realize that what he was selling was the store *and* the library too. The day after the papers were signed and we had our money in hand, John Anders sent me an eviction notice that said I had thirty days to clear the premises, after which he wouldn't be held responsible for any damage to the contents of *his* property."

"What about the dry goods store and the post office?" I asked.

"Those are safe from him, I guess," she said. "Apparently those two are a separate property altogether. Widow Hart owns the dry goods store. There's a double wall between her section of the building and my library . . ." her voice faltered, "my former library. From the front the only difference you can see is in the paint."

It wasn't polite to ask, but I wondered if she'd be able to get by, what with not having any children to take care of her as she got older. She may have read my mind, like that mesmerizer at the county fair the year before. "Mr. Stybard and I have plenty of money from the sale, so we'll be just fine." She waved her hand to take in the piles of books that spilled from the utilitarian front room onto the porch. "It does seem such a shame, though."

"What I don't understand," Jethro handed his glass back to Mrs. Stybard, "is why on earth John would want to close the library. He already has enough room in that general store."

"I wish I knew," she said. "I wish I knew."

We found out soon enough. People started complaining about not having a library in town, and it finally blew up at a town meeting. Mayor Anders informed us all in no uncertain terms that he had the right to use his building any way he saw fit, and that he was doing the work of the Lord, because "that library had the devil's own work in it." He ranted on for some time about the irreverence of Huckleberry Finn and complained about those uppity females in *Little Women.* He as much as accused us of being in cahoots with Satan if we opposed his decision. I thought Mrs. Stybard was going to expire from indignation, and I felt fairly indignant myself. Who was he to keep me from reading books I was interested in? Or even books I didn't care about very much; I still should be able to look at them and decide for myself. Jethro argued with him for some time, but John had already expanded the general store into the library space, so the damage was done beyond repairing.

Mary Louise kept prodding Jasper to get up and say something, but I guess as deputy sheriff he felt he had to remain impartial. Also, he might not have wanted Mary Louise to get too upset, since she was expecting their first. She'd told me only that morning when she showed me a length of the softest white cotton I'd ever felt. Mrs. Hart—we'd bought all our fabric from her for years—had just gotten in a bolt that she'd ordered from Philadelphia. I imagined a baby would do nothing but sleep if it was wrapped in a blanket that soft. Maybe that was the idea. When Mary Louise showed me the fabric, she asked me if I'd knit booties for her baby. Poor Mary Louise. She could sew alright, but she just never got the hang of knitting. So I ended up knitting all the booties and hats for all my sisters' babies.

I never had much use for them—babies, that is. I liked the challenge of birthing them, but after that, they struck me as being an awful lot of work, and all the mother got out of it was a good chance to die giving birth to one and then a lot of mess to clean up after. Babies smelled just fine right after they'd been washed, but then they grew up and a goodly percentage of them turned into stinkers like John Anders. His mother should have drowned him when she had a chance, but I suppose she didn't know at the time how he'd turn out.

The argument for and against the lending library raged around me while I was thinking about babies, glad that it was Mary Louise and not me, so I missed noticing who all was on John Anders' side. Probably only people like that stuck-up Dotty Farraday. I doubted that reading was high on her list of priorities. Jethro could tell me later, I supposed. Mrs. Hart, who'd kept quiet through the first part of the meeting, stood up and waited for the voices to die down around her. "None of this matters anymore," she said in that querulous nasal voice of hers that might have prompted her husband's early death. She held up her wrinkled hand to stifle the comments. She sure had aged prematurely; the skin of her hand looked as rough as the bark on a river birch tree. "This afternoon," she said, "I had a talk with Mr. and Mrs. Stybard" she nodded in their direction, "and I'm happy to tell you that the lending library will be reopening next month in the back of my store. It won't be as roomy as it was before, and my fabrics are going to be a good deal more crowded, but those of you who *love* books . . ." she raised her eyebrows toward where John Anders sat, "won't mind a little inconvenience."

Jethro started the cheering, and I was the next one on my feet. John's shouts of *you can't do that* were largely inaudible due to the general din. Jethro shouted, "Meeting adjourned," and we all thought that was the last of it. Jasper ushered Mary Louise out. I think the only reason he married her was that he felt sorry for her being single when all her friends were getting married. But I suppose he was nice enough when it came right down to it, at least for the first few years they were married.

Slip stopped to clear her throat. Nancy said, "I'm surprised to hear you say that. He seemed like a very nice man when he was testifying in court."

"Oh, Jasper puts on a pretty good front, so people who don't know him tend to think he's the cat's pajamas."

Nancy couldn't resist asking. "I saw some pajamas in the Sears Roebuck catalog. Have you ever tried wearing any of those things?"

"Pajamas? Of course not. Don't you worry; they won't last. Give me a good old flannel nightgown any day."

Nancy wanted to ask what Slip wore at night in the prison, but she wasn't quite comfortable enough to broach the subject. That was the problem with being a reporter. She knew she was supposed to ask hard questions, but she didn't like doing that. The strange thing was, she could ask about murdering someone, but she couldn't bring herself to say *What do you wear to bed here at night?* She shuffled her note pad around and went back to the topic. "You were talking about Jasper and Mary Louise. Do they really not get along?"

"Land sakes. They're not important to this story. I was telling you about Mrs. Stybard's library. Let's go on with that."

In between chores and late into several evenings, various townsfolk helped the Stybards haul all the books back. The new shelves—we had to build those because John Anders had put something in the bill of sale that said anything built in was his, and Mr. Stybard had built in every one of those library shelves himself. He'd been really proud of them. The new ones were narrower than those in the old place, but we had our books back.

One morning a couple of weeks after the library opened, Mrs. Hart found the back door broken open and most of the books dumped on the floor. No sooner had we gotten that straightened out when a whole nest of grasshoppers must have hatched on the top of one of the bookshelves. Mrs. Hart came in to find them chewing the book bindings. She'd hired Mrs. Stybard to work in the dry goods store part time, and between the two of them, they managed to shadow John Anders every time he walked in the door. He started visiting the library several times a day, and poor Mrs. Hart was at her wit's end. She finally revoked his library card, but he threatened to sue her for abridging his rights as a tax-paying citizen of Baynard's Mill. Who ever heard of such a thing? Nobody sued anybody back then, and other than Mr. Colper, the nearest lawyer was in Statesville, more than fifteen miles away.

John Anders lost the race for mayor that year, and that seemed to make him more determined than ever to close the library. In a way, it was good that the general store was connected to the dry goods building. That way he couldn't set fire to the library without risking burning down his own place of business. I wouldn't have put it past him. He put up signs about the godless material being disseminated in plain sight. He accused Mrs. Hart of doing the work of Satan. He complained to the new mayor, who listened with great apparent sympathy and then did nothing. John Anders harassed Mrs. Hart and Mrs. Stybard ceaselessly, but nobody could stop him. What he did wasn't exactly illegal, and nobody could ever prove that he'd been the one who broke into the library that first week. It was just downright irritating to those two good old women.

Jethro wanted to boycott the general store, but riding fifteen miles to Statesville in a wagon to get supplies was more than anyone in town was willing to do.

The weather started getting a good bit cooler as autumn settled in. My kid gloves were just the right weight for that time of year. They said afterwards that it was a robbery. His horse pulled the bloodstained buggy home with the reins trailing in the dust. The men who went searching found his body lying a couple of miles out of town on the road from Statesville where he went every month on business. His gold pocket watch was gone, and all the money he'd been carrying. There must have been at least two of them, Jasper and his deputies guessed— one to distract him and one to sneak up and cut his throat from behind. A suspicious man like John Anders would never have let a man get close enough to do a thing like that unless somebody else was holding his attention.

Nancy put down her pen and pushed her hair back from her face. She almost couldn't believe that she kept asking for more of these stories. The woman sitting across the table from her was far more cold-blooded than the newspapers—including the *Clarion*—had reported. Nancy wanted to leave and never come back. She wanted to applaud Slip for protecting her family so diligently. She wanted to print these stories and get that woman convicted to seven consecutive life sentences. "So, how did you manage it?" She wanted, despite her reservations, to hear the answer.

Slip smiled. "John Anders' death? It was that invisibility factor at work. He thought I was as inconsequential as I looked. When he saw me walking along the road toward town, he stopped to give me a ride. He even helped me into the buggy and put my basket of herbs—the ones I'd been gathering along the roadside—behind the seat. All I had to do was mention the library and he went into one of his tirades about the evil being spread through the community by godless authors and upstart women. Then I pulled out my knife and slit his throat. He hardly had time to feel it. Just toppled over. Well, I guess I had to push him a bit so he'd land in the road."

She threw back her head and . . . gloated. Satisfaction fairly poured off her body. "He went so easy. I felt like an avenging angel sending him on his way, and there was nothing he could do to stop me.

"His mare took off running, then, but I stopped her and carried my basket with me back to the body. I needed to make it look like a robbery, so I took his pocket watch and all the money he had on him. Then I walked home the back way, figuring the horse had enough sense to head back to town for its dinner."

"What did you do with the watch?"

"It would have been too risky to keep it, so I smashed it with a rock and tossed it back in the woods. I figured if it was found, they'd think the robbers broke it accidentally and threw it away."

"And the money?"

Slip looked Nancy up and down like an artist examining a particularly ugly bug. "I am *not* a thief," she said. "I spent every penny of that money over the next three years, always at Mrs. Hart's store, never enough at one time to raise any questions. And I made clothes with all that plain fabric and left them on the church doorstep for Pastor Jacobs to distribute to the widows and orphans in the town. I tell you again, I am not a thief, and I wanted no credit for my good works, since those clothes came from the proceeds of John Anders' crimes against the library."

"Did you save something for your treasure box?"

"Of course. I picked up a small pebble that had a tiny splash of blood on it. I held it carefully all the way home so the droplet dried without smearing. I wrapped it in a bit of brown paper that night to protect it."

"May I ask you something?"

"Yes."

"How did you just happen to have your knife with you that day he offered you a ride?"

"Oh, Nancy, you should know by now that I am a very careful planner. Everybody knew that John Anders drove to Statesville once every month or two, always on a Friday. It took me five Fridays of long walks before I hit the right day. I gathered a lot of herbs that year."

"What if someone had seen you?"

"Never. He was trying to destroy our library," she said, as if that explained it all.

Nancy squeezed her writing to fit this information on the last few lines of her notepad. It was a good thing she had some extras back in her room.

When she left, her car was as hot as the hellfire Pastor Jacobs had preached about to Slip and her family. She sincerely hoped that she, Nancy Lou Remington, wasn't headed in the same direction. The trouble was, while Slip was talking, she made so much sense.

Mrs. Cappell didn't object to Nancy's staying up late to bake cookies, particularly after Nancy agreed to make extras to share with Mrs. C. "It's such a shame you haven't met any of the other guests, dear. I meet so many lovely people who come through here, you know. Those two sisters, for instance. Lovely women. And that gentleman who works for the newspaper, just like you do. He's a lovely young man, and I'm sure you'd have plenty in common."

Not likely; not since he's the competition. "Thank you for thinking of me, Mrs. Cappell, but I'd rather spend my time writing," she looked at the spoon in her hand, "and baking." *And I think I might throw up if I hear the word* lovely *one more time.*

"I think you're such a lovely person, Miss Remington. So dedicated. I'm going to tell my brother how helpful you are." She turned toward her room. "You be sure to turn the oven off before you go upstairs."

"Thank you, Mrs. Cappell, and don't worry. I'll clean up after myself. It's . . . lovely being here."

STATESVILLE COUNTY CLARION

YOUR MORNING SOURCE FOR ALL THE NEWS WORTH READING

Sunday, July 17, 1932

Letter to the Editor of the Clarion

The murder of our beloved Senator Dominick Kingsley was obviously politically motivated. His farm bill was unpopular only with people who are ignorant of the wider implications of that sweeping legislation. I strongly suggest that certain misguided individuals, who seek to absolve Miss Packard from the legal consequences of her dastardly act, be required to take one of my political science courses at our nearby College, where Dean Kingsley so ably filled the position of Director of Admissions.

Sincerely,

Professor Joseph L. Lumerton

Chapter 7 - Feathered Friends

William F. Jennings, Plaintiff, vs. Mabel Maddox Jennings, Defendant - September 1938
. . . that he had a good home when Defendant left in which was provided all the necessities and comforts of life and he did everything in his power to make her comfortable and happy; notwithstanding this, Plaintiff shows that Defendant completely turned against him and told him she did not care for him anymore and would not return to live with him. . . .

--from the 1938 archives of the
Gwinnett County Superior Court

The next day Nancy once again had the breakfast room to herself. Mrs. Cappell had put out a selection of food on the sideboard since she never missed church on a Sunday morning. Before she left, she gave Nancy directions to three churches nearby, for which Nancy had thanked her quite politely, knowing full well that she was going to skip church. She wasn't in her own home town, and she doubted anyone would miss her. She packed another lunch, big enough for two people this time, making sure to slice the cheese before wrapping it up. Four new steno pads went into the bottom of her handbag and she tucked the lunch on top of them.

On the way to the prison, Nancy saw a stand of luscious blackberries growing beside the road. She couldn't resist, and snapped off several whole branches, not wanting to risk breaking open the juicy berries by pulling them loose. Luckily she had a day-old copy of the *Clarion* on the front seat, and she sacrificed four of the back pages to hold the berries.

Officer Sullen, as she'd begun to think of him, motioned for her to lay the bundle of berries on the desk. First he opened her bag and peered inside. He pulled out the wrapped items and inspected each one thoroughly. When he turned to the blackberries, he muttered *thorns* and began methodically removing the berries and piling them back onto the newsprint. When he mangled yet another one, Nancy pictured him drowning in a vat of blackberry juice. First it covered his chin, then his mouth, then began inching up his nostrils . . .

"That's that, miss. These thorny branches could make a nasty weapon . . ."

Not as nasty as my fountain pen.

". . . and I have to be sure you're safe in there." He swept the denuded branches into the trash can.

Nancy stopped him before he could put the juice-stained packet of berries into her bag. "I'll carry these separately, Officer." *And when I come back out I'll shove all this wet paper down your scrawny throat.*

He motioned her through the swinging half gate to the barred door that marked off Matron's realm.

The matron patted her down once again. Nancy declined coffee and asked for a cup of water instead. She walked confidently toward the interview room, as if she lived there. She felt that she almost did. *My Sunday morning Church of the Barred Windows. Does bread and water count as some sort of communion?* Nancy giggled at her irreverence. Where would the blackberries fit into such a service?

Slip was already seated. She lifted her metal cup of water and gestured to the soggy bundle Nancy set on the table. "That looks like it has a story behind it."

Nancy's laugh was dry. "Not every story is worth telling." She considered sharing her murderous thoughts with Slip. *No, no sense going there.*

Susannah opened her mouth as if she might reply, seemed to think better of it, and settled for, "I never thought the people here at the prison would be so accommodating, but I think I found out why they are."

"Oh? Why?"

"The funding from the state is being cut back because of the hard times, and . . ." She paused while the matron came in and set another cup and a tin pitcher of water in front of Nancy.

"They're cutting funding," Nancy prompted once the door shut behind Matron's ample rear end.

"Yes, and the prison officials must think it will help to have a reporter on their side."

"If they want me on their side, maybe they should increase the quality of the food they give the inmates."

"But that's the point, don't you see? They don't have the budget for it, and they probably hope you'll lobby on their behalf."

"Why are you suddenly on their side?"

Susannah looked up at the barred window. "I'm going to be here a long time, and I'd like to have you on my side too. I'm pretty sure the second verdict will be another life sentence. That means I could be here seventy or eighty years—assuming I live to be a hundred and thirty. Don't you think I'd want improved conditions?"

Nancy lifted her handbag from the floor. "We need to brighten up a bit. I have enough food in here for both of us. I hope I'm still invited to lunch."

"Maybe later. I'm ready to tell you another story now."

Nancy set the food aside.

"I should be in Sunday School." She laughed at the look on Nancy's face. "Every week for the past forty years, I've taught Sunday School."

"Do you miss it?"

Susannah's sigh oozed out of her and seemed to fill the bleak room. "If you were *me*, if you were *here*, what would you miss the most? Other than your freedom, that is."

"I'd have to think about that." She tried to picture an ordinary day, her usual day. Freedom was the first thing she'd thought of, the freedom to go wherever she wanted, to set her own schedule and her own boundaries. She certainly wouldn't miss the press room. That thought jolted her. The press room was the hub of her chosen career. Yet the thought had been so strong, so sure. It was the daily pressure she wouldn't miss, and the constant cut-throat competition. The picture of Dominick Kingsley's bloody throat flashed briefly, but she put it out of her mind. That competition was a big part of it, but even more was knowing that no matter what sort of factual, well-balanced story she wrote, George would change it, spice it up, and make her by-line somehow less valuable, even occasionally embarrassing. She couldn't always be proud of her stories, or at least not the way they ended up in the printed version. What she really wanted, and she found herself almost afraid to admit it, was to have a small weekly newspaper of her own in a town not too far from Statesville. She still would want to be able to see her dad often. She would hire women to staff the office, women to do the reporting; women who would respect each other and who would work together. She would pay her staff well, maybe even have everyone share in the profits. It wouldn't be a publishing empire, but it would be hers.

But that wasn't what Slip had asked her. What *would* she miss the most? Her car? Her clothes? Her tiny apartment or, much more likely, the bakery below it? She lingered over the thought of fresh cinnamon buns and felt her mouth begin to water in response. Her family? No. She felt certain that her father would visit her if she were in prison. Her mother, long deceased, was not a factor. Nancy didn't have to be in prison to be deprived in that way. Missing her mother so much was almost like a lifetime prison sentence, one that couldn't be commuted by the governor.

She glanced around the room. There would be sunshine through that high window by mid-afternoon. Not much, but enough not to say *I'd miss the sun*. Good food. She'd miss that certainly, but maybe once this Depression was over, they'd improve the quality of the prison fare.

"Flowers," she said at last. "I'd miss seeing flowers every day. Even in the middle of Statesville, flowers grow at the feet of the trees along Main Street."

Susannah settled back in her seat. "I know exactly what you mean. We have that in common. I think I miss the flowers the most too. I used to gather armfuls of them every week to take to the church, and of course we always had flowers from my garden throughout the house."

"You had a flower garden?"

"I'd be willing to bet I grew your favorite flower. What *is* your favorite?"

"Irises."

"Then you would have loved my garden. I had dozens of bushes."

Nancy looked at her more closely. "Irises don't grow on bushes."

"I know that. You didn't let me finish my sentence. All this interrupting. I had dozens of bushes covered in roses, and irises growing all around."

"That must have been beautiful."

"Of course it was. I always tried to make beauty wherever I went. Like the flowers I planted all around the town fountain. Are you ready for this story?"

Nancy lifted out her note pad, pen, pencils, and two hankies. "I'm ready when you are."

"Let's talk about Holden Smith, then. *The Holden Smith Memorial Fountain* was a mouthful to say. You'd think we'd just call it *the fountain*, but somehow or other there was a conspiracy to keep Holden's memory alive. His widow, Meribelle Smith—she's the one who had all those rose petals strewn around the Cotillion—wanted to rename the school in his honor too; but when someone—I won't mention who—pulled out his old grade cards and refreshed everyone's memory about Holden's dismal record in English and Geography and Arithmetic, to say nothing of his disgraceful penmanship, the school name stayed the same: Baynard's Mill Academy."

"Are you the one who found his report cards?"

"Not exactly. I had a small conversation, though, with the school principal, and she knew exactly where to look for them. She was a stickler for academic excellence, and all I had to do was point out the discrepancy between his academic record and the idea of him as a role model for our young people."

"I've never heard of Holden Smith," Nancy said. "Who was he?"

Slip paused with the metal cup halfway to her mouth. "I keep forgetting you're not from Baynard's Mill." She raised her voice to a piping falsetto. "He was God's own gift to the town, if you believe what most of the home folk say, because he saved two children from freezing to death in the blizzard that hit just before Christmas in 1903. He was out that night with his shotgun. He never exactly explained what he was doing out in such a horrible storm, but the Turner boys are alive now because of him. They'd been returning from a trip to town when their wagon broke an axle. They tried to lead the mare home, but something spooked her and she broke away from them and hightailed it down the road. They should have known the horse had more sense than they did. They tried to take a shortcut across a field and got turned around. That wasn't surprising considering the wind and snow that night. They ended up huddled in a ditch not half a mile from our farmhouse. Holden stumbled on them in the middle of the night. The horse got back to the barn well before Holden Smith brought the boys home."

Slip dropped her tone to a melodramatic stage whisper. "That's what most people remember him for, but if you ask me, he was lower than a skunk."

"I *am* asking you."

Slip pulled her gloves out of her pocket and laid them on the table, in that reverent gesture Nancy had seen before. A pigeon, or maybe it was a dove, cooed from the window ledge above and pecked at the heavy wire that separated it from the two women. Nancy looked up at it, but Slip hardly moved. "Funny the bird should sing right now," she said. "Holden Smith killed birds for the fun of it."

"Pigeons make good eating, don't they?"

"I'm not talking pigeons, Nancy. He killed song birds. He'd take pot shots at them when he was a kid, out practicing with his rifle. If anybody happened along, he'd sit a tin can on the fence post and pick it off with a single shot. But I watched him enough to know that he hardly ever wasted a bullet on a can when he could shoot something with feathers. When he grew up, it was even worse."

"He was a good shot?"

"He was accurate, if that's what you mean. Of course, sometimes he used a shotgun. He had to be closer, but he could kill more at a time." She fingered one of the gloves, bunched it up, smoothed it out. "Emmeline turned sixteen in September of 1903."

"Your little sister."

"Yes."

Emmy liked to feed the birds. Pa thought it was silly, but he always did indulge that child, her being the youngest. She grew those big sunflowers, dried the seeds, and spread them out in the winter. Seemed like we always had a whole swarm of birds warbling around our yard. I'd see Emmy sitting out there with birds perched on her shoulders and eating seeds out of her hands. They seemed to be entranced with her singing. She could trill her voice, so she sounded like an angel.

You're too young to remember the storms at the end of 1903—I doubt you were even born yet—but they were something fierce. I don't think I've ever seen snow like that before or since. It was a good thing Emmy had a bumper crop of sunflowers that previous summer. She worked like a fiend to get the seeds all saved. Everybody was saying we were coming up on a hundred-year winter. That's what they called it—the kind of winter that comes along only once in a century. Of course those predictions are usually about as worthwhile as a cherry pit—way too big for its fruit, you know. But that year they were right, at least around these parts. We seemed to get all the storms concentrated in this one county. They started early, in late October, and didn't let up until almost April. The good news was that Pa had taken the predictions seriously. He and the boys built an addition onto our woodshed, and they'd spent all summer chopping wood and filling the shed right up to the roof.

Emmy talked him into helping her build some shelters for her bird friends, small barn-shaped boxes that she filled with pine boughs and perches on the inside, good places where the birds could congregate to get out of the wind. They were grouped all over the yard, tucked under the eaves of the woodshed, hanging in little communities from the large lower branches of the mulberry trees. On the fence posts too. We had a tall, misshapen tree that grew behind our barn. The trunk had this twist in it that made the tree look as if somebody had cut off its top and added a totally different tree up there. Emmy about threw a fit when Pa told her she couldn't hang a bird house in that tree. The bottommost branch was too high . . . much too high . . . for anyone to reach. He told her he'd nail one of the houses to the trunk, but Emmy didn't want to hurt her tree friend, she said. Still, there were plenty of those little shelters for the birds to choose among.

At any rate, the birds flocked to our yard after the first storms hit, and they sure used those shelters of Emmy's. You've never heard such chirping from as early as Emmy got outside in the morning until the last light of day. When neighbors stopped by, they joked about the racket from the bird palaces in the Packard's yard, and the boys teased Emmy mercilessly about how the birds turned the snow black with their droppings—black and white. I've always thought it was interesting that bird droppings are two colors. But there was enough of the black to darken the snow and absorb what little sunlight there was. That was sometimes enough to melt the snow a bit, and the birds would congregate around the little puddles that formed in the wagon ruts to drink and preen their feathers. We got so used to the sound of doves cooing, it was like a radio playing all the time.

"Why was it almost always December?" Slip asked, looking in Nancy's direction. Nancy was reluctant to interrupt the flow of her words, but she needn't have worried. Slip's eyes were still focused somewhere else far away. "There's always been something about Christmas time that . . ." She picked up one glove and examined the stitching on the index finger. "It almost always pointed to Christmas time. Only three times was it summer."

Slip stayed quiet for so long, Nancy thought the interview might be over for the day. Finally she shifted her legs around so she could stand, and that small movement broke Slip's reverie. "Almost always Christmas," she said again.

Three French hens, two turtle doves, Nancy thought. *And a partridge in a pear tree.*

That year there was one storm in the middle of December that tore at our house as if the wind wanted to flatten us all, as if the snow was trying to bury us. Nobody went anywhere, of course. The only time we opened the door was for Pa and the boys to go outside to tend the livestock or bring in firewood. Emmy insisted on going out with him so she could throw seed out in the few sheltered places where the wind eddied the snow into deep drifts and left almost bare patches of ground right up beside the house. The howling of the wind sounded like Sylvia Telling's demented aunt, who used to scream out for no reason at all in the middle of Sunday services, until they stopped bringing her to church at all. We could hardly hear each other talking. Even when the wind let up, the farm house, sturdy as it was, still creaked and groaned, and every once in a while a board would settle or bend with a sound like the crack of a rifle.

Emmy wanted to go out during the storm to check on her bird friends, but Pa stopped her. Said she'd let so much heat out of the house we'd all freeze to death. "Don't worry," he told her. "Your birds are smart enough to stay in those houses you built them. They'll be fine." He chucked her under the chin. "We still have a whole wagon load of your sunflower seeds to get rid of, and I'm sure they'll oblige us by eating the lot of it once the storm clears." We all ducked when another loud crack reverberated through the house. "If I didn't know better, I'd think that was a gunshot," Pa said. "Funny what a storm will make you think, but nobody would be stupid enough to go out in this blizzard to hunt."

"Let's sing," Emmy said. "That will take our minds off the wind." We gathered around the spinet and sang hymns and popular songs too. Since it was nearing Christmas, we sang carols, but we added in a rousing rendition of "Daisy, Daisy, give me your answer, do. I'm half crazy, all for the love of you." Emmy sang louder than any of us, and laughed harder than us all when Pa mixed up the words. "It won't be a stylish carriage," he sang. "I can't afford a marriage." I think he did it on purpose, just to hear her laugh.

The wind tapered off during the night, several hours after our songs petered out, and the next morning dawned clear and bright. I was stoking up the fire in the cook stove when Emmy's first scream tore through the morning quiet. I never knew one small person—Emmy was always petite—could produce so much volume. She plowed through the drifts from one tree to another, from fence posts to the woodshed, from the mulberry trees to the old oak, picking up tiny bodies or pieces of bodies as she went. She'd opened her coat so she could get at her apron. By the time I reached her she'd piled twenty, thirty, maybe fifty of her dead friends in the sturdy cotton folds of her pinafore. Pa tried to hold her back, but she had to see all the devastation. Most of the loose feathers had blown away in the heavy wind, but the little bodies—what was left of them was frozen solid—were pathetic. Their blood was glazed on their feathers, like a skin of ice around the pond edges after the first freezing weather. When she brought them in, doves and finches and robins, they began to thaw out, and the blood stained her apron so that we never could wash it out. We tried to convince her to throw it away, but she wouldn't hear of it. She began to sleep with the apron curled around her.

My sister's heart broke that morning. She was never the same after that. Every noise scared her. Every footstep terrified her. And a gunshot—even one from far across the pastures—drained all the color out of her cheeks.

I knew who had done it, of course. I doubt Emmy ever suspected it; she was one of those sweet beings who always thought well of everyone, until somebody slaughtered her birds. Then she drew into herself and wouldn't talk to anyone except us in her family. We were the only ones she knew wouldn't—couldn't—have done it, since we were all inside with her that whole evening.

I couldn't let on that I knew it was Holden. I even let him open the door for me at church the following Sunday. I didn't say thank you, though. I just nodded, afraid that if I opened my mouth to speak, I would shatter like glass and rip his heart out with the shards, right there in front of the whole congregation. Pastor Jacobs praised him from the pulpit for saving the lives of the two Turner boys. I wanted to throw up, knowing that if he hadn't come out to slaughter Emmy's birds, he never would have stumbled across the two boys. I wished I'd stayed home with Emmy, who had been too sick at heart to get out of bed.

When we got home after the services, three wrens had found their way up to the porch. They huddled on the crosspieces above the steps, puffed up to insulate themselves from the bite of the wind. I turned around and went to the barn to scoop out a cup of seeds and laid it in a shallow bowl by one of the rocking chairs. Emmy would have been happy to know that there were three birds left, although when I tried to tell her, she turned her head toward the wall and wouldn't say a word.

Slip shook her head and started in the middle of the song. "What fun it is to ride and sing a sleighing song tonight." Her singing voice was higher pitched than Nancy would have expected, considering how mellow her speaking voice was.

"Why didn't you tell the whole town?"

"Just what do you think anyone would have done about it? There aren't any laws protecting birds. Nobody could have understood what those little animals meant to Emmy. Only us in the family. We saw it every day, her going deeper and deeper into a tunnel of anguish."

"I'm so sorry Emmy had to suffer," Nancy said. Privately she wondered if Holden Smith might have been out with the search party looking for the boys, and just happened to kill the birds on impulse. Not that that would have made any difference in the end. But why didn't he knock on their door to ask if the boys had taken shelter there? No, the man probably *was* the monster Slip had made him out to be.

"It was another couple of weeks before I happened on Holden out walking," Susannah said. "I was returning from taking a batch of soup to Widow Macomb. He had his shotgun with him, naturally. He almost walked right past me, but I stopped and asked him if he would show me how to shoot. He made some fun of me for wanting to learn a man's job, but I convinced him that I was only curious to feel how powerful the gun was when it went off. He pointed across the field to where four crows squabbled above a snow drift. "Think you could hit those?"

Nancy raised her left hand, almost like a school girl. "Four colly birds?"

"What are you talking about?"

"You know. From the Twelve Days of Christmas. The four colly birds."

"That's *calling* birds."

Nancy paused, hoping this contradiction wouldn't bring on another spate of anger. But facts were important, so she plowed on. "*Colly* is an old English word meaning *black*, probably from the word *coal*, so four colly birds would be four blackbirds or four crows."

The furrow between Slip's eyebrows deepened. Funny that Nancy, with her artist's eye, hadn't noticed it before.

"If you'll stop interrupting, I'll go on with my story."

"Yes. That's fine." *If you don't care about the facts, at least I do.*

"As I was saying, he asked me to shoot at the crows." She brushed the curl back from her face and kept talking.

"I'd rather try to hit a fence post first," I said. "Fence posts can't fly away while I'm taking aim."

"You ought to take off those gloves of yours."

"I don't want my fingers to get cold. Anyway, my finger is so slender I can fit it, glove and all, here where the trigger is."

He laughed. "Come here, and let me show you how a man shoots off his gun," he said, but his leer told me he wasn't talking about his shotgun.

He made a point of putting his arms around me to help me hold the shotgun level. It was all I could do to keep from pushing him away. "This here's too heavy for a little thing like you to support," he told me, all the while he was pressing himself up against me. I was so glad of my heavy coat. "You wouldn't want to get your pretty little arm all bruised," he said as he nestled the stock of the gun into that hollow at the front of my shoulder. "Hold it here real steady." His breath stank of the bacon he'd had for breakfast. The stubble of his cheek, even this early in the day, rasped against my jaw and that silly half beard of his—he called it a goatee, but it looked more like a goat—tickled my neck. He pushed his knees against the backs of mine. "Bending your knees a little bit like this will keep the recoil from throwing you off your feet." Then he added, "Of course, I wouldn't mind catching you if you fell on your back."

He was so sure of his attraction, so sure of his power, it never occurred to him that I would turn with the gun that had blown apart Emmy's birds, shove the barrel up under the scraggly half-beard on his wrinkled chin, and pull the trigger. It was such a smooth move, I almost might have practiced it.

Of course, there was a lot of blood. It was like a magic show, watching it spray everywhere. It sparkled in the winter sunlight and painted the snow that surrounded us. I had no way to clean the blood off me, so I did the next best thing. I ran to the nearest farm, screaming all the way. "Holden Smith shot himself," I told them. "We were walking along and he tripped and the gun went off." They believed me. They cleaned me up and wrapped me in blankets and clucked over me and plied me with hot cider while the men went down the road in the direction I'd indicated. Two of the women went to get Holden's wife. That was Meribelle Smith, the woman who had the roses strewn around at the cotillion. One of the boys rode over to get Pa, who came and bundled me into the wagon, glad that the barrel hadn't been pointed in my direction, and disgusted with the stupidity of anyone who'd walk with a loaded shotgun.

The following summer they wanted to rename the school and dedicate the new town fountain to Holden's memory over the objections of my father, who said there was no sense honoring anyone dumb enough to trip on his own two feet and shoot himself into the bargain. Nobody listened to Pa, though, not until the grades on Holden's report cards came to light, but by then the name was carved into the side of the fountain, and Holden Smith was a town legend. At least he was dead, as dead as Emmeline's sparrows and wrens and finches. Other birds eventually came back, but Emmy never sang again.

"Poor Emmy. I'm so sorry." Nancy waited just a moment. "May I ask something?"

"Yes."

"If you hated Holden so much, why did you decorate his fountain?"

"What do you mean?"

"With all the flowers. You said you planted flowers all around it."

"Well, I didn't plant anything there for years, but then I noticed the mess Meribelle, his widow, was making of it. All the wrong plants. No taste at all, so I took it over."

"You must have been devastated that you hadn't recognized those sounds as gunshots."

"What sounds?"

"The ones during the storm. If you'd known they were shots, you—or rather your father—could have gone outside and stopped Holden."

"Are you saying it's our fault he killed her birds?"

"Of course not. I just thought . . . well . . . it would have been nice if the story had come out differently."

"You don't like my stories?"

"I'm not saying that. I just felt sorry for Emmy."

Slip examined the fingernails on her left hand. "Everybody always felt sorry for Emmy."

Nancy couldn't categorize the tone. It wasn't exactly bitter. It wasn't sarcastic. It was *out of place* somehow. "Your treasure box," she asked, not knowing what else to say. "What did you save from Holden's death?" *His murder.*

"The morning after Holden died, four crows showed up in our yard. You know how crows love shiny objects. One of them had a button. I saw him drop it into the bowl on our porch. I always figured they were those same crows who'd seen me shoot Holden. One of them must have pecked the button off of Holden's shirt before the men got there to take up the body. Maybe that wasn't true; it was only a plain old metal button, after all, the kind that could have been on anybody's shirt. But I kept it anyway, along with the blue jay feather, and the pebble, and the clothes pin. The ivy leaf—"

Matron stuck her head in the room. "You two want to eat in here today?"

Nancy looked at Slip and was surprised to see her lip curled up in what looked like a snarl. Almost immediately, the surly expression changed to a blank stare, and Nancy wasn't sure of what she thought she'd seen. She turned back to the matron in confusion. "Eat in here? Uh, certainly. I brought enough for both of us. Thank you for thinking of that."

"Saves me time. This way I don't have to haul in some food she's not going to eat anyway. Do you want more water?"

"That would be nice. Thank you." Nancy waited for Matron to close the door. "I had one more question for you, Slip, but I can't remember what it was. Let me look back a few pages. I know it's in here somewhere. Oh yes, who played—"

"Here's your water."

"Thank you, Matron." Nancy smiled. "I have some extra cookies today. Would you like to have some?"

Matron shuffled closer and set down the tin pitcher. "Sure would. Thank you kindly." Nancy unwrapped the paper-shrouded parcel, and

Matron scooped up five of the eight cookies. "I'll save these for my dessert," she said as she left, locking the door behind her.

Nancy crossed her eyes. "If we were both on the outside," she said, "would that act of larceny have signed her death warrant?"

"Depends on what kind of cookies they were. Sugar cookies— she lives. Those new Toll House chocolate bit cookies—she dies."

"Well, this is her lucky day. We won't have to kill her, and I can now offer you one and a half sugar cookies."

"Sure," said Slip in a nearly perfect imitation of Matron's flat nasal twang. "Thank you kindly. I'll save these for my dessert."

Nancy produced the parcel of blackberries like a magician plucking a rabbit from a top hat. "I'm glad I didn't offer her any of these."

"We might have had only one berry apiece if you had." Susannah raised her cup in a silent toast. "That question you had, before we were interrupted?"

"Who played the piano?"

"What piano?"

"You said everybody gathered around the spinet to sing during the storm."

" I always called it the spinet. That's why I didn't understand your question."

"Was Emmy the one who played it?"

"Of course not. I was the only truly musical person in the family. I started on the spinet when I was four or five."

"Too bad there isn't a piano here. I'd love to hear you play."

"Use your imagination, Nancy Lou."

Maybe she was reading it wrong, but Nancy heard an insult in Slip's tone, confirmed a moment later when Slip added, "if you have any."

More cheese, more bread, a pitcher full of water, and one and a half sugar cookies each. It was a feast indeed, but Nancy's concerns wouldn't fade into the background, even though just outside the high window a peaceful-sounding pigeon cooed.

After the meal, Nancy tucked the oiled papers back into her handbag so she could wash them off when she got back to the rooming house. Next time she would bring Toll House cookies. Her notebook was already on a fresh page. She knew better than to write a name at the top. This was bizarre. She'd have to watch herself. Otherwise she'd start to think that murder was normal. Of course, in Slip's world it appeared to be just that.

Chapter 8 - Sewing Wild Oats

William F. Jennings, Plaintiff, vs. Mabel Maddox Jennings, Defendant - September 1938
. . . Plaintiff shows that this cruel treatment coming from one whom he had the right to expect complete devotion and care seriously effected *(sic)* his mental and physical wellbeing and that such treatment by Defendant towards Plaintiff makes it impossible for him to ever live happily with her again. . . .

--from the1938 archives of the
Gwinnett County Superior Court

Susannah leaned BACK in her chair and crossed her legs, the first time Nancy had ever seen her do that. "The next one was about three years later. She was somebody who was pretty much a stranger to me." She stopped talking and looked at Nancy. "You're enjoying these stories, aren't you?"

"I must admit I'm surprised by the . . . I had no idea you had ..." Nancy didn't know how to finish her sentence.

"Killed all those other people?"

Nancy hadn't noticed before how much Slip's gaze looked like a snake's. Her pupils, even in the relatively dim light of the interview room, were constricted. "How many were there altogether?"

Slip's mouth twisted in a parody of a smile, as if she knew a joke that was too delicious to tell. "Promise me you won't say a word about these, and I'll tell you all of them."

"I already did agree to wait until I could print the whole story."

"Well, say it again! Promise!"

Nancy tightened her grip on her fountain pen as Slip shouted at her. Surely Slip wouldn't lunge across the table at her. Why did she feel so threatened by Slip's request? "I promised you already, Slip, and I always keep my word."

"Do you now?" Susannah pressed the knuckles of her left hand against her chin. "If there's one thing I've learned in my fifty-seven years, it's that nobody keeps their word. Nobody. Do you hear me?"

It would be hard not to at that volume. "I keep mine. I told you I'd wait to get the whole story before I share it with anyone, and I intend to hold up my end of the bargain. I . . . I don't appreciate it when you threaten me."

"Threaten you?" Slip rested her cheek in the curve of her right hand. "Whatever are you talking about? All I did was ask for your promise."

Nancy waited for her heartbeat to slow down to normal. "You have my promise. You've had it all along." She thought back to a time when she was eleven or twelve. Her mother had pointed out to her that the only people who were consistently afraid of being lied to were liars themselves. A sweeping generalization, naturally, but Nancy wondered if she could manage to keep her promise, yet still check the facts before turning in her story. She'd definitely have to check the dates. How could she do that without going to Baynard's Mill? Obituary columns. They'd come in handy. Nobody would lie about having murdered someone, of course, but maybe she . . . Nancy couldn't think why she would doubt Susannah's word. The woman had *killed* these people. Maybe if Nancy went to verify all the dates, she could check other facts as well. The newspaper accounts of the deaths ought to have details. Surely Susannah couldn't remember every little detail after all these years.

She read the last few lines she'd written. "You said your next victim was a stranger. Is it easier to kill people if you don't know them personally?"

Slip thought a bit. "The killing itself is easy, no matter who it is. I never killed anyone without a good reason. I don't believe in killing for the fun of it. Although I must admit . . ."

Nancy waited for her to finish her sentence. "Although *what?*" she asked.

"Marjorie McDonald was about the closest I ever came."

"To what?"

"To killing just for the sheer pleasure of the killing. It's quite an experience, you see."

"No." Nancy wrote *Marjorie McDonald* at the top of a fresh page. "No, I don't really see."

"Well then, you'll just have to try it someday. For the sake of learning something new. I simply don't know how to describe it so that you would understand. Having the power to let someone live or to snuff out his life as if it were an oil lamp after bedtime—there is so much crowning glory in that achievement that it will change you forever. You'll never want to go back to the way life was before."

Nancy thought about her life. Her boring, fairly predictable life—except when she was getting lost and finding a tornado—felt mundane indeed. *What would it be like? What sort of thrill would it be?*

"You think about it, dear." Susannah reached across the table, seemed to think better of it, and put her hand back on her lap. "In the meantime, let me tell you about Marjorie."

Marjorie would still be alive today if she had left Lucy alone. Lucy's the oldest of my sisters, seven years older than I am, and has led a somewhat sheltered life. She'd been away from home only once, on a brief trip here to the state capital, just before she married William Lewis. The first four children came along right away after that and grew up, the way children do. I thought Lucy was as happy as a prairie dog with a new hole, until she came to me that day.

"You have to help me, Slip. I don't know what I'm going to do." She waved something that looked like a letter under my nose. "Do you believe the unmitigated gall of this woman?"

"Slow down and give me a chance," I told her. "You're too excited."

"She claims that Barnaby, my oldest son—"

I held up a restraining hand. "I know who Barnaby is, Lucy. I was there when he was born twenty years ago, remember?"

Lucy's eyes, which I had to admit had been rather out of focus, seemed to settle back into some semblance of normalcy. "Here." She shoved the letter at me. "You read it, and tell me what to do."

I'm a methodical person, so first I studied the envelope. The postmark was indistinct, as if the letter had been in the rain and the ink had run. The address, written in a large round hand, was still readable. It was addressed to Mrs. William Lewis. There was no return address. I opened the flap and unfolded three sheets of common white paper.

My dear Mrs. Lewis:

I am writing to you in the hopes that we can come to some sort of mutually beneficial agreement. It would be in your best interest, I am sure you will agree, to keep this communication private.

Your son, Barnaby Lewis, came to the state capital four months ago. It was at that time that he and I met outside a small store, where he was kind enough to assist me with conveying some of my heavier packages home. Because I live in an upstairs apartment, he very politely offered to carry them up the rather steep steps. Naturally, I felt it would be impolite not to offer him some refreshment.

We had a lovely conversation, in which he told me a great many details about his family. One thing led to another, and he was rather late getting back to his hotel that evening, as I am sure the desk clerk can attest, since your son was in a rather advanced state of inebriation when he left my place. When he reached the hotel, I understand he created a bit of an uproar upon being asked to lower his voice. The manager is a friend of mine.

I have no way of knowing whether you would be interested in caring for your upcoming grandchild, but I am in no position to raise the child myself, and am particularly interested in avoiding the unflattering publicity that always accompanies the birth of a child out of wedlock.

I have no interest in either moving to Baynard's Mill or in marrying your son. I would, however, be open to discussing an arrangement that would compensate me for the time I will need to withdraw from my work as a seamstress and clothing designer. I will lose a good many commissions due to my "illness," and that resulting loss of income will be substantial.

I assure you that any arrangement between us would never be referred to again. I leave it to you to decide whether you want your grandchild to grow up in your own home or in an orphanage, for I'm sure your kind heart would break at the thought of what sort of life orphans usually face.

I have no choice in this matter, and I write to you confident that you will see the power of my proposal.

Yours most respectfully,

Marjorie McDonald

Slip looked down at her hands and stopped speaking.

"Are you giving me the gist of the letter, or did you memorize it?"

"I remember every single word. Lucy was so distraught, we both read the letter and re-read it, hoping to find a contradiction or another interpretation. We took apart every sentence, hoping to find a flaw."

"What about Barnaby? Was he truly the father?"

Slip chuckled. "He certainly could have been. That boy had bedroom eyes from the time he was just a tyke. Every woman in town gushed all over him whenever he was around."

"But had he been in the city when this Marjorie said he was?"

"You don't understand, Nancy. He and his father had come up here so Barnaby could get familiar with the livestock sales. He'd never been before. They took a room in a small hotel for the week, and Lucy's husband was pretty worried on the third night when Barnaby didn't show up until so late. Five days later, when they got home to Baynard's Mill, William told Lucy that Barnaby had taken off one night and sowed some wild oats, although I'm sure he never guessed just how apt that old saying was. Lucy never had a bit of doubt that Barnaby had fathered that child. In fact, he admitted the possibility when Lucy and I confronted him that evening."

"He must have been horrified at the thought of the mother of his child attempting blackmail."

"Oh, Lucy never read the letter to Barnaby. She just told him she had heard from a Marjorie McDonald who thought she might be expecting."

"His reaction was—what? Disbelief? Anger?" Nancy thought about a great number of the men she'd met. "Pride?"

"He was terrified at the thought of having to marry Marjorie."

Nancy looked back through her notes. "I thought Marjorie McDonald said she didn't want to marry him."

"That's right, but Barnaby didn't know that. Furthermore, he was already engaged to a very proper young woman he'd known all his life. If she'd found out about an out-of-wedlock child, well, the marriage would have been cancelled. We told Barnaby we'd speak with Marjorie and see if we could come to some sort of agreement, that perhaps her family would take the child and rear it."

"She didn't mention her family in the letter."

"That's because she didn't have any to speak of. She wanted an *understanding* with Lucy. That meant money."

"So, did you come to that understanding?"

"Oh, yes. We most certainly did. I traveled up to the city. I told people in Baynard's Mill that I'd been invited to visit with Mrs. Reynolds. She's the one who moved away a few years after her Maude fell into the privy and drowned." Slip's eyes twinkled a bit. "She'd kept in touch with me by letter. For some reason she thought I was the nicest young lady she'd ever met, the way I used to help Maude with hanging out the laundry."

"You only did that twice—once when you milked her for information about the tomatoes and once the day you killed her."

"Mrs. Reynolds didn't know that. She only remembered the good parts. At any rate, she lived just outside the state capital, so it was easy for me to write and ask if I could visit her. That way I could stop in the city on my way north. . . ."

Marjorie had included her address in the letter she wrote Lucy, so I stopped by. I was particularly lucky to find her home alone. I should have thought to check out the house first, to be sure nobody would see me. Of course, as I've mentioned, I do tend to be invisible for the most part. Naturally, I had prepared several options. I couldn't be sure how she would react, you see.

I introduced myself as Barnaby's aunt, and she invited me in for tea. The room she ushered me into doubled as a fitting room. There were dress dummies in each corner and a few exceptionally exquisite gowns in various stages of completion draped over racks here and there. I admired the workmanship, and she took a moment to show me some new lace she had just received from Paris.

She was barely showing. If I hadn't known what to look for, I might not have guessed that she was expecting. When I told her that, she turned sideways and cupped her hands around her belly so I could see the protuberance. I told her she shouldn't be carrying anything heavy in her condition, so I offered to transport the tea pot into her small dining room. She was most willing to let me pour.

We had a civilized conversation about the possibilities. I told her that I hadn't brought any funds with me on this trip, but that I often passed through the city and, once we reached an agreement on the amount, I could deliver half of the money in two weeks, the next time I was planning to be up that way, and the other half when I came with a wet nurse to collect the child after the birth.

She was amenable to that, and we agreed rather quickly on a most generous sum. I even said I would add in enough so she could pay her rent to keep her apartment and workplace while she went to stay in a home for unwed mothers. She gave me the home's address and said she would write as soon as the baby made its appearance. We talked about a written contract, but I assured her that I trusted her implicitly.

I was lucky that she was one of those modern women who lived and worked alone. We parted with a cordial handshake, and I left without a backward glance. There was nothing in writing to tie me to her, and when she died we were not notified.

Nancy waited with her pen in mid-air. "If you weren't notified, how did you know she died?"

"There was a small note about her death in the newspaper. Mr. Reynolds received the paper every day, and Mrs. Reynolds was kind enough to let me read it. I clipped out the notice and brought it home for Lucy. She was a bit distraught at the loss of the baby, but finally admitted that it was probably for the best."

"If you parted . . ." Nancy looked back over her notes . . . "*cordially*, then how did you kill her? Did you go back that night?"

"Nancy, Nancy . . ." Slip wagged her finger and pointed to the notebook. "Didn't I say I had prepared several options?"

"Yes, but I still don't see how you did it."

"The tea, of course. I poured, and it was the work of an instant to slip some wort weed in with the tea leaves. I didn't drink any of my tea, but she was so anxious to talk about the money that she never even noticed. Greed must be thirsty work. She drank four cups. Wort weed takes at least fourteen hours to do its work, so I was already at Mrs. Reynolds' house before Marjorie would have had any idea that she was dying. As I sat on the train, I had the joy of picturing what that woman went through in her death throes. I'm sorry I couldn't be there to see it happen."

"Wort weed? What is that?"

"Some places it's called rock poppy. It's a common enough plant if you know what to look for. I even insisted on washing out the teacups and rinsing the pot for Marjorie before I left, so you see, there was no indication of what had caused her end."

"But you killed the baby too."

"Lucy didn't need a baby to take care of at her age, and Barnaby, handsome as he was, had no use for it. It might have been the ending of his marriage. What's the difference, anyway? I saved that baby from a horrible life in an orphanage."

Nancy couldn't look Susannah in the face. Not while thinking about that baby. "Did you put something in your treasure box?"

"Oh, yes." Susannah thought for a moment. "I forgot to mention that. Marjorie gave me a small sample of her Paris lace. She said I could trim the corner of a handkerchief with it. What in tarnation would I ever need with a lacy hanky?"

As Nancy checked out that evening, she handed the soggy, blackberry-stained newsprint to Officer Heavybrow. His mouth was closed too tightly for even a minor smile. He chucked the wad of paper in the trash, and Nancy drove to the rooming house, hoping she would be able to find some chocolate on Monday, and hoping just as much that she wouldn't have nightmares about Marjorie McDonald's baby. Why was she even thinking of baking cookies for this . . . this murderer? She knew she was just imagining it, but a voice echoed deep inside her head. *Nancy, you're cooking these for yourself. Every time we cook, we do it with love. That way we get fed twice.* Her mother stood beside ten-year-old Nancy in their sunny kitchen and seemed to banish all the nightmares, because that night, Nancy slept well.

      After that marathon weekend of murder stories, the trial ran late each day, well past the end of visiting hours, leaving no time for an interview, which as just as well, since Nancy hadn't been able to find any chocolate until Thursday. Her nightmares were predictably gory, filled mostly with knives and bears and shotguns, but Nancy chose not to dwell on them. She contented herself through the week with transcribing and organizing her notes, planning how she would present the finished article. The fact that it was turning into something approaching book length did not deter her. *We'll serialize it,* she thought in a burst of creative energy. She even broached the possibility to George, when she phoned in one of her daily reports, although she couldn't allude to the other murders, because of her promise to Slip. She wouldn't have trusted either the telephone or the mail with such explosive information, even if she had been willing to break that promise. George was understandably reluctant to commit. "Two trials just aren't worth that much space," he told her. "Just keep up those daily reports and that will be enough." *You'll change your tune when you have all my notes in your hand,* she vowed.
      Each day, Nancy tried to sit someplace where Slip would see her readily when she was ushered into the courtroom by the broad-faced limping bailiff. Slip would nod before she settled into her chair, folded her gloved hands in her lap, and withdrew into that implacable shell of inactivity that set her aside from every other inhabitant of the court. Each evening Nancy phoned in a fair reporting of the day's events. She doubted anyone would understand how hard it was for her to give a clinical summary of what happened at the trial each of those days. She

would much rather have been telling what had really happened all those years ago. She found herself wanting to skip the trial and spend all her time in the interview room with Slip. Each morning she deplored the hokey headline the *Clarion* placed above her story. That Thursday, the defense finally rested. The jury was dismissed for the night, instructed not to discuss the case, and told to return the next morning for the closing arguments.

On the way home, Nancy tried one more store and found chocolate. She stayed up late, baking, although she wasn't sure why she was putting so much effort into getting on Slip's good side. The stories would come, she was sure, without the gifts of cookies. Nancy didn't think she was so hard up for friends that she'd have to convince a murderer to play that role. Her mother had been right. The baking was therapeutic. Mix flour and butter and salt and you'd get cookies every time. It wasn't nearly as unnerving as mixing people together and getting sometimes a happy family and sometimes a monster. Sometimes a bird lover and sometimes a slaughterer. Nancy had always believed that putting the facts on paper helped to keep order in her world; but with Slip, the words seemed somehow elusive, as if there were meaning in there somewhere, but Nancy couldn't see it clearly. Were cookies a lifeline or a call for help? Not for the first time, Nancy wished her mother had survived the 1918 flu epidemic. They could have baked cookies together and then sat down at the kitchen table to talk. Nancy envied Slip that connection to family. Something, though, seemed off-kilter. Two batches later, Nancy still didn't know what it was.

STATESVILLE COUNTY CLARION

YOUR MORNING SOURCE FOR ALL THE NEWS WORTH READING

Friday, July 22, 1932

RUPERT RESTS WHILE PACKARD PACES

By Nancy Remington

The State Capital: The sensational trial of convicted murderer Susannah Lou Packard is expected to come to an end today. The prosecution's panel of experts has included many prominent members of the medical world. District Attorney Paul W. Stevens paraded a bevy of doctors who testified to the particular atrocity of the murderous attack on State Senator Dominick Kingsley last December. Photographs of the carnage, including scenes of a blood-spattered wash room and multiple views of the Senator's torn throat, were again prominently displayed for the jury. On Wednesday afternoon, the prosecution rested its case.

On Thursday, Defense Attorney Rupert Z. Pinkney proceeded to plead his client's innocence. He produced character witnesses who testified to her exemplary standing in the community of Baynard's Mill where Miss Packard has lived her entire life and where she has taught Sunday School for the past forty years. In a surprise announcement, he informed the court that Miss Packard's niece had been, at the time of the murder, engaged to the son of the victim, and argued that no loving aunt would act in such a way as to endanger her niece's future happiness. According to Mr. Pinkney, however, that engagement was terminated when Miss Packard was arrested.

Closing statements will be issued today, after which the jury will be charged and sent to deliberate. Their charge will be to examine the evidence and then to return a verdict of either guilty or not guilty. If not guilty, Miss Packard will still remain in prison, serving her term for the 1926 murder of Senator Button Kingsley. If the jury finds her guilty, they will most likely be asked to recommend a sentence, since that is Judge McElroy's usual practice. Both attorneys declined to comment on their expectations for this trial.

Miss Packard remains incarcerated at the State prison.

Chapter 9 - You Can Bank on It

William F. Jennings, Plaintiff, vs. Mabel Maddox Jennings, Defendant - September 1938
. . . that neither Plaintiff nor Defendant own any property of any consequence and that there is no question of division of property at issue in this proceeding . . .
--from the 1938 archives of the
Gwinnett County Superior Court

On Friday, Nancy opened a new steno pad as the prosecuting attorney stood and approached the dais. Mr. Stevens began his closing argument quietly. "Ladies and Gentlemen of the Jury, I must thank you for the diligent attention you have given throughout this trial. I know you have other things, important things, you would rather be doing, but serving on a jury is one of the most important services you can offer your country. I will try not to prolong your stay here." He paused to let the wave of gentle laughter rustle through the jurors' ranks.

"I am fairly certain that it will be suggested to you that the State has failed to show overwhelming evidence that Susannah Lou Packard is guilty of the crime with which she has been charged, since my esteemed colleague has suggested as much each day so far. For that reason, I would ask that we go over the evidence in this case, because that evidence is what you will use as a basis for your final decision."

He turned to his table and held up a knife. The blade glittered in the harsh electric light from the bulbs in the ceiling fixture. "Please bear with me as I repeat the scenario I asked you to imagine on the first day of this trial. I would like you to pretend that you are an elected official, doing what you think of as your best to steer this county and this state through the most devastating depression in the history of our country. You may have made some errors in judgment. Some of them may have been grievous errors. But you are trying your best. One day, just before Christmas, your secretary is preparing to leave for lunch. You look at your wristwatch, as we heard that secretary testify, and you tell her that she can take an extra long lunch hour, since the day has been slow and you plan to work through lunch. During that lunchtime on that particular day, into your office comes a woman who the defense counsel described in his opening remarks as unprepossessing." He turned and looked at her. "Yes, she is. In the same way that a dog might look innocent, until it turned and bit your child in the face. Just so, Miss Packard entered Mr. Kingsley's office on December 23rd and locked the waiting room door behind her. Of course he took no measures to protect himself from her. If a man—that rabid, angry, and completely illusory man that Mr. Pinkney has proposed—had entered the room, don't you suppose that Mr. Kingsley would have taken steps to keep his large, heavy desk between the two of them? But no, he must have stepped around that desk, to greet this unassuming woman with the hearty handshake for which he was well-known.

"Ladies and Gentlemen, it was during that handshake, we can surmise, that the woman you see sitting before you pulled this razor-sharp knife," he held it out before him at arm's length, "and plunged it into Mr. Kingsley's neck. We have proven to you that she is left-handed. You can see it, can't you? She allowed him to grasp her right hand in friendship, and then she whipped forth her deadly knife. Before he could react, he lay bleeding on the floor, unable to call for help, his windpipe had been severed, and blood gushed down his throat and over his chest. We have shown evidence that someone used the washroom. You saw photographs of the blood spattered in the wash basin and on the floor. You heard evidence that the back entrance to Mr. Kingsley's office was found unlocked. Can you see Miss Packard walking through that doorway after she washed the blood of Mr. Kingsley from her hands? Every day of this trial you have seen her sit here dressed in dark blue. You have heard evidence that she wears nothing but dark blue. Dark blue would hide splashes of blood sufficiently for her to leave the premises, return home unnoticed, and hide the evidence."

He replaced the knife on his desk and lifted a gold wristwatch. He turned it over. "*To Dominick Kingsley, upon your graduation.* That's what is engraved on the back of this watch that was found in a wooden box that Sheriff Fordyke found beneath Miss Packard's bed. I'm sure you noticed that my colleague," he glanced around toward the defense table, "has tried to shift the blame onto Dominick Kingsley's political beliefs and his Farm Bill. Mr. Kingsley, however, is not on trial here. No matter what you think of his legislation, Mr. Kingsley was the victim in this heinous crime. Mr. Kingsley is dead, at the hands of that woman," he turned and pointed, "that woman who cold-heartedly unbuckled his watch from his lifeless wrist and who undoubtedly gloated over it as she placed it in a box filled with innocent mementos—a feather, a bit of lace, a bottle of poison."

Nancy was hoping for a short recess before Mr. Pinkney spoke, but that didn't happen. Judge McElroy might have been impatient to get to lunch, or he might have been truly curious as to how Mr. Pinkney would summarize his defense of Miss Packard. "The floor is yours, Mr. Pinkney," he intoned, as soon as Mr. Stevens concluded his remarks.

Mr. Pinkney stood, adjusted his bow tie, and approached the jury box. "Gentlemen of the jury," he began. Nancy gritted her teeth. Women had been eligible to serve on juries for the past twelve years. You'd think he could make an effort to remember that three of his jurors wore skirts. "That is to say, Ladies and Gentlemen of the jury; you will remember that at the beginning of the trial I told you that there was no burden of proof on the defense. That means that we did not have to prove to you that the death of Mr. Kingsley was not perpetrated by my client, Miss Packard. The burden of proof is clearly, yes, it is clearly and by force of law on the office of the prosecuting attorney. When you retire to the jury room to deliberate this case, I have the utmost faith that you will find that there is reasonable doubt as to whether my gentle client committed any crime. The honorable Mr. Stevens has failed to show any reason why Miss Packard would have wanted to see Dominick Kingsley dead. He has failed to define any motive whatsoever. Without motive, where is the reason for murder?"

For once he was using complete sentences, unlike his usual style. Maybe he'd been drinking. Illegal it might be, but that didn't seem to stop many people. He looked too relaxed.

"You strike me as being well-read individuals," Pinkney continued. "I can imagine each of you with your morning newspaper, being sure that you are well-informed as to the important news of the day. You will remember that Mr. Kingsley was instrumental in proposing and implementing the legislation that has come to be called simply the Farm Bill. Its effects were deplored by many, and some would say that it was the Farm Bill that led this great state more deeply into the paralyzing effects of this great depression we suffer under.

"Miss Packard, however, did not feel the effects of that Farm Bill. She lives on a thriving family farm. They have not felt the strangling consequences of the Kingsley legislation. Miss Packard would have no motive whatsoever, could have no reason to wish the demise of Dominick Kingsley. I would suggest, however, that there are many persons, yes, many persons as yet unknown, who felt the abhorrent noose of starvation on their families as the effects of Mr. Kingsley's ill-advised Farm Bill led to the destruction of so many family farms. Mr. Kingsley's action in pushing through this legislation was reprehensible. He was a criminal!"

Mr. Stevens sprang to his feet. "Objection, your Honor!"

The heavy mane of Judge McElroy's white hair waved back and forth. "Who is on trial here, Mr. Pinkney?"

"I insist on being able to call the deceased a criminal, your Honor, for it was his legislation that has so adversely affected this entire county, no, this entire state. I intend to show that there are grounds for reasonable doubt about Miss Packard's guilt. She is innocent of this crime, but that can more easily be seen when one is aware that there are many persons as yet unnamed who had far greater reason than she to wish this . . . this . . . this despicable so-called public servant dead and buried, and his loathsome Farm Bill with him."

He was back to dithering again. Maybe the gin was wearing thin.

Judge McElroy looked at Pinkney long enough to make that gentleman squirm. "I will allow you to make your point."

Nancy studied the jury. They looked ready to make Pinkney squirm as well. Perhaps the judge knew what he was doing in allowing the diatribe to continue. She had to remember that Susannah Lou

Packard *was* guilty. She couldn't sit here and hope they would think she was innocent. Anyway, Pinkney was slowly digging his own grave, so to speak. Well, let him do it. It seemed heartless, on the other hand, to hope that quiet-looking woman would be convicted. Then again, a second life sentence wouldn't make a bit of difference to Susannah Lou Packard. Nancy's thoughts teetered back and forth. If she hadn't been sitting so firmly rooted to her chair, she might have felt dizzy.

Mr. Stevens sat, and Mr. Pinkney continued, encouraged no doubt by his seeming success. "This criminal who sat in the State House of Representatives betrayed us all with his ill-intentioned legislation. Is it any wonder that someone—someone other than my client—entered his office at noon last December 23rd and exacted his own form of justice?

"Look at my client, gentlemen—ladies and gentlemen. You have heard the testimony of upstanding people such as her pastor, the pastor's wife, the school teacher, and the mayor of Baynard's Mill. My client, Miss Packard, has been a Sunday School teacher for the past forty years. How can you possibly think that a lady as unassuming, as unprepossessing, as gentle as she obviously is, could possibly wield a weapon with such ferocity? No, I propose to you that this heinous crime was committed by a man who is as yet unknown. A man who took the law into his own hands, that is to say, yes, into his own hands and committed an act of singular determination, in which he took vengeance . . ."

Even from the balcony, Nancy could see the spit that sprayed across the edge of the jury box. The jurors leaned farther back in their chairs.

"Vengeance," he repeated, "on that criminal politician who never represented the will of his constituents, but who wrung the life out of the good people of this county.

"I rest assured that you will sleep better tonight knowing that you have acquitted Miss Susannah Packard of this crime, a crime which she is obviously in no position to have committed, and a crime which the district attorney has by no means proven. I trust that you will base your decision on the reasonable doubt—a doubt which Mr. Stevens will undoubtedly lie about—"

"Objection, your Honor!"

"Counselor, please restrain yourself. This is a civilized courtroom, or it was until you began your summation."

And so it went, for another twenty-five minutes. Nancy timed it.

Mr. Pinkney finished his closing arguments just before the lunch hour. When the judge sent the jury to deliberate, he asked them to consider each piece of evidence. "You will have the photographs in the jury room with you. You will have the wooden box, with all its contents except the vial of poison, which has been removed for your protection. You will have the blood-stained dress, the knife—please handle it carefully—and the wristwatch." He further warned them that if they did not reach a verdict swiftly, they would be sequestered and required to continue deliberating on Saturday. After that, the court would be recessed until the following Tuesday, because Monday was a state holiday, the birthday of some historical figure who'd made a big name for himself, a clear case of the biggest fish in a little pond, since nobody outside the state seemed ever to have heard of him. That suited Nancy fine, though, since it would give her three and a half days with Susannah Lou Packard.

No shade in the parking area. No pleasantries at the front desk. Officer Protection-Without-a-Smile neglected to check her bag. "Any more of those thorny berries," was all he said, and it didn't even sound like a question.

"No." *Instead, I brought four sharp knives, three stout clubs, two straight razors, and a partridge in a pear tree, tra-la-la.*

"The matron's waiting for you right through there."

"Thank you, Officer." She hummed as she walked away from him.

Once again they shared a mid-day meal in what Matron referred to as the *interrogation room*, much to Nancy's chagrin. Slip just laughed. "Interrogate away," she said.

Nancy had a fresh notebook page in front of her. "Are we ready for Button now?"

"Let me see. The next one would have been Sylvia." She frowned. "No, I take that back. Henry was the next one."

How many more are there? Nancy dutifully wrote *Henry*. "Last name?"

"Markham. Henry Markham."

Markham, Nancy wrote and looked up. "Wasn't he the town banker when John Anders took in all those figurines stuffed with money?"

"No, but you're close; Henry never worked at the bank, even though he was the banker's son. It was the grandson, Able Markham, who took over the bank. I'm glad you've been paying attention." She brushed idly at the dark blackberry stain on the wood between the two of them. "Tell me," she asked, "are you a good writer?"

"I . . . I suppose so. Writing is important to me, and I've always wanted to get my facts straight and get the tone of the story just right."

"Hm. I suppose that's important," she drummed her fingers on the table, "but can you tell the story behind the story?"

"I'm not sure I know what you mean."

"Never mind. I'm not sure what I mean either." Susannah pulled out the gloves once more and stared at them. "I never really wanted anyone to know about what I did, because until I met you, I never thought *anyone* could understand." Nancy felt a surge of guilt. Did she understand Slip, or was she simply pretending to do so in order to get a good story? Half of her hoped it was the former case, but the other more logical half of her brain knew it was really the latter. She was using Slip mercilessly. Maybe that was why she kept bringing cookies. To assuage her guilty conscience. Slip laid one glove on the table and toyed with the position of the thumb. Once it seemed to meet her satisfaction, she laid the other beside it. "I almost told Jethro once. I know I've said before that he was the best friend I ever had. When it came right down to it, though, I didn't quite trust him to see into my heart and know that what I did was right, was necessary, was important. At least, not about something like this."

"Do you think he ever suspected?"

Susannah fiddled a bit with the second glove, turning it this way and that. Finally she turned both gloves palm up, and they lay there side by side. "These look like they're praying, don't they?"

They look more like they're begging. "I've never been very religious," she said. "What about you?"

"Oh, church was something we had to do each week, but it always seemed to me that most people went just to see their friends or, in the good years, to show off any new clothes they happened to have. I went because I taught Sunday School and because Ma and Pa expected it. After they died I kept going because it was such a habit." She reached up to the wayward curl that had once again escaped her bun. "Pastor Jacobs is a kind man in many ways, but I'm fairly certain he would judge me worthy of hellfire if he knew what I did." She leaned her elbows on the table and rested her chin on her clasped hands. "He'd baptized most of them, you know. They were his flock and he the shepherd. It would never have occurred to him that all his preaching never stopped any of them from doing the things they did. No, he would have thought that I was the one who deserved hell, when all I did was keep them from hurting anybody else's family the way they hurt mine."

"He and his wife certainly gave you a good character reference in that courtroom, and I'm sure they were aware of the verdict in your first trial."

"Yes. Well, Pastor Jacobs never liked Button Kingsley one bit, and Mrs. Jacobs didn't have a thought worth thinking about in that head of hers. She was . . . well, let's not go into that."

Nancy waited to be sure Slip was through with her comments. "We got a bit sidetracked. I had asked if Jethro ever suspected you."

"Ah, Jethro. Maybe he did, but he was such a loyal friend, he never would have voiced his suspicion. No. No, suspicion is too strong a word. Jethro never really suspected me. He was too much in . . ."
Susannah looked at Nancy, fell silent for a bit, and then continued.

When Minnie fell and died, Jethro did make a comment to me about how convenient it was that Mary Louise's competition was out of the way.

"Jethro Fordyke," I said quite forcefully, "you couldn't possibly suspect Mary Louise of engineering Minnie's death. There's no way she could have done that. Minnie fell from her own balcony."

"Maybe Mary Louise climbed up the trellis," he said. "Jasper found a lot of broken ivy."

"In that case, if I were the sheriff, I'd look for somebody wearing pants." I swished my skirts back and forth. "How could a woman possibly climb a stupid old trellis wearing these things?"

"I guess you have a point," he said.

Then when Holden died, I know Jethro and Jasper both wondered if I might have had something to do with it. After all, I was right there when he tripped and set off his own gun, and his blood was splattered all over me. But they couldn't find a single reason why I might have wanted to kill Holden. You see, we never told anybody about Emmy's birds. She begged us not to. Said she couldn't bear people's pity. Even worse, she said she would kill anyone who told her that they were *only birds* and that birds didn't matter. A lot of people would have had that reaction, I'm sorry to say. They didn't know our Emmy.

I'm sure Jethro never thought twice about the others who died in Baynard's Mill. Of course he never heard of Marjorie, since she was from up north. Most of the killings were three, four, even five years apart, so there was no pattern for them to point to and say *there's a killer in our midst.* Now, John Anders did get robbed on the road from Statesville, but that was obviously some vagrants passing through. The only other one that might have made them think about a killer was that man, the first one, being stabbed way out in the woods behind his farm. He had nothing to rob. After that, I was always reluctant to use my knife. Thank goodness that bear took care of him.

Slip yawned and stretched. "I've been sitting too long."

"Me too. If we were smart, we'd go out and walk around the block once or twice."

"Miss Nancy Lou Remington," Susannah said as she stood, "just how am I supposed to do that?"

Nancy could feel her ears heating up. They tended to turn pink when she was embarrassed. "I'm sorry. I wasn't thinking. It's just that it's so hard to think of being inside here . . . well . . ."

"Until I die? You didn't want to mention that, did you?"

"It's a little awkward."

Susannah laughed, a dry chuckle that didn't last very long. "Yes, you could say that." She sat back down. "Let's keep going, shall we?"

Nancy took a deep breath and looked back a page or two. "You said a few minutes ago that you almost told Jethro the truth once. When was that?"

"It was right after I killed Henry Markham. He had a son named Able—the one who became the banker. I was Jethro's best friend, but Able was his second best friend, right up until his father did what he did."

"What did he do?"

Slip stood up again and paced around the room, talking as she went.

Able and Jethro always sat together in school. We had those wide desks back then that let two children sit side by side. The boys' desks were lined up in two rows on one side of the classroom and the girls' desks were in three rows on the other side. The teacher always started the school year with us in alphabetical order, but then she'd move people for one reason or another. I always sat close to the front in the row nearest the boys. Jethro and Able always sat two or three desks farther back on the boys' side.

They couldn't have looked more opposite if you'd colored them from two different paint cans. Jethro Fordyke had that yellow-white corn-shock hair; Able Markham's was as black as a crow's eyes. Jethro was skinny when he was a kid; Able was padded all over. Jethro grew up tall and lean; Able stayed short and just got rounder every year. Jethro loved to read; Able loved numbers. Jethro never missed a day of school; Able tended to feel poorly on occasion and he'd be gone a day or two, but he was smart enough to catch right up. None of those differences mattered, though. They hung around together, laughing and pulling outrageous stunts. Never anything mean to hurt anyone. They didn't bother to cover their tracks, so they got caught every time. Those two had to whitewash the town hall fence more than once to cover up the words they'd scrawled on it, but that never seemed to slow them down. The first time they wrote something from Shakespeare. The writing was juvenile, and Jethro was the only nine-year-old boy interested in the Bard. Everybody knew it had to be Jethro, and if Jethro was involved, so was Able.

Able looked a lot like his mother. Maybe if he'd taken after his father, things might have been different in that household. You see, Henry Markham, as gaunt as one of those white storks and just as sharp-nosed, thought he was God's gift to the world, personally appointed by the Lord Almighty to keep everyone else in check. We didn't know at first that every time Able and Jethro got caught for a prank, Able was practically skinned alive by that father of his. Able hid it all behind a jolly smile and a carefree attitude.

As the boys grew up, the pranks pretty much stopped. Jethro still lived with his family, managing the livestock. Able lived at home too. He handled all the accounts for his father's extensive holdings. Henry was the largest landowner around, and when Able showed no leanings toward farming, Henry groomed him to take care of the business side of the farm.

Able had a natural aptitude for numbers, you see. When Able made a few mistakes at first, his father punished him severely. Pretty soon, Able's mind was as precise as one of those newfangled adding machines.

By this time the boys were in their middle thirties—not boys any longer. Along about that time Pastor Jacobs was called out of town, and he asked Henry Markham to deliver the sermon in his absence. He suggested Genesis 22:1-13 as the text, the story of how God provided a ram for the sacrifice so Abraham wouldn't have to kill his son Isaac. Able heard his father practicing this sermon and told Jethro about it. It was too good a chance to pass up.

Mrs. Meribelle Smith, who was in charge of the flowers for the altar, just about fainted when she walked in early Sunday morning. She dropped her bucket of flowers, and water spilled all over the new rag rug that had been pieced together and donated by the ladies of the church. That water wasn't the only thing on the rug. When Henry showed up a few minutes later, his face turned as red as a cardinal bird.

You see, Jethro and Able had wanted to put a ram in there to fit right in with the sermon, but they knew enough about the destructive possibilities of a male sheep that they decided against that course. Then they thought maybe a nice ewe would work, but they didn't dare, because it was lambing season, and they didn't want to harm any of the livestock. So they installed one of the Fordyke's placid cows instead.

Believe me, those two had some cleaning up to do, and that was one mess that couldn't be fixed by a simple layer of whitewash. No real harm was done, and we all thought it was pretty funny, but Able had crossed a line and had embarrassed that self-righteous father of his.

When Able got home late that afternoon after working a good part of the day to clean the church, Henry took him out behind the barn and gave him a beating. Not a switching, mind you, but an honest-to-goodness beating. He ripped Able's back open with a birch rod and then took to him with the buckle end of his belt. By the time Able got away and ran to Jethro's house, blood almost filled his shoes. Mrs. Fordyke helped clean his back and bandaged it, and they tried to put him to bed there for the night, but Able wouldn't have anything to do with staying in Baynard's Mill. As soon as his clothes were clean, he asked Jethro to go with him, but Jethro had the main responsibility for the lambing on his family's farm, what with Mr. Fordyke getting so poorly.

Jethro and his mother tried to talk him out of it, but Able swore he'd never come back until his father was dead. He walked to Statesville and caught a train. Rode the rails like a hobo. He ended up rousting for a traveling circus for a while. He even played a clown. He could balance a straight-backed chair on his chin. Amazing trick.

When Able left, though, I'd never seen Jethro so upset. It was like his right arm had been sawn off. He blamed himself for not knowing what had been happening to Able, but you know how men are. Even when they're little boys, they hide their hurts and act like nothing bothers them. Then one day they blow up. Able hid all his bruises and scars—oh yes, he had scars aplenty. Mrs. Fordyke saw them when she was patching up his back. We finally figured out that all those times Able missed school, it was because his back needed to scab over so he wouldn't bleed through his shirt.

This last beating, though, and him a grown man, was too much for Able, and he had to leave. It about broke his poor mother's heart. Henry Fordyke blamed her for raising him wrong. I walked over their way one evening and heard him shouting at her, accusing her of laughing at Able's pranks and encouraging him to embarrass his father. He said Able was a sorry excuse for a son and they were better off without him. When she tried to object, he hit her. I could hear it all the way out on the path.

Able sent Jethro a postcard now and again. That's how we knew he was working in a circus. After a couple of years he included an address care of general delivery in some podunk town out west. Jethro finally could write to tell him his father was dead and he could come home. So he did.

"You killed Henry?"

Slip's smile grew. "His bull stepped on him. Nobody knew why he'd been stupid enough to go into the stall like that, without other men around to help keep the bull under control."

"Why did he?"

"Well, he didn't exactly. I'd gotten very good at using a hammer, and I'm a lot stronger than I look. Once he was stunned—it's surprising how often men are alone in a barn—I pushed him under the bottom rail to keep the bull company. And I waited around long enough to see the carnage. That poor bull really is a sweet animal. He's fairly placid except when it's time to mate, of course. But he doesn't like unusual activity in his stall. A man lying on the straw was just too confusing, and naturally had to be investigated. I was lucky that there were so many footprints in the snow around the barn that nobody noticed my tracks. I had to wait for winter, you see. Christmas killings had become such a habit by then. Henry came to for just a moment before the end," again, that slow, knowing smile, "so I could tell him that this was what he got for hurting Jethro."

"Jethro?" Nancy glanced back at her notes. "You said that Henry beat up Able. Did he go after Jethro too?"

"He didn't have to beat Jethro to hurt him. When Able left. that hurt Jethro. Something light and happy went out of his life with Able gone, and Jethro mourned like a man losing a brother." Susannah ran her hand over her face. "Don't you see? Henry's death brought Able back to town. He got a job at his grandfather's bank working his way up to manager. He did real well for himself, and Jethro was happy again. Eventually, Able took over as president when his grandfather died."

"What happened to the Markham farm without Mr. Markham to run it?"

"Poor Mrs. Markham had to sell it. She was mighty grateful to the Fordykes for patching up Able's back that night and giving him food for the start of his journey. She sold the farm to Mr. Fordyke for a reasonable price."

"I thought you said Mr. Fordyke was doing poorly."

"Oh. Yes." She wrinkled her forehead. "Yes, he was. And when he died, Jethro was the new Mr. Fordyke. He's the one who ran the farm, and he's the one who bought the Markham spread. He had all the respect from the community now."

Nancy waited for more, but Susannah was silent. "Slip? What did you take for your treasure box this time?"

Susannah spread her hands about ten inches apart. "A piece of straw about this long. I picked it up from the floor of the stall before the blood and gore got splashed around. A fully-grown bull weighs quite a bit, you know."

Nancy baked more cookies when she got back to the rooming house that evening, while visions of bull hooves danced in her head.

STATESVILLE COUNTY CLARION

YOUR MORNING SOURCE FOR ALL THE NEWS WORTH READING
Saturday, July 23, 1932

PINKNEY PLEADED. NOW JURY JUGGLES

By Nancy Remington

The State Capital: The jury is still out on what is being called the Trial of the Year, in which lurid evidence from the prosecutor clashed with the decorous, almost prim appearance of the defendant. Miss Susannah Lou Packard's defense attorney, Rupert A. Pinkney, Esq., pled for her release yesterday in his closing statements. A swift verdict was expected, but as of press time late on July 22nd, no answer had yet been made as to the question of Miss Packard's guilt or innocence. A source close to the defense attorney, who asked to remain anonymous, said that if Pinkney's client is found not guilty of the December 23rd murder of Dominick Kingsley, Mr. Pinkney will appeal the verdict in her first trial.

Chapter 10 - Packed with Care

**William F. Jennings, Plaintiff, vs. Mabel Maddox Jennings, Defendant -
September 1938**
We, the jury, find that sufficient proofs have been submitted to our consideration to
authorize a total divorce.

--from the 1938 archives of the
Gwinnett County Superior Court

Who could have known the jury would take so long? For
some reason, before Nancy left Statesville for this assignment, she had
packed two blue cotton shirtwaist dresses she'd found in the back of
her closet. Her older sister had given them to her several years before.
One was a dark blue, the other a lighter shade. She'd never worn either
one, because a hand-me-down shirtwaist didn't fit her vision of herself
as a slick reporter. She thought she'd wear them only for going down
to breakfast at the rooming house each morning, but she'd found that
for these interviews in a prison room that was hotter than bread out
of the oven, the short-sleeved shirtwaist was comfortable in a way her
suits never were, and she could forego the high heels, at least on the
weekends. George wasn't around to lecture her about the suitability of
her attire, no other reporters had managed to worm their way into the
fortress, and the matron couldn't have cared less. On trial days, she
could still wear her suits. Thank the good Lord for Saturdays, Sundays,
and slow juries. Whatever was taking them such a long time, though?

They had to reach a verdict, which seemed obvious, given the ineptitude of Susannah's lawyer. And with what she now knew, Nancy had to admit that *guilty* would be the right verdict. Then, if they found the defendant guilty, they had to make a recommendation for the sentencing. Again, pretty obvious. Life in prison. Maybe they were hung up over whether to allow parole after a certain number of years. Yes. That had to be it.

Nancy was tired of bread and cheese for lunch, but it was the easiest menu to pack in her handbag. She added two hard-boiled eggs and some salt twisted in a bit of paper. She was going to need to find a bigger purse. She thought idly about packing an axe and skewering the sullen guard if he pawed through her lunch. She could nail his head to the wall . . . *Stop it, Nancy! Get a hold of yourself.*

Cookies? She wrapped five sugar cookies for Matron in a double layer of paper. Then she packed six of those Toll House cookies with the luscious chocolate bits in four layers of paper. It wouldn't do to have melted chocolate coating the inside of her bag. The smell of them was enticing. She salivated a lot but restrained herself. She'd have plenty of them this afternoon.

Looking over the *Clarion's* front page, she sincerely hoped that people who knew her wouldn't use the *Clarion* as their source of news about this trial. George had leaned heavily on the word *lurid.*

"Yes, thank you, Matron. Coffee would be great. You do make a good pot of java."

"I'll have it here in a minute or two. It's still brewing."

"I brought you some dessert." Nancy reached in her bag and extracted the packet of cookies. Matron took it eagerly.

A few minutes later she stuck her head back in the room. "Here's your coffee. Say, those Toll House cookies are my favorites! How did you know?"

Nancy gritted her teeth before she turned around. "Just lucky, I guess."

Matron bustled into the room. "Look at what we have here. My mother gave me and my twin sister each a new model thermos for our birthday. I've had fun with it for a few days, and I decided to let you use it today. It's full of hot coffee, and it'll stay hot for hours."

"Thank you." Nancy took the cups and set them on the table. "That was very thoughtful of you."

Susannah narrowed her eyes and waited for the door to close and lock. "You gave her my Toll House cookies?"

"I must have mixed up the packages. I could have sworn I put the sugar cookies on top."

"Next time," Susannah took her coffee and nodded her thanks, "wrap mine in the front page and hers in the funny papers."

"I brought five sugar cookies. You can have three."

"Are you trying to bribe me or merely placate me?"

"Well," Nancy rubbed her forehead, "you did say that issues with Toll House cookies would be an executable offense."

"I said that?"

"Or words to that effect."

"You've been reading too many novels."

"Maybe the cookies are the only reason she brought us this thermos." The trouble was, Nancy felt so thoroughly comfortable with this woman who had, with no apparent reluctance whatsoever, killed— murdered—nine people, maybe even more. Unfortunately, Nancy saw the sense in Slip's arguments. Oh, sometimes the logic was a bit skewed, but Slip was fiercely loyal to her family. Nancy was just as glad she'd never met any of them. It probably would strengthen her story if she interviewed the whole lot, but she wasn't sure she could face them now that she knew about all these other murders. Then too, Slip had specifically asked her not to talk to anyone in Baynard's Mill.

Why hadn't any of Slip's sisters come to visit her? It wasn't that far from Baynard's Mill, and the roads weren't usually very bad this time of the year. Slip had done so much to protect her family, and they didn't appreciate her. Of course, it was true that they didn't *know* what she'd done for them. They probably thought she was just a cold-blooded woman who had killed two men.

Nancy glanced up at Slip, who was looking at her intently. She *was* a cold-blooded murderer. *Since that is so, why do I feel such a kinship with her?*

"What are you thinking, Nancy? Your face has been contorting, and your thoughts are obviously at war with each other, if I'm any judge at all."

Nancy ran her hands through her hair and gathered up handfuls of it. When she tightened her fists, the pressure on her scalp seemed almost to iron out her thoughts. She let go, relishing the tingly feeling. "I don't know if I can do justice to this story."

"Why do you say that?"

"I feel as if it's not complete. I should be interviewing Sheriff Fordyke—"

"Don't waste your time. He won't talk with you. Not while this trial is going on."

". . . and your family."

"I told you to leave my family out of this."

"But they're—"

"You leave them alone! I will not have them bothered any more than they already are."

"Don't you wonder why they haven't visited you here?"

"I know *exactly* why they haven't visited me, and that's their business, not yours."

"But don't you see that I can't tell the whole story if I don't know their side of it?"

"You don't need to. Believe me. Leave it alone. Promise me."

Nancy was painfully aware of the isolation of the room, and of the sound of Susannah's heavy breath. The last time she'd called Matron for a bathroom break, she'd had to wait almost a minute for the door to be unlocked. During those few seconds, Slip could have eased up behind her, wrapped her hands around Nancy's throat and—

"Nancy!" Slip spoke with quiet urgency. "I think you're getting upset, and I'm not sure why, but I'd like it better if you returned to your senses."

Nancy shook her head. "You're right. My imagination was running away with me there for a moment."

"While you were off in a dream, I ate four of the sugar cookies."

"I thought you didn't like sugar cookies."

"I prefer Toll House cookies, but since you gave mine away..." She drew her index finger across her throat, and laughed at Nancy's horrified expression.

"Now," Susannah said, relaxing against the back of the chair, "let me tell you about Sylvia. First, though, I want you to promise me something."

"What?"

"Promise me that you won't contact my family. I don't want them hurt any more than they already have been."

Nancy thought about her story. Could she justify telling only one side of it? This was pretty complete in and of itself. "I already did promise."

"I want to be sure."

"All right. I promise. Again."

Slip nodded. "That's good, then. And promise me you'll stay away from Baynard's Mill." She waited for Nancy's nod. "By the way, I like your dress. Now, it's funny that you got those cookies mixed up today, because there was a package mix-up where Sylvia was concerned too."

Nancy sat down, wondering when she had arisen. The last few minutes were a blur. "What kind of package?"

"There you go again, getting ahead of yourself."

"What was Sylvia's last name?

"Telling."

"Wasn't she the one with the demented aunt who yelled in church?"

"What are you talking about?"

Nancy couldn't recall where it had come into the earlier stories. She pointed at the notebooks. "You mentioned it somewhere in there. I think it was when you were talking about Minnie Colper."

"Well, yes. I'd forgotten that." Susannah stretched her arms up over her head and flexed her fingers. "Sylvia Telling was sister to Meribelle Smith, Holden Smith's widow. Sylvia married better than Meribelle did. Her husband was the town apothecary, and to tell the truth, we always thought that Sylvia made up most of his potions for him. She was half witch and half charlatan. She depended on a few easy-to-mix elixirs and lotions that anybody could have done up. But by that time—1915 it was—the people in Baynard's Mill were beginning to lose their do-it-yourself mentality. Instead of learning about plantain and comfrey and garlic, they'd rather pay Mr. and Mrs. Telling for a salve or a poultice every time any little thing went wrong. The Tellings took full advantage of that way of thinking. They made a point of letting everybody know how dangerous it was to fiddle around with weeds—that was the way they put it—because it was easy to mistake a bad plant for a good plant, and then where would you be?"

"I'd be up a creek without a paddle, I'm afraid. I know nothing about plants."

"Well, then, there you are. You're a child of this new generation, and you'd probably starve if you had to live on the land."

Nancy's grimace was only half-hearted. "You're probably right."

"At any rate, Ma and I had been making our own remedies for years. All it took was a careful knowledge of plants and strict attention to preparing the liniments and salves and tinctures, so we never paid either Sylvia or her husband any mind at all. But Joseph, my youngest brother, was a regular client of theirs. His five children were the light of his life, and he swore up and down that they were what kept him such a happy man. He and Sophie, his wife, were always doctoring those kids—they tended to be on the sickly side. Ma and I firmly believed it was because they lived in town and never got the fine air of the countryside except when they came to visit us. Nevertheless, Joseph was always willing to stop by Telling's Apothecary Shop to pick up the latest nostrum and talk about the war in Europe. The sinking of the Lusitania was big news, even in Baynard's Mill. Then Priscilla, his youngest—we all called her Prissy—caught the scarlet fever. There wasn't much that could be done short of isolating her and trying to keep the fever from burning her up.

"Sophie bathed Prissy in cool water, but that sandpapery red rash itched so much, Prissy fought her. Sophie tried to get her to eat soup, but it was hard for the poor child to swallow. Finally Joseph and Sophie were at their wits' end. Joseph called on the Tellings, and Sylvia mixed him up a salve to spread all over Prissy's little body. *You have to cover every inch of her*, she told them. They came home and coated that child with that sticky, messy concoction, and then waited through the night. Prissy had more and more trouble breathing, and every time she thrashed around and rubbed some of the paste off her, they slathered more on, thinking they were doing the right thing.

"Well, it's pretty obvious. That must have been what killed her. The child was dead by late the next day. Joseph turned to drink for a couple of years until he woke up to what he was doing to his other children, and he turned himself around right nicely. Sophie turned to religion. Said that God had wanted the child and that there was nothing else they could have done. Sophie never stopped being a royal pain, although I suppose it was the only way she could deal with losing her youngest child. Of course, Ma lost her youngest too, and she didn't turn into a preachy better-than-thou suffering martyr over it. Ma just tightened her apron strings and kept on going. That's what we all did."

"Wait a minute, Slip. You said your ma lost her youngest. That would have been Emmeline, wouldn't it?" Susannah nodded, and Nancy turned back a few pages. "There's nothing in here about Emmy dying."

"Well, that's because it hadn't happened yet when this was going on. I guess I'm mixing my stories up just a bit. Hold on to your britches. We'll get to that story later."

"Yes, ma'am." Nancy saluted her.

"You behave yourself." She chuckled and went on. "About that same time when Joseph lost Prissy, Mr. Stybard died. He'd been sickly for a long while, and to add to it, he suffered something awful from the piles. Mrs. Stybard gave us more information than we wanted about that part of his ailments, but she didn't mention any other specifics, of course, just said he had taken a horrible turn for the worse. While we were at their house for the laying out, just a day or two after we buried Prissy, I happened to go back into the bedroom. I was ferrying the women's wraps back there, you see. With war declared, most of the men had headed off to enlist, so the women flocked together for comfort, even the comfort of a funeral. It was cold as the dickens outside, but with all those women inside at once, the parlor was quite warm. Too warm, if you ask me, to keep a dead body lying there waiting two days for the burial.

"While I was in the bedroom, I happened to see a good sized jar of salve. It had a Telling's Apothecary label pasted on it, signed by Sylvia. They always signed their prescriptions; it was one of their trademarks. But part of the label on this one had started to peel off. Out of curiosity, I pulled it back a ways. Underneath, there was another label that read *to alleviate the heat and itching of scarlet fever*. The next time I visited Joseph and Sophie, I asked them what it was they had used to treat little Prissy for her scarlet fever. Sophie still had the almost-empty container. I slipped it in my pocket and examined it later. *Guaranteed to shrink hemorrhoids! Relief from that painful itching!* That's what it said under the Tellings label.

"So then I knew what had killed both of them, a little girl and an old man. Neither one of them should have died like that." Susannah put her elbows on the table and leaned forward until her head rested on her clasped hands. She sat that way for a moment and then looked up at Nancy. "She had to die."

Nancy waited, but Susannah sat quietly, seeming to be lost in thought. Nancy picked up a pencil and sketched her face, the deep-set eyes, the wispy brows, the hair pulled severely into a bun, but with that one wayward curl that would insist on escaping. *I wish I'd drawn her every day, in every mood.* The visage grew beneath her fingers. She added the frown-line between her eyebrows and smudged a bit at the shadows beneath the nondescript cheekbone. Slip *was* someone who could easily disappear in a crowd.

"What are you writing?"

"Oh, nothing." Nancy grimaced as the pencil slipped and the left side of the drawing's neck bent at an awkward and thoroughly un-lifelike angle. "I'm just doodling a bit. I like to draw."

"May I see it?"

Nancy held up the pad, making sure her hand covered the neck that looked broken. There was no need to show that to Slip. She'd erase it or scribble it out later. Susannah studied her likeness in silence. "Hmm," she said. "No wonder nobody ever sees me. Am I really that ordinary?"

Nancy turned the pad back around and studied her sketch. "No. I think you're an extraordinary woman."

Susannah smiled. "In that case, you're crazy."

Nancy turned to the next page. "So, how did you kill Sylvia?"

"I drowned her in the town fountain."

Nancy checked her memory. "The Holden Smith Memorial Fountain?"

"That's right. She used to walk her dog late every night. A useless little poodle or some such, all pompoms, with a pointy nose and beady eyes."

Nancy bit her lip to keep her mouth shut. She liked poodles. Her sister had one, and if Nancy's life had been more settled, without all the traveling, she would have a poodle too. She'd name it Toodle and keep a soft pink bow on its sweet little head.

". . . and her schedule was so regular I didn't have to think too hard about how to do it."

Nancy scrambled to catch up.

"The only good thing about that poodle of hers was that it couldn't bark. It was born with some sort of disorder that left it hoarse all the time. Sounded like the blacksmith's bellows, all wheezy and whispery. As long as I could catch her walking alone, I knew I'd succeed. It took me twelve nights of watching before she showed up alone and with nobody around to see me. The park had these high wax myrtle hedges around it, with the pavilion and the fountain near the center. Usually there were people strolling late into the night. But this time it was a real cold spell. Not cold enough to freeze the fountain, but cold enough to discourage casual walkers."

"Sounds like you were lucky."

"I was always lucky, Nancy. That's how I knew that what I was doing was right."

Nancy let that one ride. "What happened to the poodle?"

"While I was drowning Sylvia . . . That was difficult, I must say. I hadn't hit her very hard, you see, because I wanted it to look like an accident. Then that dratted little beast bit me in the leg, just above my boot. I couldn't let go of Sylvia, and I didn't have a way to kick off the dog. I needed both feet under me so I wouldn't fall in the fountain myself. You see, Sylvia had seen me when I walked up to her, so I couldn't change my mind about killing her right then. That stupid poodle. It took weeks for that bite to heal, and I couldn't tell Ma or Lucy or Mary Louise about it, so I had to act like nothing was wrong and treat it myself. Dogs have something in their saliva that makes a dog bite hurt like everything. Have you ever been bitten?"

"No." *But then I've never drowned a poodle's mommy in a fountain either.* "Wasn't it pretty obvious that she'd been murdered?"

"Not really. There were sheets of ice all around the fountain, and I threw her handbag in there so it would look like she'd dropped it and tried to retrieve it. Then the poor dear just fell in head and hit her head on the bottom."

"How did you get rid of the dog?"

"Once Sylvia was dead, I just shooed it away and it ran off. Then I limped home. Luckily I still had the bedroom on the ground floor. That window saw a lot of traffic with me coming and going various nights. Ma had offered me the bigger bedroom upstairs, but I told her the smaller room fit me just fine, so Emmy moved up there. Mary Louise was gone by that time, of course, being married to the sheriff."

"You must have been awfully wet on the walk home."

"Heavens yes. I just about froze that night. I shiver even thinking about it. I had to stay back from the road in case anyone came along, so it took me longer than usual to walk the two and a half miles. Mr. Telling went out looking for his wife when the dog showed up without her. Serves him right. If I could have gotten rid of him too, I would have."

"Did you save something for your treasure box?"

"Why are you always so all-fired concerned about that treasure box?"

"It's interesting." *It's morbid.* "It will add some spice to my story." *Spice, according to George, sells newspapers.* Good heavens. Nancy hoped she wasn't beginning to think like her boss. "The treasures you kept are a part of what happened." *And I like to report the facts.*

"I kept Mr. Stybard's jar lid. The two glass jars of salve—Prissy's and Mr. Stybard's—were identical. That may have been why she mixed them up. I washed it out and put the button from Holden Smith in it. That seemed like a nice touch, seeing as how the two of them were in-laws."

Nancy had to wonder what had really killed Mr. Stybard. She thought about keeping her mouth shut. After all, this was Susannah's story, not her own, but a built-in sense of justice, the fact that she was her father's daughter, made her object. "Isn't there a chance that Mr. Stybard might have been going to die anyway? And scarlet fever is often fatal in the young; maybe little Prissy was on her way out regardless of the mix-up in the potions."

Susannah lifted her chin. "You're a fine one to question me. You're not even dry behind the ears yet, and you think you know the answers to everything. Well, let me tell you, missy, that Sylvia Telling was incompetent from the git-go. She killed Prissy, and she killed Mr. Stybard too. Those potions were wrong, I tell you, wrong!"

"I understand that you feel very strongly about this, but isn't there the possibility that—"

"No! You think I'd kill someone who was innocent? How dare you, you little snip. I've never been so insulted in my whole life. How can you sit there and accuse me?"

"I—"

"You don't know what it's like to grow up in a farming community, where people have to be able to depend on each other."

"Maybe not, but I—"

"You have no right to criticize me, just because you—"

Keys jangled in the lock and the matron stuck her head in. "I'm just checking to be sure everything's alright in here."

Susannah straightened her back. "Of course it is. You needn't check on us."

The matron looked at Nancy. "Yes. Yes, thank you. We're fine, but I'll be leaving soon."

"Just knock on the door when you're ready."

"Nonsense," Slip said. "We still have plenty of time left."

Her tone was so reasonable, Nancy felt she'd just awakened from a nightmare.

Chapter 11 - Take the Sting Out of It

Mrs. Maybell Harris Thomas, Petitioner, brings her petition for alimony against Plennie G. Thomas, Defendant, on 26 October 1937. . . . Defendant ran Petitioner from their home without any cause. . . .

--from the 1937 archives of the
Gwinnett County Superior Court

Nancy looked at her watch. Yes, there was still time for another story before lunch, but she wasn't sure whether she should stay or beat a fast retreat.

"That's a right nice wristwatch you have there," Slip said. "I don't think I've seen one on a lady before."

This was crazy. One minute the woman was raving; the next minute she sounded like somebody's next door neighbor saying hello over the backyard fence.

"How long have you had it?"

"I felt pretty modern buying it last month. The big lapel watch I inherited when my mama died was too heavy, and this seemed like it would be simpler for me in my job. I have to be on time to my appointments." *Unless I get lost.*

"Do you enjoy what you do? The reporting, I mean." She still sounded neighborly.

"For the most part, yes. Naturally I like the big stories, like a tornado I covered once." *We'll forget that I was there only because I had no idea where I was.*

"A disaster story, then. Is that your idea of reporting?"

"No. There's a lot of value to the smaller stories as well. The ways people make do with the shortages, for instance. The businesses that go under and the ones that don't. The movie houses that are full even though the grocery store shelves are almost empty."

"You were too young to report on the flu epidemic in 1918."

"Maybe so, but I remember it. I was born in aught-two, so I was sixteen. That's when I got my old watch. I lost one of my brothers and my mama to the flu."

"Well, then, you'll maybe understand how I felt when I found out that Kennon Bluett killed some of my family. Ma never saw it that way, but she was the one who got me thinking about it. We were talking one day . . ."

Nancy opened a new steno pad and wrote *Kennon Bloot*. She would worry about the spelling later. She hoped Slip would stay reasonable. Susannah took a deep breath and began.

It was a Monday, the year after we lost Emmy and the boys to the flu. They were buried on our land, not even in the churchyard, because we couldn't risk going out among other people that year, not even to bury our dead. Yes, I found out on a Monday. Wash day. Good heavens, the washing never stopped. Ma and I had just finished hanging up the last load, and we sat down for a cup of coffee before we started getting the evening meal ready. "I miss Emmy," Ma said, much to my surprise.

"You almost never talk about her, Ma." I sat there and sipped my coffee because I felt like Ma had something to say, but Ma always did have to warm up a bit before she'd talk much.

"I blame myself for not keeping her safe," Ma said. "I thought the flu would stay away from Baynard's Mill. I guess a lot of us thought that way, but we were wrong. If I'd kept my door shut that morning, maybe Emmeline would be alive today."

"What do you mean, kept the door shut?"

"That's how the flu got to us. You know that. People spread it from one to another. Lucy was here for some reason. I can't recall now why she stopped by that morning."

"You're not saying that Lucy brought the flu that killed Emmy?"

"Oh, heavens, no. She came down with it the same time Emmy and I did, so we must all have caught it the same day, probably right here in this house."

"Why do you say that, Ma? You can't blame yourself."

"And Joseph's boys too. They wouldn't be dead if they hadn't been here. Joseph brought his children to me to keep them safe, and I'm the one who infected them. If I'd been smarter . . ." Her voice petered out and she just sat there, turning her coffee cup around and around.

I didn't know what to say to that. She was probably right, but I'd never seen her like this, all defeated-looking. "Ma, they would have gotten sick wherever they were. So many people were sick, and some of them were strong enough to fight through it, and some, like Emmy and the boys, just weren't. You mustn't blame yourself."

"Kennon Bloot came by to warn us. He said he'd heard it on the radio. They were telling people to stay home. We were lucky, I figured, because we had plenty of food set aside. We always were pretty much self-sufficient here. You and Emmy were such a help to me all those years, and of course your sisters were too, before they went off and got married."

"Kennon was here that day? Kennon Bloot?"

Ma stood up and pulled the cast iron skillet from the back of the wood stove to the front. "Yes, dear, Kennon dropped by. You must have been off somewhere on your own. Probably down in the barn. You know, sometimes I wish you'd married and had your own children to raise; but very selfishly I'm glad you didn't. It's been a real comfort having you here, Slip. Especially after we lost Emmy. You're so level-headed and such a hard worker."

"Kennon Bloot came here that morning?"

"Yes, dear. I already told you that, twice. Aren't you listening? He came to warn us. What a terrible thing . . ."

I didn't say anything. I'd never much wondered how Emmy caught the flu. It just seemed like practically everybody came down with it. Almost every family in Baynard's Mill lost one, two, or even more of their folk. Two families were wiped out completely—everybody in the house, with all of them too sick to care for each other. Of course, we didn't know all that until we started venturing out once the danger was over. But if what Ma said was true, then Kennon was the one who'd killed Emmy and, by extension, had killed Joseph's boys. If he hadn't stopped by, Emmy would still be well, and Joseph would still have his two sons.

Susannah rolled her shoulders back and rocked her neck from side to side. "This remembering is thirsty business. Any more of that coffee left?"

Nancy pushed the thermos closer to Slip. "What did your mother say about that?"

"About what? Oh, you mean about Kennon causing the deaths?" Susannah poured herself another cup. "Well, if truth be told, I didn't want to bring it up to her. It sounded like she already felt bad enough about Emmy dying without my getting really specific about Kennon's role in it. I thought she must have suspected, though, to have made the comments she did. So I just let it ride until I could do something about it. Then, once he was dead, I decided not to say anything. I didn't want anyone to think I had a motive for wanting him gone."

"So, how did you kill him?" Nancy reached for the thermos and screwed on the cap. It wouldn't do to let the coffee get cold.

"You ask that question a lot."

"That's because it's an important part of the story."

"Hm. Yes. It didn't take too long for me to find out that Kennon was allergic to bee stings. This was one of the . . ." She waved her hand in one of those all-encompassing gestures. "It was one that didn't happen in the winter. I had to wait for the bees to come out, you see. I've never had any problem with bees myself. In fact, I don't think I was ever stung. Jethro told me once that different people had different smells. Bees were attracted to some and not to others. I guess I was in that *other* category."

"Me too. Bees never bother me."

"Well, then, you can see how I could gather some bees in the middle of summer. I lured them into a small box and went to visit Kennon's place in the middle of the night. Everybody knew everybody else's house around Baynard's Mill, and it was easy to creep up outside his bedroom window. It was open, you see, because of the heat of the summer. I tipped the bees out into the room and eased the window closed."

"How could you be sure they wouldn't just fly off somewhere else in the house?"

"Oh, I wasn't sure at all. I had plans to visit his house as many nights as it took with as many bees as it took. His wife said the next day that he'd gotten up in the middle of the night to open the window—it had slid shut somehow, she said—and he must have brushed against a bee. His throat swelled up and he died before she could get help. Not that there was much anybody could have done for him."

"What did you put in your treasure box? A dead bee?"

"Oh, no, nothing as obvious as that. I didn't want anything that would tie me directly to his death. I made some honey candy drops later that season, with honey from our hives, and I wrapped one in oiled paper," she pointed to their own lunch sitting at the end of the table, "like that. It hardened over the years. I doubt it's any good to eat at this point." She patted the gloves. "Bees die when they sting, you know. I always appreciated the sacrifice that little fella made. It's too bad it was . . ." She stopped talking.

"Was what?"

"Oh, nothing. You'll learn about that later, when we talk about Button."

Chapter 12 - In the Altogether

Mrs. Maybell Harris Thomas, Petitioner, brings her petition for alimony against Plennie G. Thomas, Defendant, on 26 October 1937. . . . Defendant would constantly run after other women, he manufactured and drank liquor, he could not hold his job when given one, he would depend upon Petitioner to keep him up, and Petitioner was forced to go to work a short time after her baby was born . . .

--from the 1937 archives of the
Gwinnett County Superior Court

Nancy made a note to herself: *connection between Kennon & Button. SLP said she'd tell me. Make sure she does.* She drew a big star next to the note. "I'm not quite hungry enough for lunch yet. Are you willing to wait, or do you need to eat now?"

Susannah shook her head. "With all this sitting around and waiting, I don't seem to need as much fuel. Plus, it's almost too hot to eat. Isn't it funny how people can drink hot coffee on a hot day and not mind it?"

Nancy nodded.

"You write down Tosser Jones. Last night before I went to sleep I remembered that I'd forgotten to tell you about him. He happened the year after Maude fell in the privy."

With a little help from a rock to the head and a lift to the ankles. "Tosser. What kind of name is that?"

"T-A-W-S-E-R." Susannah laughed. "His parents couldn't decide which relative to name him after. They were connected to half the people in the county, it seemed. So they named him Thomas Arthur William Samuel Edward Robert and called him by all the initials. They thought that order would be better than Robert Arthur William Samuel Edward Thomas, which would have been spelled R-A-W-S-E-T. I suppose they could have named him Samuel William Edward Arthur Thomas Robert, but S-W-E-A-T-R would need another E to be correct—maybe Edwin? And SWEATER's not a name for a boy anyway."

Nancy played with SWEATR a bit. "It's a good thing Robert wasn't York; then he would have been . . ." She let it dangle.

Susannah thought about it for a few seconds. "What on earth are you talking about?"

"If . . ." Nancy hated having to explain jokes. "If you took SWEATR and replaced the R for Robert with Y for York, you'd get SWEATY."

Susannah stared at her. "No wonder you're only a writer."

"What do you mean, *only* a writer?"

"You have to admit, what you do has absolutely no value. My family raised food. You wouldn't know how to do that if your life depended on it. You probably come from a family that gets by feeding off the hard work of people like me."

Has it occurred to you that I'm the one feeding you here? She kept that thought to herself, but said in her family's defense, "My father owns a hardware store, the kind of store where your father probably had to buy most of his farming implements."

Susannah stared at Nancy in silence for a long moment. "Now, about Tawser," she said in a reasonable voice, as if nothing had happened, "why don't I start the story and if we need to, we'll take a break in the middle of it to eat."

"Fine with me." *You old witch.*

"Tawser was another one of those home-town boys. He was a few years older than I was. Other than my little brothers, he was the first boy I ever saw with no clothes on."

Nancy stopped writing.

"It's not what you think. It was one of those sultry summer days, and Mary Louise and I were walking home from doing some errand or other; I don't even recall now what it was. We took a shortcut through the woods. We were going to follow the creek down to Possum Hollow . . ."

Nancy smiled at the quaint pronunciation of *holler*.

Susannah chewed on her lower lip. "We had our baskets with us. We never went anywhere without our baskets because we never knew what we might find. In the summer it might be berries, nuts in the fall if we could beat the squirrels to them. It's hard to outguess squirrels. Almost always there were herbs to gather, things like plantain and comfrey. Once we found a nest of quail's eggs." She settled back in her chair. "Where was I headed with this story?"

"No clothes?"

"Oh, yes. There was a beaver pond in a meadow about halfway down the hollow."

"The meadow with the fallen hickory tree?"

"You mean the one where that man had the run-in with that bear?"

The knife, then the bear. "Yes. Was that the one?"

"No. The beaver pond meadow was closer to our farmhouse. The creek cut right across the meadow and fed the pond. All sorts of berries grew in thickets around the edge of the meadow. As we got closer to it, we could hear boys shouting at the old swimming hole. We didn't mean to sneak up on them, not really. We just slowed down and stopped talking as we got near the edge of the woods. Mary Louise led the way along the creek bank, her being a year older, and I was trying to creep along in back of her. All of a sudden, she ducked behind a tree to her right, leaving me standing there next to the creek in full view of Tawser Jones. He must have heard her when she dove for cover, because he looked up right then before I could react. He was wearing his work shoes, and not one other blessed stitch of clothing."

"What was he doing that close to the woods?"

"Tawser was always hungry. He'd left the other boys—I could see them off by the pond—to gather handfuls of blackberries. When I saw him, he was stuffing his face. He mashed those berries into his mouth and grabbed to cover his privates. There was dark juice running off his hands and arms. I always did wonder how long the stain lasted. Of course, I didn't stick around to find out. I lit off running up the creek and made it almost back to the road before I noticed that Mary Louise wasn't with me."

"Where was she?"

"She stayed hidden behind that tree until the boys gave up their swimming and went home. I would have had a hard time explaining to Ma why I came home without her, but when I reached the house Ma was in a tizzy over Joseph's broken arm. That boy broke more bones than you could believe. This time he fell out of the mulberry tree. Last time it was off the shed roof. Needless to say, Ma didn't notice Mary Louise's absence. Naturally, the boys at the swimming hole got hungry well before dark, so Mary Louise wasn't too late. She did have the forethought to fill her basket with blackberries before she cut through the meadow."

"What happened the next time you saw Tawser?"

"He turned red as a prairie sunset, but neither one of us ever said a word about it. It was a couple of years after that that he shot up in that way boys have of doing. He turned broad and tall and powerfully strong."

She fell silent. Nancy set down her pen and inched her fingers over to her pencil. Those shadows around Slip's jaw were just too delicious to ignore—they said something of Slip's ability to disappear—and Nancy often found herself drawing the shadows instead of the substance.

A minute or two later Susannah seemed to recollect herself. She looked at the fountain pen lying on the table. "Drawing again?"

"Yes. I like the way the shadows fall on your face. Do you mind?"

"I suppose not. Use these drawings to illustrate your book, will you?"

"My book?"

"Don't pretend you haven't considered it."

"I thought my editor might agree to serialize the story in the paper."

"I'd rather have a book; I want to read it as I sit on my cot in my cell." She smiled as if at an inward joke. "Yes. It will be great to read about all my exploits."

Exploits? "Are you ready to tell me why you killed Tawser, and how?"

"Why?" She sighed. "Why, why, why, why. I'm not sure you'd understand this one."

"Try me."

"You know that my brother Silas came six years after me."

Nancy nodded.

"The only reason I'm willing to tell you this now is that Silas died last year."

"I'm sorry."

"Yes. Well, Silas wanted so much to be a grown-up man. It would have been about 1893, I think. Our older brother was married and gone by then, which meant that Silas was the oldest boy left at home. He took on responsibilities early and was real dependable, except when he used to run with Johnnie Reynolds, Maude's brother."

"The cowbane and the poisoned knife?"

"Exactly, although that wasn't Silas's fault. I think Silas really missed his big brother, and he transferred his loyalty to Tawser. But Tawser wasn't worth it. He misused my little brother something terrible. Took advantage of him." She stopped speaking and appeared to be waiting for a question.

"How did he take advantage of Silas?"

"Since you asked me, I'll tell you, although I've never told this to another soul. One day I snuck away from the house after the evening dishes were cleaned up. It was the middle of the summer, and the sun stayed late in the sky. I had a little room carved out of the hay in the loft, and I was curled up reading when I heard the barn door close. I stayed quiet, thinking it was Pa come to check on the cow, but it wasn't Pa. It was Silas. Naturally I'd recognize my own brother's voice, even though I couldn't hear much of what he said, just a word here and there. He was talking with Tawser."

"How did you know it was Tawser?"

"His voice had started to change later than most of his friends, and he had that funny squeak that boys get around that age. It sounded silly. He already had a beard, but his voice was still so little-boy."

"Did you ever hear what they were saying?"

"Not exactly. . . . I tried to creep closer to the edge of the loft, but I must have made a noise because Tawser looked up at me when I peeked over the edge. There he was again, in the altogether. Well, that's not quite true. He wasn't *completely* naked, but his britches were down around his knees. He whipped those up so fast and scooted up the ladder quicker than I would have thought possible. I had no way to get away from him, nowhere to go. He grabbed me and twisted my arm behind my back. 'If you ever say a word about this, Slip Packard, I will hurt your little brother so bad he'll never walk again, and it'll be your fault.' That's what he threatened, and I believed him. He made me vow that I'd never speak a word of what I'd seen.

"Silas must have heard us, but he didn't say anything. When Tawser went back down the ladder, I heard him tell Silas, "I saw a rat up there, Silas, but I took care of it. You run back to the house now and remember—this is our secret. If your Ma knew what you were doing, she'd turn you out of the house and never let you come back home again." Susannah took a big breath, but before she could finish her story, Matron opened the door and ushered Susannah's lawyer into the room.

"Yes, well, that is to say, we need to go to the courthouse. The jury has, yes, they've indicated that they have reached, yes, they have reached their verdict."

Susannah let out her breath slowly, which made Nancy aware that she'd been holding her own breath ever since the door opened. Nancy looked down at her notes. "How much time do we have?" she asked the lawyer.

"None. We . . . uh . . . we have to leave now. There are guards outside, that is to say, they're in the corridor." He mopped his forehead. "It won't do to keep the judge waiting. No, it won't do at all."

Susannah swept her gloves from the table and put them on, slowly and with great deliberation. Nancy watched her and felt prickles of fear inching up her spine. "I need to go back to my cell," Susannah said, "to get my hat." She looked and sounded calm, but Nancy saw her hands tremble before she clasped them together.

"Ladies and gentlemen of the jury, have you reached a verdict?"

The bald foreman stood, somewhat reluctantly, Nancy thought. "Yes, we have, Your Honor." He began to unfold a piece of paper, but the judge held up his hand and motioned to the bailiff, who had already stepped forward. He raised his hands, palms upward, as if he were conducting a choir to increase their volume. Both attorneys and the defendant rose. Stevens braced his fingertips against the prosecution's table. Pinkney adjusted his bow tie. Susannah simply stood. The bailiff stepped to one side.

Judge McElroy waited for everyone to settle into place. "Please read to us the verdict you have reached."

The man seemed to be studiously avoiding looking at the defendant. In fact, Nancy noticed, all of the jurors seemed intent on watching the judge. The foreman unfolded the paper once, twice, three times. Each time it doubled in size. By the time he reached the fifth unfolding, Nancy was on the edge of her seat. He must have been nervous indeed to have mangled the verdict in such a way.

"We . . ." He cleared his throat and started over. "We find the defendant guilty."

The court clerk wrote briefly. So did the judge. "And did you reach a recommendation for sentencing?"

"Yes, Your Honor."

"Please read it to the court."

"We recommend the . . ." he glanced to his left at the juror seated beside him. That man nodded. "We recommend the death penalty."

Susannah grabbed the edge of the table. Pinkney reached to steady her, but she shook his hand away.

The judge polled the jury, asking each member if the verdict was reached without duress. The twelfth *yes* sank into a silence that was immediately broken by excited conversation from the audience.

Judge McElroy steepled his hands for a moment and cleared his throat. The bailiff stepped forward. "Quiet in the courtroom!"

"Miss Susannah Packard, you have been found by a jury of your peers to be guilty of the crime of murder with malice aforethought. You have heard their recommendation for sentencing. Therefore I sentence you to be taken out and hanged by the neck until dead. And may God have mercy on your soul."

Reporters scrambled to get out of the courtroom, but Nancy sat still. She knew that Slip hadn't expected to be found innocent, but Slip had said something, jokingly almost, about how, with two consecutive life sentences, she'd be in prison until she was one hundred and thirty. Two life sentences. That was what she had expected.

While the judge thanked the jury, Nancy watched Slip sink slowly into her chair. Pinkney remained standing, and he frantically motioned to Slip to stand as well, but to no avail. Slip had developed a tremor. It started with her head, moved down her neck and to her shoulders, and proceeded down her back. In the heat of the courtroom, Susannah Packard looked like she was freezing.

The verdict hadn't been a surprise, of course, but the death penalty? Nancy felt some of that same chill inch its way into her joints. She wanted to run screaming from the room. She wanted to sit unmoving until this was all over. Both at the same time. Then she thought about Old Ned and almost applauded the jury.

As the bailiff walked stiffly forward to remove his prisoner from the courtroom, Susannah looked up at Nancy and shook her head in disbelief. Nancy mouthed, "I'll see you in a few minutes," and gestured in the general direction of the exit.

Susannah nodded, shook off the bailiff's hand, and turned to leave.

They must have taken Susannah out through a back entrance. Nancy waited with the other reporters for a long time, but Susannah and her guards never came out. The boutonniere was long gone, probably phoning his story in to the *Midwest Times* while Nancy stood there unmoving. She watched the woman with the green scarf leaning on the arm of the woman with all that red hair. They looked resigned somehow.

Finally, Nancy shrugged and trudged toward her car. "At least I can take her some lunch," she muttered to her steering wheel.

Something had conspired to cloak the roadsides in glory that day. Nancy couldn't remember ever having noticed so many wildflowers. A profusion of butterflies wafted over the blossoms. It wasn't far to the prison—it stood just outside the city—and Nancy drove as slowly as she could, stopping at the rooming house on the way to phone George with her story. He'd heard it, naturally. The news was everywhere, and he already had ideas for a special edition, something the *Clarion* rarely put out.

The young fresh-faced guard at the outer fence asked her to identify herself, as if he hadn't gotten the same information just a few hours before. A few hours that felt like a lifetime.

The gravel parking area hosted a convention of small birds, fluttering around the puddles left by the rain. They scattered before

Nancy's car, up into the lone tree, leaving a few feathers drifting down in the wind of their passing. It made Nancy think about Emmeline's bird friends. She just didn't see how anyone could hurt a song bird.

She turned off the ignition and sat for a few moments, not quite brave enough to face Susannah. She couldn't abandon her like this, though. She had to go in. She wiped her eyes, blew her nose, and wondered why she had so many stiff, laced-edged hankies.

The stairs seemed longer and dirtier than they had just that morning. The entryway felt drearier. Officer Jolly looked even less like his name than usual, hard as that was to believe. "I'm sorry, miss. I can't let you in this afternoon."

"You're joking, right?"

"Afraid not, miss. The rules are pretty strict. From now on, the only people she can see on the weekends are her immediate family, her lawyer, and her minister."

"I can't come back tomorrow?"

"Not on Sunday, miss."

Matron stuck her head around the corner. She held out the package of cookies. It looked smaller than it had earlier in the day. "I didn't eat all of these. There are still three left. Do you want them back?"

Nancy recoiled at the thought of Toll House cookies without Slip. "Give them to Miss Packard," she said. "She'll appreciate them."

Matron nodded. "I guess you two were close?"

Nancy thought she detected a tone of pity, but she couldn't be sure and didn't want to ask the reason. "We still are." She turned to go, but then thought she'd give it one more try. "She hasn't had any lunch, and neither have I. It's still here in my bag. Can't I just go in and eat with her?"

Matron looked at the guard, who shook his head. "I'm sorry," Matron said. She really *did* look sorry, Nancy thought. "The rules, you know. Only immediate family—the rules define that as parents, brothers and sisters, and the spouse, so you don't qualify."

Well, of course I don't qualify, and I know what immediate family means. "Miss Packard's parents are dead, and she doesn't have a husband."

"I'm truly sorry. You can come back to visit your . . . to visit Miss Packard on Monday, and on Wednesdays and Fridays too, but only in the afternoon."

Nancy set her handbag on the desk. "I told her I'd be here this afternoon."

Matron shook her head. Officer Stick-to-the-Rules mirrored her action.

"Will you at least tell her what happened, that I tried to bring her lunch?" Nancy felt an unaccustomed tightness in her throat. "I don't want her to think I lied to her."

Nancy pulled out the packet of food, unwrapped the bread, and broke it into little pieces. She scattered them in the gravel at the edge of the parking area. Sparrows, wrens, finches, and one fat pigeon fluttered down from the tree and gathered around the crumbs in feathered disarray, twittering and cooing, but Nancy couldn't smile. Susannah was a murderer. Susannah deserved to die. But they'd eaten lunches together. Even if Slip had been testy at times, and to be perfectly truthful, she'd been downright obnoxious at other times, still, she was a woman facing death for trying to protect her family from harm.

STATESVILLE COUNTY CLARION

YOUR MORNING SOURCE FOR ALL THE NEWS WORTH READING
Saturday, July 23, 1932

EXTRA! EXTRA! SPECIAL EDITION!

GUILTY!

Chapter 13 - Regrets

Mrs. Maybell Harris Thomas, Petitioner, brings her petition for alimony against Plennie G. Thomas, Defendant, on 26 October 1937. . . . Defendant expected to keep his brother living with them at the expense of your Petitioner, all of which caused Petitioner mental pain and anguish, and resulted in their separation. . . .

--from the 1937 archives of the
Gwinnett County Superior Court

Nancy didn't want to crawl out of bed that Monday morning. Sunday had crept by, more slowly than one of those three-toed sloths she'd seen in *National Geographic*. Yet here it was, already Monday; one less day to the final countdown.

What could she possibly say to Slip? She knew pity would be unacceptable, but what about compassion? Maybe there was somebody Nancy could contact for Slip. Funny that in all this time she hadn't asked where Slip's family was now. All she knew about them was what she'd gathered from the stories. Why was she lying in bed when she could get up and write out a list of questions? With every moment counting now, it wouldn't do to forget to ask her for even a single vital piece of information.

Why do you always wear blue?
How do you feel about the sentence?
Do you want me to contact anyone for you?
What are your fears?

What happened to Tawser Jones?

What do you want people to remember about you?

How did Jethro get that scar?

Are you going to appeal the sentence?

How did Silas die?

Did you choose not to marry, or did things just work out that way?

Have you written a will?

Nancy worked on the list until she had two pages filled with questions. She prioritized them all, rewrote the list in order of importance, and went downstairs to eat breakfast.

Mrs. Cappell glanced up from where she was rearranging food dishes on the sideboard. "How about some nice bacon with a soft-boiled egg? I'm afraid I overcooked the bacon. It's awfully crisp. I apologize for that."

"I like it crispy."

"Well, then, you'll enjoy this." She filled a plate and set it in front of Nancy. "It's too bad you never met those two sisters. They packed up yesterday afternoon and went home."

I couldn't be less interested. "Yes, I'm sorry too, but I was just too busy."

"I know, dear. You're so good at what you do. George is very pleased with your work. Have a seat, and I'll bring you some coffee."

After breakfast, Nancy loaded her handbag with cookies.

Officer Grumpystiltskins smoothed back his sparse hair as Nancy walked in. "Leave your umbrella over there in the corner." He pointed and Nancy did as he instructed. "I have to check your handbag." *You thought I'd forgotten how we do it here?* He must have seen her eyes flash, and he had the good sense to look a bit sheepish, but Nancy still resented being talked down to.

"It's mostly cookies in there. That and my note pads."

"I never knew any woman to come in here without her lipstick and powder."

Make one more condescending comment like that and I'll run you through with a pirate's cutlass. "I don't use a lot of that stuff, so I never carry it with me."

His mouth closed in a grim line as he poked the cookies around.

Nancy could practically hear them crumbling. *Where did I put that darn sword? Maybe I could just use the umbrella. It has a nasty-looking point on it.* "Is Matron ready for me?"

He felt underneath the note pads and nodded. "Right through there," as if she hadn't already done this a dozen times.

Matron must have been feeling the strain. She didn't even hint about cookies. Still, Nancy felt obliged to offer her a few. "Thank you. We don't see many treats around here unless we bring them in ourselves, and I've been working a double shift three times a week. We're short-handed, you see." She unlocked the interrogation room. "I'll bring in some coffee, shall I?" Nancy nodded. "Your . . . I mean, Miss Packard will be right along. I sent one of the guards for her when I saw you walk in. I knew you'd want as much time with her as possible."

In some ways, it wasn't as awkward as Nancy had thought it would be. In other ways it was hell in a bucket. After Nancy stuttered and stammered a bit, Susannah held up her hand. "Let's just get on with it, shall we?"

"All right. I have some questions I put together . . ."

"Want to get them all in before the end, eh?"

"I wouldn't have put it that way."

"Oh, don't go all stuffy on me. I know what's coming." Her left hand crept up to her neck like a spider scaling the side of a building. "But I'm hoping the appeal for clemency will come through."

Nancy crossed the second question off her list. "Then, can I ask these?" She held up the note pad. When Susannah nodded, she asked, "What happened to Tawser?"

"He died when he fell into the hay baler. . ."

"A hay baler?"

"One of those big machines that packs hay into square bales. It has a big metal plate that rams against the hay and mashes it none too gently into a chute. Once there's enough hay in there, the bale is tied with heavy twine. Then the end of the chute opens and the bale is pushed out. People fork the hay in through an opening in the side, but they'd better be quick about pulling their pitchfork out. I know somebody who lost an arm once."

Nancy turned away from the gleam in Slip's eyes. This was just a bit too graphic for her. She had a feeling she knew what was coming.

"It was too hard tricking him into letting me get close to him. He never did trust me. But I'd been practicing for quite some time with a slingshot. Sort of a David and Goliath story it turned out to be. I hid in the shadows of the barn and hit him with a good-sized stone in the back of the head just as he was leaning forward to pitch a forkful of hay into the baler. He fell in head first, pretty as you please." She giggled, like a child, and Nancy was startled by the inappropriate sound. "I had wanted to wait until Christmas time, but I couldn't decide how to kill him, and the hay baler was just too good a chance to pass up. The men working with him never saw me."

"Where did you get the slingshot?"

Susannah blushed, much to Nancy's surprise. "I'm ashamed of this, but I suppose you've got a right to know." She rubbed her throat. "I stole it. I know I've said I'm not a thief, and I'm *not*; but I did steal this one thing. I stole it from Johnny Reynolds."

"How did you do that? I thought boys were cemented to their slingshots."

"He left it lying on our porch one day when he came to see Silas. I picked it up and slipped it in my pocket." She nodded, as if to herself. "I'm not proud of that, as I already said, but it's the only time I ever really stole anything. The only time."

"What happened to it?"

"After Tawser was dead, I threw it away in the outhouse." She smiled. "Privies were a wonderful invention."

Nancy waited, but Slip had apparently finished. "What do you want people to remember about you?"

Susannah pursed her lips. "I guess if they'll just remember me, period, that will be enough. This is not a happy way to get recognition, but at least my name will be known. I won't be invisible—for a while at least. Your book will help a lot." She smiled. "Be sure you get it printed right away. I want the first copy."

Nancy shook her head. "I'm a newspaper reporter."

Susannah's face hardened. "I told you I want my story in a book. I don't want it strung out in a series of newspaper articles. If you won't agree to that, you can leave right now, and I won't let you print any of what I've already told you."

"Leave? Do you mean that?"

Susannah pulled out her gloves and kneaded them. "I've never meant anything more. I want my stories in a book, I tell you. Not in a paper that will get thrown out or used to wrap up the garbage." She stopped abruptly. "Or cookies," she said in a softer tone, and smiled. "So, will you agree to a book?"

Nancy's hands were in her lap. She knew George would never give up on the stories, not once he saw how incendiary they were. It really was not her choice to make, but Susannah didn't need to know that. Anyway, there was no way Slip could stop her. Not now. She crossed her fingers and hoped her parents would understand. "A book," she said. "All right." *Why does this woman, this murderer, have me lying every time I turn around?*

"Have you ever wondered . . ." Nancy hoped that this question wouldn't stop Susannah from making any more revelations, ". . . what your family will think when they read my . . ." she paused and crossed her fingers again, ". . . my book?"

"My sisters are tougher than you'd imagine just based on what I've said of them. I spent so much time and energy protecting them, and now, when I need them . . ." Her face, so vulnerable a moment ago, tightened. "Next question?"

Was that the story-behind-a-story that Slip had asked her about back at the beginning? Nancy looked at her list. "What are your fears?"

"Fears? Oh, you mean about what's happening? I'm trying my hardest not to think about it." She swallowed and wiped the back of her hand across her lips. "Mostly, I don't want to cry. Nobody's ever seen me cry."

Nobody except Old Ned after he ate the tomatoes. "Did you choose not to marry, or did things just work out that way?"

"Jethro wouldn't have understood my need to go out some nights. He was . . ." she placed the fingertips of her left hand just above that hollow at the base of her throat. "He was the only one I would have considered, but when he asked me I had to say no."

"He asked you to marry him?"

"Does that surprise you?"

"Not really. I can see that he always favored you." Nancy searched for the right words. "It seems to me, though, that you set up a certain . . . boundary . . . that would have kept him at arm's length, right?"

At first Nancy thought Susannah wasn't going to answer. When she did speak, every word was weighted, but whether it was with anger or with resignation, Nancy couldn't tell. "Yes. I set up barriers. Would you have wanted to be me and have the sheriff as a brother-in-law?"

"I see what you mean." She glanced at her list. "Have you written a will?"

"Mary Louise and Lucy will get everything I own."

"Mary Louise and Lucy? What about Estelle?"

Susannah swallowed. "She's been gone four years now."

"I'm sorry." *I would like to have interviewed her about her husband's death. It's been so many years since the bear in the clearing, maybe it wouldn't have hurt her to talk about it.* Nancy pulled herself up short. It wasn't a bear that killed Franklin. It was a knife, Susannah's knife. Why was she starting to think like Slip?

Susannah hadn't noticed Nancy's inattention. ". . . two remaining sisters will divide everything. My brothers wouldn't want any of it. I only have one other bequest." She stopped speaking. Nancy waited. "You'll find out what it is soon enough."

Nancy wrote *BEQUEST – FIND OUT.* She thumbed back to her list of questions. "Have you ever had any regrets?"

The sun that had streamed in the window moments before dimmed. A shadow passed over Susannah's face. "Funny you should ask that. I was awake for a long time last night. A place like this," she swept her arm in a gentle arc, "makes a person think." Susannah reached across the table and laid her hand over the steno pad, effectively stopping Nancy from writing. "Yes. I did have some, as you call them, *regrets.*" She pulled the pad gently but firmly out of Nancy's reach. "I don't want you to write about this."

"You're not giving me much choice in the matter." Nancy set her pen on the table. That pad was pretty well full anyway.

"I really mean this." Susannah turned the pad face down, picked up the pen, and laid it on top of the note pad. "Even if you have my words memorized, I don't want you to leave here and write them down. I want your promise on that."

Nancy had visions of her coveted Pulitzer Prize going down the drain. A prize for investigative journalism. Was there such a thing? Maybe *this* was another story-behind-the-story. "I guess so," she said. "I promise."

"Okay then. I can tell you what really happened. It was about Emmy and the flu epidemic." Susannah stood and leaned on the back of her chair. "A few years ago—" She pulled out her gloves and laid them across the pad. "We were talking about regrets. As I was saying, a few years ago, in the summer of 1926, I dropped by Lucy's house to take her some preserves I'd put up. She always did have a fondness for the taste of raspberries. She asked me to sit with her a spell. She showed me an emerald green scarf William had bought for her. She was planning to wear it only on special occasions, maybe over her black winter coat. With her dark hair—she took after Pa's side of the family—it would look striking. While I admired the scarf, she put a kettle of water on to heat. . . ."

Lucy and I sat there for a while, discussing her children and my Sunday School classes. The talk finally got around to the flu epidemic of 1918 eight years before. That time was such a horror for everyone concerned. It seemed like it didn't leave any family untouched, and it didn't seem to matter whether people lived in fancy homes or in hovels, whether they were in town or in the countryside. It hit everywhere. We didn't see it in Baynard's Mill until late September or maybe it was early October of 1918. We'd heard about it sweeping the nation, but up until then I thought our town might be spared. "I was surprised at how suddenly it hit," I said to Lucy. "Isn't it strange that we never talk about it much?"

"Not so strange," she said. "It was a sad time. Ma always thought Button Kingsley brought the infection to our house."

"I don't remember Button being there," I said to Lucy. "I thought it was Kennon Bloot that did it."

"Kennon? No, of course not. It was Button. Kennon stayed out by his wagon—remember?—and just shouted to us to listen to the radio and keep everybody away. He did so much to try to keep everyone safe, but then he died that horrible death from the bee sting the next summer."

"Are you sure it was Button?"

"Oh, yes." She took a slow sip of tea. "Without a doubt."

"You say Kennon did so much to help, but his warning obviously didn't keep Ma from letting Button into the house."

Lucy stirred her tea. "If I remember right, Button had already dropped by early that morning, a few hours before Kennon showed up. Button came in and had a cup of coffee with us. I seem to recall him saying he wasn't feeling well. He probably already had it." She closed her eyes, as if trying to picture who had been there around the kitchen table. "Ma and Pa, Emmy, Button, and me. You must have been out at the barn reading in that cubbyhole you fixed up in the hayloft."

"How did you know about that?"

"Oh, Slip, you didn't really think you were fooling anyone all those years, did you? We all knew you spent every minute you could out there, from the time you could first climb that ladder until . . . well . . . you never gave it up, did you? I'll say this for you, though, you never packed down the hay too much. You've always been such a little slip of a thing." She looked me over. "You still are."

I wasn't convinced. "Joseph's boys both caught it and died too. Where were they when Button came to the house?"

"The good Lord only knows, Slip. It's been—what?—seven, eight years? Do you want more tea? I'll pour. Here, hold your cup up higher." We sipped our tea in companionable silence as Lucy thought. "I think it was that afternoon. Joseph brought all four of his children in the wagon and asked Ma to watch them and keep them safe. He'd heard on the radio that the flu had come to the county, and he was living in town by then. He said he wasn't going to take any chances where his youngsters were concerned. That's what he said. I remember it like it was yesterday. Not going to take any chances, especially since he already knew what it was like to lose one child to scarlet fever."

"But if the boys weren't there, how could Button have infected them?"

"Button didn't infect them. He infected Emmy and Ma and me. Remember how sick we got? Somehow you and Pa got passed over, just like the Hebrews with the plagues in Egypt. Emmy and Ma must have passed on the infection to the boys, because I left to go back to my own family right after Joseph brought his kids by." Lucy stopped talking and reached across the table toward my hand. "Slip? Slip? Are you alright? You look pale all of a sudden."

"It's just the memories, Lucy. They're getting the best of me, I guess."

"I know, you poor dear," Lucy told me. "You were sitting with Emmy when she died, weren't you? I'm sorry I brought all this up."

Susannah pushed the gloves and the note pad farther away from her toward the end of the table. "I left to walk back home soon after that, but I couldn't get rid of the thought of Kennon dying, suffocating like that. I thought about those bees I'd let loose in Kennon's house. The bees I'd used to kill him because Ma had said—or I *thought* she had said—that Kennon was the one who brought the flu to our farm. She never told me he stayed out away from the house. And I know she never even mentioned Button. I thought about Kennon's wife saying that his throat swelled up so much he couldn't breathe. I'd thought at the time that it was an appropriate way for him to die since that was how Emmy ended, unable to breathe."

Nancy felt her own breath catch in her throat. "How could you have known, though?"

"I could have asked some questions. I could have done some research. I should have noticed there were things Ma didn't say about that morning, and I could have insisted that she fill in those blanks."

"But how would you have even known to ask those questions?"

"I guess I couldn't have, but that didn't stop my mind from whirling around all the way home from Lucy's house and late into the night. If Kennon had been the one who killed Emmy, he would have deserved to die. If it was Button, though—if Kennon had been trying to save us, but Button had already brought death to our house—then it was Button who deserved to die, don't you see? Ma never told me Button had stopped by that morning." Susannah walked over to the window and reached up to the small ledge. "I wish I could see outside."

"It was raining when I came in." Nancy picked up her coffee cup, but it was empty.

"I wonder if I'll ever feel rain again." Susannah let go and dropped her arms. "I sat with Emmy while she was dying from the flu. I watched her choke, held her as best I could. Do you know how helpless you feel when there is absolutely nothing you can do to stop the death of someone you love?"

Nancy massaged her left hand. The skin was dry, but she had no lotion with her. "I was there when my brother died. My mother too. I know that feeling."

"Then maybe you'll understand how angry I was at Kennon, until I found out it wasn't Kennon after all; but he was already dead when I learned the truth. Button killed him too, in a way. If he hadn't brought the flu to our house, then Emmy and the boys would have lived and I wouldn't have been mad at Kennon. It was really Button who caused all those deaths."

"You can't mean that." Nancy reached for her notepad. *Now I know what her motive was.*

"No!" Susannah grabbed up the notepad before Nancy could touch it. She turned away, toward the wall. "I told you I don't want any of this written down." Susannah slipped the gloves into her pocket. "You asked if I'd ever had any regrets. Well, I'm telling you that I did. They should have tried me for the murder of Kennon Bloot. That's the only one that was really murder, even though it was all Button's fault." She turned back, and sank into her chair. "I do regret killing Kennon, because he didn't deserve it. He's the only one who didn't, though. The others were just scum. I was ridding the earth of scum."

Nancy ran over the list in her head. A dozen deaths, from Franklin to the two Kingsleys. "So why did you kill Dominick? I know what they said at the trial, but why did you really?"

"Such a hurry you're always in. There was Evelyn—she came after Button and before Dominick. Would you like to hear her story?"

Change that to a baker's dozen. "Only if I can write it down."

"Of course you can." Slip slid the note pad back within reach. "Here."

Keys jingled in the lock. "Tomorrow?" Nancy asked.

"I'm afraid not." Matron clasped her hands behind her. "You'll have to wait until Wednesday."

STATESVILLE COUNTY CLARION

YOUR MORNING SOURCE FOR ALL THE NEWS WORTH READING

Tuesday, July 26, 1932

Letters to the editor of the Clarion

Dear Editor:
She got what was coming to her. God's commandment is clear. Thou shalt not kill.
Sincerely,
Robert Vining

Dear Editor:
Can we not find some Christian compassion in our hearts for this forsaken lamb? I pray that our Governor will grant her appeal for clemency.
Respectfully,
Mrs. Arthur Fountain

Dear Editor:
I cannot sign my name to this letter. I would fear for the safety of my life and property if it was known that I applaud Miss Packard. She rid this state of two of the most insidious leeches our political system has ever seen.
Name withheld

Dear Editor:
This past week has been a demonstration of the equity of our judicial system at work. Even if someone is so obviously guilty as Miss Packard was shown to be, it still behooves us to give her (or him) the benefit of a belief that one is presumed innocent until proven otherwise. Her trial was fair, and the verdict was just.
Most sincerely,
Stephan Keiser III

Chapter 14 - Mistaken Identity

Mrs. Maybell Harris Thomas, Petitioner, brings her petition for alimony against Plennie G. Thomas, Defendant, on 26 October 1937. . . . Immediately after Defendant ran Petitioner off, he sold all their furniture and house-hold goods, and went away out of state for three months. . . .

--from the 1937 archives of the
Gwinnett County Superior Court

On Tuesday, with nothing else to do, Nancy found a dry goods store and bought half a yard of soft blue cotton and a spool of dark blue thread. She had to borrow a needle and a pair of small, sharp-pointed scissors from Mrs. Cappell. Her sewing skills were minimal, amateurish at best, but she carefully ripped the seam out of the bottom of the completely inadequate pockets in one of her shirtwaist dresses. She cut four rectangles that measured fourteen inches by nine inches and folded each in half. After a great deal of experimentation, she shaped one piece into a serviceable pocket by sewing up the two sides, leaving the top open. She then stitched that open edge onto the bottom of the dress pocket, thereby extending the depth of it by about six inches. Her stitching was a bit ragged, but she was inordinately proud of the result. After she'd repeated the process with the other pocket, she tackled the pockets on her other shirtwaist, and began to wonder how she could alter her suits once she got home.

The result of her Tuesday afternoon and Wednesday morning's

exertions was thoroughly satisfying. She packed a lunch, assuming that Slip might not have eaten. If she ever got out of this routine of running from rooming house to prison and back again, she was never going to look at bread and cheese again as long as she lived. Her new pockets held four hankies with plenty of room to spare, but when she looked for her fountain pen, it seemed to have disappeared. She hoped she hadn't dropped it in the prison parking area, where it could have been smashed by the Willys or the Ford. She settled for a couple of pencils instead.

Officer Snarlsalot looked at the collection of steno pads that weighed down Nancy's handbag. "How could you possibly write this much about two murders?"

Nancy smiled sweetly. *Watch it, mister. Your own might be the next one.* "You'd be surprised, Officer Jolly. There really is quite a story here."

"She's getting what she deserves."

And what do you deserve? "The jury seemed to think so."

He scowled even more, like a sudden thundercloud blocking out the sun over the prairie. "Don't you?"

"Oh, I'm glad I wasn't on that jury." It wasn't an answer, but Nancy didn't care for the conversation. She put her umbrella in the corner. "May I go in now?"

He waved her through the gate to the barred door where Matron waited.

"No cookies today, I'm afraid."

Matron ran her hands over her own hips and belly as if she were searching herself for hidden weapons. "That's probably just as well. These hips of mine are wide enough already. I do love those chocolate bits, though."

"Me too."

"She's already in there waiting for you."

Evelyn. She had already written the name before Matron threw her out on Monday. She'd been writing out the names in block letters and reserving her shorthand for Slip's dictation. "Last name?"

"Ingalls. Evelyn Ingalls. It may seem like this story is roundabout, but there's a connection here. An important connection. Just let me tell it in my own way, and then you can ask questions later, okay?"

"That's fine with me."

"I think I need to walk for this one." She circled the table and peered over Nancy's shoulder. "That's i-n-g-l-e-s."

Nancy struck through *Ingalls*. She'd have to go back and double-check every one of these names. The obituaries should help. She had the approximate month and in most cases the exact year for each of the . . . the events.

"Dominick Kingsley ran for reelection in November of 1930."

"I thought this was about Evelyn?"

"There you go again." A clap of thunder punctuated her remark. "Sorry."

"As I was saying, he ran for reelection. Just a week before the voting, there was an awful rainstorm." Susannah looked up at the window as she passed it. "Like that one out there now." She resumed her pacing.

It would be nice to blame it on the weather, nobody's fault, but when Evelyn Ingles said that she'd come around the turn so quickly that she hadn't had time to stop before she hit the man in the road, I didn't believe it. After the accident, I'd gone out there myself, to look at where it happened. I could still see skid marks that the rain hadn't rinsed off the macadam yet. There would have been plenty of time for her to stop, or at least to swerve around him. He was changing a tire, and yes, he may have been farther onto the road than was safe. With the thunder that was raging at the time, he most likely never heard Evelyn's car approaching until it was too late, and she said herself that her headlights didn't give much illumination, so they wouldn't have given him more than a second or two of warning. Not nearly enough time for him to jump out of the way. But plenty of time for her to pull to her left and avoid hitting him.

Jethro never had a chance. She hit him full on. Oh, he lived a few excruciating, pain-filled hours, long enough for me to make it to the hospital. He'd called my name, you see, so they sent for me.

Jasper arrested Evelyn, but couldn't make a serious case against her. I could tell he suspected that she wasn't telling him the truth, but she had no reason to kill Jethro, and maybe she was innocent after all. He charged her with involuntary manslaughter, and the judge slapped her wrist and told her not to let it happen again. Poor little thing, looking all pathetic in the courtroom. Well, I was sitting there, and I watched Dominick Kingsley through the proceedings. He may have told the newspapers that he was there because she was a campaign worker of his, and he wanted to show his belief in her innocence, but I saw the looks that went between the two of them. Put that together with what Jethro told me as he lay dying, and I knew what I had to do.

Susannah stopped her pacing and stood beneath the window. The sound of the rain was still just as insistent as before. Ordinarily Nancy liked rain, but this storm felt menacing. She hoped it wasn't leading up to a tornado. She needed to focus on the issue at hand. "What did Jethro tell you?"

"The funny thing was that his first words were *I never took you up in a hot air balloon.* I told him that was a bunch of nonsense, but he asked me to promise to try it some time." Her eyes clouded, and she blinked rapidly. "He told me that Dominick was the one who hit him. Dominick got out of the car on the driver's side. A woman came around from the other side. Jethro didn't know who she was. All he knew was what he heard. I think that if Dominick had known Jethro was conscious, lying there in the road, he wouldn't have said what he did. This is what Jethro told me."

Susannah's voice dropped into the singsong of memory, lowering to approximate what Nancy assumed must have been Jethro's voice.

If anyone finds out I was driving, Dominick said, *I'll lose the election. I'll have to withdraw, especially if they find out that you and I were . . . were here together.*

We're not that far from town, the woman said. *You run off through the woods, and I'll tell them I was driving, that it was an awful mistake. I haven't had nearly as much to drink as you have. What with the weather, nobody will blame me. You run on now, before somebody comes along.*

"Jethro took hold of my hand as best he could. *Find her,* he said. *Make her tell the truth.* Those were almost the last words he ever spoke. After that, I started following Dominick."

Thank goodness for shorthand, Nancy thought, and scribbled *Find out what last words were.* She started to speak, but paused to write *Ask her if she cried when J died.* "How did you follow Dominick without being seen?" She paused. "Wait. I know. Invisible, right?"

"Pretty much so, although I did take extra care since he was such a public figure. I waited around outside the places where he was having evening functions—dinners, speeches, things like that. He and one particular woman were often the last ones to leave, and I'd follow them."

"How did you do that?"

"I had a car by then, a Dodge, which was a good name considering what I did with it. I'd drive with the lights out, and for somebody who thought he was so smart, Dominick Kingsley was certainly dumb. Every time he'd start by going around a block twice. Once I figured out his strategy, I'd just pull over to the side and pick him up on the second time around. He was easy to follow. He and Evelyn would go someplace secluded and then drive back out a half hour or so later. He'd drop her at her house and he'd head on home where his bird-brained wife waited for him."

"Why did you kill Evelyn if Dominick was the one who ran over Jethro?"

"I had to. Of course I had to. She was as guilty as he was. They were fornicators, and she tried to hide the evidence of his guilt. She deserved to die."

Nancy didn't see it that way. She opened her mouth to object but saw that Slip had that look on her face, that look of completely enjoying herself, and Nancy decided not to risk another tirade.

"My sister Lucy's scarf gave me the idea. Remember five years ago when Isadora Duncan strangled herself accidentally? Her long scarf got tangled in her automobile's wheel. I had to strangle Evelyn first and set it up to look like an accident, and I had to sacrifice a perfectly good scarf to do it with. I bought two identical ones up in Statesville. One of them I mailed to her from Statesville with a card that I had typed. It said, FROM A SECRET ADMIRER. She started wearing that scarf everywhere. The other one I yanked and pounded and stretched until it was thoroughly messed up. Then I wound one end of it around my own car's wheel and got it covered in grease.

"When the time came to kill her, I used the ruined scarf to strangle her, wound the other end of it around her axle, and pushed her car off the road so it ran into a tree. It was real obvious to everyone that she had died the same way poor Isadora did. You'd think people would learn from the mistakes of others."

"What kind of a car did she have?"

"That was the beauty of it. She had one of those brand new Willys convertibles, so it was easy to see how the scarf could have blown back behind her."

"And for your treasure box?"

"I thought about a piece of fringe, but that would have connected her to me, so I chose a tiny model car I found in the general store."

"Was it a Willys, like Evelyn's car?"

"No. It was a Ford, but that was close enough."

"What happened to the other scarf?"

"What other scarf?"

"The one she was wearing. The one that wasn't damaged."

"Oh. Didn't I tell you that already? I untied it from around her neck after I strangled her. I burned it so nobody would get suspicious."

Nancy set down her pencil and flexed her fingers. She wished she hadn't lost her fountain pen; it fit her hand so much better than a pencil did. "When Jethro died . . . did you cry?"

Susannah clasped her hands behind her neck, supporting her head as she stretched her back into an arch. "I might have, but a nurse bustled in right about then and took over. She told me it was time for me to leave. I never really said goodbye. I was . . ."

The keys jangled once again in the lock, and both women sighed. "I hate that sound."

Nancy nodded. "So do I."

Matron bustled in. "I'm afraid it's time for you to leave," she said.

"I'll be back on Friday," Nancy said, and Slip nodded, but didn't say goodbye.

Her car was worse than an oven and unbelievably muggy, probably because of all the rain, so Nancy rolled down the windows and waited for the excess heat to dissipate in the half-spirited breeze that disturbed the wet leaves above her.

Why wouldn't Slip cry? Did she ever cry when she was alone at night in her cell? Had she ever cried at home in bed, turned away from Mary Louise at night so her sister wouldn't hear her?

When, Nancy wondered, would the governor announce that he was commuting Slip's sentence? Surely that wouldn't take too long, although every day must seem like an eternity for Slip, there in that barren prison. Slip seemed so certain that the governor would rule in her favor, and Nancy had to agree. Surely they wouldn't execute a woman.

If Slip *had* been able to cry, was there a chance that she might not have bottled so much of her anger inside? Maybe then she might have taken her despair and laid it at the sheriff's feet. *What a sappy image,* Nancy reprimanded herself. The facts were that, for whatever reason, Slip had not cried, had not gone to the law, and had not resisted the impulse to take that law into her own hands. Susannah was a murderer, and Nancy appeared to be the only one who knew just how very true that statement was.

Chapter 15 - The Last Time

Citation in the case of Mrs. Maybell Harris Thomas vs. Plennie G. Thomas
Defendant Plennie G. Thomas cited for contempt of court for refusing to pay $2.50
each Monday to Petitioner

--from the 1937 archives of the
Gwinnett County Superior Court

Nancy hated limp bacon. The boiled eggs were fine. So was the toast. But the bacon was pathetic. She wanted it crispy, but after all she'd been going through, she felt starved, so she ate it anyway. Maybe all that bread and cheese was refusing to digest.

If she'd glanced at the front-page story before she paid for the paper, she would have saved her nickel. George had added two more paragraphs—more blood and guts—that made Nancy cringe. Everyone who read the *Clarion* had already been bombarded by these details countless times. They didn't need to see them one more time.

"You're early." Officer Not-So-Jolly seemed to take it personally. He shook his head slowly, like a bewildered sheep watching stray dogs close in.

"Only a few minutes."

"Five."

She tapped her wristwatch. "Three and a half."

He looked at the clock on the wall and grimaced. "Four," he conceded with very little grace.

"So could I go on in?"

Nancy thought she'd won a small battle, but Officer Molasses-in-January took a full minute to examine the outside of her handbag and four minutes to inspect every single item in it. Finally, he handed over the bag, glanced at the clock, and said, "You're late."

Ooh, if I had half of Slip's gumption, you'd be dead meat, and I'd fry your liver and feed it to Toodle. Nancy walked silently and with studied dignity through the barred gate. To her great satisfaction, Officer Petty did not look any happier after his minor victory.

She pulled all the note pads from her bag. "I've been putting together a timeline, and I'd appreciate it if you would look it over and tell me if I've missed anything." She unfolded a large sheet of paper with columns. YEAR / AGE / VICTIM / METHOD / TREASURE

Skip glanced over the notations, took Nancy's pencil, and crossed out *Bloot*. B-L-U-E-T-T she wrote above it in precise block letters. "Forty years," she said. "It doesn't look like much of an accomplishment for that long a time, does it?"

Thirteen bodies, thirteen families. Knife, poison, hammer, gun, bull, bee, scarf, three French hens, two turtle doves, and cyanide in a ma-ar-ti-ni, tra-la-la. "I think you've accomplished quite a lot."

"Thank you, Nancy. I'm glad you feel that way."

Nancy stacked all but the most recent note pad at the end of the table. "How have you been getting along with the other prisoners?"

"There aren't many people like me in here. Women, I mean. There's only that one small ward for us, and none of the other women are there for . . . for what I'm there for."

"Do you talk to each other, or are you isolated?" Nancy remembered the sneeze that came from the woman in the cell next door that day she'd eaten lunch with Slip.

"What would I have to say to someone who's been convicted of prostitution? Or someone who, according to her, got away with writing so many bad checks she had a fortune before she got caught."

What a wealth of story material. "I should think you could ask them lots of questions."

Susannah shook her head slowly. "I'd have to be interested

in their answers before I could do that. I've been spending my time sitting on the cot and thinking." She sat up a bit straighter and rolled her shoulders forward and back. "You can call this chapter *The Last Time.*

"Really?" Nancy turned to a blank page. "Are we up to Dominick?"

"Dominick." There was a wistful tone to her voice for just a moment, but then she cleared her throat. "I already told you how I stabbed him there in his office, and now you know why I did it, but I still have some other things to say. I'll bet you can guess what they're about."

Nancy thought back over all the stories while Slip sat patiently. "There *was* something different about Button and . . . uh . . . Dominick too. You kept items for your treasure box that were directly traceable, that linked you to both of them."

"That's right. I changed my method. That's why I got caught. I saved the cyanide bottle that killed Button, and I took Dominick's wristwatch. I had a rule not to take anything personal—or anything that could be traced back to the one who died."

"What made you do it differently with those two?"

"I guess it was because Button killed Emmy, and Dominick killed Jethro. They were family. It was somehow more personal with them. I wore Dominick's watch to sleep the night I killed him." She encircled her right wrist with her left hand. "I used to take that cyanide bottle out and admire it before I'd go to bed. You might remember that one of the waiters there that night was arrested. His family had lost their farm because of that ghastly farm bill that Button pushed through the legislature. The bill was all Button's responsibility. His son . . . Dominick . . . had nothing to do with that."

"You sound as if you . . ."

"As if I what?"

"As if you missed him?"

"Nonsense. Where did you ever get a ridiculous idea like that?"

From the tone of your voice when you said his name.

"Well, you were asking about that waiter. Jasper tried to pin the murder on him, since he was the only person there who had an obvious motive, but that never went anywhere because he was setting up the table for dinner downstairs the whole time cocktails were being served in that supposedly hidden room upstairs. Prohibition has been such a silly idea. Do you think it will ever be repealed?"

"There's a lot of call for it," Nancy said, "but the Temperance leagues are still strong."

"Tell that to Al Capone and his mob."

Nancy nodded. "That's not exactly the legacy the prohibitionists had in mind. How did you feel about being around all that liquor?"

"It didn't bother me. I was too intent on what I had to do. It helped that everyone there was tipsy, so their memory was affected."

"As I recall, while they were sorting out the murder, they arrested quite a few prominent people."

"Yes; but it all came to nothing. Jasper was furious. All his hard work, and his lawbreakers walked away with minor fines. And the murderer had somehow slipped," Susannah smiled, "slipped away." She sighed, and the lines on her face seemed to smooth out by a giant eraser. "It was almost too easy. He always did drink too much. I wore my darkest blue dress with a white pinafore. I went upstairs as if I belonged there, picked up a drink, slipped in the cyanide, and tied a ribbon around the stem while I waited for the crystals to dissolve. When I handed it to him, that was my only moment of fear, in case he looked at me and recognized me, but he ignored me. I was only the hired help, or so he thought. I waited until I saw him toss down his drink, and then I slipped out before the furor erupted. "

"If . . ." Nancy hesitated. "If that waiter had been tried for the murder, would you have spoken up?"

This time the silence seemed never-ending. Susannah leaned forward and propped her elbows on the table. Her face stilled again and took on that blank inward look of total concentration. "I suppose . . ." Each word dropped slowly. "I suppose we'll never know the answer to that question." She settled her right cheek into her open palm, and curled her left hand into a fist beneath her chin. "I will say this. I'm glad I never had to make that decision."

Keys jingled and Matron opened the door. "Time's up. Visiting hours are over."

Nancy closed her note pad. It felt heavier than usual.

As she signed herself out, Officer Gloomy-Gut made a smart-aleck comment about little old ladies with knives. *And hammers and bees and rocks and outhouses*, Nancy thought. He raised an eyebrow at her, as if he expected an answer, but she walked on to her car. On the way home, she stopped and bought some of that new waxed paper.

Chapter 16 - The Last Day

Deposition
Personally appeared before me the undersigned Mrs. R. Stonecypher, who being duly sworn, deposes and says that a certain tract of land to wit: [description of land] and which tract of land is advertised by the administrator to be sold on the First Tuesday in May 1938, is not the property of the estate of the deceased, but is the property of the deponent, Mrs. R. Stonecypher.
Sworn to and subscribed before me this 15th day of April 1938
--from the 1938 archives of the
Gwinnett County Superior Court

Nancy spent the weekend holed up in her room, writing. Mrs. Cappell knocked at her door on Saturday and tried to entice her down for breakfast. "There is a very personable young couple who have taken a room for several days. They're simply lovely people. You might enjoy the conversation."

"No, thank you, Mrs. Cappell. I'm sorry, but I'm not feeling sociable. I'll go down to the kitchen later and get myself something to eat." But she skipped lunch and found herself hungry only for a cup of tea in the evening.

Knock, knock on Sunday morning. "It's time for church, my dear."

"Thank you, Mrs. Cappell," but Nancy stayed put, leaving her room only to grab some toast and jam after she was sure the well-intentioned landlady had left. She paused in the door of the kitchen and went back for more bread. She might as well be in prison herself and on a starvation diet of bread and water. And, she had to admit, some mighty fine blackberry jam. This so-called starvation was completely self-imposed. And completely uncalled for. Why was she punishing herself? Her mother's voice sounded a gentle suggestion. Nancy made herself some scrambled eggs.

George called her mid-afternoon with news of the latest announcement from Prosecuting Attorney Stevens. Together they worded one short paragraph for the next morning's issue. She sincerely hoped George would keep his hands off it.

That night she crept downstairs and baked one more batch of Toll House cookies, using up the last of her flour and the final chunky pieces of chocolate.

STATESVILLE COUNTY CLARION
YOUR MORNING SOURCE FOR ALL THE NEWS WORTH READING
Monday, August 1, 1932

MURDERER TO BE MOVED; WHEN AND WHERE?
By Nancy Remington

The State Capital: District Attorney Paul W. Stevens announced late yesterday afternoon that convicted murderer Susannah Lou Packard will be transported sometime today to a different facility within the state, where her sentence will be carried out within the next two weeks. He declined to give either the exact date or the location of that facility. The Governor's office has yet to announce a decision on the appeal for clemency that was filed on Miss Packard's behalf.

On Monday Nancy could barely wait to leave for the prison, but she took the time to prepare another simple lunch and to package the cookies with a jaunty blue ribbon tied in a big bow. At the newsstand she read her unchanged paragraph with astonishment. He hadn't added a single word. Would wonders never cease?

Officer Plug-Along went through the usual motions with even less enthusiasm than usual. "Berries?" he asked. "Weapons?"

"No." *Ah, but I'd love to have brought along a polished razor-sharp saber with a braided gold cord hanging from the hilt. I could run it through your bowels. And then I could chop off your head and place it on the window ledge for the pigeon to peck at.*

He opened her bag, took out the cookies, and removed the ribbon. "She could strangle somebody with this."

"She wouldn't do that to me."

"There are other people here." His scowl deepened. "Think about Miss Char . . . Think about the matron."

"She wouldn't . . ." *Maybe she would, though.* "I see what you mean."

"Have a good day, then, miss. Head right on in."

"She's waiting for you," Matron said through a smile that didn't quite reach her eyes.

"Are you okay?" Nancy asked.

"My mother is sick bad, and I'm afraid for her. I had to work all the weekend, a double shift on Saturday. I guess I'm worn out with worrying." She placed Nancy's hat pin in an envelope and signed a receipt.

"Would cookies help?"

"You've been awfully sweet to us here, but I'm beyond cookies right now. I don't want to face the rest of the day."

"I'm sorry." Nancy looked down at the floor and turned to the interview room.

"I'm sorry I couldn't come over the weekend. I would have been here if they had let me." *All I seem to be lately is sorry.*

"That's all right. Mary Louise came. She brought Lucy."

"Your family was here?"

"Just those two. Estelle sent word she never wanted to see me again. Funny, isn't it? All this time of the trial, both trials, we never spoke even once, although I saw them in the courtroom each day, of course. They were here the entire time, staying in a rooming house somewhere.

They left the day the verdict was announced."

The two sisters in the rooming house. Why didn't I take the time to meet them? "The woman with the green scarf?"

"Yes. That was Lucy."

"And the one with all the red hair must have been—"

"Mary Louise would put you on her Rectification List if she heard you call her a redhead. It was red-gold. That's what she always insisted on."

Red-gold, she wrote. "It never occurred to me that they were your kin." *It never occurred to me that I could have interviewed them without breaking my promise to Slip about not going to Baynard's Mill. My reporter's instincts must be slipping.*

"I'm not surprised." Susannah had developed a tic that made her eye twitch. "You didn't know who they were. Every morning, they'd look at me when I came into the room, but other than that, they never tried to make any contact with me."

"Why do you suppose they acted like that?"

"You heard what my attorney talked about during the trial. Lucy's youngest daughter, Caroline, was engaged to Arnold, Dominick's son. When Arnold's father died, and when I was arrested for it, Arnold broke off the engagement. Lucy's convinced that her precious Caroline will be an old maid now, and Mary Louise agrees with her. They think it's all my fault."

"I remember that. I put it in one of my reports, but surely they can't blame you."

"They do."

"Maybe Caroline is better off this way, especially if Arnold was anything like his father."

"You see it that way, and I agree with you, but Lucy doesn't have our sense of perspective. It will be interesting to see . . ." After a long pause, she spoke again. "Once they know how much I did for them and the rest of the family, I imagine they'll both be feeling pretty bad."

Nancy tilted her pencil back and forth between her thumb and index finger. "Why didn't you tell your lawyer the real reasons why you killed Button and Dominick? He might have been able to make a case for you."

Susannah lowered her head and peered at Nancy from under her sparse eyebrows. "My lawyer? Mr. Bumble-around himself? Surely you jest."

"I see what you mean."

"Anyway, I couldn't see that a jury would understand, and if I told about Dominick killing Jethro, Jasper would have looked into Evelyn Ingle's death, and I . . ." She pushed back the cuticle on her right index finger. "I thought if they found out I murdered a woman, it would get me the death sentence."

Nancy drew in her breath and let it out slowly. "You're probably right. It would have."

"There was something wrong with my plan, though. A fatal flaw, wouldn't you say?" Susannah brushed her hands several times over the front of her dress, as if clearing away a cobweb of useless ideas. "They're moving me today, did you hear?"

Nancy nodded, not quite trusting herself to speak.

"They don't have the facilities here for . . . for what they're going to do."

"I know. Let's hope the appeal comes through soon." Nancy glanced down at her lunch-laden handbag. "Have you eaten yet?"

"I'm not hungry, but don't let that stop you from eating."

"I can wait. There's plenty of time." She stopped. "I'm sorry. I didn't mean that the way it sounded."

"You can't make this not happen, you know," Slip said. "We might as well keep going without fretting." She pressed her lips together. "It would bother me less if I could keep active, but there's nothing to do in that cell. I feel like a lion in a cage at the zoo. All I do is pace and think. As hard as wash days were growing up, I think I'd prefer a week of Mondays to this eternal boredom." Letting out a shallow breath she asked, "What did you bring?"

Nancy pulled the top packet out of her handbag. "Toll House cookies." She laid the gift on the table between them.

Susannah looked at the small bundle. The outline of the chunky cookies was visible through the milky wrapping. "You bought some of that fancy waxed paper?" She touched it gently and watched the paper fold in at the pressure. The crinkly sound was magnified in the bare room. Nancy wished she'd brought a tablecloth.

"I thought you might want to . . . to . . . to take them with you, and this looks more . . ." She searched for a word. *More festive. More final*. ". . . more formal than newspaper."

Susannah nodded. "They haven't told me when it will be. Maybe a couple of weeks, maybe a month."

"The appeal will be granted. You'll see."

"If it doesn't, will you be there?"

Nancy reached impulsively around the cookies, but stopped short of touching Susannah's hand. They had never touched, had never even shaken hands, and now this simple gesture of comfort and connection seemed like it might be an intrusion. Instead, she laid her hand flat on the table, just inches from the kid gloves. Could she go through with this? She'd never seen a hanging, but she'd read some gruesome accounts by people who *had*. Still, it would be the final chapter in her series. She had to go. "Of course I'll be there."

Susannah looked at Nancy's hand. "I'd like to think that it's more than just . . ." She nodded in the direction of Nancy's note pads. "More than just a newspaper story."

Here I go with another lie. "Yes, of course it is." *It's my prize winner.* Immediately she rejected those thoughts, but they were there nevertheless. She hoped Slip hadn't sensed it. "Wait a minute. You said 'newspaper story.' I thought you were insisting on a book."

"I may not have time to wait for a book to be printed. Promise me you'll get those articles out right away, so I can read them. See them in print."

"I will, as fast as I can, and . . ." Nancy spread her fingers apart as wide as she could stretch them, ". . . and I'll be there to . . ." she relaxed her hand into a loose fist, ". . . to say goodbye."

Susannah laid one fingertip on Nancy's thumbnail for an instant. "Thank you." She gathered up the package and opened it with deliberation. "Let's see what we can do about this meal."

"That's not a meal," Nancy objected. She trembled as she pulled herself together. "I brought a real lunch too."

"I think I'd rather just take one moment at a time. We'll call this a meal for now." She handed the first cookie to Nancy and lifted the second one to her nose. "Ah, yes."

Nancy munched slowly. "You never told me how you got the kid gloves. Are you willing to talk about it?" She pulled a clean hanky from her bag and laid the unfinished cookie on it.

Susannah looked at the handkerchief. "Lace trimmed, I see."

A vision of Slip's treasure box hung there between them for a moment. A blue feather, a button, a clothespin. One ivy leaf and a small stained pebble. A piece of straw. A toy car and a lid from a prescription jar. Honey candy and cyanide. A wristwatch and . . .

"Lace!" They both burst into laughter—no, not laughter—something more primal, more primitive that grew from their fears and erupted into high-pitched cackles as they fed off each other's hysteria.

Matron opened the door. "You okay in here?"

Nancy nodded, pulling herself into a semblance of calm. "Yes, Matron. We're fine. We were just discussing . . ." she looked over at Slip, ". . . lace hankies."

Matron glanced from one to the other. "Doesn't seem too funny to me."

Nancy nodded again. "You'd have to know the whole story."

As the door closed, Slip spoke up. "Let's finish that story now, shall we?"

Nancy pulled out her pencil.

"What happened to your fountain pen? It was right pretty."

"I lost it somewhere. I've looked through the car and on the ground between here and the parking lot."

"Did you check your room where you're staying?"

"Yes, I did. I loved that pen. My father gave it to me when I graduated from high school."

"Well, now, that's too bad that you lost it. Carelessness never pays off." Susannah patted the gloves gently. "I've taken good care of these gloves," she said, "cleaning them each time, stitching up any small rents in the seams before they could get any bigger. A stitch in time— you've read that, I suppose. I always keep them with me, and *I've* never misplaced them."

I'm probably imagining things. Surely she's not trying to insult me for losing my fountain pen.

Susannah held the gloves out, but Nancy didn't touch them.

"When did you get them?"

"I thought I'd already told you."

"All you said was that you were a child."

Susannah put her left hand flat on the table beside the gloves. They looked brown against her skin. "I hadn't realized they'd turned quite this dark." She took a deep breath. "It's all about Hattie, you see."

She was silent for a few moments, so Nancy prompted her. "You've mentioned Hattie several times, but I still don't know who she was."

Susannah stuffed the gloves into her pocket before she spoke.

Hattie was just a little slip . . . no, I won't label her with my nickname. She deserves her own name. Hortense Alice Turner was small-boned. Her sisters, though, looked like their father. They came from sturdy stock, and their hands were too big for such delicate gloves.

I loved Hattie. Even though she was a year or two older than my big sisters, she never minded if I tagged along with her. The morning of her funeral, all three of her sisters stood in the back bedroom arguing about which one would get the gloves. Our whole family sat in the crowded parlor, waiting to follow the funeral wagon to the church for the burial. Everybody tried to pretend that they didn't hear Hattie's sisters yelling like that. I always hated to sit in one place for very long. Even then, when I was so young, I was almost invisible, so I just left Ma and my sisters and walked down the hall to where the argument raged. I hovered near the doorway and watched Hattie's mother snatch the gloves from the oldest sister's grasp.

"My child is gone," she said. "My firstborn is dead at seventeen, and all you three can do is snip at each other, dividing the booty like a bunch of heathen pirates." She plowed through them, and they scurried to protect their black bombazine skirts from her onslaught. "Here." Mrs. Turner thrust the gloves at me. "You'll grow into these soon enough," she said. "In the meantime, take care with them." Then she shooed me out of the room, back to where my sisters sat looking at their friend in the coffin. I hid the gloves in my pocket, not sure if Ma would make me give them back. Estelle was still crying. Lucy's eyes were red and puffy, and Mary Louise was hiding her face, curled up in Ma's lap.

Lucy had sat up with me all the night before, and Ma was there with me the night before that. I never used to wake up at night when I was little, until that week when I saw Hattie die. Then I couldn't sleep without nightmares. I guess it was hard on my family, all my screaming, but they thought they understood, and they were real caring about it.

"You saw Hattie die? No wonder you were traumatized."

"Oh, the dying was bad enough, I suppose. But it was what came right before that that gave me the nightmares."

"Before?"

"Remember when I asked you about the story behind the story?" Nancy nodded. "You have to know this in order to write it." She sat unmoving for a moment, and then stood and started pacing.

One minute I was playing hide and seek with Hattie. She had taken me out with her to gather wildflowers. That day I was too impatient to stay in my hiding place, so I crept along behind her while she searched for me. I'm sure now that she knew I was there, because she'd slow down every once in a while and I'd almost catch up with her, and then she'd be off again, calling out *Slip! Slip! Where are you?* That's what grown-ups do for small children for their delight.

The next thing I knew she stepped out into a pretty little clearing just bursting with wildflowers. It was a real windy day, and the flowers bent over almost to the ground. We hadn't felt the wind while we were in among the trees, but now she looked up at the sky and frowned. "I need to find Slip," she sang out. "This wind is brewing up a storm." Then she bent down, broke off a white daisy, and turned back to look at me. She smiled real big, but before she could take a step in my direction, a huge old hickory tree snapped off and fell on her, just like that. I've never seen a tree fall so fast.

Afterwards the men said it had a rotten center. It looked fine on the outside, but it couldn't stand up to the wind.

I was afraid to step close to her. The tree pinned her down by one arm and had smashed her shoulder to pieces. She had a bloody gash on her head, and a small branch stuck right into her eyeball, but once she stopped screaming she could still talk through her crying. *Go get help,* she told me.

I was four, maybe five. I looked back at the woods and listened to the screaming of the wind, and I was scared. *I can't,* I said, but she yelled at me. *Get me some help, or I'm going to die.* I turned and ran, and for a little bit I was okay, but then all the trees began to look the same, and I couldn't see a path anymore. I'm surprised I ever found my way back to her. I must have walked in a circle. Once I was pretty much back where I started, I could see someone with her.

I'm not sure why I didn't call out. Maybe things would have been different if I had, but I didn't. I crept behind a big old oak and peeked around the side of it. That man . . .

Slip's voice had gradually risen in pitch, as if she had gone back to her childhood through the memory. Nancy almost recoiled at the look of abject fear that seemed to take over Slip's face as she talked about *that man.* There were no tears in Slip's voice. There was terror.

. . . that man stood there talking to Hattie. That was years before he married Estelle. While I watched, he leaned his rifle up against the fallen tree. I could hear Hattie's breathing. It was ragged and rough.

Seems like you owe me something, he said.

Help me. I could barely hear her.

He laughed at her. That man laughed at Hattie lying there. *You're never going to be much good to anyone with your arm and shoulder all smashed like that.* He sounded clinical. I didn't know that word at the time, but remembering back, that was what it was like. *And your eye's gone,* he said. *You used to be a looker. Too full of yourself to go to the harvest dance with me. But look at you now, begging for help.* He looked around the clearing, and I cringed back, hoping he wouldn't see me behind him. *I'm all you've got now, and like I said, you owe me something.*

I watched him take down his suspenders. He kicked her legs apart and knelt down between them. Then he dropped his pants down and settled himself on top of her. The last thing I ever heard from Hattie was her screaming.

When he was done, he stumbled to his feet, yanked her dress

back down over her legs, and spit at her. He left, with his gun slung over his shoulder, and I stayed hidden behind my tree for a long time. I stayed really well hidden so he wouldn't see me. Finally I followed his footprints until I could see the edge of the woods. Then I waited until he was out of sight before I ran the other direction, toward home.

When I came home without Hattie, Pa and my older brothers ran to get her. I told them a tree fell on Hattie in the clearing. Ma thought that was what gave me the nightmares. I was too scared to say anything about that man—terrified that if I told, he'd think I owed him something more too. There wasn't any way that I could have said anything. Anyway, I was pretty sure that Hattie would tell on him, but by the time Pa found her, she was dead, so that man got away with it. Or he did until I was old enough to pay him back, right there in that same clearing.

Matron opened the door. Three burly guards stood behind her. "It's time now," she said.

"Wait." Nancy held up her hand to stop Matron from entering the room. It didn't work. "Slip? What was the last thing Jethro said?"

"The last thing?" She stood, turned away from the phalanx of guards, and lowered her voice to a wistful tone. "Nancy Lou, I'm surprised at you. You can figure out the answer to that one. Be sure you print it in your newspaper." She reached in the pocket of her blue dress. "You asked me if I had written a will, remember? And I told you I had only one bequest." She pulled out the kid gloves and handed them to Nancy. Then she walked to the door, glanced back one time, and was gone without saying goodbye.

A few minutes later, Matron returned to usher Nancy to the front. "I guess that's the end of something, isn't it? You're going to write a book about her?"

"Newspaper. I'd like to tell her whole story. We may need to serialize it."

"We'll keep an eye out for it. We like to read things like that. It might even brighten up Officer Jolly."

Nancy raised her eyebrows at that.

"Poor man. He lost his wife a good six months ago, and he just can't seem to get over it. I don't think I've seen him smile even once since then. And he used to live up to his name. He was one of the happiest men I ever knew until his wife got so sick and there was nothing he could do to help her. Even now in all his pain, he's so considerate. He's really a sweet man." A faint pink tint crept upward from her neck to her hairline. "You just never know about people, do you?"

Nancy looked down at her handbag. "That's right. You just never do know."

"I know you'll miss her. It's good that the two of you had all this time together, isn't it?"

"I had a lot of questions for her."

"Of course. Of course you did. Oh! One more thing. I had to pack up your aunt's belongings before the guards came to get her."

"My aunt? She's not my aunt."

"But she said . . ." Matron clamped her lips together, and turned her head away. A moment later she said, "Well, that explains why she asked me not to mention it. Anyway, while I was gathering her clothes, I found this. It was in her dress pocket." She held out a fountain pen. "I recognized it. It *is* yours, isn't it?"

Chapter 17- The Kid Gloves

On the 10ᵗʰ day of April in the year of our Lord Nineteen Hundred and Ten, the Defendant in the presence of Mrs. C. Blair, a female, did unlawfully use the following obscene, vulgar and profane language, to wit: "I'll be damned if I'll do it till I get ready." And "By God, wait awhile."

--from the 1910 archives of the
Gwinnett County Superior Court

The day of the hanging, Nancy stood near the gallows in the rosy light of dawn. She couldn't decide whether Susannah Lou Packard deserved to hang. Susannah had never looked like an avenging angel, with her simple blue dress and comfortable shoes. When Nancy first asked if she could write Susannah Lou Packard's story, she thought she'd be forced to listen to hours of self-serving platitudes as Susannah tried to justify her two crimes. Over the past week Nancy had sorted through all seven steno pads, planning how to serialize her story, and she'd been struck by how little Slip seemed to care about defending her actions or the reasons behind them, despite the fact that she had confessed to thirteen murders instead of only the two she was tried for. She seemed simply to want to be understood. To be *seen*.

She knew the seriousness of the charges against her, although she definitely had not expected the judge's sentence. Still, throughout the interviews, until that very last morning, she'd acted as if it didn't matter.

Maybe she was tired after so many killings, and yet Nancy never had the feeling that Susannah's crimes had been a burden. Once Nancy understood the first murder and why Slip did it, she couldn't help but lean toward agreeing with the boys in the copy room, who thought Susannah Lou Packard should have received a medal instead of a noose. Nobody in the copy room had liked the Kingsley men. *Too bad Susannah never came across the drunk who shot my best friend when I was in fourth grade.* Of course, he'd been caught and convicted, Nancy's father had told her that, so maybe Slip hadn't been needed in that particular case. Susannah *was* a killer, though. Thirteen people dead at her hand. Was any of it justifiable? What if Slip had taken her knowledge to the sheriff? But much of what she had done avenged something that wasn't truly illegal—the spreading of the scarlet fever germ, running a son out of town, the slaughter of song birds. The law wouldn't have cared.

At any rate, Slip would soon be gone. Nancy was sure that Slip had never lost her appetite for that—what did she call it?—that divine moment. The killing. Even as old as she was when she told Nancy her story, her eyes always lit up like a path of moonlight across the surface of a still pond each time she got to that instant, that line of demarcation between life and death. And now Slip would experience that fine line.

Nancy felt a kind of kinship with Slip. She thought she understood her, but then again, there was the fountain pen. Slip had clearly stolen it, and then had pretended to be concerned about Nancy's loss. Why? Why? Nancy stood dry-eyed as Susannah was led out into the courtyard. Nancy's stomach cramped as she watched Susannah climb the steps of the scaffold. Why had she ever agreed to be here? What, after all, did she owe this woman? Her mother's voice sounded, low and sure. *We're all in this world together, Nancy dearest, and if we can't be there when someone needs us, then we might as well give up.* That was why Nancy had gotten up in the dark and had driven all those miles. She was her mother's daughter, after all. She could be kind.

Just before the guards placed a hood over her head, Slip looked at Nancy and began to laugh. Guards with pistols at the foot of the scaffold; the minister Susannah had brushed past; three silent crows perched on the crosspiece at the top of the gallows; and one woman laughing maniacally.

The body swung and twisted in an eerie dance to the sound of urine falling onto the paving stones. It took every ounce of self-control

Nancy had to keep herself from screaming. At the same time, a more detached part of her thought she might have stayed forever, frozen to that spot beside the gallows in the center of the prison yard, watching the crows circle overhead. At the end, a soft-spoken guard had to take Nancy's arm to usher her out.

After the hanging, Nancy sat in her car, shivering from the cold of the dawn air—and from something more. She slipped Susannah's kid gloves out of her deep right-hand pocket and tried them on. They fit. Perfectly.

Nancy stuck the car key in the ignition slot, pulled it back out, and took a good look at the brown-stained gloves. She shuddered and took them off.

Chapter 18 - Mary Louise

"Mrs. Fordyke? I'm Nancy Remington from the *Clarion*. May I talk with you a few minutes?"

"I don't think so." She stood immovable behind her screen door, her red hair pulled back in a braid that was wound around her head like a crown. A big floppy-eared yellow dog sat beside her leg. "You want to write about my sister?"

"Yes, and I'd like—"

"You'd like me to tell you what a poor, sweet, misunderstood girl she was."

"Not exactly—"

"Because that's not what I'd tell you. They hanged her this morning."

"I know, and I'm sorry about that."

"Why? Do you think she was wronged by the verdict?"

"No, ma'am. I'm convinced that she committed the murders. I saw you at the trial, so I know you heard the overwhelming evidence. I'd like to understand more, and I think it would help if I had your side of the story."

"You're the fifth pushy reporter to show up on my porch this morning."

Nancy cringed inwardly, but tried not to show it. Pushy reporters made a lot of people unwilling to talk. "I'm sorry to add to your distress, Mrs. Fordyke, but I don't think any of those other reporters ever spoke with your sister."

"You're saying you did?"

"Yes, ma'am." Nancy held up the stack of note pads. "She told me a lot of her life story. I've been interviewing her at the prison ever since the first day of the trial."

Mary Louise looked Nancy over from head to foot. "She even got you to dressing like her, didn't she?"

"Shirtwaist dresses are comfortable in this heat."

"Uh-huh. Well," she held the screen door open, "don't just stand there. You've got me curious now. You might as well come in and sit while I do some cooking. I have a couple of men to feed." She held out her hand and Nancy took it. "Pleased to meet you, Miss . . . what did you say your name was?"

"Remington. Nancy Remington."

"Welcome to my house, Miss Remington. Don't mind Cheyenne. Once she's sniffed your shoes, she'll go lie down."

"Thank you. I'm sorry to intrude," she inhaled the deep rich aroma of roasting chicken, "especially while you're cooking."

"Oh, land sakes, it's no intrusion. You just caught me off guard there." She waited as Nancy leaned down to pat the white-muzzled dog, who flapped her paddle-shaped ears and wiggled her yellow-haired body in pleasure. "You've found a friend for life."

"She's quite a watchdog."

Mary Louise chuckled. "That's right. You could steal the whole house, and she'd watch you do it." She led the way down a wide picture-lined hallway toward the back of the house. Nancy caught glimpses of photographs and pen and ink drawings. She wanted to ask about the artist, but Mary Louise walked briskly ahead. The delectable smell got stronger as they went.

"You said you have men to feed." Nancy looked around the sprawling kitchen and felt instantly at home. "Do you and the sheriff have children?"

"Four grown sons and two daughters with families of their own. They all live in Baynard's Mill, and the whole raft of them are here every Sunday. The two youngest sons have farms. Fortunately they're doing quite well, despite the hard times. They're the reason we have chickens to eat on a regular basis. And the sheriff brings one of his deputies to eat here three or four times a week and every Sunday. He's a young man with no family to speak of and we sort of fell into the habit of feeding him. We're old enough to be his parents." She looked Nancy over. "I'd say he's about your age, maybe a year or two older."

"I'm twenty-eight."

"That's the age of our youngest."

You don't look old enough to be my mother. Of course, since Mom died twelve years ago, I don't know what she would have looked like now.

"Allon will be thirty next month. At any rate, he calls me Mother Fordyke. It makes me sound ancient, but then he's respectful, so it's not so bad. And my Jasper says Allon Mercer is one of the best deputies he's ever had. Very dependable. Very steady." She motioned to a straight-backed wooden chair. "Sit there, at that side of the table."

"This is a lovely kitchen." Nancy set the note pads on the sturdy, somewhat scarred oak table and placed her handbag on the floor beside her.

"You'd better pick that up or Cheyenne will have her nose in it. Put it on the sideboard over there."

Nancy did as she was told. A framed photograph of a much younger Mary Louise and a youthful sheriff sat on the shelf below the glass-fronted cabinets. "Your wedding picture?"

"Yes, indeed. I swear we were just babies. Where has the time gone?"

"I'm glad you're willing to talk with me." Nancy sat down and turned her chair slightly so she was facing the cast iron wood stove where Mary Louise stood.

"You wait and hear what I have to say before you go getting all thankful. You may change your mind. And the only reason I'm willing to invite you in is that you talked with her. I think I'd like to hear what she had to say about herself."

"Slip told me—I'm sorry if that sounds presumptuous. That's what she asked me to call her; I hope you don't mind."

"Of course not. Ma was the only one who called her anything else. Always Susannah Lou. So formal." She pumped water and sang in rhythm with the handle. "S-L-P, S-L-P, dangling from a rope."

Is this woman as crazy as her sister? No, she doesn't seem crazy.

Just angry. Very, very angry.

Still facing the window, Mary Louise said, "You must think I'm crazy, singing *Jingle Bells* like that. It was Slip's favorite tune for some reason."

Nancy placed her hand on the note pads. "She mentioned that to me."

"Did she now?" Mary Louise reached for a rock that sat on the window sill and studied it for a moment, then set it back down. She hoisted the pot of water onto one of the front burners. "Here, the sink's free now. You can wash your hands, and then I'll put you to work."

"Slip spoke so highly of you, Mrs. Fordyke. You must miss her a great deal."

"Miss her? I haven't missed my sister since she was about six years old." She put a lid on the pot. "That rock over there on the windowsill is a geode. Do you know what that is?"

"It's a rock that has crystals on the inside, isn't it?" Nancy smiled, but the smile faded when Mary Louise turned. Bitterness seemed to have etched itself into the lines around her mouth and eyes.

"Yes. My mother found it years ago and had it on her kitchen window sill for the longest time. One day when I was about seven years old, it wasn't there anymore. I thought I might know what had happened to it, so while Slip was out collecting eggs, I looked under the bed. We both had treasure boxes. Well, you know about hers, since they brought it up at the trial. I'd never looked in hers before, but that day I found Ma's geode in the box."

"What did you do?"

"I left it there. But I knew where it was. I never looked in her box again until last Christmas, right after Dominick Kingsley was found murdered." She paused, as if wondering what more to say. She moved to the squat icebox and pulled out a two-pound chunk of cheese. "Here. You can make yourself useful. There's a knife in that drawer and a cutting board behind the sink. Cut this up in cubes. I'm making a big macaroni cheese pudding." Then she turned back to the stove. "She probably told you how close we were growing up."

"She did say you talked a lot in the bedroom the two of you shared until you got married."

"Did she tell you how often she was gone at night?"

Nancy glanced at the stack of note pads. "Yes, she did mention that."

"Did she tell you where she went?"

Nancy stilled the knife and rested it on the cheese. "Yes, she did."

"Uh-huh. I'll bet she ran you around the maypole with her stories. Let's try one of her favorites. Did she tell you about sitting with Old Ned, our horse, when he died?"

Nancy nodded.

Mary Louise nodded right back at her. "Really sad story, wasn't it? All about how she cried and how she sat next to him until his body turned cold."

Nancy picked the knife back up and cut one more slice of cheese into chunks.

"She never knew that I followed her out to the barn that night. She fed him poison. Did she tell you that?"

Nancy laid the knife aside. "Yes. The poisoned tomatoes that you and she had canned."

"Poisoned tomatoes? That's a good one. Horses won't eat tomatoes."

"She said she mixed in sugar."

"Sugar? Well, that's inventive, I suppose." Mary Louise turned to the pantry and pulled out a glass jar filled with macaroni. "Old Ned had gotten pretty feeble, and Pa was planning on taking him out to the swamp to shoot him the next morning. Right after we went to bed, as soon as Emmeline—that was our younger sister, she was just a baby at the time—as soon as she was asleep, Slip pulled off her nightgown and got into her best Sunday dress. She even put on those kid gloves of hers. I asked her what she was doing, and she said she thought that it must hurt to get a bullet through the head, and she felt sorry for Old Ned, so she was going to be sure he died faster." She scooped out handfuls of macaroni into a yellow bowl. Once the water came to a boil, she dumped in the pasta. Nancy watched her quietly. Mary Louise stirred the pot vigorously. "I tried to talk her out of it, but she wouldn't be dissuaded. I waited until she was out of sight, and then I climbed out the window and followed her down to the barn. She opened a can of rat poison—we kept it on a workbench just inside the barn door—and took a scoop of the poison to Ned's stall." Mary Louise wrapped her arms around her middle and bent forward as if she were in pain. "I wish I had stopped her, but I couldn't believe she'd really do it. I loved that old horse."

"It's true, though, that he was going to be put down the next day, wasn't he?"

"Oh, yes, but did she tell you what she did in the barn?"

Nodding, Nancy moved the knife and the cutting board over to the edge of the table and stook up to retrieve the first note pad. She thumbed her way through to the story of Maude and the tomatoes. "She said she brushed him gently and sang to him. Then she knelt beside him once he fell, and brushed some stray bits of sugar off his chin after he died. Then she cleaned up the stall and sat beside him until her father and brother showed up."

Mary Louise rolled her eyes. "She always could play people like violins. Too bad she never took up an instrument. She would have been very good at it."

"Except the piano."

"What piano?"

"You said it was too bad she never took up an instrument."

"That's right."

"She played the piano, didn't she?"

Mary Louise bent her head and looked at Nancy from under her furrowed eyebrows. "I'll bet you enjoyed her stories, didn't you?"

"Enjoyed isn't exactly the word I'd use. I'm a reporter, so I'm used to sad stories." Nancy rubbed her eyes. "I can usually tell, though, when someone is spicing up a story, embellishing it."

Mary Louise shifted an iron skillet from the back burner to the front. "Slip never played a piano in her life. There really *is* a sucker born every minute, and Slip was a master at finding suckers."

Nancy bridled at that, but then her reporter's instincts took over. "So, what *did* she do that night at Old Ned's stall?"

"I watched her. She twisted a long piece of straw into her hair and . . . danced . . . outside . . . his . . . stall." Her hands twisted in her dress, wringing the material into tight wads. "She *danced* up on her tiptoes while Old Ned was in his death throes."

"Danced?" Nancy choked on the word.

"Oh, yes. . . ."

Nancy picked up the knife again, gripping the handle so tightly she could see her flesh turn white. "She told me a completely different story," she finally managed to say. "She sounded so believable."

"I'm sure she did. That night, she had her knife in her hands, and I was afraid to let her see me. She finally got tired and went back to bed. Ned wasn't dead yet. That dear old horse who had carried us on his back when we were little, who pulled the wagon without ever balking, that sweet boy who always snuffled his wide nose in my hair, he . . ." Mary Louise lifted the edge of her apron and blotted her eyes. "I went in the stall with him. He'd fallen on his side. I couldn't help him. I couldn't make it better. I couldn't make it not happen. If I'd had a gun I would have put him out of his misery, stopped his pain. I thought about running to get Pa, but as I started to stand up, Ned let out a whimper, like he was afraid of the dark, and I just couldn't leave him. His eyes had rolled back and I knew he couldn't see me, but I rubbed his chin and that big curve of his jaw. I think maybe that helped him some, so at least he knew somebody loved him. At the end he was just shivering, little waves of convulsions running up and down his body. I hated her! I hated her so much; and right then, if I could have, I would have killed her and sent her to the hellfire she deserved." She pulled a hanky out of her apron pocket and blew her nose. "It was such a relief when he finally died. At least I knew he wasn't hurting anymore. I just lay across him with my arms around his big old neck and my face buried in his mane. . . . He had a star on his forehead. A white splotch. Pa told me once when I was little that an angel patted him when he was born and left that white mark. I believed him then, and I still believe it. So, I was the one who cleaned the stall. I was the one who sat curled up against Old Ned's body until Pa and Silas came down at dawn. I was thirteen at the time. Slip was twelve years old."

Nancy moved the cutting board back into place. "She told me a completely different story," she finally managed to say. "She sounded so believable."

"My sister always had a tale to tell about how this person or that was doing us wrong, and how she'd like to take care of them. That's how she put it—take care of them."

"Is that why she killed the Kingsleys?"

"The good Lord only knows why she took it in her head to kill them. Usually it was just animals."

"Like Old Ned?"

"Yes. And like Emmeline's birds."

Nancy sat down rather quickly. "She said Holden Smith did that. Shot them during a snow storm, which is why she killed him with his own shotgun."

"Oh, Miss Remington, you have a lot to learn about my sister Susannah Lou. It's true that there was a big snow storm that year, when Emmy was five—"

"I thought that happened when Emmy was sixteen?"

"No, she was just a little tyke. Pa helped her build some shelters for her birds. During the storm, after we all went to bed, Susannah snuck out the back door. Our window was frozen shut, so she couldn't use her usual route. We had extra people sheltering in the house that night. I'll never know why nobody except me heard a thing; by then the wind had died down to nothing. The moon even came out. I could see her through our bedroom window. I remember it kept fogging up from my breath, and I kept wiping it with the edge of my sleeve. She went to the first little barn-like shelter, reached in and pulled out something. I guess it was a bird, although I couldn't see clearly that far away. She wrung its tiny neck and reached in for the next one. She left a trail of bodies and went on to the next little house where it hung from a mulberry branch."

"What did you do?"

"When she came back to bed, I pretended to be asleep. Then I went out early in the morning, while Slip and Ma were cooking breakfast, and I picked up every little body I could find. Their feathers were beautiful, all different colors and patterns. I cried almost as much over those birds as I did over Old Ned. I hid their tiny bodies behind the barn under a pile of snow. And when Emmy woke up and went looking for her bird friends, I told her they'd all decided to fly to a warmer place. She was young enough that she believed me."

"So all this business," Nancy touched the note pads, "about Emmy never singing again was just . . ."

"Just a bunch of nonsense. Emmy was the happiest child I ever knew. I was glad I could protect her from knowing Slip's viciousness."

"Did you ever talk to Slip about it?"

"About the birds? Yes, and she just laughed at me." Mary Louise turned aside to lift the pot and pour the cooked macaroni into a strainer.

"I tried to stop her once, a long time before that, when she had a blue jay she was tormenting, breaking the bones in its wings. I screamed at her and told her I thought she was disgusting and that I was going to tell Pa about it." She poured the pasta into a bowl and added the cheese cubes Nancy handed her. "She threw the bird down on the ground and grabbed me by the throat—she was so petite, you'd never know she had that kind of strength in her. She told me if I ever told on her, she'd make me sorry for it."

"What would she have done?"

"Well, that was the trouble; she never specified it. She just said she would do something that would make me regret it forever, and I believed her. She whipped that knife of hers out of her pocket when she said it. It was a real threat. When she let me go, she picked up that wounded blue jay and yanked out one of its tail feathers. The poor little thing died right there in her hand, probably of fright. I could see why too. I was scared every day after that until I married Jasper."

"Did you ever tell him?"

"Tell him what? That I had a sister I didn't like who was mean to birds and horses?"

"He might have been able to do something."

"Like what? Tell her to quit?"

Nancy leaned her elbow on the table. "Maybe he could have talked to Jethro about it."

"Jethro? Jethro Fordyke?"

"Wouldn't she have listened to him?"

Mary Louise perched her left hand on her hip and waved the long-handled wooden spoon in the air with her right hand. "Just what did she tell you about Jethro?"

"That he was the best friend she ever had. That he asked her to marry him once, but she turned him down. That he was killed by a driver who ran over him beside the road when he was changing a tire in a rainstorm."

"That last statement was true, about his being run over and killed. I thought Minnie would never get over his death."

"Minnie?"

"Yes. Jethro's wife. She's a sweet little thing, bright as a button and smart as can be. Always did love Jethro, from the time she first set eyes on him."

"Was that Minnie Colper?"

"Yes. Did Slip tell you about Minnie?"

"She said Minnie was dead." Nancy fingered the pile of notebooks. "She said that she killed Minnie by pushing her off the Colpers' balcony."

"Balcony? That's a good one." She fiddled some more with the macaroni pudding, scraped it into a pan and slipped the pan into the oven beside an iron skillet that held the chicken. Nancy almost fainted with pleasure as the fragrant steam billowed forth. "A good one," she repeated. "The Colpers lived in one of the only houses in town that didn't have a second floor. Mrs. Colper had bad legs, and Mr. Colper built her a house that was all on one level. He was such a dear man."

Nancy closed her eyes and rested her head in her hands. She'd been a fool. If what Mary Louise said was true, and she had no reason to believe it wasn't, she, Nancy Lou Remington, so proud of her credentials as a newspaper reporter, had been completely hoodwinked. "Slip told me that Minnie was engaged to Jasper."

"Jasper? My Jasper? That's another good laugh. Jasper and I married a year before Minnie and her parents moved to town." She stepped closer and patted the top note pad on the pile. "I think my sister played you for a fool." Her smile took some of the sting out of the words. "She played a lot of people for fools, Miss Remington. That was just her way. Slip would rather tell a lie than breathe. She had a way of figuring out what a person wanted to hear, and then she'd string them along with a tale as tall as the hotel on Main Street."

"Did you ever tell Emmy—after she got older—who had slaughtered her birds?"

"No. If I had, Emmy probably would have killed Slip. Maybe I should have let that happen, but I didn't want Emmy to end up in prison."

"The way Slip did."

"Slip deserved it. I have no doubt that she killed Button and Dominick Kingsley."

"But did she ever tell you why she did it?"

"Even if she had, how could I have believed her? My sister was so far gone in her own little world, with herself at the center of it, that she stopped caring what was true and what was false a long time ago."

Mary Louise lifted the heavy lid and stirred something that smelled like green beans. "I think she got to where she believed her own stories."

"I need to ask you something." Nancy shuffled through the stack and pulled out two note pads. She opened the first one just as Sheriff Fordyke came through the kitchen door.

"Good evening, miss. Didn't I see you in the courtroom during Slip's trial?"

"You have a good memory."

"Dear, this is Miss Remington, from the *Clarion*. She wants to write Slip's story."

The sheriff rubbed his hand across his chin. Nancy could hear the rasp of his beard-stubble. She could tell his beard would grow in darker than his almost yellow-white hair.

"Another reporter? There were three here before breakfast."

"And another one showed up about three hours ago, dear. I sent him packing, him and his ridiculous boutonniere."

"Nothing personal, Miss Remington, but I'm not interested in talking to a reporter. You can write that justice was done. You can quote me on that. Now," he turned and gestured down the hall toward the front door, "although I don't want to seem inhospitable, I'll ask you to leave."

Nancy looked quickly at Mary Louise, who remained silent. "I'm sorry I bothered you, Mrs. Fordyke." Headlines loomed in front of Nancy's eyes. REPORTER EJECTED. ALL LIES, NO STORY. REMINGTON FAILS. Her chin lifted. "Sheriff . . . sir . . . it's important to me to write the truth, and I have some serious questions about the information Miss Packard gave me."

He frowned. "She talked to you?"

"Yes, sir. I interviewed her in prison. During the trial," she added. "Her attorney approved it."

The sheriff looked over at his wife. "Didn't I always say Pinkney was a fool?" He raised his index finger and turned back to Nancy. "You may *not* quote me on that."

"Yes, sir . . . I mean no, sir. I won't." Sensing a slight opening, she asked, "Wouldn't you want me to report the truth?"

Mary Louise came to the rescue. "She's been telling me some of what Slip said, dear. You may want to hear this."

"Yes, sir. From what your wife has already told me, you may find this entertaining."

"Or appalling," Mary Louise put in.

"If it has to do with Slip, I'm sure it will be a little bit of both. You're planning to write her story?"

"Her *whole* story. We thought of serializing it, but I needed to check some facts first, and I'm coming up with more questions than answers."

Sheriff Fordyke grinned at his wife and hugged her to his side. "I'll just bet she is, wouldn't you say?"

"Where is Allon? Couldn't he come tonight?"

"No, he had some reports to write and wanted to get them finished. Two of the keys are bent on the typewriter, and Mrs. Connors has just about given up, so Allon's going to try to straighten the keys. Otherwise he'll never get his reports typed, even if he does get them written." He chuckled as he removed his tie. "You don't mind if I get a bit more informal, do you, Miss Remington?"

"Go right ahead. I'm the one intruding on your evening."

"It's no intrusion," Mary Louise said. "You'll stay to eat with us—there's plenty, especially since Allon isn't here—and maybe you can read your notebook to both of us."

"I'll start with the last one first, if you don't mind. I think it will help to explain what's been going on."

"Notebook, you said?"

"Yes, dear." She pointed at the pile. "Miss Remington has Slip's stories all written down."

"That should be educational, but let's wait till after we eat. I don't think I can deal with Slip's ideas on an empty stomach, and that chicken smells mighty inviting." He winked at his wife. "I don't know how I ever got by while you were gone."

"Neither do I, considering the shape of the kitchen when I got back."

"I washed the dishes."

"You forgot the counters. And the floor. Now, go get yourself washed up. We're having macaroni pudding, green beans, and fresh bread to go with the chicken."

"I must have died and gone to heaven."

"Yes, dear. Wash up, and it'll be ready."

Nancy moved all the note pads onto the sideboard beside her handbag. "What more can I do to help?"

"You've been sitting here for quite a while. I imagine you need to take a little break?"

Nancy crossed her eyes. "Yes," she said. "I'm getting a bit desperate."

"The outhouse is right down the back path. There's plenty of paper. We just got a new Sears & Roebuck catalog, so I put the old one out there."

"Thank you. I'll be right back."

"Hattic was Estelle's dearest friend," Mary Louise said later after Nancy stopped reading. She wiped her eyes with the edge of her apron. "That much of the story is true. She *was* killed when an old hickory tree snapped off in a heavy wind."

"Was Slip with her at the time?"

Mary Louise glanced at her husband. "I think she was. I was still pretty little myself. I seem to remember that Slip came running back home all in a panic. After that everything was such a blur. And I'm not surprised that Mrs. Turner gave Slip the gloves. Slip was so quiet; she always made a good impression on adults. I don't remember her leaving the room that day, but I suppose she could have easily. Part of the reason we kept calling her Slip was that she could glide in and out of a room without anybody ever noticing."

Sheriff Fordyke studied his wife. "You don't suppose . . ." He formed his left hand into a fist. "You know, before he retired, Sheriff Lundstrom told me something that he thought I might need to know. He told me that Hattie Turner had been molested. Your father could see that right away when he found her, and he told the sheriff. Hattie was already dead, but she'd definitely been . . . well, the sheriff hoped that I might find out someday what happened, and he told me to string up the bas. . . the man who did it and left her there to die."

"You think that if Slip was right about what happened to Hattie, then she might have been . . ." Mary Louise stumbled over her words, ". . . maybe she didn't hide well enough. Maybe he caught her and . . ."

"Yeah. That's what I'm wondering about. It sure might explain a lot of her anger."

"My poor baby sister." She rocked quietly for a moment. "No wonder she was such a mess."

"Wait a minute, Mrs. Fordyke. You can't be certain."

"It sure sounds like it. Look at how many times there she said she'd stayed hidden, almost like she was trying to convince herself that she *had*."

Nancy looked back at her shorthand. "She said—here it is—*I was too scared to say anything about that man—terrified that if I told, he'd think I owed him something more too.*" Nancy chewed at her lower lip. "If she was afraid he might think she owed him something *more*, then maybe he had already . . .*"

Jasper stroked Cheyenne's head, then pulled out a pipe and spent a few minutes filling it and lighting it to his satisfaction. He pointed the stem at Mary Louise. "I think that tomorrow I'm going to have a talk with your brother-in-law."

"Who?" Nancy set the note pad on the couch cushion beside her.

"Franklin."

"But wasn't he mauled by a bear when Slip was seventeen?" She held up the first note pad. "She told me she killed him and then a bear ate him."

"Another one of her flights of fancy," the sheriff said. "But don't you think it just might be possible that she spent a good deal of her life wishing she'd been able to do that to *that man*, as she called him."

"You know, Jasper dear, thinking back, as we grew up I never did once hear her call Franklin by name, and come to think of it, she never went to Estelle's house by herself. She always talked me into going with her." She pulled her knitting out of a bag sitting beside her rocking chair. "You might be right, but how could you prove it after all these years?"

Jasper shook his head. "I think I'm going to have to sleep on it. Maybe I'll get an inspiration. First, though, I'd like to know what else she told Miss Remington."

Nancy reached past her handbag and picked up the other steno pads. "It's rather lengthy," she said.

"We're not going anywhere." He leaned back in his chair.

Halfway through the Maude story, Mary Louise laughed. The dog snorted, yawned, and shifted her head from one of Jasper's feet to the other. "Sorry I disturbed you, Cheyenne." She smiled. "Lord, yes, that county fair we missed. I remember that, but it had nothing to do with the tomatoes being ruined. They were just so ripe, full to bursting with juice. In fact, the ones I'd planned to enter in the fair actually *did* burst when I went to pick them that morning. That's the only reason we stayed home to can. Slip was mad as a hornet at having to miss the fair. She complained all day long. There wasn't anything for me to enter, though, and we didn't want the tomatoes to go to waste."

Nancy read a bit farther. When she got to the part about Parsella's death, Mary Louise let out a whoop. "Land sakes, whatever was Slip thinking?"

"You have to admit, my dear, it shows a good deal of rather gruesome forethought."

"Jasper, she was crazy out of her head and you know it."

Nancy broke into their repartee. "What really happened to Parsella? Is she still alive?"

Mary Louise's smile faded. "No, I'm afraid not. She died in childbirth. Their fourth child it was, a little girl. The baby died too." She lowered her head, but Nancy could see frown lines deepen in her forehead. "Slip was there, you know. She delivered that baby girl." She looked at her husband. "Do you think . . ."

"I don't know. It could be, but at this point it's too late to tell one way or the other."

"Trip died too, right about that same time." Mary Louise rubbed the back of her neck. "That was Ronald's old hound dog. Ronald said he thought it looked like poison."

Jasper leaned forward and rested his hand on Cheyenne's head. The old dog thumped her tail twice and went back to snoring.

Nancy waited while the couple looked at each other. "What about Parsella's husband Ronald?"

"Ronald," Jasper took up the tale, "took Dottie Farraday for his second wife. He needed somebody to raise his three sons."

Mary Louise nodded. "She was young, but she's been a good mother to those boys."

"The Dottie Farraday who was Maude's friend?"

"That's right, and before you ask, yes, they did do that twirling around and dancing in the schoolroom. Everybody thought it was a fun joke," Jasper's face turned grave, "but I guess Slip didn't see it that way." He pointed to the note pad. "Did she kill off Dottie in there?"

"No. She poisoned Maude and then drowned her headfirst in the privy."

"I'm sure Maude would get a big kick out of hearing how she died," Mary Louise knitted a few more stitches, "but I'm not going to be the one to tell her." She looked up at Nancy. "Oh, you poor thing, are you all right?"

Nancy rummaged in her pocket—her deep pocket—for a hanky. She pulled out one with a lace edge. "I feel like such an idiot. If I'd sent these stories to George—he's my editor—I would have been the laughingstock of the newspaper industry. Here I thought I had a first-class, prize-winning news story, and all I have is the ravings of a lunatic—oh! I'm sorry; I didn't mean to put it that way."

Mary Louise leaned forward, as if to give her words more weight. "Don't feel too bad about it. She *was* messed up more than any other person I've ever known. Maybe something did happen to her out there in that clearing, and maybe, because she was so little, she grew up warped somehow. I'm not saying that excuses what she did, but heaven knows I've spent many years hating her."

"You don't mean that, honey."

"You hold your tongue, Jasper Fordyke. I most certainly do mean that. I've told you about every spiteful thing she ever did. You know how hateful she was. But I guess now I'm a little bit sorry that we could never do anything to maybe get her some help. Oh, fish! I dropped a stitch." She fiddled with the yarn for a moment. "Things might not have turned out the way they did if we'd known."

Nancy tapped her pen on the edge of the note pad. She always thought better with a pen in her hand. "This must be why she kept making me promise not to visit Baynard's Mill and not to bother her family."

Mary Louise's laugh had not a shred of humor in it. "I'll just bet she did. She wouldn't want something as inconsequential as the truth to mar your story."

"I know your sister was messed up, my dear, but even I am

surprised at the depth of your cynicism." He waved his left hand, the one without the pipe, in the air. "What do you think she had against Miss Remington here, to feed her all these lies?"

Mary Louise shook her head as Nancy spoke. "I thought she liked me, and trusted me."

"The way you trusted her?" Mary Louise rested her knitting in her lap. "Maybe that was the problem. She couldn't abide people who had a sense of integrity."

"She called me a city girl."

"Hmm." Mary Louise slowed her rocker. "Did she complain about how hard she had to work growing up?"

"Yes, she did."

Mary Louise bent her head to one side. "That girl could hide out in the barn any hour of the day. We were always after her to finish her chores. It's a wonder the old homestead didn't fall down around her ears when it was just her and Pa left. Even something as simple as washing the dishes after they'd eaten seemed to be too much for her to manage."

Jasper lit his pipe yet one more time. Nancy sniffed quietly. "May I come back tomorrow and talk about more of . . ." she indicated the pile of note pads, ". . . of these? I don't think I can take any more tonight."

"Of course. You're welcome anytime. Do you have far to go? Where do you live?"

"Statesville."

"Oh, that's fifteen miles, and you don't want to be driving on those holey roads in the dark."

"Holy roads? What do you mean?"

Mary Louise laughed. "Full of holes. Holey."

Jasper swung his head from side to side, like an old horse nosing familiar food. Nancy was sure he'd heard that one before.

"Don't pay any attention to me. I get silly sometimes. But it *is* too far for you to drive this late. Why don't you stay the night? I'll loan you a nightgown and a robe. We have plenty of room now that the children are up and grown."

Nancy thought about driving back to her dark apartment. If she had Toodle, she'd never be able to leave her alone this long. But, of course, she *didn't* have Toodle. Yet. "Thank you. I'd be happy to stay." Cheyenne's feet began to jerk, the way they do when dogs are chasing something in their dreams, and the three people laughed.

SUSANNAH SWINGS

By Nancy Remington

The State Capital: In one of the swiftest carriages of justice ever seen in this state, twice-convicted murderer Susannah Lou Packard was executed by hanging early yesterday morning at an undisclosed location. The Governor denied clemency. District Attorney Paul W. Stevens read from a prepared statement yesterday, stating that "Miss Packard's execution brings to a close the nightmare of a one-woman vendetta against two of the most powerful political figures in the history of this state." Miss Packard had been convicted of the brutal 1926 poisoning of State Senator Button Kingsley and was sentenced to life imprisonment. Her subsequent conviction for the grisly December 1931 murder of State Representative Dominick Kingsley earned her a death sentence. Miss Packard's attorney declined to be interviewed, but reliable sources indicate that no appeal other than the request for clemency was ever instituted.

Representative Kingsley's limp and bloody body was found by his secretary, Mrs. Anna Brown, when she returned from lunch two days before Christmas last year. "I'll never enjoy Christmas again," she told the Clarion. Mr. Kingsley's throat had been cut, and his wristwatch was discovered two days later by Baynard's Mill Sheriff Jasper Fordyke in the bedroom of Miss Packard.

Chapter 19 - Baynard's Mill

Nancy's underwear wasn't quite dry yet. She'd washed it out in the kitchen sink and hung it behind her bedroom door overnight. Mary Louise had loaned her a long chenille bathrobe, though, and had apparently explained her dishabille to Jasper, for he didn't blink an eye when she walked up to the kitchen table, where Cheyenne sprawled with her head on the sheriff's feet. He set aside the newspaper he'd been reading, but not before Nancy saw the usual lurid headline. George had been at it again. She wondered what extra touches he had added to the simple, one-paragraph story she had called in yesterday after the execution, before she'd driven to Baynard's Mill.

Except for his tie, Jasper was dressed and ready to go. "Sorry," Nancy said. "I waited until I heard someone leave. I wasn't expecting . . ."

"Don't you worry about anything. I've seen women in their nightclothes before."

Mary Louise harrumphed from her place at the stove.

"I was referring to my sisters, my dear. I've seen them in all sorts of casual wear."

Mary Louise held up a big glass jar half filled with what looked like milk. "Our youngest son just brought by a jar of fresh cream. That's who you heard leaving. He tends to slam the screen door, no matter how many times I've told him not to." She eased the jar into the icebox. "Sit down, Miss Remington. I hope you slept well."

"Yes." *I tossed all night, wondering what else Slip had lied about. No story. No prize. No nothing. Just a wasted two and a half weeks.* "Yes, thank you. I was very comfortable."

The sheriff cleared his throat. "I think you're just being polite. People who sleep well don't wake up with dark circles under their eyes."

"Jasper, that's not a kind thing to say."

"I think Miss Remington needs to know that it's safe to tell the truth in *this* house."

"Sorry." Nancy pulled out a chair, making sure she avoided Cheyenne's tail. "You're right, Sheriff. I hardly slept at all. The bed was comfortable, but my mind wasn't."

"Miss Remington . . ."

"Would you call me Nancy?"

"Yes. Thank you." Mary Louise filled three plates and set them on the table. "Nancy, I . . . we . . . we don't want you to feel bad about being fooled by Slip. She was a master at leading people on. We got so used to it that we just never believed anything she ever said to us. Maybe we weren't fair to her, but she was a hard person to live with."

Jasper raised a hand. "Hold on. I plan to say grace and then to eat this fine breakfast without thinking about Slip. We can talk about her afterwards. Allon should be by in a little while to pick me up. So let's eat." He bowed his head. "Thank you for this bounty and for the loving hands that prepared it. Help us to be grateful for all the good that we have and for all the ill that we have avoided. Amen."

Unusual blessing. Nancy picked up her fork as the kitchen door clattered open.

"It's a beautiful morning, Mother For . . . Whoops!" A tall young man with a rapidly reddening face stared at Nancy.

She clutched the robe closer at her neck. "Hello," she said.

Mary Louise laughed. "Miss Nancy Remington, meet Deputy Allon Mercer. Allon dear, we haven't finished breakfast, as you can see. Can you sit and have some coffee with us?"

Allon pulled himself straighter, but seemed unable to speak.

Jasper set his fork down. "Allon can't stay for coffee. He needs to go on in to work. Something's come up, Allon, and I'm going to be doing some research here this morning. I'll come down to the station as soon as I'm finished. If you need me, you can telephone me. That's what those contraptions are for. Just don't say anything on the line that you don't want everybody in town to hear about. You know how Miss Emily does love to spread news."

"Research, Sir?"

"Yes. Miss Remington is a newspaper reporter."

"I'm with the *Clarion*," Nancy put in.

"She's helping us with some background on the . . . um . . . the Kingsley murders."

"I thought that was all taken care of, Sir." Nancy could almost hear the capital letter. Allon was a bit less red-faced, but still as rigid as a fireplace poker.

"Some new evidence has come to light, and Mrs. Fordyke and I want to talk with Miss Remington about it. Now, you scoot on downtown and I'll see you later."

"Yes, Sir. Goodbye, Miss Remington. Goodbye, Sir. Goodbye, Mother Fordyke." He turned to leave. Turned back. "Goodbye, Miss Remington."

Nancy inclined her head, but held onto her robe.

Mary Louise watched his retreating back. "Well, now," she said after the screen door slammed shut. "Who would have thought it?"

Jasper narrowed his eyes. "Who would have thought what? And what's gotten into Allon? He looked like he'd seen a ghost."

Mary Louise smiled. "Men," she said, but that word was full of affection. "You can let go of your collar now, Nancy, and start eating."

Jasper tapped the newspaper. "After meeting you, Miss Remington, I have to say I'm a bit surprised at the news stories you write. You don't seem like the sensational sort."

She set him straight on that with no hesitation whatsoever. "Look at that," she said after reading the offending article. "I never interviewed this Mrs. Brown. George probably called her, got the quote, and stuck it in where he thought it would have the greatest effect." Exasperation leaked out of her in a big sigh. "I wish I had some control over what gets printed under my name."

Mary Louise passed her the bacon. It was deliciously crispy.

Streams of early morning sun filtered through the lace curtains and settled in puddles on the wide oak floorboards of the sitting room. A cool breeze wafted in, carrying the scent of roses and the sound of birds chattering in the nearby elm tree. Nancy went back to the same end of the couch where she'd sat the night before. "Where do you want me to start?"

Jasper patted Cheyenne's head and leaned back in his overstuffed chair. It looked as substantial as he did, Nancy thought. He wasn't fat, not portly even. Just a big man, sturdy. She felt comfortable with him. "What about where we left off? We can deal with the Franklin business later on, once we know the whole story. I doubt he's going anywhere after all these years." He sent one of those married-people-eye-messages to Mary Louise, and she nodded.

Nancy reached for the second note pad. She had taken the time to number and label them before crawling into her sleepless bed, so she wouldn't have to shuffle around to keep them in order. She flipped through the pages about Minnie. She already knew that was false. "There's a story here about John Anders. Should I start with that?"

Jasper picked up his pipe and apparently decided against it. "The mayor? Sounds as good as anything. Let's hear it."

Mary Louise drew her knitting bag closer to her rocker. "I'm ready."

Nancy read quietly for some time, then sat back expectantly.

Jasper nodded in time to his wife's rocking. "We did love Mrs. Anders," he said. "She really was like a grandmother. And those china figurines of hers—we played with them all the time, until Slip was over there one day and broke one of them. I wondered at the time if she did it on purpose, but I hadn't actually seen it happen, so I couldn't be sure. Still, it was the sort of sneaky thing Slip tended to do. After that, Mrs. Anders began to fuss at us a bit, so we pretty soon stopped playing with them. They were hollow, of course, and easy to tip over."

"No rocks?" Nancy asked.

"No rocks. And no money either. John Anders was already loaded with cash when he came home to Baynard's Mill after the war. I often wondered if he'd gotten it gambling—he was that sort of man—but he settled down pretty well."

"What about the library?"

Mary Louise spoke up. "Mayor Anders . . . well, he wasn't the mayor at that time yet. He didn't run until about fifteen years ago. He did buy Mr. Stybard's general store, though. And when the little library next door to it started bursting at the seams, he bought it too, and put up the money to build a brand new library. Even designed some rather pretentious white columns in front of it to hold up a little roof over the porch. He calls it the portico. It looks sort of Greek, wouldn't you say, dear?"

Jasper nodded, but the way he screwed up his mouth led Nancy to believe he didn't agree. "The two of you should take a turn through town later on today. My wife makes an excellent tour guide."

Nancy looked back at her notes. "What I don't understand then, is why Slip would have wanted to think about killing John Anders. What did he ever do to anger her?"

Mary Louise rocked. The sheriff picked up his pipe again, scooped tobacco from a ceramic humidor on the small stand beside him, and tamped it down with a fat wooden dowel. "What do you think, my dear?"

She knitted a few more stitches. "Remember that time he caught her trying to steal a pair of scissors from his store? Maybe that was it. We never could figure out why she'd steal a pair of scissors. She couldn't sew worth a hoot."

"She couldn't sew? She told me she made all her own clothes, so she could have those deep pockets she wanted."

"Nonsense. Oh, the pocket part was true enough, but that was Ma's doing. She and Lucy and Estelle always did the sewing. The only thing Slip seemed to do well was fishing and cooking, and I think it was only because she enjoyed killing things and chopping them up. So it didn't make sense for her to steal scissors."

"If I recall, though," Jasper said, "Mr. Anders never filed a complaint." He lit the pipe and puffed to get it going. "I wasn't a deputy yet, but I probably would have heard about it if he had. I used to hang out at the sheriff's office as often as I could get away with it."

"You're right. I remember he stopped by the house one evening and told Ma and Pa that he'd caught her sneaking out of the store with some scissors in her pocket. Pa liked to have had a fit. He never would put up with anything like stealing."

"So, John Anders embarrassed her when he caught her stealing from his store, and she wanted to kill him for it?" Nancy ran her hands through her hair and down the back of her neck, trying to still the ache.

"Seems so," Mary Louise said.

"She kept telling me she wasn't a thief."

"'Methinks the lady doth protest too much.'"

"Sheriff? Slip said that Jethro was the scholar." He started to reply but seemed to think better of it. "In fact, she said that you never read a book after you got out of school."

He chuckled softly. "Well now, did she? I'm the one who taught Shakespeare to both my brothers, and if you'll look around," he pointed his pipe stem at the bookshelves lining the sitting room, "you can see that I've kept up with the reading just a bit."

Nancy swiveled around on the couch and looked at all the other bookshelves behind her. This was no showcase library, with perfectly aligned volumes. The books leaned higgledy-piggledy against each other in a sort of comfortable disarray. Nancy had the feeling that every volume had been well-read and well-discussed. "I can't believe I was so blind. She told me once—where was that? Oh, I don't recall which story. It was in here somewhere." She laid the notepads back down. "She said she'd checked out *Middlemarch* from the library."

"Ah, *Middlemarch*," Mary Louise murmured. "One of my favorite books."

"Yes, mine too. But I should have seen then that she was lying to me."

"How so?"

"She made a disparaging remark about Jethro when he said something about the woman who wrote it."

"George Eliot?" Jasper said. "Everybody knows George Eliot was a woman."

"My thought exactly. But Slip didn't know that. She made fun of Jethro for his mistake, or what she thought was a mistake. I should have picked up on that."

"If you had," Mary Louise said, "she'd have come up with some perfectly plausible explanation."

"She had me completely in her power. Even though I saw inconsistencies, I didn't question them."

A Slaying Song Tonight

"The important point, Nancy, is that you *did* see that things didn't add up. That's why you're here, isn't it?"

Jasper sucked on his pipe for a moment and blew out a perfectly round smoke ring. Nancy was impressed. He watched the ring dissipate. "I think she was crazy enough that she might have done these things if she'd had the opportunity to, only she never got the chance. And let's don't forget that she did manage to kill two people. Maybe more that we're just not sure about."

Nancy balanced her pen on her outstretched index finger. "Like Parsella and her baby girl?"

"All those poor animals too," Mary Louise added.

"Maybe I'm lucky," Nancy said, and the pen fell into her lap.

"What do you mean?"

"All she did to me was lie and steal my fountain pen. The matron found it hidden in Slip's cell when she . . . when it was time to . . ." Her voice faded out.

"You can say it, Nancy. When they took her off to hang her." The rocking chair speeded up noticeably. "To think she might have gotten away with it. Makes me so mad I could spit."

Cheyenne lifted her head at the sharp tone and inspected her mistress. Jasper soothed the old dog with a few quiet words. "We would have caught her eventually, my dear."

"You didn't—" Mary Louise shut her mouth abruptly.

"You're right. I didn't catch her. *You* did. I had no idea she'd poisoned Button in '26." He scratched at his chin. "My wife is the one who cracked the case; both cases, in fact."

Disparate pieces of dialogue clicked into place. "The treasure box," Nancy said. "You're the one who turned her in, aren't you?"

"Yes. I'm not proud of that. I made Jasper wait with me behind a stand of cottonwoods until we saw everybody leave to go to Lucy's for Christmas dinner, and then we went in her bedroom, and I showed him where she kept the box. I was sure that she'd still keep it under her bed. Then we drove to Lucy's house and Jasper arrested her."

"Must have put quite a crimp in the family Christmas."

"My sweet husband wanted to wait till after we'd eaten, but I told him I refused to break bread with a murderer. He and Allon took her into town and locked her up in the jail cell."

"Did she ever get Christmas dinner?"

Jasper smiled. "My wife isn't nearly so hard-hearted as she'd have you think. She brought a plate of food for Slip and a much bigger one for Allon. Then she kidnapped me and took me back to Lucy's."

"So, Allon had to stay there with the prisoner on Christmas Day?"

Mary Louise inspected her, smiled, and said, "Yes, he did. A good man, that Allon is. It was a subdued celebration for all of us, that's for sure." She squinted at a knot in her yarn and spent a few moments untangling it. "I wish I could unravel the Slip knot as easily as this one. She's better off dead."

Jasper coughed out some smoke. "A Slip knot? You're witty even when you're bitter, my sweet."

Nancy wrote that down, waited a moment, then said, "It must have been hard to turn in your own sister."

The sheriff leaned forward and pinned Nancy with a hard stare. "You weren't planning to write about these conversations of ours, were you?"

"I . . ." she felt her ears turning red. "I thought . . . Yes, I suppose I was. It would be a good . . . almost like an epitaph for her." In the face of his obvious displeasure she ran out of ways to justify herself.

"We spoke to you in good faith."

"You knew I was a reporter. I didn't try to hide that."

"I didn't expect you to turn us into a circus sideshow."

"I told you I was here to get some questions answered. Your sister-in-law lied to me, stole from me, gave me a royal runaround which would have embarrassed me completely if I had printed it under my byline, but I'm conscientious enough to check my facts, even though she ordered me not to, and now you're telling me I can't write about her perfidy? How . . . how dare you?"

Jasper puffed on his pipe. Nancy grabbed a handkerchief. She hated it when she cried. It was so unprofessional. Mary Louise sat stock still. Cheyenne chose that moment to pass an appreciable amount of gas, loudly.

Jasper caught the brunt of it. His face turned as red as Nancy's. He spluttered a bit, and finally let out a roar of laughter. "Cheyenne, you did it again. Perfect timing."

"I'm sorry, Sheriff. I shouldn't have gotten so upset."

"No, no. I was the one in the wrong. I hate to admit it, but you've got a perfectly good point there. We did agree to talk with you. I just hate to have my wife's name dragged through this."

Mary Louise spoke up. "You think people will brand me as a traitor because I tattled on my sister? My sister the murderer?"

He bent over to scratch Cheyenne. Nancy was pretty sure it was just a ruse to stall for time. "When you put it that way, I guess I'm overreacting."

"I'm glad you want to protect me, dearest, but I *did* turn her in. I know you kept it out of court, but I would have been happy to testify if Mr. Stevens had called me as a witness."

"I can't even begin to imagine what the cross-examination would have been like," Nancy said. "Mr. Pinkney probably would have tried to prove that you weren't her sister or that you had a long-time grudge against her."

"We all know that would have been right."

Jasper leaned back in his chair. "You know, I agree with you that Pinkney is a horse's . . ." he looked sheepishly at his wife. "That is to say, he's ridiculous a good bit of the time. I'm just glad he didn't think to ask me how I knew to look for that wooden box. But in this case, what else was he to do? He had a client who was so clearly guilty. I think even he would have been embarrassed if he'd gotten her freed on a technicality."

"Pinkney as hero of the day? What a novel idea." Nancy clasped her hands and stretched her arms forward. "If you want to go on with these stories . . ." she looked a question at the sheriff and he nodded, "I think I need a little break first."

Mary Louise stuffed her knitting into the bag. "I'll bet I can beat you there first."

"Cheyenne, let's you and me stay here and wait for the womenfolk. Maybe they'll bring us some coffee on their way back through the kitchen."

"Shall we, Miss Remington?"

"I think we might be able to arrange that, Mrs. Fordyke; but first things first."

When Nancy returned, she folded up the John Anders note pad and looked through the next one. Pad #3 / Holden / Margie / Week of Trial she'd printed on the front. "We already know the business about Holden shooting the birds was a lie. I have to ask, though, is there a town fountain named for him, even though the school wasn't? And . . . did he get shot?"

One of those looks passed between Mary Louise and Jasper again, a shared memory, perhaps. Mary Louise pursed her lips. Jasper spoke first. "Well, now, the fountain. Yes. He did save those two boys in the blizzard. They were his nephews. Their father was dead, and the boys and their mother lived with Meribelle and Holden. He certainly risked his life going out to find them, although I think he never should have let them drive off to Statesville that morning with a storm so clearly on its way."

"Holden Smith had about as much sense as a pea pod."

Nancy had heard that same expression from Slip. She wondered if they'd both gotten it from their mother.

"The boys were hunkered down in a ditch. Holden took them to the Packard farmhouse for refuge. They stayed overnight, didn't they, dear?"

"That's right. They were all three asleep in our sitting room when my sister snuck outside to slaughter Emmy's birds."

"As to the school, no. It's still the Baynard's Mill Academy, although there was some talk about renaming it. You see, Holden Smith was the first person from Baynard's Mill to attend college. He was something of a legend around here. Smarter than either my brother Jethro or Able Markham, and that's saying something." He glanced over at Mary Louise. "Whether he had good sense or not is another subject altogether."

"So that business about the bad report cards was made up?"

"Sure was."

"What do you suppose she had against him?"

"Beats me," Jasper said, just as Mary Louise said, "I'll bet I know." He waved his arm at her as if conceding the floor to a fellow orator.

"Remember when Slip was in the spelling bee? She must have been twelve or thirteen at the time. Holden Smith was conducting the bee, and she missed a word halfway through the competition. Architect or architecture, I think it was. He told her that she'd gotten it wrong but that women couldn't build houses, so there was no need to be able to spell a word like that." Jasper cringed as Mary Louise went on, her voice growing in volume. "Every man and boy in the audience laughed."

"I didn't."

Her face softened briefly. "You have always been an exceptional man." She turned her knitting to a new row. "I tell you, I was ready to string him up by his thumbs, making a stupid comment like that. Slip was absolutely livid. She hates . . . she *hated* to be laughed at or belittled. I wonder if she just never forgave him for that."

Jasper looked at his wife's flushed face. "I don't think *you* ever forgave him, my dear."

"Well, no, I didn't. Even so, I've never considered shooting him with his own shotgun."

"Is he dead?" Nancy asked.

"Might as well be," Jasper said. "He went all doddery a few years ago. His wife, long-suffering creature that she is, has to feed him and clean up after him. Meribelle is a saint, if you ask me."

Mary Louise lifted her eyebrows. "Nonsense! She's a martyr, and she thoroughly enjoys all the pity she gets."

Jasper raised his hands. "If you say so, dear. I bow before your superior knowledge of human foibles, particularly of the female kind."

"You're laughing at me, but I love you anyway." Mary Louise looked over at Nancy. "You'll just have to forgive us. We get like this once in a while."

"I don't mind. I think it's nice."

"We've been this way for years," the sheriff said. "Not likely to change anytime soon. But I'm curious. What's next in the notes?"

"The rest of this pad is all the trial goings-on. That was the week I couldn't visit her because the trial went so late each day."

Jasper relit his pipe. Why did men even bother with those things? Pipes seemed like more trouble than what they were worth. He looked up at Nancy and she felt herself flushing. "You think it's foolish to fiddle around trying to keep a pipe lit, don't you?"

"Is what I think that obvious?"

"You're no poker player, that's for sure." He chuckled and

scratched at the skin just above his shirt buttons. A wispy tuft of blond hair showed there. "I think most women probably think about pipe smoking the same way. But this gives my hands something to do when my mind freezes up. Makes it look like I'm doing something important, when all I'm really doing is trying to think of something to say."

Nancy grinned and felt her flush receding.

He gestured toward her note pad. "You have quite an output there. You know, as many times as I've testified at trials, I've always wondered about how those poor court reporters keep going. They work nonstop. While everybody else is taking a break, waiting for someone else to speak their peace, those reporters have to stay right on track, writing away furiously."

Nancy thought about her own shorthand notes. "They probably have to stay up half the night transcribing their shorthand into English."

He rested the stem of his pipe against his upper lip. "I know in some courts they're using typewriters, and I suppose that's a bit faster, but all that clickety-clacking is distracting."

"I wonder if Blattnerphones would help."

Mary Louise looked up from her knitting. "What are they?"

Nancy explained the newly-invented recording devices as she thumbed back through the first notebook. "Here's a sketch I did of the court reporter on the first day." She passed it to Mary Louise, who took a look and handed it to her husband.

He studied it. "Looks like our houseguest is quite talented. May I?"

"Of course. You're welcome to look through it." She pulled on her earlobe. "I enjoy sketching."

"I can tell that." He held the pad so Mary Louise could see it. "Look how she drew the jury box. Every time one of them steps up there, they always grab hold of the top rail. Look at how the pressure from their hands has worn through the varnish. She shows it plain as day."

"You're the one who did the pen and ink drawings in the hallway, aren't you?"

He waved his hand deprecatingly. "Just a little hobby of mine. I think it helps me remember people better. Not a bad habit to have when you're in my line of work."

Mary Louise brought them back on track. "You were showing us the court reporter."

"Oh! Right." Nancy took note pad number five and looked through it until she found what she wanted. "Here is the same reporter while we were waiting for the jury to be led in on the day they gave their verdict."

Mary Louise glanced at it and gave it to Jasper, who said, "I'll be jiggered. Looks about a year older, wouldn't you say?" He held onto the pad and looked through the next few pages of sketches. "I hope the people at the newspaper appreciate your talent. Look at this, Mary Louise. Remember Willie Kenston, the bailiff? You met him that year I took you up to the capital."

"And we spent most of our trip in the police station and the court building," she said drily.

"It was historic," he countered. "All right, parts of it were boring. But Willie gave us both a tour of the offices in back." He gestured to the sketch and looked over at Nancy. "He has an awful limp. Said his leg hurt him all the time. He fought in Flanders during the Great War, and the battlefield conditions were terrible. Most of the men who were injured either died or ended up with amputated limbs. He never did get his leg cared for properly, but at least he didn't lose it. That was a miracle. Still, you've managed to show something of his spirit here. I can almost tell his leg's still hurting, just looking at your drawing."

Nancy smiled. "I did wonder why he limped, but I figured I'd never know. I had no way of talking with him. About all I saw him doing was leading Slip in and out, and doing the same for the jury." She thought back. "He had a nice smile, though. It seemed to fill up that wide face of his, I noticed it once when he was talking with the prosecutor before the judge came in. I should have sketched that."

She set those two pads back on the stack and held up number three. "The next person she killed was Margie McDonald. Do you want me to read it to you or just summarize it?"

Jasper rubbed his hands together. "This should be interesting."

"You know the name?"

Mary Louise harrumphed again. "I should say so. She—"

"Don't tell her," Jasper interrupted. "First, let's see what Slip did to Margie."

"I think I'm going to feel foolish again," Nancy said.

"Oh, don't bother worrying about it." Mary Louise turned her knitting to begin another row. "Think of it as a script in a play we're reviewing."

"Hmm." Nancy recounted the tragedy of Margie McDonald. The blackmail letter to Lucy, the confrontation with Barnaby, the trip to the state capital, the wort weed in the tea, the snippet of lace, the brief obituary. When she set down the note pad, Jasper and Mary Louise looked at each other and burst out laughing.

"Another lie?"

"Plenty of them," Mary Louise said. "That lace in her treasure box was a piece she cut off my dress after I went to a dance with Jasper before we were married. Slip was so angry about something—I never knew what for sure. I think it was that I had a new dress and she was going to have to wait for me to hand it down. It's a good thing she didn't get her hands on that dress *before* the dance."

"You would have looked lovely anyway, even with your lace in tatters."

Mary Louise grinned at Nancy. "He's making sure he stays on my good side."

"It's all because of your fried chicken," Jasper said.

"You know, Jasper, we ought to have a dinner party while Nancy is here and invite all the people Slip killed off. Nancy could read the accounts as the after dinner entertainment."

"I doubt we could fit that many bodies in here at one time, my dear, but I must admit it sounds like it would be an enjoyable evening altogether."

"So, who is Margie, really?"

They stopped laughing and echoed each other: "Barnaby's wife." Mary Louise added ". . . and mother of his seven children," as Jasper said ". . . completely alive and well." He guffawed one more time and went on, "Slip never did get along with Margie."

"I'm getting the feeling there were a lot of people she didn't get along with. Did she like anybody?"

Mary Louise nodded slowly. "She liked Joseph. He was our youngest brother, two years after Silas, and four years older than Emmy. Our mother had three stillborn children in there as well." Her hands paused between stitches. "Joseph was the only one who could get Slip to laugh."

Joseph. The one who brought his children to the farmhouse to get them safely through the flu epidemic but then lost his two sons despite his caution. What a tragedy. "I'd like to meet him."

"I wish you could. When he was just a boy—it was shortly after Old Ned died—he and Slip went fishing over at the mill pond. Only Slip came back. If she hadn't liked him so much, I think I might have wondered about his death happening so soon after that nightmare time with Old Ned, but I know Slip was genuinely distressed by his loss. It's the only time I ever saw her cry, so that must have meant something."

He died? Another lie.

Jasper leaned forward and laid his wide hand across his wife's long fingers. "I don't think we need to worry about Joseph's death. Sometimes sad things just happen." He seemed suddenly aware of Nancy's presence. "Joseph was a little slow, but Slip was always patient with him. He adored her. That boy loved to fish better than anything, and she'd take him to one of the ponds—we have several around here—as often as she could."

"Yes. We had a lot of good meals from the fish they caught. They never came back empty-handed." She rearranged the sweater she was working on and set the needles down. "That day he tripped on a stone and fell in. Slip had never learned to swim. She was dreadfully afraid of the water. Even so, she waded in up to her knees and tried to reach him, but the mill pond has a deep heavy current, and he was swept out of her reach."

The telephone jangled, and Jasper went to answer it. After a few moments he returned to the sitting room. "That was Mrs. Connors. Allon's on his way to pick me up. Why don't you two take that tour around town? Leave the note pads here; I don't want to miss any of this. You can stop in at the station when you're finished. I should be ready by then to come home for lunch."

He reached for his tie, put it on, and tightened it into place. Mary Louise stood up and adjusted his collar. "You men," she said. "Never can get your collars folded over right."

"That's why I keep you around, my dear. Whatever would I do without you?"

"You'd look downright disreputable, that's what," she poked him in the middle, "and you'd be skin and bones without my good cooking."

Jasper winked at Nancy over his wife's head. "Right you are about that." A car clattered into the front yard. Jasper kissed Mary Louise on the forehead, picked up his hat, and sketched a wave at Nancy.

"Men," Mary Louise said again as the screen door slammed. "Well, let's get that kitchen cleaned up and then we can go touring."

"Jasper's automobile isn't working right now. That's why Allon came by to pick him up this morning. Usually I just walk everywhere. We're only half a mile east of the town square. If you're not comfortable walking, though, we could take your car, I suppose."

Nancy glanced out the kitchen window. Light clouds left the sun a bit pallid, but it didn't look like an imminent storm. "Walking is fine with me. I'd just as soon not waste the gasoline. It's not too hot outside, and I think we can see more if we walk, wouldn't you say?"

"I'm glad you feel that way." Mary Louise put away the last of the dishes. "Thank you for your help."

"It's the least I could do. You're feeding me and loaning me clothes. I'm glad we're the same size." She patted the front of the borrowed dress. "And you're listening to all these useless stories."

"Not useless, Nancy. They're helping me understand my sister a little bit better. I could never get through to her when she was alive. Maybe now that she's dead, I'll be able to come to a sense of peace about . . . well, about everything that happened."

"Or didn't happen, as the case may be."

Mary Louise smiled. "As you say. Why don't we start with the old farm house where she and I grew up? It's two and a half miles southeast of town, but we can cut across the pastures and be there in no time at all."

Nancy tried to imagine the triangle, was only partly successful, and gave up. With her sense of direction it was lucky she'd found Mary Louise's house to begin with. "That's fine with me. I like walking. You just lead the way and hope there's not a tornado."

"What?"

"It's a long story."

"Fine. You can tell me as we walk." She bent to pat Cheyenne. "Do you want to come with us, old girl?" Cheyenne looked completely willing to accompany them, but when she tried to stand up, her back legs didn't want to cooperate. "Poor old girl. Why don't you stay here and guard the house while we're gone? Keep out the marauding hoards."

"Is she sick?"

"No. Just old. Some days she can prance around like a pup, and then she hits a day like today when she needs to lie low. Maybe the weather's in for a change. Cheyenne is like a barometer."

"I had an aunt like that. She died five or six years ago. Her rheumatism always told her when a storm was coming."

Mary Louise shook her head at Cheyenne. "You keep the storms away for this afternoon at least, you hear?" Cheyenne wagged her tail and settled back down in the corner.

Mary Louise slowed as they reached the rise of a small hill. "There it is."

Nancy drew in a long breath. The farmhouse was a comfortable weathered gray. Shutters a darker shade of gray sided each window. Gables protruded from the roof line, and two stone chimneys, one at each end of the house, guarded the roof like prairie dog sentinels. A wide porch wrapped around the two sides of the house that Nancy could see.

Mary Louise seemed to be as intuitive as her sister. "Our bedroom was on the back side, near the far end. The porch wraps around three sides."

Beyond and to the right of the house, the barn squatted in the farm yard surrounded with outbuildings, like a hen in the middle of her chicks. In back of the barn, Nancy saw a flock of crows settling into a tall tree. It looked just like Susannah had described it, misshapen somehow, as if someone had tried to graft one left-leaning tree onto the top of a tree that needed to go to the right. Even with all the leaves, Nancy could easily discern the outline. She imagined it would be even more dramatic looking in the winter when the branches were bare. A tree like that had to have a history.

As Nancy watched, a man left the barn and headed toward a

small shed. "That's Ethan Harbin," Mary Louise said. "The one who just came out of the . . . the . . ." Her voice dropped, and Nancy held her breath. Mary Louise passed a hand over her forehead. "We'll talk about that later. He bought the farm shortly after Pa died. We'll see how that fits into your collection of stories."

She started forward, but Nancy laid a restraining hand on her arm. "Slip never mentioned selling the farm."

"I don't know why not. We had to sell it when Pa died. The boys were . . . were all gone." Mary Louise paused, then went on briskly, "Slip could never have kept up that big old place all by herself."

"Where did she live?"

"Tom, our older brother, took her in." Her face went grim as her mouth settled into a thin line. "His wife Evelyn had to talk him into it. Evelyn was a saint to put up with her, if you ask me."

Evelyn, Nancy thought. *Evelyn Ingles, who was strangled with her own scarf? No, if she's married to Tom, she'd be Evelyn Packard.*

"But that's enough about the old house. We can either drop down there for a visit so you can see the inside, or we could head off to the right here and intersect the road."

Nancy might not have been very intuitive, but she could tell an implied request when she heard one. "I suppose I could always visit the farm later if I needed to. For now, why don't we head on into town?"

Mary Louise heaved what sounded suspiciously like a sigh of relief. "Thank you. I didn't particularly want to go in there. I always think I will be comfortable with the idea of visiting, and heaven knows I've come over this way many a time, hoping to be able to do it, but something always stops me. I think there are just too many ghosts."

"Ghosts?"

"You know. Memories that aren't all that happy. Once Ma died, and after Silas . . . there I go again, saying what I didn't want to talk about. Let's just say I haven't been back in a long time. Mrs. Harbin must think I'm downright unneighborly."

"Maybe she understands. If there were deaths there, surely she'd know how reluctant you'd be to stir those memories back up."

"I'm not sure she knows about how they happened, unless some busybody from town told her. There's a little family cemetery," she pointed, "on that far hill over there."

Nancy looked and saw a narrow path that wound up through a pasture carpeted in a purple haze of wildflowers. She could just make out a picket fence that surrounded a small plot of land. A solitary tree beyond the cemetery shaded five or six cows, and flowering bushes on the graves brightened the scene even more.

"The graves go back more than a hundred years. Mr. and Mrs. Harbin came here from the west end of Kansas. They got a right nice deal on the farm." She looked back in that direction. "There. See that one with the red bandanna around his neck? That's their oldest son. They have six boys and two girls, enough to keep the farm running smoothly. I'm glad they're taking care of it. These times make it hard to maintain a place."

"Do you ever miss the farming life?"

"I was ever so happy to be finished with it when I married Jasper. I have my kitchen garden, of course. That's enough for me."

"It's pretty good-sized, from what I could see."

"Oh, it's nothing like the gardens we had on the farm. All I have is onions and beans and cucumbers and squash." Her voice took on a liturgical quality as she half-closed her eyes. "Tomatoes and pumpkins. Lettuce and peas in the spring. Leeks and turnips and cauliflower."

"I don't see how you do it all."

"Well, it's not that bad. I don't have to take care of goats and chickens or sew Jasper's shirts anymore. I don't even have to churn butter unless I want to. I do love fresh butter, you see. What about you? Do you like fresh butter?"

"I've never had it. All we ever get comes from the market. I was pretty much raised on oleomargarine, to tell the truth, until the prices went so high because of those government regulations."

"Sometimes I think we have way too much government for our own good. But, child, you just haven't lived. We'll have to do something about you and real butter. I'm going to set you to work this afternoon." She laughed. "Don't look so terrified. There's nothing to churning butter the way I do it. Life is pretty easy now compared to farming. The one thing I made Jasper promise me was that he'd never try to farm." She walked a few more steps. "And that he'd give up chewing tobacco. I can't stand spittoons." She shuddered. "Vile things."

Nancy stopped short. Mary Louise sounded for a moment so

much like her sister that Nancy heard the echo of Slip's words. *Vile drink.* The echo was only an unfortunate coincidence of word usage. *Vile.* Anybody could use that word. She was not, definitely was *not* hearing Slip's voice.

"Are you okay, Nancy? Have we walked too far? Do you need to sit down?" Mary Louise led her farther along the lane. "There's a stile just up ahead. Here. You sit on the bottom step and catch your breath." Mary Louise rubbed Nancy's back and patted her hand.

"Mrs. Fordyke—"

"Mary Louise, please."

"All right. May I ask you something?"

"Why, of course you may. Anything."

"Did Slip ever," Nancy chose her words carefully, "ever touch anyone?"

"What a strange question." Mary Louise leaned back against the second step and looked out over the pasture in front of them. Wildflowers, seemingly cloaked with butterflies, sprung up along the fence line in glorious abandon, bright reds mixed in with hot oranges and sprightly yellows. One fence post was entwined with morning glories, another with cardinal vine, where hummingbirds darted after each other in an iridescent display. Small white wild asters danced in the sporadic breeze. "Did she ever touch anyone? I can't say she did. Even when we were birthing a baby, she usually left it to me to guide the babe out into the world. She hauled water and sponged off sweat and cleaned up blood, but I can't say I ever saw her reach out to comfort anyone." She clasped her hands on her lap and arched her back. "Whew! The older I get, the stiffer I get." She stood up. "You look like you've gotten some of your color back. If you feel up to it, let's walk some more while I think about this."

Nancy got to her feet, checked her sense of balance, and joined Mary Louise. "I was just wondering about it, because she and I never even shook hands."

"Mm-hmm. You know, I've never really thought about it, but one time when we were out gathering raspberries for jam, Slip tripped somehow. I rushed over to help her up, but when I grabbed her arm, she wrenched it away from me like I was some sort of leper. I remember thinking at the time that she had a fine way of thanking a body for helping her. But you may just be right. We slept in the same bed for years after Estelle left home to get married, but even on the coldest nights of the winter, Slip would curl up on her side of the bed while I shivered on my side. And if Emmy wanted to crawl in bed with us, Slip always made her stay over close to me. I just thought she liked bossing us around, but I do think you're right. She didn't like to be touched. At barn dances she always wore those kid gloves of hers. Square dancing is a lot of fun. Did you ever do it?"

"No. I never had the opportunity."

"There's a barn dance planned for Saturday night. You're welcome to stay, and we'll show you some country fun. But I'm getting off the subject. Nobody dressed up much for the barn dances. Nobody except Slip. She'd show up wearing those kid gloves of hers and, well, people thought she was snooty. But I think you have a point. She never wanted to feel anybody's skin on hers."

"That last day, before they moved her to . . . to where they . . . to where they hanged her, before they took her away," Nancy held out her right hand, "she touched my thumbnail, right here, with the tip of one of her fingers. It felt like an electric jolt going right through me."

Mary Louise frowned. "I wonder what it felt like to her? That may have been the only time she ever chose to touch another living soul with her bare skin. Now that I think about it, she never even held Joseph's hand when he was little. He'd tag along everywhere beside her. Sometimes he'd hold onto her skirt." Her lips pressed together briefly. "Maybe she didn't try all that hard to reach him when he fell into the millpond." She shivered, even though her face was flushed with the walking. "What a ghastly thought."

Nancy rubbed her thumb. "Let's walk a little faster. Where are we going first, now that I've seen the farm?"

"I thought we'd start at the school. The original building is still there, although they've added several extensions onto it as the town grew. Then we'll check out the town square. You can see the house on Havering Street where Minnie lived—the one without a balcony." She grinned. "Then we can stop by Barnaby and Margie's house."

"Oh, I couldn't do that. I don't think I could keep a straight face. I'd keep imagining all that Paris lace. I didn't ask earlier. Is Margie a seamstress, like Slip said?"

"I've never seen her sew a stitch, but she can knit circles around me any day."

"I'd still like to pass on visiting her."

"All right. We'll skip meeting Margie, but I swear we're going to have a party for all of Slip's victims. It doesn't seem right to celebrate her death, but by golly a dark shadow passed out of this world when she left it."

"Is she going to be buried here in town?"

Mary Louise's ruddy face paled. "Lucy and I never discussed that. I have no idea what they did with the body."

"Do you suppose Mr. Fordyke knows?"

"Land sakes, Nancy. You call him Jasper. He wouldn't mind. In fact, I think he'd be pleased. And yes, he might know. Funny he hasn't said anything."

They walked on, speaking of desultory things and allowing a number of comfortable silences between them. Before long, an imposing brick structure, rather obviously built up around a simple shingled house, loomed on their left. Nancy didn't even have to ask. A sign out front proclaimed it to be Baynard's Mill Academy. In smaller letters was the motto: *Let Knowledge Be Our Foundation and Wisdom Will Be Our Guerdon.*

"Stuffy, isn't it?"

Nancy agreed, but wasn't sure it would be politic to say so. "What's a guerdon?"

"Most people wonder that. It means a reward."

"You're right. It's stuffy. Wisdom doesn't necessarily come from knowledge."

"Book learning surely does add value to a life, though," Mary Louise said.

"You're right, but that doesn't mean you always know how to use it wisely." Nancy clasped her hands behind her and rolled her shoulders back, relishing the feeling of release when her spine popped. "Did you really have a Rectification List, the way Slip said you did?"

"No. I've always kept what I call my Thankful List. That's how I first knew I was going to marry Jasper. He kept showing up on it every single day. He still does." She thought for a moment. "Most days," she added.

"Is Slip the one who had the Rectification List?"

"You know, I don't think she ever put anything down in writing. Maybe she was afraid to leave a record of her thoughts."

"I can see why," Nancy said. "She figured she could always get some fool newspaper reporter to write down all those stories and save herself the effort. My revenge will be to burn the note pads."

"Nancy Remington, I think I like you a great deal."

The town square was just about what Nancy had expected. The pavilion in the middle of it was somewhat the worse for wear, times being what they were, but Nancy could still imagine the ropes of ivy wound around the white poles and could see waltzing couples in the candlelight. They passed around the pavilion and stopped at the fountain. No poodle in sight. No body. No handbag wavering under the water. It was something of an anticlimax. Nancy wanted to say something about Sylvia, but Mary Louise hadn't heard that story yet. So all she said was, "Nice fountain, but I don't see any dogs."

Mary Louise cocked her head to one side, started to say something, and closed her mouth. "I assume there's a point to that," she said a few seconds later.

"Oh, yes, but I have to wait for the sher . . . for Jasper to get home."

"Goody. I love a mystery. Who could she have killed in the fountain? The principal, perhaps? Mrs. Connors, perhaps? Mrs. Connors did not approve of Slip at all. Saw right through her, I think."

"Mrs. Connors?"

"She's the widow lady who works in the sheriff's office. You'll meet her in a little while." She walked a few steps farther. "I know. It was Lucy she killed in the fountain! Did she kill our sister Lucy?"

Now it was Nancy's turn to cock her head. "You are enjoying this entirely too much. Speaking of Lucy, though, Slip said that when she was arrested for Dominick's murder, the engagement between Lucy's daughter and Dominick's son was called off. I hope that was true because they mentioned it in court and I reported it in the paper."

"Yes. She told you one truth at least. As to why it happened, I think Arnold used the arrest as an excuse to weasel out of something he wasn't all that enthusiastic about to begin with. Being married might have cramped his style. Thank goodness they broke apart. I never did know what Lucy's daughter Caroline saw in the Kingsley boy. He was a charmer, just like his father—and his grandfather too, for that matter. You never knew Dominick Kingsley, did you?" She went on without waiting for an answer. "He had most of the women in the county hanging on his every word. Even Slip, although I know she would have denied it if I'd ever said anything to her."

They turned down Havering Street. One block farther on stood a modest one-story brick dwelling, surrounded by a green lawn that separated it from two imposing white mansions on either side. A stately woman in a silver gray dress stood on the porch of the first big house, watering a potted rose bush. Mary Louise sketched a wave at her, and she nodded in return. They walked on past and stopped in front of the one-story house. The walls were covered with ivy. She got that much right, Nancy thought. She looked at Mary Louise. Mary Louise was grinning like a leprechaun, and that pile of red hair—she caught herself—red-gold hair heightened the illusion. "You're right. No balcony."

"I don't know about you, Nancy, but my old bones need to be fed on time. Let's go roust up that husband of mine and get some grub."

"Sounds good to me."

Mary Louise led them by a circuitous route around a couple of blocks, past the rather pretentious-looking pseudo-Greek temple of a library and the squat, sturdy general store to the other end of the town square, where the sheriff's office stood like a rock between the Congregational Church and the town hall.

"Separation of church and state," Nancy muttered, much to Mary Louise's delight.

The Baynard's Mill Sheriff's Office, as the sign above the door proclaimed, was a sturdy stone-faced building. Aside from the bars on the windows, it looked fairly friendly with its pot of pink and red geraniums, mixed with orange zinnias, beside the door. "Who's the gardener?" Nancy asked. "Those colors sure do clash."

"Guilty as charged." Mary Louise laughed. "Don't look so stricken. I know what they look like, but I can't help thinking they brighten up the place, so it's worth the derision I get from the garden club ladies."

"You have a garden club here?"

"Yes, we sure do. Meribelle Smith started it years ago. That's why the town square is so pretty." She waved a hand in that direction. "They won't let me in the club."

She sounded so cheerful about it, Nancy wasn't sure whether or not she was joking.

"Was Slip in the gardening Club?"

"Heavens, no. Slip hated flowers. She thought they were useless." Mary Louise opened the door. "Head on in. I'll introduce you around."

Allon Mercer jumped to his feet. "Miss Remington!" He pulled out a chair. "Here. Have a seat. Hello, Mother Fordyke. Can I get you a glass of water, Miss Remington? The sheriff said you were touring the town. Did you like it?"

Mary Louise stepped in front of him. "Settle down, Allon. We came to see my husband. Would you tell him we're here?"

"Oh, I'm sure you can go right on back. I'll keep Miss Remington company."

Mary Louise tilted her head back and pinned him with a stare. "Allon. Go get the sheriff. Please."

"Yes, ma'am." He headed down a hallway, tripping only once.

"Is he always that nervous?" Nancy whispered so the two other people in the room wouldn't hear her. A gray-haired woman, most likely Mrs. Connors, the secretary who had been frustrated by the bent typewriter keys, sat with her hands on a piece of paper she appeared to have been feeding into the machine. She examined Nancy without apology or pretense.

"Only when you're around." Mary Louise gave another one of her leprechaun grins.

Before she could introduce Nancy, Jasper strode down the hall with his hat in his hand, followed closely by his red-faced deputy. "I'm famished. Let's go. I'll be back tomorrow, Allon, but maybe not until the afternoon. Call if you need me. George, I'd like that report ready for me to review it tomorrow." George nodded without saying anything. "Hold the fort and don't take any wooden nickels. 'Bye, Mrs. C." With that, Jasper ushered the women out the door and down the street.

"What on earth was that about," Mary Louise asked after about half a block. "And will you slow down? We're not in a foot race here."

"I'm sorry, my dear." He held out his arm, and she twined her hand onto his forearm. "I thought you wouldn't get here soon enough. Sylvia telephoned the station this morning to say that she'll be coming in to make a report about the vandalism at her house, and she expects me to take it to the city council meeting next week. I want nothing to do with that, so I told George to take her statement, get it typed up, and I'll look it over tomorrow."

Mary Louise turned to Nancy. "Somebody tipped over her outhouse—"

". . . and now she wants me to make this crime wave a town issue." He lengthened his stride. "If we hurry, we can be out of sight before she drives up."

"It won't take her long. She was on her front porch when we passed by." She turned again to Nancy. "She was the woman in the gray dress."

"The one built like a schooner?"

Mary Louise guffawed. "That's right, with a huge prow up front." She waited until she was under control, and turned back to her husband. "Slow down, dear. You're going to have to deal with her eventually. You know she'll be at that meeting to put in her two cents' worth."

"Then let her present her own case."

Nancy hadn't seen the sheriff looking so nonplussed before.

"I'll deal with her eventually," he said, "perhaps, unless I can wiggle out of it. But not today. Not when I'd rather be hearing about Slip's adventures. Did you discuss any of them without me?"

"Shame on you and your suspicious mind, Jasper Fordyke. Of course we didn't."

Jasper grabbed her hand before she could free her arm. "Just making sure."

They chatted amiably on the walk home. The fresh air and the exercise left Nancy famished, which was hard to believe considering the substantial breakfast she'd eaten just a few hours before. She helped Mary Louise make sandwiches from the leftover chicken.

Once again, Jasper said grace, ending with, "Save us, Lord, from women who want to run the town. Amen."

Mary Louise kicked him under the table. "Sylvia's not that bad, and you know it."

Jasper chewed thoughtfully. "You're right. She's not that bad." He winked at Nancy. "She's worse," he said, and took another big bite.

Chapter 20 - The Bull and the Poodle

🛷 **"I'm going to perk us some fresh coffee and we can take it** into the sitting room."

"I'll clear the table while you do that." Nancy stood, once again avoiding Cheyenne's tail, and ferried the plates to the sink.

"Just let those soak a bit in the dish pan," Mary Louise said. "We can wash them later."

Nancy centered the tin wash basin under the pump spout and piled in the dishes. Three good strong pushes on the handle, and water flowed into the basin. She added some soap powder for good measure and dried her hands on a white dish towel hanging to the right of the sink.

"I never even thought to offer you cream and sugar," Mary Louise said as she filled three big mugs.

"This is perfect. I drink it black. Slip did too, didn't she?"

Mary Louise picked up two of the mugs and headed toward the sitting room. "That's true. She did do a few things right."

Yellow rays of sun reflected off the mellow wood floor and danced up the rounded side of the pot-bellied stove. Nancy could imagine how cozy the sitting room would be on a winter evening, with the stove pouring out its heat. She was just as glad at the moment for the cold stove and the cross-breeze through the open windows. Jasper pulled the ottoman away from the couch and placed it in front of his chair before he sat down. "You weren't using this, were you?" Nancy waved her hand dismissively. Cheyenne padded in from the kitchen, looked at the human feet up on the ottoman, gave a big doggie sigh, and wriggled beneath the pipe stand. Jasper grabbed the humidor and a stack of books to keep them from toppling.

"Nice catch," Mary Louise commented.

He sketched a small bow, which Nancy thought was quite an accomplishment, considering the fact that he was sitting down, and released his hold on the humidor. "Who did she kill next?"

"Henry Markham. She hit him with a hammer and pushed him into the stall where his bull was penned up."

"Now, I doubt the hammer part, but Henry surely did get stepped on by that bull of his. Ground his belly to a pulp. He lived for a couple of minutes after they dragged him out of there, but he was so torn up, he didn't stand a chance."

Nancy grimaced. "Do you know if Slip was there?"

"I'll have to look into that and see if anyone saw anything before they heard his screams."

"Don't waste your time, Jasper. I can vouch for Slip on this one. That was when she had the chicken pox so bad."

He set his coffee mug next to the humidor. "Now, I don't mean to dispute your word, but how can you be so sure of that? It was years ago."

"I know that. I distinctly remember stopping by that day to see how Ma was doing. Ma nursed Slip through that whole time, and if I recall right, Slip was not an easy patient. Ma was plum wrung out. Slip had a fever something awful. She could barely lift her hand, much less a hammer, but that didn't stop her from complaining incessantly about the itching. We'd already heard about Henry—the word went around town like wildfire that morning—and I remember joking with Ma about Henry dying of the bull pox. She didn't think that was very funny, and as I remember, she gave me a lecture I'd never forget, all about respect for the dead and honoring our elders and all that. Later on, Pa told me that she'd laughed with him about how clever I was to come up with *bull pox.* I was a bit put out with her."

"You and your mother were too much alike. That's why you butted heads so often. Two redheads like that—"

"Jasper Fordyke—"

"Sorry, my dear."

Mary Louise lifted the unfinished sweater onto her lap. "Here we go again, leaving Nancy in the dust. You'll just have to excuse us."

Nancy grinned. "Doesn't bother me a bit."

"My husband's right, though. I was a lot like Ma. Emmy and I both inherited her red-gold hair, while Estelle and Lucy and all the boys took after Pa with his coal-black mane and quiet ways. Slip was the only one who didn't fit, with her hair that pale brown."

"Slip said she kept a piece of straw for her treasure box."

Mary Louise looked up at Jasper. He nodded. "There was a piece of straw in that box all right. Must have been her wishful thinking."

"It could just as easily have been that piece of straw from Old Ned's stable."

"What a horrible thought," Nancy said. "Would she really have kept something from such a dreadful crime?"

The sheriff ran his fingers through his hair. Nancy noticed how thick it was. "I wouldn't put anything past her."

"You know," Nancy said, "I kept wondering, during the interviews, why she had never reported any of these incidents to you before she took the law into her own hands."

Jasper covered a yawn with his blunt-fingered hand. "It's hard to report something you've made up, especially if the local sheriff knows the people involved, and your victims aren't even dead."

Mary Louise drained her mug. "I'm going to get a refill. Anyone else?"

Jasper stretched and yawned. So did Cheyenne, with no regard to the fact that she was under the small table, and Jasper had to grab the humidor again. The books toppled over. "Guess I should have read these and put them back on the bookcase."

"You're never happy without a stack of books at hand, and you know it."

"Maybe you should tell that to Cheyenne here."

Hearing her name, the old dog wriggled out from under the stand and plopped her head onto Jasper's lap. Everybody laughed. "I've been sitting too long. Need to stretch my legs. Let's all mosey out to the back porch with our fresh coffee and sit there for the next story."

"You call a walk to the back porch *stretching your legs?*"

"It sure beats sitting down the whole time."

Cheyenne sneezed and Mary Louise harrumphed. Nancy took one note pad with her and filled her coffee cup on the way to the porch. A slight breeze ruffled the leaves of the geraniums in their ceramic pots. Nancy combed her fingers through her hair and blessed the breeze.

Mary Louise paused in the kitchen and came out onto the porch a few minutes later carrying a large glass jar with about four inches of white liquid in the bottom of it. "You're going to learn how to churn butter the easy way," she said and nestled the jar into Nancy's lap. "Now, you just rock away all you want to. Eventually the cream will clabber." She must have noticed the bewildered look on Nancy's face. "That means it will separate the butter from the milky part of the cream. Once that happens, we'll deal with it. For now, just rock."

She went back into the kitchen for the coffee, then settled into her own rocker with her own jar of cream. Cheyenne lay basking in a pool of sunshine in front of Jasper. Nancy could have taken a nap, but she began to rock determinedly and opened the note pad. "I didn't read you the whole Henry story. She killed him, she said, because he beat Able so much that Able finally ran away from Baynard's Mill. Could that part of the story be true?"

Jasper's rocker squeaked the loudest, sounding like a field full of crickets on a summer evening. "Able did leave town for a while, but it was so he could go to the state college for—what was it?—two years?" He looked a question at his wife.

"I think you're right. As to the beatings, no. Henry was so scrawny and Able was so hefty, I don't think it would have been much of a match there."

"Then what did Slip have against Henry?"

More cricket sounds, joined by the shush-shush of Mary Louise's rocking chair. Nancy sat still until she remembered the butter churning. Finally, Mary Louise said, "He was a deacon in the church, and used to give the sermon when Pastor Jacobs was called out of town."

"Yes! She mentioned that." Nancy flipped back several pages and read the account of the cow in the church vestibule.

Jasper threw his arms up in the air. "Why didn't that woman write these stories down? She could have sold them to a magazine."

"No cow in the vestibule?"

"I'm afraid not, but I would have loved to see Meribelle Smith's face if she'd run into one." He chuckled some more. "She *was* in charge of the flowers each Sunday. Still is, for that matter."

Nancy started rocking again with a gentle squeak-squeak. "But what would Slip have had against Henry?"

"Honey, would you mind running in and grabbing my knitting bag for me, since you're so in need of a good walk? I know the answer to this one, I think, but I'd just as soon have something for my hands to do while I'm telling it."

"Slip told me you never learned how to knit."

Mary Louise opened her mouth, expelled a loud breath, and shook her head. "Will we ever get to the bottom of that woman's lies?" She rocked quietly until her sweater was in her lap. The cream gurgled endlessly. "Now, about why she hated Henry. I've been thinking about this ever since you started telling us about Henry and his bull. I know we told you that John Anders never charged Slip with stealing those scissors from his store, but he might have told Henry about it. Maybe he thought Henry should know, him being a deacon and all. But not long after the stealing incident, Pastor Jacobs was called out of town and Henry preached in his place. He talked about the eighth commandment."

"Thou shalt not steal," Nancy murmured.

"Exactly." She finished her row and turned the piece around, frowning in concentration as she changed to a different color yarn. "Whether or not he meant it for Slip isn't the point here. I think maybe she thought he had meant it for her. As far as Slip was concerned, she was the center of the universe. If Henry was preaching about stealing, it was because he knew about her. I remember she stalked out the side door that day, wouldn't even speak to him. I do remember being shocked by her actions. They were so rude." She looked over at Nancy. "In those days, we always filed by the preacher and thanked him for his sermon, no matter what we'd thought of it." She looked her question at her husband.

"You just may be right about that." He studied Cheyenne for a minute or so. "Wouldn't the world be an easier place to live in if we all acted like dogs?"

With that perfect coincidental timing that occasionally happens, furious barking broke out in front of the house. Cheyenne scrambled to her feet, and Jasper grabbed her before she could bolt down the steps. "Those mutts sound like they're at it again."

"The dog from down the road," Mary Louise said with a tilt of her head to the left, "seems to think that our front yard belongs exclusively to him, while the dog from up the road," her head tilted to the right, "believes it's his territory."

Jasper pushed Cheyenne down onto her side and held her there. "About once a month they have to dispute it until one of them backs down." He sighed. "Sometimes that takes awhile unless I go out there and douse them with a bucket of cold water." He sniffed the warm breeze. "I think I'll let them work it out today. Water's too warm this time of year, anyway."

Within seconds there was a yelp, followed by the sound of a noisy retreat.

"As you were saying, sweetheart?"

"Wouldn't this world be easier on everyone, I said, if we all were as relaxed as old Cheyenne here."

"Right." Mary Louise watched Cheyenne settle back into the sunshine. "What's the next story about, Nancy? Is it a good one?"

"The next one is Sylvia Telling."

Jasper slapped his thigh. "I just knew she'd get around to Sylvia. I can't wait to hear this."

"Now, dear, restrain yourself."

"Nope. I've been waiting for that woman to die on her own for years now. If Slip kills her off sooner, it'll be just fine with me. That way she won't make it to the council meeting with her complaints about an outhouse-tipping crime wave."

"You don't mean that, Jasper Fordyke."

"It's all right for me to wish, isn't it? Why don't you read us the whole thing, so I can gloat."

They listened in silence, except for the sound of the rockers, the cream, and the dog snores, while Nancy read. Occasionally Jasper interrupted with a laugh or a snort or a chuckle. "Mixed up prescriptions. Sounds just like her." Nancy read on. "A poodle. That's cute." Nancy read on. "The fountain," he muttered. "Good touch."

When Nancy settled back and tucked the pad under the jar in her lap, Mary Louise said, "Except for the fact that they turn the fountain off every winter so it won't freeze, I suppose it's a good story."

"That and the fact that little Prissy was Tom's daughter, not Joseph's, and she didn't die of the scarlet fever."

"She didn't?" Nancy smiled. "I'm glad. She sounded like such a sweet little thing."

"You're right," he said. "She grew up into a fine young woman. She married Able Markham's son. They live in that big yellow house down the block from the bank."

"I forgot to show that to her on our walk."

"Is that the one with all the honeysuckle covering the porch?"

"Yes, but we didn't pass it on our tour."

"That's where I stopped yesterday to ask directions to your house."

Mary Louise tilted her head. "I thought you said you came directly here from Statesville."

"Yes, I did."

"But Prissy and Able live way on the other side of town. You couldn't have come in from that direction."

Nancy looked at the jar in her lap, as if something truly interesting lay in the cream which was, she noticed, beginning to look lumpy. "I got turned around."

"You got lost in Baynard's Mill?"

"Jasper, do not make fun of her. This is a growing town. It's easy to get turned around."

"That's okay, Mary Louise. You don't have to make excuses for me. My dad always says I can get lost between the back door and the outhouse. At least I stopped and asked for directions."

Mary Louise looked sideways at Jasper. "Yes. Isn't that funny? Women are the ones who are willing to ask for directions."

"Now, honey, there's no call to bring that up."

"Would I mention the number of hours we spent roaming around the capital looking for that little restaurant you seemed to remember was somewhere near the courthouse? Would I mention that?"

He rubbed at the day-long whiskers beginning to darken his chin. "Little lady, what am I going to do with you?"

"You are going to take me back there sometime, because once

we found it, the food was delicious."

"Yes, ma'am."

"Of course, by the time we found it, I was starving, so anything would have tasted good."

Jasper cleared his throat. "So, you'll have to take another tour of Baynard's Mill tomorrow. You can deliver party invitations along the way to all of Slip's victims."

"Hush your mouth, Jasper Fordyke." Turning away from her husband, she said, "Please tell me you'll stay another night, Nancy. Allon will be here for dinner, and you can read us more of your stories. Who are the next ones?"

Nancy thought about it. She'd left the other pads inside. "Tawser, I think. No, wait. It was Kennon Bluett. Then Tawser Jones."

Mary Louise stopped rocking. So did Jasper.

"I think it would be a good idea if we stopped now and I spent some time getting dinner ready. You're welcome to sit out here, Nancy."

Jasper stood abruptly. "I think I'll take Cheyenne for a short walk, maybe up to the mill and back."

What did I miss there? Nancy cradled the jar of cream—butter?—in her arms. "I'll be happy to help. Just point me toward the kitchen and tell me what to do with this." Her voice was as subdued as Mary Louise's had been brisk.

Mary Louise bustled around the kitchen in silence, broken only when she gave Nancy curt instructions. Keep shaking that jar until the butter is in a firm lump. Pour off the liquid into this pitcher. Shuck this corn. Pump water into this pot; we'll boil the corn in it once the meatloaf is almost done. She screwed a grinder onto the edge of the counter and ground three pounds or so of beef. Two eggs. Some bread cubes. Salt and pepper. A little of the thin milk that Nancy had poured off the butter. All her movements were brisk. All her words were clipped. Finally, Nancy couldn't stand it anymore. "Did I do something to anger you?"

Mary Louise stopped and pulled her fingers from the meat loaf mixture. She used the back of one wrist to push a stray lock of hair off her forehead. "You'll have to forgive me, Nancy. I wasn't prepared to hear that name, and you just caught me off guard." She pointed with her nose to a pan standing on edge at the back of the counter. "Would you grease that pan, please?"

"Where do you keep your lard?"

"It's in the pantry. There's a jar right in front on the shelf about chin high."

The pantry was a model of good order. Canned fruits and vegetables, each with a date on the lid, stood in orderly ranks. Bins of potatoes and onions. If there was a Depression going on, it didn't seem to have hit here too hard. Maybe there was hope. She located the lard, greased the pan, and set it on the counter beside Mary Louise.

"Thank you." Mary Louise lifted the mixture into the pan and formed it into a loose loaf. "I'll be able to talk about this once I've settled down a bit. After dinner, as long as Jasper is here." Mary Louise raised her hands as if to rest her face in them. At the last moment she noticed the mess of meat and egg that coated her fingers. Shaking her head, she washed her hands and turned to face Nancy. "I truly do appreciate all you've gone through with Slip." She slid the meat loaf pan into the oven and eased the heavy door closed. "I guess I'm sorry she had to be alone at the end, but I couldn't go there. I couldn't watch."

"But—I was there. I drove home first, but then I had to find out the truth, so I came here that . . . that same day."

Mary Louise leaned back against the counter and fanned her flushed face. "That must have been hard. Was she . . . all right at the end?"

Nancy remembered the three crows taking flight from the scaffold when the trapdoor dropped open under Slip's feet. She saw the dawn light turning the undersides of two high clouds golden. She felt the pull of Susannah's kid gloves in her pocket as she stood there. She remembered how the guard had come over to take her arm and lead her away. *You don't want to watch the rest, miss*, he had said ever so kindly, as he guided her away from the sight of the dangling corpse and the sound of its urine cascading onto the paving stones. She took a deep breath. "At the very end, she laughed at me."

Mary Louise opened her arms, and Nancy burrowed into them like a newborn pup seeking warmth and succor. "You poor, sweet thing," Mary Louise murmured. "You poor, sweet thing."

The screen door banged twenty or thirty minutes later, and Jasper walked in with a thoroughly happy dog at his side. "You okay, honey?"

Mary Louise nodded. "The coffee's ready, if you'd like some."

"Think I'll get washed up a bit first. Cheyenne took me on quite a hike." The old dog heard her name and thumped her tail against his leg. "I do believe she'd be ready for another walk if I were willing to take her."

"She'll settle down soon enough once you sit. Still, she does look pretty perky for such an old girl."

"Where's Nancy?"

"She's in her room, crying, most likely." She brushed a stray bit of dandelion fluff from the front of his shirt. "She didn't understand what was happening, and I think we frightened her."

"I'm sorry about that. I didn't know what to say."

"Yes, well, I told her we'd explain it after dinner. You'll have to send Allon home right after dinner, dear. I don't want him to hear this."

"He knows about it."

"Yes, dear. Half the town knows, but I still don't want to talk about it in front of him, so you send him home early."

"If you say so."

"Nancy told me that she was there for the hanging. She watched it, Jasper." Mary Louise shrugged. "Why didn't we go?"

"I've seen hangings before, honey. It's not a pretty sight."

"But Slip was my sister."

"I'd say she stopped being your sister a long time ago. She was somebody who was born to your mother, but when was she ever a sister to you?"

"Still, we were about all she had left."

Jasper took two strides across the kitchen and lifted Nancy's stack of note pads in the air. "This is what that woman had left. These insane, destructive wishes of hers were what she chose. She could have had the love of a whole family. Have you forgotten how she threatened you? Have you forgotten how she mangled Emmy's birds? Have you forgotten how she danced while she was killing Old Ned? Have you forgotten?" He slammed the pads onto the sideboard, and moved back to her side, enveloping her in his arms. "Sweetheart, don't waste a moment of regret about Slip. She may have had reasons for going astray like that, but at some point she must have had a choice. And she made the wrong one. All along, she chose to turn away from you and the rest of her family." He bent and kissed her forehead. "We have us. She never could tear us apart, no matter how hard she tried. And I will not let that twisted woman hurt you from the other side of the gallows."

Nancy moved back from the edge of the door and tiptoed back to her room. She'd come out again in a few minutes and make more noise, so they'd know she was there.

Allon hung around after dinner, making all sorts of excuses for why it wasn't time for him to leave yet and repeatedly complimenting "Miss Remington" on the quality of her butter. Finally, Jasper handed him his hat, said, "I'll see you in the morning, deputy," and ushered him out the front door. He watched the young man's receding back and muttered, "I'll be jiggered if I can figure out what's wrong with him." When he turned around, Mary Louise was laughing at him. They walked back into the kitchen.

"He's in love, dear. It hit him like a fence post this morning. Didn't you notice?"

"I've noticed him making a fool of himself all day long."

"Yes, well, that's part of the process. He is totally, completely smitten and will probably return to his senses only after Nancy is long gone."

"Where is she anyway?"

"She went to the outhouse while you were getting rid of Allon. Now you behave yourself when she comes back."

"What do you mean behave myself? Would I do anything?"

Mary Louise stood on tiptoe for a kiss. "Men," she said.

Nancy paused outside the back door. Now what was she going to do? This was getting to be a habit. She eased back a few feet and scuffed her shoes on the porch floor. Mary Louise turned from her husband. "Let's go sit and get comfortable."

Jasper stood back to let his wife and Nancy precede him into the sitting room. Cheyenne had no such qualms. She led the way and plopped down in front of Jasper's favorite chair. The ottoman was back at the couch. Cheyenne was happy.

Nancy stepped around the dog and around the ottoman so she could curl into the corner of the couch, dropping her shoes and tucking her full skirt around her legs. She rubbed her hands and crossed her arms. What was she supposed to say?

Mary Louise rescued her. "Nancy, I'm right sorry about how I reacted this afternoon. You had no way of knowing that Tawser's name is not welcome in this house." She glanced over at Jasper, but he worked away at filling his pipe. "I think I'd like to hear the story of Kennon first, and then we can talk about . . . Tawser."

Jasper set his pipe aside without tamping down the tobacco. Nancy wondered if he was saving that step for the next time he wasn't ready to say anything. She picked up note pad number five. "Kennon's story came in two parts. First she told me about how she killed him, and why. Then she said that she learned later that he wasn't guilty the way she thought he was. She even said that his death was the only true murder she committed, because Kennon didn't deserve to die the way the others did."

"This sounds intriguing. Let me get my knitting going, and I'll be all ears."

"How women can knit and listen at the same time is beyond me."

"That's because most men can only do one thing at a time, dear. Knitting gives my hands something to do so my mind isn't fretting about things."

"I suppose that makes sense to you two women," Jasper said, "but it sure doesn't sound right to me."

"Go ahead, Nancy. I'm ready as I'll ever be."

Chapter 21 - Yellow Jackets and Hay Bales

Nancy read them the story of Kennon's murder by bee sting, and then she told them as much as she could remember about how Slip learned that Button was really the one who had brought the flu that killed Emmy and their two nephews. "She didn't want me to write any of this down. I thought she was ashamed for having killed the wrong person." She fell silent and leaned back to wait for their reaction. Jasper looked at his wife, but she remained quiet.

"I'm not sure why she'd want to hide this lie and not all the others she told you. Maybe it just made this sound more dramatic."

Nancy thought back to that day. "I know why she didn't want me to write this next story down. That was when she stole my fountain pen, and I never even noticed because I was feeling so sorry for her."

"That sounds just like her," Jasper said. "As to the story, though, Kennon definitely was allergic to stings. And that's what killed him. But it wasn't a bee through the window in the middle of the night." Jasper scratched at his chin. "He was out working his field one day and stepped on a nest of yellow jackets. You know they nest in the ground, don't you?"

Nancy nodded. Everybody knew that.

"He tried to outrun them, but they swarmed around him. He swelled up something terrible. His sons tried to get the insects off him. They got stung badly in the process too, but it was too late for Kennon."

"He was a good man," Mary Louise added.

Nancy sat quietly for a moment out of respect for their feelings. "What about the flu? Was that part true?"

"Nineteen eighteen was a terrible year," Mary Louise said, and her husband grunted his agreement. "Kennon and Button both drove around town warning everybody. Neither one of them came anywhere near any of the houses, but Emmy caught it somehow anyway. We never did know where it came from. Sometimes I think the wind carried it to us. Our older brother Tom brought his children to us to keep them safe. Joseph never had children, remember? He died in the mill pond." She paused in her knitting. "Emmy came down with the flu first. She was so sick, so weak, but she made it through. Tom's two boys got sick next. Then Pa and Slip. Those of us who didn't catch it quite so bad were worn out trying to clean up after the ones who did have it. It was like slogging through a nightmare, the kind where you're trying to run away from some monster, but you can't get your feet to move because they're stuck in the mud. Do you know what I mean?"

"Yes, I think so." She twisted a few inches of her dress hem. "I lost my brother and my mama in the epidemic, but they both died fairly quickly. I never caught it. I tried to nurse them, but they died anyway." She rubbed her eyes and brushed her hair back from her face. "You said Emmy survived. That's wonderful. Will I get to meet her?"

"I'm afraid not," Mary Louise said. "She married Minnie's younger brother and they moved to eastern Pennsylvania some time ago. The funny thing is, they ended up in the town that our great-great-grandmother Thornton came from years ago."

"The one with the green glass tray?"

"How did you know about that?"

"I guess Slip told me one thing that was true."

Mary Louise smiled. "Getting back to the flu epidemic, though, I'm sorry you lost your brother and your ma. That must have been hard for you to go through. We were luckier than most. I think the Packard stock is strong." She nodded at Jasper. "So are you Fordykes."

"We're too ornery to die," he said, picking up his pipe and setting it down again. "Are you going to be okay with this next part?"

Mary Louise pressed her lips together. "I can do it," she said.

Nancy looked down at the pad in her hands. "I don't know what to say and what to leave out. I don't want to hurt you."

"It's all right. I'm ready, and it's just a big bunch of bad memories. I can deal with them."

"We can deal with them together," Jasper said. Leaning to one side, he worked a handkerchief out of his back pocket and handed it to Mary Louise.

Nancy read the whole story straight through. Jasper and Mary Louise sat almost without moving, except for once when Jasper leaned forward and took his wife's hand. She didn't even try to knit, and he left his pipe sitting on the stand beside him.

The pond, the blackberries, Tawser wearing nothing but his boots. Then the scene in the barn while Slip tried to listen without being discovered. Tawser's threat to her. His threat to young Silas. The slingshot and the hay baler.

When it was over, there was nothing to do but listen to Cheyenne snoring. Mary Louise patted Jasper's hand and pulled free from him. She ran her fingers over her face and adjusted a few hairpins. She blew her nose. She picked up her knitting and set it back down. She smoothed out a wrinkle in her dress. "That wasn't quite as bad as I feared," she said.

"Do you want to tell her, or shall I?"

"You go ahead, dear. I may add a bit later."

Jasper scrutinized his wife, apparently was satisfied with what he saw, and turned to Nancy. "I think this explains a lot. I can't say whether the beginning of the story is wrong or right. Mary Louise might be able to verify the part about the blackberry picking near the swimming hole, but whether or not that happened isn't the point. You see, Tawser . . . Jones," he stumbled a bit over the name, "did die in a hay baling accident. He got into a fight with one of the farm hands, who slugged him so hard he toppled back into the baler head first. Those machines are nasty and dangerous. One mistake can kill a man, and it certainly did kill him. He was almost ripped in two when the baler pushed forward before they could turn the fool thing off."

"Served him right," Mary Louise muttered.

Jasper glanced at her but kept on with his explanation. "About a week after his funeral, Mary Louise went out to the . . ." He touched his wife's hand. "Are you sure?"

"Yes. Go on. Get it over with."

When he swallowed, Nancy could see the knob on his throat go up and down. Adam's apple. Adam was supposed to protect Eve. "It was Silas's job to milk the cow. He took longer that morning than he generally did, so Mary Louise went out to the barn to get the milk. The door was closed, which was unusual. She could hear the cow stomping and lowing."

"We called her Bess. The cow. Her name was Bess."

"That's right. Bess was fussing inside the barn, and when Mary Louise opened the door, the first thing she saw was that the . . . that Bess hadn't been milked."

"The second thing I saw was . . . Silas wasn't there so I walked through to the back door of the barn. It was open, even though we usually kept that back door closed. I saw . . . I . . . ."

Jasper waited a moment and then took up the narrative in a quiet voice tinged with anger. "She could see her brother hanging from the tree out back. There was a tall ladder on the ground. As best we could tell, he must have climbed way up onto the first big branch, kicked over the ladder, and jumped off."

"I hate that tree," Mary Louise said. "It looks evil, somehow. Twisted."

Cheyenne rolled over and yawned. Jasper stilled the dog with a gentle hand. "Mary Louise's father climbed up and managed somehow to get hold of Silas's body and cut it down. They carried it . . . they carried him . . . "

"It," Mary Louise said. "By that point it didn't look like my brother."

Nancy thought of Slip's body dangling from the rope. Thank goodness they'd put a hood over her head.

"They carried the body up to the house, and when they went to undress him so they could wash the body, they found a note attached with a straight pin to the front of his undershirt, right over his heart. It had just one word on it . . . in Silas's handwriting."

"Tawser." Mary Louise unclenched her hands. Nancy could see where her nails had dug into the palms. "We never knew what it meant. Now, hearing this, I can see how Silas might have been ashamed. Or maybe he didn't want to live without Tawser. Now it makes sense."

"We still might not know for sure, sweetheart. Slip could have been lying about this too."

Mary Louise reached for her husband's hand, but addressed her words to Nancy. "Do you know what it's like to wonder why for so many years? I've spent a lot of time blaming myself. If only I'd gone to the barn sooner . . ."

"Honey."

"I'm all right, dear. I know it was a wasted thought, but it was there nonetheless. I might have stopped him."

"But he would have found another way." Jasper's voice was gentle. Nancy had the feeling he'd said the same thing before, possibly many times.

Nancy wanted to know what Slip's reaction had been to this whole tragedy, but didn't have the heart to ask. "I'm sorry," Nancy said and left to use the outhouse. They didn't seem to notice.

Chapter 22 - Conversation over Coffee

"Good morning, sleepyhead." Mary Louise set aside the beans she was shelling. "Have a seat and I'll get your breakfast for you."

"Please don't go to any trouble. I'm so sorry. I don't usually sleep this late."

"First of all, it's no trouble at all, and the only time eight-fifteen is late is if you're a farmer." She pulled the skillet onto the front burner and cracked three eggs into a green glass mixing bowl. "Jasper went ahead down to the station for a few hours. Allon was here at six-thirty, and the two of them worked on the automobile. Allon is a handy young man. He got it working in no time."

"I never heard a thing."

"It's a wonder you didn't. Allon kept shushing us so we wouldn't disturb you, but he made more noise than a flock of turkeys doing it." She looked sideways at Nancy. "He did ask about you in a roundabout way while we were eating breakfast."

Nancy felt her ears heating up. The day would probably be another hot one. This chenille robe was too heavy for a summer morning.

Mary Louise chattered on. "Allon loves my biscuits. He asked specifically for some of the butter you made. It's a good thing I set three biscuits aside for you. Otherwise he would have eaten them all. They left around seven-thirty. Jasper told me not to talk to you about anything until he got back."

Nancy grinned and poured herself a cup of coffee. "As if women could ever not talk about anything."

"You know what he meant. Open that jar, would you? It's fresh raspberry preserves."

"Yes." Nancy reached for the lid. "We won't talk about Dominick or Button or Evelyn."

"Evelyn? What about her?" Mary Louise clamped her mouth shut and crossed her eyes. "He's gone half an hour and I'm already pumping you for a story."

"We'll be good. Anyway, I can't talk and do justice to those scrambled eggs. They look delicious."

"They'll be ready in a minute."

Nancy crossed her arms and sighed. "I wish I had a real kitchen."

"What *do* you have?"

"I live in a small apartment. My kitchen is about the size of your outhouse."

"You are joking, aren't you? Here. Sit down and get started."

"Not by much." She spread some of the rich reddish-purple jam on half a biscuit. "The good thing, though, is that it's right above a bakery."

"Sounds like heaven."

"It would be if I didn't spend most of my paycheck there." Nancy chuckled and started on her eggs.

Mary Louise eased into the chair across the table from her and picked up the bowl of beans. "Are you getting all your questions answered?"

"I suppose so, but I don't know how I'll ever manage to craft the articles. George said he'd let me start the series with the funeral. Thank you for letting me call him long distance yesterday, by the way. I still have my job, despite how long I've been gone. George seemed to think we can make a story out of the way she lied to me. He's proud that I took the time to check all the facts, or fiction, as it turns out." Nancy set her fork down and stretched her arms over her head. "I still don't understand *why*, though. Why would she lie so consistently? And so hurtfully?"

Mary Louise nodded at the implication behind the words. "It would have hurt you terribly if you hadn't come here. If you'd printed those stories just as she told them to you."

"I would have lost my job for sure. And nobody else would ever have hired me. There may be a lot of camaraderie among news reporters in the press room, but the competition is fierce." She squeezed her eyes shut and rubbed them gently. "Particularly if you're a woman in a man's stronghold."

Mary Louise slapped the bowl down on the table, startling Nancy. "I think women will move into more and more jobs. Now that we have the vote, our daughters will grow up believing in themselves more. It's not always going to be like . . ." she looked around her kitchen, ". . . like this."

"Do you ever have regrets?" Nancy was aware of the echo of that same question when she had asked it of Slip, but she put that firmly out of her mind.

Mary Louise took a deep breath and let it out slowly. "No. Not really. It's just that sometimes, especially now that the children are grown, I wonder if this is all there is left for me. Cooking, cleaning, tending the house and the garden." She rubbed her hands together and shelled a few more beans. "But then Jasper comes home and I thank the Lord for how lucky I am to have such a good man." She reached across the table and took Nancy's hand. "When the time comes, young woman, you choose yourself a good man, a man you can respect and one who respects you. A man you can laugh with." She pulled her hand back. "Right at first, love can make you blind to what a man really is underneath. You be sure to wait long enough for him to show his true colors. That frothy first love can turn to acid if you're not careful."

"Can't that happen anyway, even if I do wait?"

"Well now, yes it can, I suppose. But there's a deep kind of *knowing* that you need to listen to." She rubbed her forehead. "Tell you what. When you find a young man, you bring him here to meet me and Jasper. If we both like him, and if *you* like him, then that just might be a good way of deciding."

Nancy laughed. "I'll do that." They chatted amiably as she finished her breakfast. By the time she went back to her room, her underwear was pretty much dry, and Mary Louise loaned her an old skirt so they could gather more beans.

They spent a few pleasant hours working in the garden. Nancy swiped a lock of hair back from her face and could feel the trail of dirt left across her cheek. "I've been too much of a city girl. I never thought I'd enjoy getting dirty."

"You think this is fun," Mary Louise pointed to the row next to Nancy, "just try biting into one of those tomatoes."

Nancy twisted around, careful not to knock into any of the bush bean plants she'd been weeding, and plucked a ripe tomato from its vine. She took a moment to sniff it before she bit into the succulent flesh. Her eyes widened considerably. "I never knew I was missing so much."

Mary Louise laughed in appreciation. "You can come work in my garden any time you want to, And you can eat as much of it as you like."

"Sorry it took me so long at the station, my dear." Jasper hung his hat on the peg beside the kitchen door. "What have you two been up to?"

Mary Louise gave a knowing smile and pointed to the bowls of snap beans. "We've been busy. I have trained a farm hand for our future harvests, and we did not talk about Button or Dominick." She paused. "Or Evelyn."

"Evelyn? What did she do?" He kissed Mary Louise on top of her head.

"She's the woman who confessed to running down Jethro," Nancy said.

"Did she now? Would that be Evelyn Packard, Tom's wife, the woman who offered Slip a home after Slip's Pa died?"

"No," said Nancy. "This Evelyn's last name was Ingles."

"That," Mary Louise said, "was Evelyn's maiden name."

Jasper loosened his tie and soaped up his hands at the sink. "You said *confessed to*. Does that mean she didn't really do it?"

"That's right. She was protecting Dominick. He was the one driving the car."

"You're still hoping that maybe something Slip told you was the truth, aren't you?"

Nancy lowered her eyes.

"Well, I hate to be the one to smash your hopes, but Dominick Kingsley did not run over Jethro Fordyke."

"How can you be sure?"

Jasper turned halfway to face Nancy, but held his drippy hands above the sink. Mary Louise stepped closer and handed him the hand towel. "The night Jethro was killed, I was working at a political rally, keeping an eye on the crowd and helping ladies find seats and such. A husband and wife left halfway through the main speech and found a body lying in the road. The man stayed there to keep cars away and the wife drove back to tell me what had happened. I went directly there."

"You had to deal with your own brother's body? That must have been so hard for you."

Jasper knocked the dead tobacco out of his pipe by tapping it on the edge of a heavy ashtray. "Yes," he said. "It was hard. If only I'd gotten there sooner."

Nancy wasn't sure whether she should try to continue the conversation or let it die right there. She looked at Mary Louise for direction.

"Dear, you know the doctor said he died the moment he was hit."

Jasper nodded, but remained silent as he refilled his pipe and struck a match to light it.

Nancy lowered her voice to almost a whisper. "How do you know it wasn't Dominick who hit him?"

He took a moment to be sure the pipe was drawing properly. He blinked several times, more than seemed accounted for by the thin trail of smoke that drifted toward his eyes. "Since I left early, I missed the rest of Dominick's speech." He paused. "He'd been speaking for over an hour already, and socializing an hour before that, so I doubt I missed much."

Mary Louise twisted her mouth to one side. "There goes Slip's motive." Her wry tone lightened the mood in the sitting room.

"No," Jasper said. "Let's keep that motive. I like it. Evelyn Ingles Packard and Dominick Kingsley together killed my brother. Of course, that would mean I arrested the wrong person. Too bad."

Nancy threw her hands up in the air. "I give up! Did she ever tell me *anything* that was true?"

He examined the bowl of his pipe, as if he had never noticed it before. "Sure she did. Sylvia has a dog. Of course, it's not a poodle. It's a dachshund."

"Henry did die from being stepped on by his bull," Mary Louise said, "but Slip wasn't there to hit him with a hammer first."

"It's true that Kennon died from being stung. Yellow jackets, though, not bees." Jasper looked at Mary Louise. "I can't think of anything else, can you?"

"Well, she's kept true to the relative ages of all her brothers and sisters."

"It probably would have been too confusing even for Slip to keep her lies straight if she'd started making Emmy the oldest and Tom the youngest."

Nancy noticed that neither one of them mentioned Tawser having died in the hay-baler accident. She didn't say a word, though.

Mary Louise stopped laughing abruptly. "You said you wanted to look into that story about Franklin and Hattie."

"True," he said.

"Three, maybe four, truths," Nancy said, "and partial truths at that out of two weeks of interviews. I'm trying hard not to feel bitter about this."

Mary Louise pointed her toward the flatware drawer. "Look at it this way. You had a chance to meet us, . . ."

". . . and set the table and harvest beans," Jasper added.

"I weeded the garden." Nancy smiled. "And I ate a fresh tomato."

"And you met . . ." Mary Louise's eyes crinkled up as she studied Nancy. "You met Cheyenne here." Cheyenne look up expectantly and thumped her tail. "There now, life is complete, isn't it?"

Nancy ate lightly, relishing the fresh butter on her bread almost as much as she enjoyed the easy banter between Mary Louise and Jasper, and joining in herself occasionally.

Once the dishes were set to soaking in the dish pan, Mary Louise made fresh coffee. "What did we ever do before this bean was invented?"

"We never had to worry about that," Jasper said. "It's been around longer than we have."

"You know what I mean."

"Not always, but sometimes I get a glimmer."

She threw the dish towel at him.

Nancy waited for them to stop laughing.

"It might not be a good time to mention this, but do you know when Slip's body will be released for burial?"

Jasper's smile faded. "Yes. I do know that. The body's already been transported to Telling's place. That's the funeral parlor in town. Sylvia Telling's son is the undertaker." He paused. "No wonder," he said, under his breath, "with a mother like that."

"Jasper!"

"Just making a comment."

"Why didn't you tell me about this? We need to get—"

He reached out and put a restraining hand on her arm. "That's precisely why I didn't tell you. We're going to have a short, quiet service on Sunday afternoon. We're not inviting anybody. Just family, if they even want to come."

Mary Louise tightened her lips.

"I know you want to do it properly, sweetheart, but keep in mind that Button and Dominick were related to half the people in this town."

"The same half we're related to, most likely."

"Exactly, so let's just have her sister Lucy and her brother Tom over here, and we'll lay Slip quietly to whatever rest she can find."

"Nancy too." Mary Louise raised her eyebrows in a query. "Will you come?"

"Yes. Thank you. I'd be . . ." *Happy to be here? Honored? Gratified? Determined?* "I'll be here."

Jasper reached for his pipe. "I'll stop by Telling's tomorrow and let them know."

"Jasper, dear?"

"Yes, sweetheart?"

"I'm not cancelling our Sunday family dinner just because we need to bury Slip."

He filled his pipe, so obviously stalling for time that Nancy almost laughed. "Well," he finally said, "we'll let everybody come as usual, and whoever wants to ride over to the cemetery will be welcome. Then we'll all come back here and eat."

Nancy waited until Mary Louise nodded. "May I ask another question?"

"Do you think we could stop her, sweetheart?"

"Behave yourself, Jasper. Go ahead, Nancy."

"How did Jethro get that scar on his chin?"

"What scar?"

"Oh, no. Here we go again. Slip said he had a scar on his chin. That was about the only way people could tell you two apart, since you were identical tw . . ." She stopped talking as Mary Louise and Jasper both exploded yet once again in merriment.

"Jethro and Jasper," Mary Louise gasped. "Identical?"

Jasper stood and beckoned to Nancy to follow him. Cheyenne scrambled to her feet and tagged along. The picture-lined hallway was illuminated by indirect light from the tall windows in the sitting room. He pointed to an old-fashioned family portrait photograph. A tall, rather gaunt white-bearded patriarch sat stiffly beside an equally stern hawk-nosed woman who held a dark-haired infant in her lap. Behind them stood a couple, clearly husband and wife, since her hand rested lovingly on his black-suited forearm. Seven children were ranged around the four adults. Two light-haired boys and four girls sat or stood in front of or beside their grandparents. Jasper pointed to the shorter of the two boys, a freckle-faced youngster of about two or three. "That's me," he said.

Nancy peered at the taller boy in the photo. "Yes. I can see how you two looked alike, but you were obviously not identical."

Jasper tapped the photo. "That tall one you're looking at was my brother Tobias."

"Tobias? I don't understand. Where is Jethro?"

"There." He pointed with his pipe stem. "The baby with the black hair. Sitting on Grandmother Fordyke's lap."

"Well, you certainly weren't twins." He shook his head. "No scar?"

"No scar, at least not on his chin. He did have one on his—"

"Jasper!" Mary Louise hollered from the sitting room. "She doesn't need to hear about that."

Jasper winked at Nancy and called out to his wife, "You're right as usual, my dear." As they retraced their steps down the hall, he pointed to Jethro at seven wearing a sailor suit, Jethro at fifteen holding a baseball. There was Jethro at twenty-two, standing beside his diminutive bride, with the wind blowing his black hair back from his narrow face. At forty, he stood with his arms around the shoulders of two young men who were obviously his sons, and finally, a photograph of Jethro's coffin. "He had a good life. It wasn't long enough, but it was good."

Once they settled back in their seats, Nancy picked up all the note pads and balanced them on her lap. She ran her hand over the top one. "In this whole collection of stories, we don't have even a hint of a real motive for why she would kill Button or Dominick, either one. Button didn't spread the flu germ, and Emmy survived, so there was no motive there; and Dominick didn't run down Jethro. Once again, no motive." Something was tickling on the edge of Nancy's memory, but she couldn't put a finger on it.

Mary Louise switched yarn colors again. "Maybe she was just crazy, after all. Losing her home after Pa died, maybe she had imagined killing people for such a long time that eventually she felt she had to try it for real."

"If that's the case, my dear, let's hope she didn't inspire anyone else."

Cheyenne snored. Jasper puffed quietly on his pipe. His wife's rocker squeaked softly. Nancy fished around in her right-hand pocket and pulled out the kid gloves. "She tried to recruit me. I don't know what to do with these now."

"Would you mind if I looked at them," Jasper said. It wasn't a question.

She handed them over, feeling a tug of unexpected pity for Slip as she did so.

"We never could find out where she bought the cyanide," he said, examining the thumb of one glove.

Mary Louise stopped knitting. "Does it matter that much?"

"Probably not. I just wondered for a moment if the source might give us a clue about what she was thinking, why she killed Button. And with Dominick, I never believed that nonsense about her being so angry when she was denied admission to the college." He offered the gloves to Mary Louise, but she shook her head. He handed them back to Nancy. "She really carried these around with her in prison?"

"Yes. Every time I saw her, she had them with her." She folded them in half and slipped them between two of the note pads. "Mary

Louise? You said something when we were taking our walk. Remember? I asked you about the engagement being broken off between Arnold Kingsley and Lucy's daughter."

"Yes?"

"Didn't you say that Slip was as charmed by Dominick as a lot of other women in town were?"

Jasper cleared his throat rather loudly.

"She's not referring to me, dear. Just Slip and Sylvia and Meribelle and people like that. They were always fawning over Dominick."

"Do you think perhaps . . . No. That's ridiculous."

"You know, Nancy, there may be something . . ."

"And she told me she wore his watch to bed that night . . ."

"I think you're right . . ."

"Yes. It seems obvious, doesn't it?"

"A woman scorned . . ."

"What in tarnation are you two females talking about?" Cheyenne lifted her head and looked around, as if she expected to see a threat looming in the doorway. "All these half sentences, and you aren't saying a dad-gummed thing."

"Yes we are, dear. Settle down. We're coming up with a possible motive."

"Motive? For what?"

"For Slip to kill Dominick. If she tried to make advances to him and he rejected her, don't you think she'd want to kill him?"

"That makes about as much sense as anything else I've heard in the last three days."

"But still," Nancy said, "we don't know for sure."

"And never will, I'm afraid." Mary Louise went back to rocking. "Maybe it doesn't matter at this point, with her being dead now."

"Do you ladies have any theories about why she killed Button?"

Nancy looked at the stack of note pads. "Not a one."

Cheyenne lay back down across Jasper's feet. "We also never answered the question of what, if anything, Franklin had to do with Hattie's death."

"Uh-huh," Mary Louise grunted. "And what if anything he had to do with my sister's insanity. Do you want me to invite Franklin over for dinner?"

"We could, dear." Jasper picked his words slowly. "But I really don't want to interrogate him over your fried chicken."

"I see what you mean."

"What about Estelle?" Nancy asked. "What's she liable to do when all this comes out in the open?"

"Estelle died six years ago."

"Slip told me that Estelle refused to visit her at the prison, which was why you and Lucy were there, just the two of you. But earlier, I could swear she told me that Estelle had died. I'll have to look through the notes again."

"I wouldn't bother if I were you. You'll just get all tied in knots trying to second-guess what she was thinking. By the time Estelle died, their children had all moved away, far away, except for the youngest girl. The others all left home as soon as they got old enough. Mary is still there, keeping house for her father." She looked at Jasper and raised her eyebrows.

The rocking chair squeaked; the dog raised her head. Jasper set down his pipe and hauled his big frame out of the chair. "Looks like I'm going to drive over there to talk to Franklin."

"Would you stop by Allon's and take him along with you, just in case?"

Chapter 23 - Goodbyes

Mary Louise hugged Nancy warmly. "You come back anytime, you hear? You're always welcome in Baynard's Mill. I'm sorry you can't stay for the barn dance on Saturday."

Jasper rested his hand on Mary Louise's shoulder. "There will be other dances, my dear, and I'm sure she'll be back to visit." He reached out and shook Nancy's hand gently. "You will, won't you?"

"Of course. If I'd had more clothes with me," she looked down at her shirtwaist, somewhat the worse for wear, "and if I didn't have to go back and get started on a story for George before he fires me, I'd stay."

"You will be here for the burial on Sunday, won't you?"

"I'll be here. As I told you, we're going to start the newspaper story with her funeral. Have you, uh, decided on a headstone yet?"

"Jasper thought a simple wooden cross with just her name and the two dates would be more appropriate; why do you ask?"

"Nothing. I'm sorry I mentioned it. She told me she wanted a college education so she could have a headstone with letters after her name."

"Well, then," Jasper pulled Mary Louise closer to him, "I'd say she waited a little bit too long to get started on that degree."

"She hated reading," Mary Louise said. "She never would have made it through college."

"I thought she always hid in the hayloft so she could read."

"Not Slip. I don't know what she did there, but it sure didn't involve books."

Jasper cleared his throat. "She probably spent that time dreaming up ways to kill us all off."

Mary Louise elbowed him gently, and he doubled over in mock pain. "Hush now, Jasper, or Nancy will never want to come back. You be careful driving home, Nancy. We'll see you Sunday." The two women hugged once more.

"I won't be able to stay but just the afternoon, but I will come to . . . to see Slip laid to rest."

Jasper nodded. "I guess we won't have time to read all those stories to the victims then, will we?"

"Jasper Fordyke, you behave yourself."

"Sorry," he said, although Nancy didn't think he looked sorry at all. "You have to admit, Susannah is a lot more fun dead than she was alive."

"Pastor Jacobs would be scandalized if he could hear you."

"Pastor Jacobs, may I remind you, is about two hundred and thirty years old, and probably couldn't hear me even if he were standing right beside me."

"You're terrible."

"You're lovely."

"Oh, here we go again. Nancy, you'll just have to forgive us."

Jasper's smile faded. "I know it wasn't easy for you," he pointed to the stack of note pads she'd placed on her front seat, "going through all this. I must say, though, if you hadn't brought these stories to light, I might never have found out who hurt Hattie all those years ago and left her to die. Justice may be forty years slow at times, but in this case, it was well-served. Sheriff Lundstrom would have been pleased to know you had helped us find the guilty party."

Mary Louise beamed at Nancy. "That's high praise indeed. Jasper just about worshipped the ground Sheriff Lundstrom walked on."

"He was a fine man, and a good friend."

"I wish I knew what to do with all these notes." Nancy smiled ruefully. "My newspaper story is going to be considerably shorter than I thought it would be."

Mary Louise stepped closer to Jasper, and he put his arm around her. She grinned her leprechaun smile. "Save them. Some day you might want to write a novel."

"I do have one more question."

"Only one?" Jasper grinned and ran his free hand through his hair. "What is it?"

"If she climbed out the window a lot at night, where did she go, since we know she wasn't out killing people."

Mary Louise looked down at her feet. "Remember I told you how much little Joseph used to adore Slip?"

"Yes."

"She fixed up a little nest for him out in the hayloft. They used to sit up there for hours and she'd tell him stories."

Jasper cleared his throat. "Probably about murder and mayhem."

"I don't know about that, dear, but after he drowned in the mill pond, Susannah spent most nights out there, except in the coldest part of the winter. She had a stack of quilts and blankets. I know because I climbed up there once to look. She would have been furious with me if she'd known I peeked. It was her private place."

"A perfect place," Jasper added, "to hatch her nightmares about exterminating perfectly good people."

"Sounds like she really needed *me* to come along." Nancy tried not to sound bitter, but she couldn't help it. The tone was there.

Jasper smiled. "I'd say you were the perfect audience. We'll install a second fountain and engrave your name on it."

Sunday, August 7, 1932

Mary Louise, Jasper, and Nancy. Three people to say goodbye to Slip. Even Mr. Telling seemed loathe to remain near the grave once the coffin had been lowered into the ground. He and his assistants retreated outside the picket fence and stood there in a clump while Jasper walked forward and removed his hat. "Bless us all, Lord, and help us to learn from the mistakes of others. Keep us from hasty judgments . . ." He scratched the side of his jaw. "Keep us from judging others unfairly." He paused and twisted his hat in his hands. "We've all made mistakes, Lord, some worse than others, but we're all guilty of one thing or another.

Have mercy on us all. Amen." He bent and scooped up a clod of dirt and tossed it onto the coffin. Mary Louise, dry-eyed, did the same. Nancy stood for a moment and then reached into her pocket. She dropped the kid gloves into the grave and stared at the worn leather on the white pine box. Her eyes burned.

Jasper and his wife started back toward the car—they'd driven the mile and a half to the old family graveyard on the hill—but Nancy held back. "I need some time here, if you don't mind."

"How about if I take my sweetheart home, and I'll come back to pick you up in . . . would half an hour do it?"

She nodded her agreement and stepped aside to watch the gravediggers filling the hole. As soon as they drove away, she walked back to the mound of dirt. Anger started to build inside her in hot rushes until her stomach cramped and her fingers began to shake. "I hope you're happy," she said. The grave was stark and as bare of growth as the jury foreman's pate had been. Not a flower in sight, not on the grave at least, although the meadow beyond the weathered fence was rife with wildflowers. "You almost got what you wanted." The tightness of her throat forced her voice out as a whisper. "I came that close," Nancy held up her index finger, half an inch from her thumb, "*that* close to making a fool of myself." She felt the sharp prick of hot tears and breathed through her mouth to maintain control. "You would have enjoyed that, wouldn't you, if I'd lost my job because of your twisted, hateful, warped vision." Tears fell, and she did nothing to stop them. "I don't give a fig for that hard childhood you claimed to have. Lots of people survive things much worse than you did," she sniffed and swallowed a sob, "but they come out of it trusting people and telling the truth. You never had any charity in you. Not an ounce. You never gave a whit about another human being. Oh, I know you tried to make me feel sorry for you. I know you told me just what I wanted to hear." She dug in her purse for a handkerchief and blew her nose. "You practically hypnotized me, getting me to gloss over the inconsistencies. They were there. I know." Her voice climbed into that little-girl squeak she detested. "I've spent the last two days re-reading every word I took down over the last two weeks. You lied. You lied to me! You knew what you were doing every step of the way." The light summer breeze blew Nancy's hair into her eyes and she slapped it back impatiently. "What an absolute fool I was to trust you. You must have sized me up the minute you laid eyes on me. What was it Mary Louise said? A sucker. Well, that's what I was; I admit it."

Her legs felt weak, and she sank down onto her knees in the grass that filled the paths between the headstones. "To think I cried—I actually cried over your poor wounded feelings when all those horrible people hurt your loved ones. Ha! You never loved anybody except yourself." She felt the grass tickle her shins, and she sat to one side, curling her legs and tucking her skirt under them. The grass brought back a memory, something she hadn't thought about in years. Something her mother had said to her. *Grass will grow wherever it has enough soil, enough sun, and enough rain.* They were standing in their back yard, hanging up the wash. Nancy wasn't tall enough to reach the line, but she handed the clothes one at a time to her mother. *It doesn't matter whether or not the grass is welcome there. It's still going to grow.* Mother reached out and cupped Nancy's chin. *If someone encourages it, it will grow thicker and greener. If they don't want it, the weeds will invade.* Mother's voice began to fade. *The thoughts we have about ourselves are like those weeds, honey. They can choke out all the good grass in our hearts.*

Nancy stared at the mound of dirt while her chest ached. "You didn't love yourself, did you? You couldn't have. You had to have known what you were doing. You couldn't . . . nobody could have been so hateful without some of it poisoning their very soul. Nothing but weeds." She twisted the handkerchief. It felt the way her heart did, all skewed up. "I can't believe I thought you were so noble for wanting to be at that Sunday School Conference last weekend. I think I'll mention that in my story. Oh, you just bet your life I'm going to tell your story, you rotten woman." A growl, almost primal in nature emanated from some deep recess of her gut. "I'm going to show them how one twisted individual thought she could get away with lies. I'm going to quote just enough of what you said so people will know how warped you were. I'm going to make sure that everyone who reads the *Clarion* will know you were a fool."

Nancy stood and covered her eyes with her fingertips. The tears formed a slick surface as she wiped her hands down her cheeks. "Yes, that's right, Susannah Lou Packard. You were a fool. A fool to think you could do this to me. You know why?" Nancy shook her fist at the grave.

"Because I'm a better person than you. I'm willing to trust people. I don't judge people the way you did."

Officer Jolly came to mind. Nancy stopped abruptly and looked out across the wildflower meadow. She'd been ready, without knowing what he was going through, to hang him, skewer him, drown him, cut off his head and feed it to the pigeon; she couldn't even remember all the punishments she'd dreamed up for him. Of course, she never would have carried through on any of those. She never would have actually wanted him to be hurt. Would she? She kicked at a clump of dirt in front of her. What about the man who'd shot her best friend in fourth grade? If he hadn't been tried and convicted, what would she have done? Nancy shivered. No. No, she wouldn't have taken the law into her own hands; or would she? Oh, this was getting her nowhere. She turned back to the grave.

"I was too tempting, wasn't I? Walking in there all starry-eyed, the ace reporter on the scene. I should have stood up to you more, questioned you more about those things you told me that I just knew weren't right." She could almost see herself, sitting there with her little note pads and her fountain pen, like a cow just waiting to be slaughtered. "I was so eager to get that prize-winning story I couldn't be bothered to ask you why you thought irises grew on bushes, or why your sister Estelle was dead in one story and alive four stories later. You forgot that little detail, didn't you?" Nancy twisted the toe of one shoe on a small clod of dirt that had rolled off the mound. She watched it disintegrate with great satisfaction. "I should have high-tailed it to Baynard's Mill that first day when you told me to ignore the sheriff and leave your family alone. I should have known there had to be a reason you kept making me promise not to come here. Well, guess what, sweetie-pie? You lose! You got strung up, and I can't think of anybody who deserved it more. How could I have let you lead me on like that? I was stupid, stupid, stupid! And you were despicable."

When Nancy ran out of nasty names to call both herself and Slip, she backed away from the grave. Nearby an old tombstone leaned rather dispiritedly to one side, as if it had given up hope a long time ago, but the flowering bush just beside the monument seemed to hold enough spirit for both of them. *Louisa Thornton.* The great-great-grandmother who'd brought the green glass tray from Pennsylvania. "Did you have any idea that this offshoot of yours would turn out the way she did?" Mrs. Thornton said nothing, of course, but Nancy felt a sense of calmness settle over her. Slip was dead. Nothing she had said or done, nothing at all had hurt Nancy. Injured her pride, perhaps. Given her a lesson in humility. Taught her something about her own gullibility. But Nancy hadn't really been hurt by Slip. Slip was as dead as Mrs. Thornton here, and some day would be remembered even less, Nancy imagined. At least Mrs. Thornton had left a green glass tray. Slip had left—what? Seven note pads and a pair of kid gloves. Well, Slip's monument was wood that would soon weather away. The gloves were gone, and the note pads would someday be worth a laugh. Not yet, though. Nancy wasn't ready to laugh yet.

Had Slip been routinely and frequently abused by Franklin when she was a little girl? They'd never know. Nancy looked back at the mound of bare dirt. Poor untrusting, unloving, unloved Susannah Lou. Poor Slip, who was at least partially responsible for the death of her adoring little brother Joseph. Slip, afraid of the water and unable to save him. Nancy reached across the fence and plucked a branch of wild asters. She laid the flowers on the grave, straight over where Slip's heart would have been—if she'd had one, Nancy thought—and smiled. What fun it is to laugh and sing a slaying song tonight.

She walked out to meet the sheriff's car that approached slowly from the east.

The End

Notes from the Author

When I began writing A SLAYING SONG TONIGHT, I saw it as a somewhat tongue-in-cheek spoof of serial-killer thrillers. In fact, I wrote the first seventeen chapters, much as they still are, in that vein. It was a fun book, but it didn't have the depth of character or the intricacy of plot that I've come to expect of my books.

About this time I interviewed Margaret Maron, author of the Judge Deborah Knott mystery series, on my internet radio show, Mystery Matters. She spoke on Friday, August 7th, about the courtroom research she does for her series, and she suggested that it would be a good idea for everyone to sit through an entire trial as an observer. On August 31st, I went to the courtroom of Gwinnett County Superior Court Judge Debra K. Turner and over three days observed a trial for assault and battery. The entire process fascinated me. I had a chance to see the way a jury is selected. I listened to the arguments (politely labeled discussions) between the attorneys each time the jury was sent from the room. I was shown the behind-the-scenes offices by Court Reporter Beth Cappell (and I borrowed her last name for one of my characters). I observed Judge Turner's positively wicked grin and incisive (but never unkind) wit during the moments before the jury came into the room and after they left. I spent the lunch breaks and time before and after court in the Clerk's Office, where Debby Boyt, Clerk of the Superior Court, helped me locate old archives—records from 1880 to 1940. In going though those fragile and in some cases handwritten pieces of paper, I was struck with how much has changed in the past century, and how little has changed. I took the quotations that begin the first seventeen chapters directly from those records. Susannah's charge, at the beginning of Chapter One, is taken directly from a murder case that occurred more than a hundred years ago. All I changed were the names, dates, and the part about *cutting into his throat.*

On the third day I listened to the closing arguments. Assistant District Attorney Alston McNairy was absolutely passionate in her plea that justice be done, and in her argument that a reasonable doubt needs to be just that—reasonable. That short statement doesn't even begin to do justice to her eloquence and her fervent oratory. By the time she finished, I wanted to jump to my feet and applaud.

In that moment, I knew that I would be ashamed to show my book, as it was at that time, to ADA McNairy and to Judge Turner. That day I went home and began a sweeping re-write of A SLAYING SONG TONIGHT. This is now a book I can be truly proud of, for it carries, I believe, something of the spirit of Turner and McNairy both.

As to my reference to Madeleine Ames in my Gratitude List? Fans of my Biscuit McKee mystery series may recall that in GREEN AS A GARDEN HOSE, the third book in that series, a young woman moves from Atlanta to Martinsville. Madeleine is the sister of the priest at St. Theresa's. She is escaping from the clutches of her overbearing mother. For years she has been writing horror stories, in each of which she kills off someone who looks suspiciously like her mother. None of her attempts to interest an agent bears fruit, until one agent suggests that she has talent, but the story needs some work. *Rewrite it and resubmit it* is the agent's advice.

Well, Madeleine's title was just too good to pass up. She had envisioned a story about a serial killer in Atlanta who murdered people at Christmas time, and the title was to have been, naturally, A SLAYING SONG TONIGHT. With apologies to Madeleine, I really didn't want a serial killer roaming the metro area where I live, so I set the story in the Midwest and stretched the crimes from 1892, soon after *Jingle Bells* became a favorite household song, to 1931. Then, thanks to the McNairy/Turner influence, I put in a wicked twist and had great fun in the rewriting.

Madeleine always contorts her body in pretzel-like knots. I have always sat ramrod straight—thanks to teachers who drilled that into me at a time when posture was a taught skill. As I wrote, though, I found myself sitting with one leg tucked under me and the other leg crossed at an unbelievable angle. Am I Madeleine? While writing this book, I certainly was. The truth, however, is that Madeleine may have come up with the title, but she never got off her butt to write the book. If this book had ended after seventeen chapters, I would have published it under her name. Now, though, I hope you can see why I definitely want my name associated with A SLAYING SONG TONIGHT.

I've been asked why I didn't tie up all the loose ends. What eventually happened to Franklin? What about Allon? Did Nancy ever run a newspaper? And just why did Slip kill Button? Well, as Slip told Nancy, I think you can figure all that out.

Fran Stewart
from my home beside a creek on the back side of
Hog Mountain, Georgia
November 2009